MO HAYDER

After leaving school at fifteen, Mo Hayder worked as a barmaid, security guard, film-maker, hostess in a Tokyo club, educational administrator and teacher of English as a foreign language in Asia. She also has an MA in creative writing from Bath Spa University.

Visit **www.mohayder.net**
for more info and join the forum.

ALSO BY

MO HAYDER

TOKYO

Desperate and alone in an alien city, student Grey Hutchins accepts a job as a hostess in an exclusive gentlemen's club. There she meets an ancient gangster rumoured to rely on a strange elixir for his continued health; it is an elixir others want – at any price . . .

'Left me stunned and haunted. This is writing of breathtaking power and poetry'
Tess Gerritsen

PIG ISLAND

When journalist Joe Oakes visits a secretive religious community on a remote Scottish island, he is forced to question the nature of evil – and whether he might be responsible for the terrible crime about to unfold.

'The most terrifying thriller you'll read all year'
Karin Slaughter

The thrillers featuring DI Jack Caffery are:

BIRDMAN

Greenwich, south-east London. Detective Inspector Jack Caffery is called to one of the most gruesome crime scenes he has ever seen. Five young women have been ritualistically murdered – and Caffery knows that it is only a matter of time before the killer strikes again . . .

'A first-class shocker' *Guardian*

THE TREATMENT

Traumatic memories are wakened for DI Jack Caffery when he is called to a crime scene in south London. A husband and wife have been discovered, imprisoned in their own home. They are both near death. But worse is to come: their young son is missing . . .

'Genuinely frightening' *Sunday Times*

RITUAL

Recently arrived from London, DI Jack Caffery is now part of Bristol's Major Crime Investigation Unit. Soon he's looking for a missing boy – a search that leads him to a more terrifying place than anything he has known before.

'Intensely enthralling' *Observer*

SKIN

MO HAYDER

BANTAM BOOKS

LONDON • TORONTO • SYDNEY • AUCKLAND • JOHANNESBURG

TRANSWORLD PUBLISHERS
61–63 Uxbridge Road, London W5 5SA
A Random House Group Company
www.rbooks.co.uk

SKIN
A BANTAM BOOK: 9780553820508

First published in Great Britain
in 2009 by Bantam Press
an imprint of Transworld Publishers
Bantam edition published 2009

A CIP catalogue record for this book
is available from the British Library.

Addresses for Random House Group Ltd companies outside the UK
can be found at: www.randomhouse.co.uk
The Random House Group Ltd Reg. No. 954009

The Random House Group Limited supports The Forest Stewardship Council
(FSC), the leading international forest certification organisation. All our titles
that are printed on Greenpeace approved FSC certified paper carry the FSC
logo. Our paper procurement policy can be found at
www.rbooks.co.uk/environment

Typeset in 11/14pt Sabon by
Falcon Oast Graphic Art Ltd.
Printed in the UK by CPI Cox & Wyman, Reading, RG1 8EX.

2 4 6 8 10 9 7 5 3 1

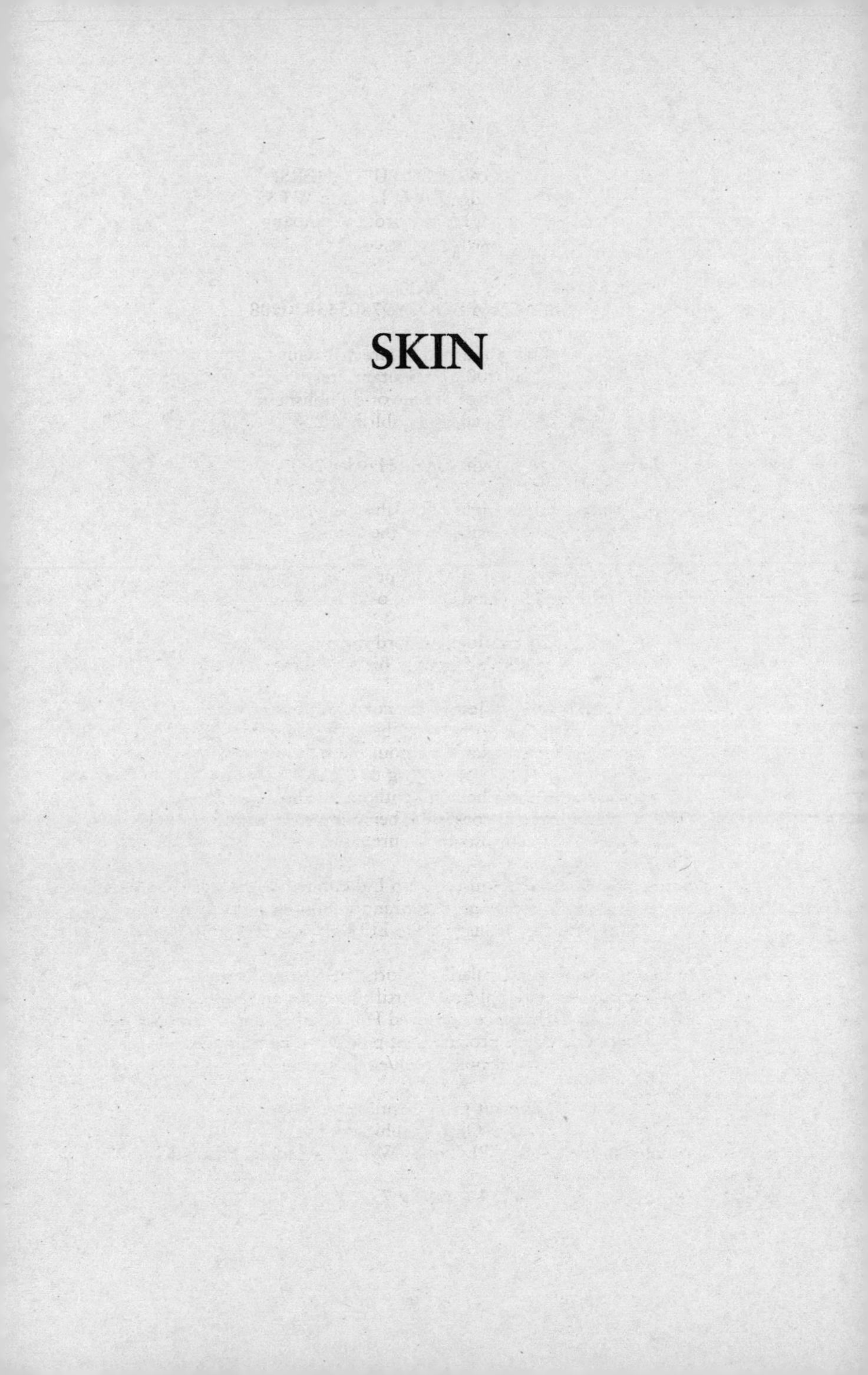

SKIN

1

Human skin is an organ. The biggest organ in the body, it comprises the dermis, the epidermis and a subcutaneous fatty layer. If it were to be removed intact and spread out it would cover an area just under two square metres. It has weight too: with all that protein and adherent fat, it has enormous bulk. The skin of a healthy adult male would weigh ten to fifteen kilos, depending on his size. The same as a large toddler.

The skin of a woman, on the other hand, would weigh marginally less. It would cover a smaller area too.

Most middle-aged men, even the ones who live alone in a remote part of Somerset, wouldn't have given any thought to what a woman would look like without her skin. Neither would they have cause to wonder what her skin would look like stretched and pinned out on a workbench.

But, then, most men are not like this man.

This man is a different sort of person altogether.

2

Deep in the rain-soaked Mendip Hills of Somerset lie eight flooded limestone quarries. Long disused, they have been numbered by the owners from one to eight, and are arranged in a horseshoe shape. Number eight, at the most south-easterly point, nearly touches the end of what is called locally the Elf's Grotto system, a network of dripping caves and passages that reach deep into the ground. Local folklore has it there are secret exits from this cave system leading into the old Roman lead mines, that in ancient times the elves of Elf's Grotto used the tunnels as escape routes. Some say that because of all the twentieth-century blasting, these tunnels now open directly into the flooded quarries.

Sergeant 'Flea' Marley, the head of Avon and Somerset's underwater search unit, slid into quarry number eight at just after four on a clear May afternoon. She wasn't thinking about secret entrances. She wasn't looking for holes in the wall. She was thinking about a woman who'd been missing for three days. The woman's name was Lucy Mahoney, and the professionals on the surface believed her corpse might be down here, somewhere in this vast expanse of water, curled in the weeds on one of these ledges.

Flea descended to ten metres, wiggling her jaw from side to side to equalize the pressure in her ears. At this depth the water was an eerie, almost petrol blue – just the faintest milky limestone dust hanging where her fins had stirred it up. Perfect. Usually the water she dived was 'nil vis' – like swimming through soup, everything having to be done by touch alone – but down here she could see at least three metres ahead. She moved away from her entry point, handholding herself along the quarry wall until the pressure on her lifeline was constant. She could see every detail, every wafting plant, every quarried boulder on the floor. Every place a body might have come to rest.

'Sarge?' PC Wellard, her surface attendant, spoke into the comms mike. His voice came into her ear as if he was standing right next to her. 'See anything?'

'Yes,' she murmured. 'Into the future.'

'Eh?'

'I can see into the future, Wellard. I see me coming out of here in an hour freezing cold. I see disappointment on everyone's face that I'm empty-handed.'

'How come?'

'Dunno. Just don't think she's down here. It feels wrong. How long's she been missing?'

'Two and a half days.'

'And her car. Where was it parked?'

'Half a mile away. On the B3135.'

'They thought she was depressed?'

'Her ex was interviewed for the misper report. He's adamant she wasn't.'

'And there's nothing else linking her to the quarry? No belongings? She'd not been here before or anything?'

'No.'

Flea finned on, the umbilical lead – the air and communication line that linked her to the surface – trailing gently behind. Quarry number eight was a notorious suicide spot. Maybe the police search adviser, Stuart Pearce, disagreed with the family about Lucy Mahoney's state of mind. Maybe that was why he'd put this particular pin in the map and detailed them to do this search. Either that or he was grasping at straws. She'd encountered Stuart Pearce before. She thought it was the latter.

'Could she swim, Wellard? I forgot to ask.'

'Yeah. She was a good swimmer.'

'Then if she's a suicide she'll have weighted herself down. A rucksack or something. Which means she'll be near the edge. Let's run this pendulum search pattern out to ten metres. No way she'll be further out than that. Then we'll switch to the other side of the quarry.'

'Uh, Sarge, there's a problem with that. You do that pattern and it'll take you to deeper than fifty metres.'

Wellard had the quarry schematic. Flea had already studied it surfaceside. When the quarry company had made finger-shaped holes to pack explosives they'd used ten-metre-long drills, which meant that the quarry, before they'd turned off the pumps and allowed it to flood, had been blasted away in ten-metre slices. At one end it was between twenty and thirty metres. At the other end it was deeper. It dropped to more than fifty metres. The Health and Safety Executive's rules were clear: no police diver was cleared to dive deeper than fifty. Ever.

'Sarge? Did you hear me? You'll be down to fifty metres at the end of this arc. Maybe more.'

She cleared her throat. 'Did you eat all the banana bread?'

'Eh?'

That morning before work she'd baked banana bread for the team. It wasn't the sort of thing she usually did. She was the boss but she'd never been mumsy with them – she was the second youngest, only Wellard was younger. And it wasn't because she loved cooking either. They'd had a bad, bad time recently: one of them was on compassionate leave and probably wouldn't be back after what he'd gone through earlier that week. And then there'd been her foul moods, too: a nightmare to live with for the last two years. She had to give them something in return every now and then.

'We ate it. But, Sarge, some of those pockets are way over fifty deep. We're supposed to get one of those maniac techie divers in to do something like this.'

'Whose side are you on, Wellard? Ours or the HSE's?'

Silence. Or, rather, the sound of Wellard's silent grumbling. When it came to being an old woman Wellard had the whole team beat hands down. 'OK. But if you're going to do it I'm turning this voice panel down. The whole quarry can hear you and we've got a viewing gallery today.'

'Who?'

'There's a traffic unit cruised by to get a look, sitting up there on the grout dunes. Think they're having their coffee.'

'I don't suppose the audience includes that tit of a search adviser, does it?'

'Not yet.'

'Nice,' she said, sarcastic now. 'Just, it's sometimes considered etiquette for the search adviser to get his arse out of bed when he's hauled a team out like this.'

She slowed. In the darkening water ahead a net was slung across her path. Beyond it was the fifty-metre section, where the water was darker and bluer. Colder. It was such uncertain territory that the company had rigged up netting to prevent access to the recreational divers who sometimes used the quarry for practice. She gripped the net, clicked on her divelight and shone it through to where the quarry floor dropped precipitously away.

She might have had only one previous encounter with Pearce but it was enough. She wasn't going to let him get one up on her. Even if it meant breaking all her professional rules and going deeper than fifty, she was damned if she wasn't going to complete the search. There was a sign set in concrete to her right, the words covered in algae. *Danger: depths exceeding fifty metres. Random checks on dive computers are in force in this quarry. Do not dive beyond your capabilities.*

Good place to hang your dive computer, she thought, touching the sign. Just take your wrist unit off, hang it on one of the nails, then collect it on the way back up. No one checking later would be any the wiser that you'd gone deeper than fifty, and the surface unit didn't generate a computerized dive record. It was the sort of trick Dad had pulled when he was alive. An extreme-sports diver, he'd do anything to push the limits, get to the depth he wanted to be.

She used her dive knife to make a cut in the netting, then carefully slipped off her dive computer and hooked it on to the sign. Switching on her torch she slid through into the enclosure, following the beam down into the darkness.

With her compass lubber line set hard against the north-west notch she began to swim down, down and down, following the lie of the rock, keeping about two metres from the bottom. Wellard paid out the lifeline behind her. The schematic was accurate – it was deep here. She went slowly, letting the torch guide her, doing sums in her head. No computer. She'd have to work out bottom times and decompression stops in her head.

A movement in the dark to her right. She whipped the torch towards it and stared into the beam, keeping herself steady in the water, letting herself float horizontally. There weren't any fish in quarry number eight. It had been flooded for years now and the company hadn't introduced any stock. No nearby rivers so there probably wouldn't even be crayfish. And, anyway, that movement hadn't been a fish. It had been too big.

Her heart beat low in her chest. She kept her breathing steady – too deep and she'd start to rise, too shallow and she'd lose buoyancy. Nothing should, or could, be moving down here: there were no currents in the quarry.

Everything should be motionless. She began to swim towards where she'd seen the movement.

'Sarge?' Surfaceside, Wellard had noticed the diversion instantly. 'Everything OK?'

'Yeah, yeah. Give me another bar.'

As she went deeper it was Wellard's job, as the panel operator, to increase the pressure of the air reaching her down the umbilical lead. She turned and shone the torch behind her, trying to see how far back the netting was. She was probably at about forty-seven metres deep and still going down. Just another three metres to the HSE limit. 'Yeah – up it to sixteen.'

'Sixteen bar? That'll put you at—'

'I know what it'll put me at. Let me worry about it, not you.'

She swam on, her hands out now because she wasn't sure what she was going to see. Forty-eight metres, forty-nine. She was at the place where the movement had been.

'Sarge? Do you know what depth you're at?'

'Just hold it,' she whispered. 'Hold me steady.'

She turned the torch upwards and looked up. It was uncomfortable with her mask wanting to lift off and let water in. She pressed it to her face with her fingertips and stared into the effervescent silvery stream of bubbles marching determinedly above her in a long column – up towards a surface that was too far away to see. Something was in that column. She was sure of it. Something dark was swimming up through the procession of darkness and air. A shiver went through her. Were those the naked soles of someone's feet?

'Sarge – that's it. You're over fifty. Can you hear me?'

'Hey, Wellard,' she whispered, looking up to where the bubbles had cleared now, dispersed into nothing but frosty jags of light. Now, suddenly, everything looked as it should. The water was empty. 'Is there anyone else in here?'

'Anyone else?'

'Yeah,' she hissed, not wanting to sound scared. She hoped he'd turned the comms panel down. Didn't want her voice broadcast across the water to every person on the quarryside. 'Is anyone swimming around in here with me? You'd have seen them getting in.'

There was a pause, a hesitation. Then the voice, a little cautious. 'Boss? You know you're well over, don't you? Maybe it's time to put the standby in.'

Narcosis, he meant. At this depth it would be easy to succumb to the disorienting, poisonous effect that nitrogen could have at high pressure – her reactions and thoughts were as they'd be if she'd been in the pub all afternoon. A hallucination like this would be classic narcosis stuff. She stared up after the bubbles. It had been something dark, the size of a large turtle. But not with a shell. It was something smooth and hairless, with agility and strength. With the feet of a human being.

'I'm not narked, Wellard, I swear. I'm fine. Just reassure me there's no one else swimming around down here. That's all.'

'There's no one in there. OK? And the standby's getting ready now.'

'No.' Her umbilical had snagged on a ledge or a rock

behind her. Irritably she lifted her shoulders, waved her right hand in the air to free it and felt it pop easily away from the rock or ledge, freeing her. 'No need for anyone else. I'm nearly done here anyway.'

Wellard was right, of course. If this was narcosis she should get out. But she wanted one more minute to check that she'd searched everything, so, tilting herself back down, liking the way it eased the pressure on her mask, she pointed the torch ahead. There, about ten yards away, was the bottom of the wall, the edge of the quarry. She'd come as far as she could and there wasn't any doubt about it: Lucy Mahoney wasn't here. Good. She'd been right. She was going to enjoy surfacing and sending Pearce the message that he'd been wrong.

The rubber seals of her mask sucked tight against her face. And locked.

She groped at the mask. Tried to take a breath. Nothing came, just more tightening of the seals and a familiar pressure under her sternum. She knew this feeling well from all her training sessions. No air was getting through. She fumbled at the side of the mask above her right ear. This wasn't going to be a problem. The surface crew were pumping air down to her – she couldn't run out. But just occasionally the umbilical got tangled with the positive/negative pressure lever on the mask and cut off the supply. It was easy to solve. If you kept calm. Easy.

Heart thudding she found the lever, flicked it down and went for another breath. Her ribs tried. Wouldn't inflate. Quickly she snapped the lever back down.

Nothing.

Up. Nothing.

'Sarge?' Wellard sounded panicky. 'What's going on? What's happening?'

But there was no air in her lungs to answer. Her arms were aching. Her head was pounding as if it had swollen to twice its size. Someone could have been standing on her chest. Her head jerked back, her mouth gaped. She groped for the switch block on the side of her vest. Tried to get her air supply to transfer to the Scuba bail-out system.

'Sarge? I've opened all my valves but there's air haemorrhaging from somewhere. Have you got pressure?'

She knew what would be happening up there. The standby diver would be fumbling himself into his equipment, getting his fingers tangled in the mask spiders in his panic, forgetting everything. Legs like jelly. He wouldn't be in time for her. She had seconds left, not minutes.

Numbly she batted at the switchblock again. Couldn't find it. Her head swelled harder and tighter now. Her limbs were tingling.

'I'm going to have to pull you out, Sarge – having to make assumptions here.'

She'd stopped listening. Time had slowed and it was in a different world – on a distant planet – that Wellard was pulling frantically at the lifeline, dragging her out. She knew her limp body was jerking backwards in the water. She felt her fingers lose their grip on the torch, felt it bump lazily against her leg as it sank. She didn't try to stop it.

In the gloom, about ten metres away, something that looked like a white jellyfish had appeared. Not the same thing she'd hallucinated earlier, but something else, something that billowed, moving up and down in eerie corkscrew shapes, like a cloud of hair. It seemed to hover, buffeted by unseen currents, as if it had been on its way somewhere – to the bottom maybe – but had stopped its descent to watch her. As if it was interested in what was happening. Interested in her struggle.

The top of the shape lifted, seemed to lengthen and slip out into long, tendril-like hair and now she knew what she was looking at.

Mum.

Mum, who had been dead for two years. The long blonde hair that she'd always kept in a knot at the back of her neck lifted and wallowed in the gloom, wafting around her face.

'Wake up, Flea. Look after yourself.'

Flea didn't answer. She wasn't capable. In the real world her body had tilted on to its side and was twitching like a fish with a broken swim bladder.

'Look after yourself.'

Mum turned in the water, her small white hands propelling her body around so her head was facing Flea's, her hair floating in a cloud around her, her thin white legs trailing like wisps. She came forward until her sweet, pale face was close up to Flea's, her hands on her shoulders. 'Listen.' Her voice was sharp. 'Wake up. Now. Look after yourself.'

She shook her, and when Flea didn't respond, she closed her fingers around her hand, moved her fingers across and flicked the lever on the switching block to SCUBA.

Air flooded the mask. Her lungs inflated in one blast

and her head shot back. Light poured into her eyes. Another breath. She threw her arms out and coughed, the air dry in her parched lungs. Another breath, panicky, feeling her heart beat again, feeling blood hammer in her temples. And another. Flailing blindly, the equipment gauges, the emergency sports valve bobbing around her like tentacles as she righted herself in the water. In Wellard's panic he'd pulled her along the bottom. Silt had come up and was billowing around her like smoke. She hung limply in the milky water, letting him bump her along the wall.

Mum?

But the water rushed past her and all she could hear was Wellard's frantic voice screaming into the communications panel. 'Are you there, Sarge? Answer me, for Christ's sake.'

'I'm OK.' She coughed. 'You can stop dragging me now.'

He let go the tension on the line abruptly and she came to a halt. She floated face down, still holding the bail-out toggle, staring into the place where Mum had been. The water was empty. It had been another hallucination.

She began to tremble. She'd been close. She'd broken the HSE's rules, she'd cocked up an emergency procedure and the whole team had heard her going into narcosis. She'd even bloody wet herself in the process. She could feel it running down the inside of her thermals.

But it didn't matter. It really didn't matter. She was alive. Alive. And she was going to stay that way.

3

Bristol's Major Crime Investigation Unit was dealing with one of the most notorious cases it had ever known. Until a few days ago Misty Kitson had been a B-list celebrity, known only to the nation as another footballer's wife who'd put enough cocaine up her nose to destroy it from the inside out, collapsing the septum. For months the press had been scrambling to get pictures of her nose. Now they were scrambling to find out what had happened to her on the day she'd walked out of a rehab unit on the other side of Somerset, never to be seen again.

The countryside around the clinic had been searched: the police had ripped open every house, every wood, every livestock barn within a two-mile radius. It was unprecedented: the biggest land-based search the force had ever conducted and it had turned up nothing. No body. No clue. Misty Kitson seemed to have vanished into thin air.

The public were fascinated by the mystery, and by the unit handling the investigation. They pictured MCIU as an élite team: a group of dedicated, experienced men, pouring every ounce of energy into the case. They pictured the men clearing their heads and their lives for the case, dedicating themselves to the hunt. On the whole they were right: the officers on the case were one hundred per cent committed to finding Misty.

All, that was, except one.

Just *one* man was having problems concentrating on Misty. One man found that, no matter what he was supposed to be doing, what time he was supposed to be giving to finding Misty Kitson, the only place his head would go was backwards. Backwards to another case, one he'd worked on the previous week. A case he was supposed to have put away and moved on from.

That man was Detective Inspector Jack Caffery.

Inspector Caffery was new to MCIU, but he had almost twenty years of experience, most of it on the murder squad in London's Metropolitan Police. In all that time he'd never had trouble letting go of a case.

But, then, he'd never had a case that had scared him.

Not in the way Operation Norway had.

At eight thirty a.m. on the morning after Flea's accident, at the other side of town from quarry number eight, Caffery sat in his darkened office in the MCIU building at Kingswood. The blinds were down, the door was locked. He was watching a DVD.

It showed two men in the unlit room of a derelict squat. Both were white. Both were under thirty. One wore a zipped-up S-and-M leather hood and was naked to the waist. The camera sat steady on him as he took some time to prepare tools and show them to the camera. This man was twenty-nine. The other man was also naked to the waist, but he hadn't chosen to be dressed like that. He was unconscious, drugged and lying strapped to a bench. He didn't move. Not until the hooded man moved the hack-saw to his neck. Then he moved. He moved a lot. He was just nineteen.

This video was infamous throughout the force. The press knew it existed and would have done anything to get a glimpse of it. It showed the death and near decapitation of Jonah Dundas. Caffery had arrived in that room just minutes too late to save him. Most officers who'd worked Operation Norway insisted on keeping the sound turned down if they had to watch the video. Not Caffery. For Caffery the soundtrack was another place to search for answers.

He let it run through to the place where he'd arrived and the hooded man had fled. Then he skipped back to the beginning, to the part he was interested in: the first five minutes when Dundas had spent time alone in the room, strapped to the bench, before the hooded man began the beheading. Caffery pressed the headphones to his ears and shuffled forward in his seat, his face close to the screen.

The name 'Operation Norway' was arbitrary. The case had had nothing to do with Norway, the country, and everything to do with Africa. The hooded man – 'Uncle', as they called him – had been running a scheme among the African community in Bristol. Through greed, sadism and chance he'd tapped into the community's ancient belief, called loosely '*muti*', or African black magic, that some parts of the human body could be used to treat certain medical and spiritual conditions. Over the last ten years there had been just eight cases like this in the whole of Europe and for the British police it was uncharted territory, but what they had learnt was that a human head, the head of a young man, especially one that had been removed when the victim was alive, would fetch a huge amount of money in some circles. That had been Dundas's misfortune.

Operation Norway was broken apart before the head could be trafficked on and the police had arrested two people: the hooded man, who was local, and an illegal African immigrant, who'd been teaching him the customs, helping him to open up a network of customers for his merchandise. The African was in custody now, still trying to convince the police that his name was Johnny Brown and that he held a British passport. They'd searched him and found he was carrying a key fob with the Tanzanian national flag on it and that the T-shirt he was wearing was by a Tanzanian manufacturer, so MCIU was combing records from Dar Es Salaam to get a hit on him.

'What's all this?' Superintendent Rolf Powers, the head of MCIU, opened the door at ten past nine. 'No lights? It's like my teenage son's bedroom in here.' He switched on the fluorescents. 'Where were you? I've just done a whole press conference on the Kitson case without you.'

Caffery froze the DVD and rotated the monitor to face the superintendent. 'Look at this.'

Powers did so. Frowned. 'That's Operation Norway.

We've finished with that. The files should be with the prosecution service by the end of the month.'

'Watch this.' Caffery tapped the screen. 'It's important.'

Powers closed the door and came in. He was tall, wide and well dressed, and must have been athletic once. The lifestyle had taken its toll, though, and his body was spreading around the middle, the neck. He put the wallet he was holding on the desk and pulled the chair up to the screen.

The freeze frame of Dundas alone in the room before the attack showed another shape, standing close to Dundas's head, its back to the camera. It was bent over, concentrating on doing something. After the arrests, when they'd got Dundas's head to the morgue and examined it, they'd discovered that clumps of his hair were missing. In the same place on which the figure in the video was concentrating now.

Powers shook his head. 'It's the Tanzanian, Johnny Brown, or whatever he's really called. The one we've got in the bin.'

'It's not him. He's lying.'

'Jack, the little shit's 'fessed to it about a thousand times. Straight cough – said he cut Dundas's hair, wanted to make some voodoo bracelet with it. And if it's not him, then who the hell is it? The support group emptied that place out, raked the place clean. There was no one. And no way out.'

Caffery stared at the shape on screen. No one who'd seen the video had ever stated the obvious: that the figure on the screen didn't look quite human. 'No,' he said. 'It's not him. I had the guys in the custody suite measure him. He's five four. Short, but not this short. The camera was set at exactly one metre fifty high and was two metres from the table. I've looked at the CSI plans. Johnny Brown would have stood here.' He pointed at a place on the screen. 'More than a head taller. And look at those shoulders. There's something wrong there, seriously wrong.'

'They dressed him up – he admitted it. They sent him out to scare people into buying their voodoo crap. Pretty crude beliefs, these people have – not that those exact words ever came out of *my* mouth, of course.'

Caffery stared at him stonily. 'How'd they "dress" someone up to look like that? Look at it.'

'Prosthetics. Lighting.'

'There weren't any prosthetics when we searched the place. And Brown didn't have Dundas's hair on him when they took him in, did he?'

'Says he tossed it. And call me slow, call me a woollie, or however you Met people refer to us, but out here in the boonies someone 'fesses up to something like that, we kind of find it easier just to go ahead and believe him. No.' His voice was suddenly efficient. 'No, Jack. Let's pretend we haven't had this conversation. Operation Norway is over, OK?' He stood. Pushed the wallet he was carrying across the desk to Caffery. 'This is where the chief wants our time spent. This is the case I'm taking the beta-blockers for now. Open it.'

Caffery did. It contained six eight-by-ten glossies. Photos of clothing laid out next to a measuring tape.

Women's clothing. A dress. A pair of high-heeled sandals. A purple velvet coat. A silver mobile. 'Misty Kitson?'

'Of course. These are reproductions of what she was wearing. We've circulated them force-wide. Every person in every office across the force is going to have a copy of these pinned above their workstation by this evening, so even if they don't read the papers or watch the telly they'll've heard of her.' Powers went to the map on the wall, put his hands in his pockets and studied it. 'I can't fathom it. I really can't. A two-mile radius, the biggest search I've ever seen in the force, every inch gone over and we haven't turned up a *thing*. Not a sausage and— Christ, you're not listening to a word I'm saying. Are you?'

Caffery was sitting forward, staring at the post-mortem photograph of Dundas pinned up on the wall, at the way his hair had been clipped.

Powers picked up a photograph of Misty's clothes and stuck it, pointedly, over the one of Dundas. 'Jack, you've got three DSs and four DCs out there waiting to hear what you want them to do. *They* all want to find her.'

Caffery opened his drawer and pulled out the photographs of another post-mortem that had taken place two nights ago. It had come to him yesterday on the Centrex Guardian database and had everything he needed. He got up and pinned it over the photo of Misty Kitson's clothing.

'Ben Jakes. Twenty years old. Student at Bristol University. Can't face his exams, girlfriend leaves him, ends up with a penknife and a case of *wkd reds*. Down in the Elf's Grotto area. It's pretty there. You can see the lights of Bristol. Very popular suicide spot.'

'What's that got to do with anything?'

'His phone was missing – still hasn't been found. He'd been robbed. Roommate said he had money, a twenty at least, plus cards, never been used. Even sandwiches in his rucksack. They were gone. Oh, and he was naked.'

'Stripped off to kill himself? What was it? A full moon?'

'No. The thief took the clothes too. At first the officer in charge had it down as a murder. It was in the "too hard for district" file for a while, even flagged up on a watch-list for us, until the PM came back as suicide. The clothes came off him more than twenty-four hours after he died, says the coroner. Plus the other evidence – depression. No one's got any doubt it was a suicide; even his parents said they'd half expected it. But this is what I want you to look at.'

Powers took off his glasses and peered at the photograph.

'See it? His hair?'

'It's been cut.'

'Shaved. Remind you of anything?'

Powers frowned again. He took the photograph off the wall and turned it over. It was stamped by the Audio-Visual unit at Portishead. 'Where did you say it happened?'

'Quarry number eight. Down near Elf's Grotto.'

'And it's the hair that's the important factor? Because it's the same as what happened to Dundas?'

'The same person did it. The marks are almost identical.'

'So?'

Caffery gave him a grim smile. 'The pathologist, being

a pathologist, is typically vague about when Jakes died. But he's admitted that whoever rolled up and stole his clothes did it a minimum of six hours after death – there's livor mortis to prove that. The roommate says it's six a.m. when Jakes leaves his room. We don't know how he gets to the quarry but it's got to take at least an hour, probably more, assuming he doesn't stop on the way, which gives us seven a.m., so our thief has to come along at one p.m. at the *absolute* earliest. Meanwhile Brown was in that place,' he jabbed a finger at the screen, 'at two that afternoon. I saw the bastard with my own eyes. Can you really see him cruising out to the quarry, shaving Jakes's head and winging it back to the other side of Bristol within an hour?'

'I take it these are on the quiet, these timings the pathologist's given you. I can't picture him writing any of those in the report. They *never* commit when it comes to time of death.'

'You're right. But I don't need his say-so. Vodaphone coughed up Jakes's phone records. They showed calls made on his mobile at eight p.m. that night. Brown had been in custody for five hours by then.'

Powers lifted the blind and glanced outside. One or two reporters had taken up permanent residence outside since the Kitson case had come to MCIU. He stared at them for a while. Then he dropped the blind and gave his DI a long look. 'Jesus Christ,' he said. 'What do you want from me?'

'A week. A week on this. Give me two men and a week off from the Kitson case. I want to know how Brown cut

Ben Jakes's hair when he was twenty miles away at the time. I want to know what he wanted the hair bracelet for. And . . .'

'And?'

'And I want to know what prosthetics you'd have to use to make a human being look like *that*.'

4

Caffery left the MCIU offices at half past ten. He used the back entrance and walked round the side, away from the Kitson reporters, and straight into the low-ceilinged car park. It was sheltered there, but even so he walked fast, head down, collar up. He didn't get into his car, an unmarked fleet Mondeo, but stopped, facing it, thighs just touching the bodywork, and took a moment to scan the car park, checking that the shadows behind the other cars were lying flat and still. After a while he crouched, looked under the car. Then he straightened, opened the car, got in and central locked the doors.

However they'd managed it, whatever tricks they'd used, the players on Operation Norway had convinced people they were seeing something they couldn't explain. Something that made them nervous. Some of the earlier witnesses didn't have a name for it – they could only describe the glimpses they'd had: something human-like, but too small and stunted to be properly human. Then there had been the witnesses who had a name: a name that came from the darkest parts of the darkest continent. A

Zulu word that Caffery hadn't spoken out loud to Superintendent Powers because the sound of it put hairs up on the back of his neck.

Tokoloshe.

Three simple syllables, but they meant something powerful to those who believed. They meant deformity, brokenness. They meant all African superstition in one creature: the size of a large baboon with the body of a monkey and the face of a human. A witch's familiar, a creature from the heart of the velds. Sitting in the shadows. Watching, unblinking.

Caffery couldn't square the shadowy figure in the video with Johnny Brown, but the alternative explanation was, of course, close to insanity: a theory he would never vocalize, even to himself. But he couldn't help thinking about whatever it was he was hunting by that eerie Zulu word: Tokoloshe.

Now he leant over, flicked open the glove compartment and checked through the things in there. All front-line officers were issued the basic self-protection standards – quik cuffs, a pepper spray, and an ASP, a metal baton that could break bones. He'd been on the receiving end of an ASP during the Norway arrests at the beginning of the week. It had hurt like a bastard, but it was laughable as protection when the lowlifes out there were carrying Mach 11s and Magnums. Now it lay on top of a buff envelope file in the compartment. Underneath it, wrapped in oil-cloth, was a gun.

Five years ago, back in London, he'd had a dodgy mate working on Operation Trident who'd put him in touch with a character who'd lived in Tulse Hill all his life, but spoke, inexplicably, as if he'd been born in South Central LA and never took off his LOCs so you never knew exactly what he was thinking. When Caffery had turned up at his place he'd taken him into the kitchen and shown him two guns in a shoebox under the liner of the pedal bin: a model 17 Glock and a stainless-steel AMT 45 Hardballer that was so shiny it looked as if it was meant to be worn as jewellery. The dealer couldn't believe it when Caffery didn't jump at the Hardballer, because he personally thought it was the shiza and it wouldn't be hanging around long because the next person through the door would be snapping it up, if Caffery didn't have the good sense to take it off him. In the end Caffery did take the fashion-statement gun. Not because he liked it but because the Glock was the same as a force-issue weapon, and although he didn't intend getting touched for it, you had to look at every eventuality. A force-issue gun would point fingers at the wrong people. It was better to get caught with a street gun, even if it was an embarrassing bit of bling.

Usually the Hardballer was kept under the bag in the kitchen pedal bin, because if there was one thing Caffery had respected about the Tulse Hill dealer, it was his choice of hiding place. He'd be screwed if he used the damn thing and, anyway, that wasn't the point. The point was there were times when he needed the sense of security it gave him. Just knowing it was there. This week was one of those times.

He closed the glove compartment and looked out of the

window at the walls, checking the shadows again, concentrating on the ones at waist height. He hadn't told Powers the whole story: he hadn't mentioned that it wasn't only the video that unnerved him. He hadn't said that ever since Operation Norway he'd had the feeling someone was watching him. If it didn't sound insane he'd say the Tokoloshe had been following him. The Tokoloshe? In the streets of Bristol?

It had started in this car. Late one night, more than a week ago, he'd been parked in a deserted alley in the centre of Bristol late and someone, or something, had leapt on the car, slammed into the bonnet. It had been gone too quickly to see what it was, but he'd had the impression of something small, something close to the ground, scurrying away. That had been the beginning. Now he imagined the damned thing everywhere. In the shadows, under cars. Even in the mirror when he shaved in the morning.

He looked at his watch again. It was ten thirty-five. Only one victim had survived Operation Norway. He'd given the police a garbled statement on the day of the arrest, but now he was in Southmead Hospital, fighting for his life. The doctors weren't letting anyone near him, especially not the police, stressing him with their questions.

So what now, you twat? thought Caffery.

After a moment or two he started the car. He knew where to go. He wanted to see where Ben Jakes's body had been on the night someone had shaved off some of his hair.

5

Every month the underwater search unit did a handful of decomposed-body recoveries. A decomposed corpse is a dangerous thing. A biohazard. The fluids it produces when the abdomen splits can transmit a number of blood-borne diseases, and if the body has been eaten by rats there are other dangers: the transmission of leptospirosis or Weil's disease. Sometimes when the corpse is moved it will 'sigh', as if it has come back to life as air leaves the lungs, maybe expelling tuberculosis spores into the air. Most police forces in the UK insist that severely decomposed cadavers are handled by teams trained to use breathing apparatus. In short, the divers. Even if the body is on dry land.

Flea's unit had a strict clean-up routine in their headquarters after a body recovery and usually they managed to keep the place smelling OK. But that morning, at ten o'clock, sitting in the office filling in the RIDDOR accident forms, she noticed that something was wrong. She sniffed the air. Not nice. She put the forms into the envelope, got up and went into the corridor. Sniffed again.

After the accident with the air lines yesterday,

paramedics had checked her over but she hadn't let them take her in. She was fine. Fine and sturdy. She'd dropped on to the pontoon and done twenty press-ups to prove it. Nothing and no one could talk her into hospital for the rest of the day, and that had turned out to be a good thing because within two hours the team had had another call-out – to collect the sixteen-stone body of a fifty-six-year-old man who'd died on the toilet in a block of flats in Redland. He'd been sitting there for eight days, pyjamas round his ankles. Toilets were the worst because there was never any room to move. It had taken them three hours, start to finish, to get him out. Back at base they'd decontaminated their chemical-incident suits. They'd laid them out on the floor and scrubbed with long-handled brushes, rinsed and sanitized and changed the five phase filters in the masks, then sprayed everything down with antibacterial solution for good measure. Everything had been done by the book.

But the smell of the man was still there.

Flea went into the locker rooms where all the team were getting changed. She wasn't thrilled about the way they'd heard her in narcosis yesterday. So far no one had teased her about it but she wouldn't put it past them. 'What's the smell, guys?'

'Your banana bread?'

'Funny. We did the decontamination. It shouldn't smell like that in here.'

Wellard shrugged. The others shook their heads.

'OK. Go on.' She made a shooing motion with her hands. 'All of you. Do it again. Use the Janitol.'

No one moved. They all gazed back at her steadily.

'What?'

'We've already done it. *Again*. While you were in the office. Done it twice.'

'Twice? Then, where's the sodding smell coming from?'

'Your banana bread?'

She went into the decon room where the suits were hanging up to dry – ghostly, like a line of people standing there – and sniffed. She went back into the hallway and sniffed again. The smell was unmistakable. She went to the dustbin that they'd used to transport their soiled suits off site, put her face into it and took deep breaths of the air in there. Wellard appeared next to her, keeping pace, watching her forage in the bins for the liners they wrapped used bootees and gloves in.

'It's not that.' He folded his arms. 'I checked. The cleaner took them.'

She straightened. 'I give up. Where's it coming from?'

'Haven't got a clue.'

She sighed, took a green apron off the hook, pulled it on and tied it. 'And I was planning to go jogging.'

'You shouldn't be jogging, not after yesterday.'

'Well, I'm not, am I? I said I was *planning* to.' She pulled on nitrile gloves. Pumped some air into the pressure spray. 'Instead I'm going to clean these suits. Again. Do your job for you.'

'Ooh. Arsy.'

'Not arsy, Wellard, *hormonal*. I'm a woman. I've got ovaries. I get hormonal.' She went to the store and pulled out some things. A cylinder. An air hose. 'Come here.'

He looked at the air hose. 'Good God, boss. I didn't mean it.'

'Give me your hand.'

'At least make it quick.'

'Attach this,' she slapped the hose into his palm, 'to the valve. That's the way. Good boy. Now, while I redo the decontamination, you go round the buildings and sniff the drains. If anything smells, run some water into it. If it backs up, use this.'

'Compressed air? In the drains? Sarge, we've got a caretaker somewhere in the building, I'm sure we have. He's a lovely man. He'll have some rods. Better for the interior decoration than air.'

'Wellard?'

'Yes?'

'JFDI, mate. Just fucking do it.'

The Arctic Monkeys CD was on the player. Flea turned it on, jacked up the volume really loud and got stuck in. Scrubbing and spraying. Sluicing water into the drain. The umbilical lines that had ruptured yesterday were in a yellow nylon bag pushed up against the tiled wall, waiting for the HSE lab to pick them up. They'd take months. The lab would subject them to a battery of tests trying to work out what had gone wrong and how she'd managed to rub a hole in both of them just like that. She stopped for a moment next to them.

It befuddled her. She'd always thought they were pretty bombproof and it made her feel really uncomfortable and *thick* that she hadn't checked her equipment. She'd been so, so close. It was starting to feel as if she was on a run of bad luck. There was this, yesterday. Then on Tuesday she'd got into a hell bastard of an arrest with the MCIU people on Operation Norway, a job that had all but destroyed the member of the team now on compassionate leave. Not to mention the day before *that* when she'd got forced into a position *again* of covering for Thom. He'd come home paralytic one night, driving her car and trailing a cop car with him. Being the sap she always was for her brother, she'd stepped in for him, sworn to the jobsworth cop she'd been driving the car, even did a breathalyser for him. Thom had dodged a serious bullet for the hundredth time, and she was left wondering two things: if he was ever going to stand on his own two feet and how long she could continue to pull him up the hill.

She pulled out the white wellingtons the team wore for body recovery and turned them inside out to check that no body fluids had run down into the absorbent interiors. As she got to the last pair, Wellard appeared in the doorway. She wiped her forehead and dropped the boots, defeated.

'I give up. I've done everything. I'm going to have to go through all your bags next. Check for disgusting *man* underwear. Socks. That sort of thing. What's the report, Dyno-Rod man?'

'Drains are as clean as a whistle. Anyway, no point worrying about it now.'

'Eh?'

'Phone's been ringing off the hook. You had the music up too loud.'

'Who's calling?'

'Your friendly search adviser, Pearce. Got another body. More overtime.'

'Yeah?'

'Yeah. They think they've found Lucy Mahoney.'

6

Quarry number eight was deserted. Caffery stood next to his car and stared at the puffy clouds and blue sky reflected in the still, cold face of the water. At the head of the quarry, on the flat perimeter where the water hadn't yet risen, two old cabin cruisers lay on their sides, chained together with a rusty anchor line. At the other end vast grey cubes of dimension stone had been abandoned in puddles of brown water. Buddleia clung to the waste tips sloping up on all sides.

Caffery locked the car, shrugged his jacket closer and went to stand at the quarry edge, peering into the water. Beyond his reflection the water was a clear twilight blue. A yellowish haze of embryonic plants clung to the rock edges and below that, about twenty feet down, the vague suggestion of something misshapen. A boulder maybe, or submerged pumping equipment, or the quarry wall, following the hewn-out rock edge.

Africans believed the Tokoloshe was a river-dweller. They believed he hung around the banks, made nests in the rushes and could stay submerged for hours. Whatever the witnesses in Bristol had seen, one thing they were all clear on: it had come out of water, from rivers and quarries, once even from Bristol's floating harbour. They swore it had simply 'surfaced', as if it had been under the water for some time, lolling on the bottom, rolling content as a crocodile in the mud. And there was no breathing apparatus – the witnesses were adamant on that point: the hellish face was naked. So how the hell had the Operation Norway gang managed to fake those unexplained submerged minutes?

Caffery straightened and looked across to the hills of grout. The sun had gone behind a cloud, and for a while something heavy seemed to hover over the water, as if the air itself had got darker. Ben Jakes had been at those slopes when he'd killed himself. A bit of old police tape was still hanging in the bushes and some dead flowers in cellophane that some of his university buddies had brought. There had been ten other suicides here in the last four years. Suicide had that effect – always seemed to spread like a virus. Someone jumps off a bridge and before long it's Suicide Bridge and people who'd never have heard of the place will drive through the night just for the honour of jumping off it. That was what this quarry was like, except they didn't jump in. Just sat on the edges with their pills and their razors, probably looking at the stars.

Jakes's phone still hadn't turned up, but the same team who'd worked on the Kitson case had analysed his signal patterns and worked out that the two calls after his death had been made from somewhere near here. The number wasn't one Jakes had used before. Caffery had called it on the work phone and it turned out to be disconnected. It was a throwaway phone, pay-as-you-go, and he was pretty sure it had been disposed of already in a rubbish chute somewhere.

Caffery picked up a stick and began to walk the perimeter, beating at the undergrowth as he went. The quarry had been searched when Jakes's body had been found, but Caffery wanted to be sure there was nothing he had missed. No hidey-holes or evidence that someone else had been there on the night Jakes had died, maybe watching him from the bushes. He searched every square inch again, kicking around among the undergrowth, and after an hour the only thing he had found was a scooter lying on its side in the bushes.

Someone had made an effort to conceal it – he had to crouch down and break branches to get at it. He dragged it out into the sunlight and set it upright, giving it a small shake. It had a tax disc, and petrol sloshed around in the tank. Jakes hadn't had a scooter, Caffery was sure of that. He took a pen from his pocket and pulled back the callipers to check the brakes. No rust, so it had been used in the last twenty-four hours. He laid it on the ground, slapped his hands together to get the dust off and was about to turn back to the car when he noticed something else.

About ten feet away to his right something blue and white was snarled in the roots of the buddleia. It was police tape, wrapped around the twigs. He went to it, pulled at it, and saw a length of blue butyl lying on the ground. It was about ten inches long and had come from a tube of some sort. He picked it up and studied it. At three-inch intervals letters had been stamped into it: USU. Underwater Search Unit. He knew the unit, and their sergeant, Flea Marley. She'd been the support unit officer who'd made the arrests on Operation Norway with him. Pretty. When Caffery had come out here to the West Country he'd made a pledge: he'd left a couple of lives ruined in London and he wasn't going to do it again. There would be no more women in his life. Not without serious thought. But he hadn't made any promise not to notice if someone was pretty.

He pulled out his phone and called Kingswood. DC Turnbull, one of the men Powers had assigned him, answered. 'I was just about to call you,' he said, spruce and eager. 'Got a couple of things. First off the Tanzanian in the bin, the one who keeps telling us his name is Johnny Brown? We've got a name. Clement Chipeta. Interpol had him in Dar Es Salaam until he came off their radar about a year ago. He was in serious trouble out there, not just with the law but with the gang he was working for.'

'Who did what?'

'Trafficking. They dealt in the ingredients for traditional medicine, mostly from endangered species, but some of it from humans. Which, I assume, is why the Operation Norway muppets found a use for him when he turned up here.'

'You've let the custody officers know?'

'Of course.'

'OK.' He turned away from the quarry, his finger in his ear so he could hear over the lousy signal. 'Listen,

Turnbull, I need you to do three things. Give me a PNC on this number, will you?'

He gave him the plate number for the scooter and Turnbull tapped keys, getting into the Police National Computer.

'And when you've done that go online and look something up for me. Ever heard of free diving?'

'Free diving? Sorry, boss, I'm from Birmingham. We don't do sea, water, rivers. We like our concrete.'

'Look it up when we're off the phone. I want to know how long someone can hold their breath. How long they can stay under.'

'Free diving.' He could almost hear Turnbull frowning. The computer bleeped. 'PNC's back. The scooter's a TWOC.'

TWOC – Taking Without Consent.

'When?'

'This weekend. From a driveway over in Bradley Stoke. Nothing else.'

'OK – let them know I've found it. Then speak to someone in the support unit. Find out what the underwater search unit were doing in quarry number eight, over in Elf's Grotto.'

Silence.

'You there, Turnbull? Give someone in Support a call.'

'I don't need to, boss. I can tell you what the search unit was doing. They were searching for a misper. A woman. Yesterday.'

'Did they find her?'

'Not in the quarry. But they have now. That was the

other thing I was going to call you about. They're not far from you. Eight minutes if you drive legally. Four if you don't.'

7

Lucy Mahoney had been missing for three days. Judging from the state of her she'd been dead for most of that time. Her body had been found by hikers out in the Mendips on the banks of the Strawberry Line, the abandoned railway the Victorians had used to transport strawberries from the fields around Cheddar. The countryside there was pretty, the poppies already out in the linseed fields, a pollen heat haze hanging over it. But there was nothing pretty about the corpse: visible from a hundred yards away, a tower of shifting flies hovering above, a blackened pile of clothing and skin.

She was lying on her back. Dressed in a distinctive stripy sweater, skirt and flower-printed Doc Martens covered with leaves, she had already decomposed enough for some bones to protrude through the discoloured flesh. Flea led the team through the wrapping of the body: batting away the flies, pulling carefully to unstick the corpse from the fluids on the ground, log-rolling it into a linen sheet, and lifting it into a white body-bag – face up because the mortuaries hated corpses arriving face down.

Mahoney had been well built and, even decomposed, she wasn't easy to lift. Inside the suits the team were sweating: Flea could see the rivulets running down Wellard's face.

Flea had had commendations for her work. Two. And she was only twenty-nine. She was scared stiff she'd only got them because she was a woman, scared stiff it was the only reason she'd made sergeant and was leading the unit. Being scared like this was why she over-compensated for her build and height. It was why she knocked herself out doing insane training circuits, running ten miles a day or working weights into the night – high weights, low reps – day after day after day. Under the water everyone was equal. On land she had to work twice as hard to hold her end up.

They sealed the body in a yellow biohazard bag – XL, because corpses sometimes bloated to twice their original size – and carried it along the quarter-mile track to the rendezvous point, stopping every so often to rest and swap sides. From time to time they'd check for long-range press lenses outside the cordons, waiting for a chance to snap her and the boys covered from head to toe in body fluid.

The rendezvous car park was packed with vehicles. The coroner's private ambulance was there – two men in grey suits and black ties standing near it, smoking – and the head of the CSI team, a woman in a red Canada sweatshirt and jeans, sitting in the opened door of a car, drinking a cup of tea. It wasn't until Flea had got the stretcher into the coroner's van, had chucked her respirator into a little wheelie-bin, and was standing next to the unit's Sprinter at the RV car park letting Wellard hose her down with bleach solution, that she noticed someone else.

He was just outside the cordon, holding a can of Red Bull. Medium height, lean. Dark hair cut short. Maybe nine or ten years older than her. DI Jack Caffery. MCIU. The last time she'd seen him, on Tuesday, they'd been making an arrest together. That day something had passed between them. She knew it, and she wondered if they were ever going to talk about it. She watched him carefully as he ducked under the outer cordon, using the CSI's aluminium tread plates to cross towards her. He wasn't limping like she'd thought he'd be.

'OK, Wellard. That's enough.' She pulled off her hood, undid the storm zip on her suit, then peeled it down, pulled her hands out so the gauntlets were left inside the sleeves and stepped free of it. Without lacing her trainers, she jammed her heels down against the backs of them, and clomped across the car park. She stopped a few yards away from Caffery.

'Hey,' he said, taking her in from head to toe. She knew what he was thinking. The mosh-pit hairdo, the trousers sticking to her. The grey T-shirt glued tight with sweat. 'How're you doing?'

'Fine. You?'

'Yes. Nice to see you without an ASP in your hand.'

'Nice to see you on two feet. Not on the floor.'

'Bad, wasn't it?'

'Not your finest hour, I s'pose. Or mine. I still don't know what axe they're going to drop on my head. Keep getting memos from Occupational Health telling me I'm due for a free critical debrief, y'know. For the trauma. I haven't taken it yet.'

'Me neither.'

'I was going to call you. I wanted to say sorry.'

'Sorry about what?'

'About that.' She gestured to his leg. 'About your ankle. About what I did. I didn't mean to give you grief.'

He glanced down at his feet and gave the trouser leg a quick shake. To stop him savaging the piece of shit they'd been trying to arrest on Operation Norway she'd used her support unit stainless-steel ASP on Caffery's ankle-bone. It'd been the only way she could bring him to his senses.

'You're not limping. I thought you might be.'

'No. Not limping.'

'I didn't tell anyone. About what you did.'

'I gathered. No rubber-heelers on my doorstep.'

'Half of me regrets stopping you. I might've liked to have seen him with his head split open.'

'Nice.'

She shrugged. 'Honest.'

'Thank you. For not saying anything.' He looked at her for a long time. And then, just when she was about to speak again, he glanced at her breasts. Only for a split second. But it was enough.

'I saw that.'

'Couldn't help myself. Sorry.'

'You're my senior officer. You're not supposed to look at me like that. It's demeaning.'

There was a pause. Then he raised an eyebrow. 'Mmm.

Is this the overture to an industrial tribunal? Sexual harassment?'

She stopped herself smiling. Suddenly she felt light and easy, as if she'd just woken up from a long sleep. 'Is that why you're here? To see if you can get a grievance accusation? Is that the sort of frathouse-initiation thing they get up to in MCIU now?'

'Frathouse initiation?' He half smiled. 'No. Sorry.' He pointed at the coroner's van. The door stood open. Inside was the bright orange blur of Mahoney's body on the stretcher. 'I'm here about her. Have you signed her over yet?'

'They're doing the paperwork now.'

'Got any spare respirators?'

'Sure. I've always got a couple spare to stop the CSI guys vomming. Why?'

'I'd like to see her before the coroners take her.'

'I thought it was District's case?'

'It is. I'm not really here. I'm just being nosy.'

She raised an eyebrow. 'Hmm. One body. Female, but fully clothed. Knickers on, skirt not pulled up or disturbed. A bottle of pills next to her, a suicide note. I pulled out of the gunk a Stanley knife she'd used to cut her wrists. Sounds to my naïve ears as ninety-nine point nine a suicide. The pathologist isn't going to work hard for his corn today, believe me.' She gave him a suspicious look. 'So what's Major Crime doing? It's totally off your radar.'

Caffery looked at the CSI woman. She'd lowered her face and was pretending not to be listening. He turned his back to her and lowered his voice. 'OK,' he murmured.

'Last week there was a suicide only a few miles from here. Young guy. Ben Jakes.'

'Not one of mine.'

'No. Well, excuse me for being rude but maybe he was a little fresh for you. They found him in hours.'

'There are suicides around here all the time.'

'Except this was different. Something had happened to the body. Someone had got to him post mortem.'

'What'd they do?'

'Cut his hair. Actually shaved it. At the back of his head. The psychologist's telling us there's something ritualistic about it.' Caffery tipped the remainder of the Red Bull into his mouth, half crumpled the can, put it into his jacket pocket. Copper habit, this: so close to a possible crime scene you do things automatically. '"Ritualistic" was the word he used. Ring any bells?'

'Operation Norway bells?'

'Exactly. And it's got me wondering. Have you ever asked yourself if we missed someone that day? When we came into the squat. Are you sure we got everyone? There wasn't a chance for someone to have got away?'

She shook her head. 'No. I mean, there was a window grille, Sitex. It had been bent back, but not enough for someone to get out.'

'What about a child? Could a child have got out of it?'

'A *child*? What would a kid have been doing in a hell-house like that?'

'Do you remember this word?' He glanced over his shoulder then turned back, leant into her and whispered, 'Tokoloshe.'

'Ye-es,' she said cautiously. 'Of course. And I remember they dressed someone up to scare the living crap out of people, but I thought you had him.'

'No. The guy we arrested was too big. Too big to be the Tokoloshe.'

Flea started to laugh, but when she shaded her eyes to study him, she saw he wasn't joking. She'd heard that some of the people in London who'd worked on a *muti* case there had developed a taste for Africa, that now they took family holidays in Botswana and Ghana, not Margate. They told their colleagues they were brushing up for a future in hostage negotiation with one of the securities agencies like Kroll, when actually they'd fallen in love with the dark continent. Maybe Caffery was like them and had started to believe in the mumbo-jumbo. She'd have liked to say something, but there was an unwritten law in the police: thou shalt never *ever* make thine superior officer look a tit. She narrowed her eyes and kept her mouth shut.

'I wanted to ask you,' he said, 'because one thing all the witnesses said was that it came out of the water like it had been submerged. I wanted to know how you think it achieved that.'

At that she dropped her arms. *Now* she got it. Now she saw what was going on. The boys had leaked she'd been narked that day and set Caffery up for this wind-up. Someone else in the water in quarry number eight? An African monster swimming around in the water? Yeah, right. She folded her arms and gave him a measured look. 'You must think I'm *spectacularly* stupid.'

'What?'

'You must really think I'm a twat. You must think all I do is . . .' She trailed off. She'd just caught sight of Wellard. He was busy hosing down the wellingtons, not looking at her. If this was a joke he'd have been watching her carefully. Smirking. And when she looked back, Caffery's face told her he wasn't kidding either. Wasn't his style. 'Oh,' she said lamely. 'You're serious, aren't you?'

'Yes.'

'No one asked you to wind me up?'

'About what?'

'Nothing.' No. She'd been at fifty metres that day. Too deep for someone without equipment. Wellard said the surface of the quarry had been like glass. It had been a hallucination. Happened all the time with narcosis. You saw any crap the imagination could churn out. And if Caffery had suddenly turned into a true believer it was nothing to do with what she'd seen. Nothing to do with her. It was SEP: someone else's problem. 'Yeah, well, that's your business. And my business is getting this body to the coroner without anything going missing.'

He nodded. 'Do you think you can spare me that respirator first?'

'You're not going to be able to see anything.'

'Humour me?'

She shrugged, went to the dive truck and got two clean respirators. They approached the van with its blacked-out window, 'Private Ambulance' in yellow letters on the side. She leant inside and unzipped the bag. A few flies crawled out. Fat and drugged. She hated the flies the most, hated their habit of laying eggs in the mouth, eyes, ears, genitals and nostrils, even the anuses of corpses. All fair game to a bluebottle. Lucy was no different. Maggots had eaten away most of the exposed flesh and taken her face back to the teeth in some places.

Caffery peered at her.

'Not much to see.' Flea's voice was muffled in the mask. 'Is there?'

He motioned for her to zip up the bag. They went over to the unit van, where the smell couldn't reach them, and took off the respirators.

'Well? What's your professional opinion?'

'My professional opinion?' She laughed. 'That you're going to have a trip to the mortuary this afternoon.'

'Then what about your personal opinion? I don't think you're short of those.'

'Personally? I wasn't looking when we did the recovery, but I don't think there was anything unusual. Not on her head. You'd need to get all that yeuch rinsed out to be sure. It's really not our business to be going through her hair out there in the field, y'know, so get thee to the mortuary, Mr Caffery.' She took his respirator from him and chucked it into the truck. 'It'll be the Royal United in Bath, I should think. The on-call pathologist's over there today.'

8

'Sir?'

Flea might have said something else to Caffery that day. She might have said a little more and things might have panned out very differently if at that moment Stuart Pearce, the rolypoly search adviser who'd ordered the quarry search, hadn't interrupted them.

'Sir? *Sir?* I'd like a word.'

They both turned to watch him come across the car park, smiling at Caffery, his finger held up in the air as if he was making a point. He stopped a few feet away, breathing hard from the exertion. He had a soft face and a thick, sunburnt neck. His hair was combed across his balding pate. He addressed Caffery, acting as if Flea didn't exist. 'You're the SIO, are you, sir?'

'No – he's gone. Wells station. You'll catch him there in about ten.' Caffery started to turn away, but Pearce wasn't going to be put off.

'Is it Lucy Mahoney in there?' He gestured at the coroner's van pulling out of the car park.

'Who wants to know?'

He fumbled in his pocket and pulled out a business

card. 'I was the search adviser on her disappearance. Today's my rest day but I thought I'd better come in when I heard they'd found someone.'

That figured, she thought. He was the type: an officer freshly trained in a new job, full of enthusiasm, such a need to be involved that he'd turn up on rest days probably for no pay. All because he liked the glory. He was the sort who'd accidentally let his warrant card drop out of his wallet on to the bar when he was trying to pull someone. Thought women were more likely to open their legs for a cop.

'You can see, can't you, now that you've got the lie of the land, how I would never have put this place on my search parameters? I'd never have found her with what I had to go on – it was like a needle in a haystack.'

'Don't waste your breath, mate,' said Caffery. 'I'm just floating here. It's not mine, it's F District's. I'm MCIU.'

'MCIU?'

'Major Crime.'

'Yes. I know what MCIU is.' He wiped his forehead. 'You must be doing the Kitson case, then. I was the search adviser on that too, before the review got it bumped up to you from District.'

Bloody celebrity junkie, Flea thought. People like Pearce loved the media scrums that the Kitson case was attracting, the spotlight on the force. God, she didn't like the guy. The more he talked, the more he ignored her, the more the fuses popped in her head.

'I heard you got a fix on her phone from the Macrocell base station?' he said. 'Used that call analysis team, right?'

'You've had your ear to the ground, then,' said Caffery.

'That mast was in the parameters I drew up, but it wasn't a good area – not well covered by masts.' Pearce put his hands on his hips and, head back, gazed out across the trees. Then he squinted in the other direction, at the horizon. 'Somewhere like this would have been better. If Misty Kitson was out on that railway line we'd have got a fix on her in no time. But her phone was switched off, wasn't it?'

'Whose?' Flea could hear irritation creeping into Caffery's voice.

'Lucy Mahoney's. It was switched off, District told me. Bizarre, if you ask me – usually suicides use their phones. Make last-minute calls, even just to hear someone speak, or texts before they pull the plug. You can see why my job was difficult, can't you? She broke all the rules.'

'What rules?'

'All the geographical profiling rules, everything. To start off, look how far away her car is – she had to walk half a mile to get here. Why didn't she park nearer?'

'She was wandering? Distressed?'

'Nah. Suicides generally know where they're going to do it before they set out. And, anyway, I spoke to the ex-husband and he said she doesn't know this area. She never walked her dog here or anything like that. There was nothing connecting her to this place. I mean, most suicides are less than half a mile from a road, and she must be topping that, surely? And they go somewhere high, suicides. They go and sit somewhere – somewhere they can see lights, buildings, so they can see what they're saying goodbye to. But not her. You can't see a thing from that embankment. I've been over there. Had a look.'

Flea'd had enough. She stepped forward. Hand up. Big smile on her face. 'Hi.' Her best, brightest voice. Waved the hand for good measure. 'Remember me? Sergeant Marley? The one who did most of your searching?'

He gave her a cool look. 'Yes.'

'We dived the quarry yesterday. You missed it.'

'I was looking at other possible sites.'

He turned back to Caffery, but she'd started now and she wouldn't stop until she'd got in his face. 'Yeah, well. Don't worry about it. I didn't think she'd be in there anyway.'

'Of course not,' he said quietly, his eyes still on Caffery, 'because you're psychic.'

'I'm sorry?'

'You knew she wouldn't be in the quarry. So you must be psychic.'

She started to laugh, but stopped when she saw the look on his face. 'What did you say?'

'I've had to come in on my rest day for this. And it doesn't help when whatever blood, sweat and tears you throw at it, whatever profiles, Blue 8 mapping you generate, some people still won't believe you. This is the second time you've undermined my authority.'

She knew what he was talking about, of course: earlier this week she and Pearce had got into what Wellard called 'a full and frank discussion' about whether the team should be searching for Misty Kitson in a lake near the rehab clinic. Flea hadn't thought Kitson would be found in the lake and she'd told Pearce so. She probably hadn't done it in the sweetest way imaginable either. 'Misty Kitson again?'

'You decided *she* wasn't going to be in the lake either. Didn't you? A bit dispiriting, that – being told I was wrong before you'd even finished the search.'

'I was right, though, wasn't I? She wasn't there. You get an instinct after a while. She was never going to be in the lake. She was never going to drown herself, a girl like that.'

'You're going to tell me the lottery numbers next.'

'Yeah, yeah, yeah. Well, I can't reason with you so I think I'm finished here.' She put her arm out, gesturing for Pearce to stand back so she could pass, but he didn't move, didn't meet her eyes. She tried to go round him the other way but he shifted his boxy body a little, hemming her in. He held Caffery's eyes while he did it, a half-smile on his face.

She stopped and raised her eyes to his. 'You know what?' She was calm. 'It's been years since I got my hair off over a case like Kitson just because the victim was a celeb. You know why?'

'Why?'

'Because I'd be just a *little bit* afraid someone would turn around and call me an effing media monkey. Now,' she paused, breathing hard, 'are you going to step out of my way, you combed-over old twonk? Or do I have to push you?'

Pearce's nostrils widened a tiny amount. There was a moment when she thought he might just take his life into his hands and stand his ground. But in the end he hadn't the balls. He rubbed his nose and stepped out of her way.

She made a small, victorious noise in her throat, slung the towel over her back, turned and trudged back to the unit van. Bloody Newbs. Probably moved up from the Specials, that one. She just didn't have the patience.

'Marley,' Caffery called. But she raised her hand, goodbye, and continued to where the team were throwing the last few pieces into the van. She got into the Focus, started the engine and pulled out on to the road. The sun was beating down on the windscreen, making patterns in the dust. As the car park disappeared in her rear-view mirror she allowed herself to smile.

Do I have to push you, you combed-over old twonk?

Good one, girl. She jacked up the volume on the end of that Arctic Monkeys CD. She liked the way Caffery had looked at her breasts. As if the T-shirt wasn't even there. As if he could see right through it, and as if her breasts were round and big and something to be respected. It was an age since someone had looked at her like that. An age. She'd like it to happen again.

She laughed and opened the window. *Combed-over old twonk*. Yeah. She was proud of that one. Really proud.

9

Back at base everyone was hot and tired. And they still couldn't get rid of the smell. Even after they'd showered and showered, decontaminated the suits over and over again, shoved their underclothing into airtight sacks, even after all that, somehow, it seemed to linger. Flea wasn't even sure she couldn't smell it on her clothing when she got into the car to go home. She sat at red traffic lights and wafted the neck of her T-shirt. Bent her face down for a sniff test.

It was hard and cold and lonely to think of a woman's life reduced to this: a smell other people struggled to wash away. There had been days, especially when she'd first started in the unit, when every dead body she handled took something vital out of her. But she'd grown more pragmatic over the years and today she put the thought of Lucy Mahoney away easily and drove with the window open, the countryside flying past. The phone sat in the central console. Caffery's mobile number was in its contacts list. She could call him any time. She could just pick up the phone and call.

By the time she got home to the house she'd grown up in, high on a hill overlooking the distant city of Bath, she was hungry. A long time had rolled past since breakfast. She parked on the gravel and climbed out, automatically going to the back to put her kit holdall in the boot for the next morning. But as she aimed the key at the lock she remembered: the boot was stuck. It had been like this for four days, ever since Thom had borrowed the car the night he had come home drunk. The lock made an odd little electronic bleep and seemed to click open, but when she tried to lift it, it jammed. She put the key in and turned it. Again it clicked. And again she couldn't open it.

Swearing now, she dropped the holdall in the gravel, squatted at eye level to the lock and saw what was jamming it. A piece of material was trapped in the latch. She gave it a tug, thinking somehow she'd shut her overalls in it, but the fabric was wrong: it was soft, velvety, not slick. She tipped back on her haunches, puzzled. Running her fingers over it, she tried to remember what she'd put in here. And then she noticed something that made everything go into slow motion.

The smell.

She stared at the lock. Sniffed the air. Now she thought about it, the car had smelt this morning on her way to work. Yesterday too. Maybe the stench in the offices hadn't been the team's fault at all. Maybe they'd cleaned the equipment properly. Her car had been parked near the air-conditioning unit. This smell could have been sucked into the building from the boot.

Four nights ago Thom had taken the car to a meeting.

Fuck, fuck, fuck, she thought. Thom? You were upset that night. Too upset. Was it really just the drinking and the police car you trailed in with you?

She straightened. Stepped away from the car. Scanned the garden, the driveway. Her parents' house was on a remote hillside, but there were neighbours, the Oscars, who often watched her from their windows high above the driveway. There was no one at them today, though. Lucky. Head down, she went to the garage door and threw it open. Then she went back to the car and swung herself into the driver's seat. Inside, the smell came back at her. How the hell had she missed it all this time?

She spun the car round under the huge wall of the Oscars' house and reversed into the garage, spraying gravel everywhere. The garage was a triple one, but even when her parents had been alive no one had ever parked in it. Instead the walls were lined with the family's detritus: old lawnmowers, a Victorian cast-iron bath, rusting shears, a freezer, a rolled-up tent and some of her father's old diving cylinders propped in a row in the corner. There was just enough space to squeeze in the Focus. Its exhaust filled the place, poisoned the air.

She killed the engine, got out and slammed down the garage door, then slid across the interior bolts – rusty because no one had ever used them. Among a pile of tools near the door was a jemmy. She took it to the car and inserted it carefully under the lock, then paused, half of her not wanting to know. Taking a deep breath through her mouth she leant on the handle. The lid flew open with a rush of stinking air. Inside was a bloated corpse.

'Shit.' She slammed the lid shut and took a step back. Dropped the jemmy with a clatter. '*Shit.*' She put her hands into the air and stared at the boot, breathing hard. What the *hell* had Thom done?

She clenched her fists. Unclenched them. She grabbed the jemmy from the floor and popped the boot again, keeping well back when it opened.

It was a woman. She lay on her side with her left arm squashed under her, the right elbow over her face at an unnatural angle. She was dressed in a purple velvet coat, a neon-green dress belted at the waist. The four days of being cooked and simmered by the sun on the car had made her limbs swell fat and shiny, enough for the straps on her high-heeled silver sandals to have disappeared into the flesh. From the small part of her face that was visible Flea could see her eyes and lips protruding. Mottled, like a frog's.

She shut the boot and went shakily into the house through the side door, kicked it closed and sank to the floor, her back against the wall. She put her arms on to her knees and dropped her face, staring blankly at her legs in the dark blue trousers. This was insanity. It was insanity.

After a while she got to her feet and went around the rooms, gathering things in her arms until she'd found everything she needed: brown paper, tape, one of the face-masks her team sometimes used for body recovery, and the blue inner gloves she wore for diving polluted water.

Back in the garage – the smell was unbearable now and already a few flies were circling the boot – she stood on a box and taped brown paper to the windows, sealing them carefully so no one could stand on tiptoe and stare in. Then she pulled on her gloves and facemask and went back to the boot. She stopped to take a few deep breaths and wipe her head with her forearm, then opened it again.

The body was still there. Yeah, right. Like it might have got up and left? She stepped nearer. Forced herself to look. Her breathing was loud in the facemask.

The woman didn't seem very old – mid-twenties maybe, with nicely manicured nails, highlighted hair and expensive gold hoops in her ears. Her arm was dropped across one as if she was trying to shield herself. The coat lay across the lock, part of it jammed into the mechanism. Flea looked hard at it, wondering if there was something important about it. Where had she seen it before? One of Thom's girlfriends, maybe?

She lifted the woman's elbow, careful not to disturb the clothing. No injuries to this side of the face. There was a long graze on the underside of the arm. With her index finger pressing the facemask tight to her nose, she bent, squinting at the graze. Something was embedded in the skin. Something dark and hard, like small stones. Or tarmac. An idea began to work in the back of her head.

Lowering the woman's arm carefully she went to the front of the car. The Focus had belonged to her parents – their priorities in life had had everything to do with experiencing the world and nothing to do with nice-looking cars: it was battered and well used. But now, and she crouched next to the headlamp to be sure, she was pretty certain this dent hadn't been there before Thom had borrowed it.

She studied it carefully. She'd seen a lot of road crashes. Only last month she'd been woken at two in the morning to cut a body out of a car wreck: a thirty-six-year-old mother of three had impaled her car on a motorway barrier. She was alive and unhurt, talking to everyone on the scene, but stuck in the car like a pig in a poke. The fire that had started in the engine had cooked her alive. Flea had been the one who had pulled out her skinless corpse and put it into the coroner's van. No one said the obvious, that she looked like an anatomy lesson with all her musculature so exposed. Yes, what a car could do to a human body was something she knew a bit about. And what a human body could do to a car – she knew a bit about that too.

She straightened and went to the other side of the Focus, checking along the sills and the doors for anything unfamiliar. She studied the bonnet, the wheels, the windows, careful not to touch. Then she stood on tiptoe, and immediately saw what she was searching for. There was a crumpled area about two foot in diameter on the roof just above the driver's seat, with a small crescent of blood caked on it. A picture was forming of the way a body could fly into the air, cartwheel through the moonlight, bounce on a roof and land on the road, tarmac and grit scraping itself into the skin. Thom had been drunk that night.

She went back to the boot and put her hands into the pockets of the woman's dress. Empty. The coat pockets too. Then her hands closed around something else, wedged just under the woman's hips. It was crackly and cool against Flea's gloved fingertips. Turning her face away because each time she moved the body a waft of decomposition came into her face, she gripped the object between thumb and forefinger and tugged gently. Surprisingly, it came away easily, dragging briefly against the clothing and popping out so fast it almost made her take a step backwards.

It was a handbag, sewn intricately with large, faceted sequins dangling and catching the light. Something about the design, the natural fabric at its base, told her it was expensive. Flea opened the clasp and peered in.

Most of the things inside it were cosmetics. She laid them carefully on the garage floor: a tube of Benefit concealer with a picture of a fifties girl on a telephone, a sachet of Hard Candy body shimmer, a stick of Chanel lipstick, colour 'Boudoir' – things Flea could never have afforded, even if she'd wanted them. Deeper in the bag was a compact Tampax tampon wrapped in green plastic, a half-finished blister pack of paracetamol, some banknotes folded into a diamanté clip. She put everything on the floor and ran a gloved finger through the rest of the bag. There was a handful of change but otherwise nothing. Just a few coppers and a bit of dust. No ID.

She was replacing everything in the bag when something made her stop. It was the diamanté clip. On one side it was straight but on the reverse side the diamanté was formed into a single letter. She stared at it. It was an M.

The letter M.

The air came out of her lungs fast. She sat down on the garage floor and put her head back, trying to breathe. She knew where she'd seen the coat before. It hadn't been on one of Thom's ex-girlfriends. It had been at work. The photo of a replica of this coat had been circulated to everyone in the force that morning. That and the green dress and a mobile phone, spread out on a table. There was even a copy of the photo pinned on the noticeboard over her desk.

Dropping the clip, she got to her feet and kicked open the door into the house. She went to the toilet, squatted at the bowl and retched, letting everything come up, heaving until it was just thin brown trickles of saliva. She stayed there for a while afterwards, one hand on the seat, the other holding her hair out of her face, spitting the taste out of her mouth, staring blankly at the bottle of Toilet Duck sitting on the floor behind the U-bend.

It wasn't the smell of that poor contorted human in her boot that was making her throw up. It wasn't any of that. It was that M on the money clip. M for Misty.

Misty Kitson. The missing footballer's wife.

Flea spat again, sat back on her heels and wiped her mouth. Thom was in more trouble than he could possibly, possibly imagine.

And she didn't know what to do next.

10

When Caffery arrived at the mortuary the remains of Lucy Mahoney were already on the central table, the lights powering down on her, the huge fans in the floor and ceiling roaring, sucking air in from the outside and drawing away the foul smell. The brown-smeared sheet she'd been wrapped in lay open on another table. In it, a scattering of maggots squirmed and crawled over each other.

Caffery put on the mortuary's bootees and gloves, came into the room, crouched at the head of the block and peered into the mess of her hair.

'You're DI Caffery.'

He glanced up. The district DI, a guy who looked as if he spent a lot of time in front of the mirror each morning, stood a pace away. He had his hands in his pockets and was half turned sideways so he didn't have to look at the body. This was a suicide but Lucy was female, and protocol put a CID officer of at least inspector level at the post-mortem: to rule out rape or sexual assault. From his face Caffery guessed the DI wasn't ecstatic at having to be there.

'We met at that SIO's investigation policy meeting in Taunton. Remember?'

Caffery straightened. 'Yeah,' he lied. 'Good to see you again. How's it going?'

'Fine.' He jingled the loose change in his pockets. Still didn't look at the body. 'But Major Crime? For a suicide? Anything about this I should know?'

'Nothing.'

'No one warned me.'

'Don't worry about it. Forget I'm here.'

'Would be nice to know, that's all.'

'Hello, boys.' They turned. The pathologist stood in the doorway pulling on latex gloves, eyeing them both. Beatrice Foxton. Caffery knew her from London – they were both refugees from the Met. A formidable woman in her late fifties and drop-dead gorgeous. Beatrice smoked, drank, raced horses and took trekking holidays in places like Uzbekistan. She also had perfect skin, cornflower blue eyes and lots of hair that she wore as it grew out of her head: long, grey and wavy.

'Lucky me. *Two* men.' She made a show of snapping on the second latex glove. Pulled it carefully down her fingers. Gave a dirty smile, as if she was going to ask one of them to bend over. 'Right. Who's first?'

Caffery gave a thin smile. 'Beatrice. You haven't changed.'

'Really, Jack. I'm insulted. I *meant* which of you has primacy? I see two DIs. I don't know which I'm working with. I have to ask.'

'It's him.' He nodded at his oppo.

Beatrice gave the DI a cool look, then raised an eyebrow at Caffery. He knew what she was thinking: she was wondering what the hell MCIU wanted with a suicide. She wasn't stupid enough to ask. 'OK, OK. Come on.' She tucked her long grey hair into a surgeon's cap decorated with SpongeBob SquarePants cartoons and gestured at the morticians. 'Shall we do it?'

As the door closed everyone jostled for space: the coroner's officer, the district DI, the photographer, who stood at the head of the table chatting quietly with one of the CSIs. The two mortuary attendants stood nearby and Caffery found a place to the right where he could lean against one of the other tables, arms folded. Back on the murder squad in the Met he'd done enough post-mortems to have learnt ways to get through them. He'd learnt how not to think about the human being the corpse had once been: how to see decomposed meat and not a person. Scraps of hair, sometimes they didn't help, sometimes they started a flicker of something, a flicker of reminding him that this was a person, but he'd even learnt to look past those most of the time.

The district DI had found a place by the sinks, as far from the table as possible, and was trying to look nonchalant. He was popping extra-strong mints into his mouth on the heel of his hand and sneaking suspicious glances at Caffery. His face was shiny with sweat.

Beatrice swung the microphone on a rotating arm out over the table so it was near her mouth. She gave the date, the time, the place, the names of those present. 'I'm looking at the remains of a woman presumed to be . . . ?' She glanced at the DI.

'Uh – Lucy Mahoney.' He tore his eyes away from the corpse, from the sodden clothing drenched in brown fluids, and forced himself to look at Beatrice. 'That's what we're thinking. Date of birth, oh two oh one 'seventy-eight. Been a misper for three days.'

'And am I supposed to be looking for an ID too?'

'Next of kin's IDed the clothing. Her-ex husband. But she's . . .' he gestured at what was left of the corpse's face '. . . not really in a state for him to ID.'

'Have we got any personal descriptives?'

'He's a bit fragile about it at the moment. Someone's trying to reach the family liaison officer from when she was a misper, hoping he or she's got something in the descriptive file, something more detailed. But on the plus side we don't have to wait for dentals from the dentist or the practice board because the department right here in the hospital has her records on file. She had an extraction under anaesthetic two months ago. Can you believe our luck? They should be here any time now.'

'In that case, if she's out of rigor . . .' Beatrice switched off the mic, lifted Mahoney's hand and flexed the arm '. . . which – ah, yes – she is, nice and bendy, I'll do some bitewings and some periapicals when we're done. Save the poor ex the trauma of looking at her.'

She switched the mic back on and checked the hanging scale digital readout.

'Clothed, the subject weighs fifty-five kilos. Usual caveat, though, that there's considerable decomposition so

I suggest it would be lunacy to take that as a reliable indicator of weight before death.' She looked up at the morticians. 'Fester? Lurch?' Caffery watched Beatrice, half a smile twitching his mouth. He'd never known anyone quite like her. Every PM she did, whatever mortuary, she always called the morticians Fester and Lurch. And always got away with it too. Incredible. 'Move her up a bit.'

The morticians shifted the body so that what was left of Lucy's neck was resting on the block there. Beatrice walked slowly around the table, talking into the mic as she went, bending every now and then to inspect any part of the body that caught her attention. 'The decedent is wearing a long green skirt – some sort of velvet – a blouse patterned with flowers, striped woollen sweater, striped tights, lace-up boots, also with a pattern of some description. Clothing has been photographed and logged, so now I'm going to remove it.'

She took her time snipping away at the skirt, peeling it away from the places it had become stuck to the skin, cutting through the sodden blouse. She used a hook to pull the bra out, it was embedded so deep into the flesh. Under the clothing Lucy's flesh was different, not black and covered with maggots, but hard and soapy – duck-egg blue. Soon all her clothing had been clipped away and passed to the crime-scene manager, who was now checking that each article was properly bagged and labelled. There was a set of door-keys in her pocket, but nothing else. No handbag, money or makeup.

'Where was she found?'

'Next to a railway line.'

'Urban?'

'Rural.'

'She's done well,' Beatrice said. 'Not been pulled around too much. Sometimes they come to me in twenty different bags – the way foxes scatter a corpse around, you'd think it was a game. Do you remember that woman on the golf course in Beckenham? You worked on it, Jack, if I recall. Took six men all day to find all of her and there were still bits missing. Still, s'pose foxes've got to eat too.' She bent over and addressed the corpse. 'All right, my love. I'm just going to move you a little.' She lifted the body at the hips. Peered under it. Fluid seeped slowly out from between the slack, yellowish buttocks. 'There are plenty of post-mortem artefacts here.'

Caffery took a step closer. 'Post mortem?'

'It's not that clear, but can you see here? On the posterior surface of the trunk there are some excoriations.' She used a gloved finger to point to an area of skin. 'Ants, I'd guess. Or some other insect.'

She lowered the corpse and slowly checked the surface of the thighs, belly and arms, running her fingers over the skin, pausing to check each area. She took a hand, lifting it and crouching at eye level with the table so she could peer into Mahoney's armpit. Something had caught her eye. She angled the little gooseneck light so it shone on to the hollow there.

The district DI took a step nearer. 'What?'

'There's a little wound. Just here.'

She poked at it, then shook her head, dismissing it. 'Surgery. Not recent, maybe a year, two years ago. Not great as an identifier, even a secondary one, but it might have popped up on the personal descriptive. If the dentals don't arrive at least we've got something.'

'What kind of surgery?'

'Keyhole – probably endoscopic thoracic surgery. Could be a lobectomy for lung cancer, that sort of thing. Maybe a biopsy incision. Nice neat mark. Made a better job of it than whoever did her Caesarean.' She straightened and ran the tip of a gloved finger across the woman's pelvis. 'Bloody awful job. Shoot the obstetrician, I say. Now, what about these other scars? These are more important.' She turned Lucy's left hand over and studied the inside of the arm. 'Incised wounds to the right wrist. On the left wrist one wound has partially incised the radial artery. A second has incised the ulnar artery.'

Lucy's arm hadn't been transected but sliced longitudinally from top to bottom, the sides like dried meat now, opened to show the intricate network of blood vessel and nerve. Not from side to side. Caffery had seen that before: it was the most effective way to end your life. He bent over, hands on his knees, and peered into the hair again.

'So she was serious about what she was doing,' Beatrice said. 'At least on this wrist. Not so hot on the right side – which is what you'd expect. This second wound is gaping. It's transacted the volar carpal ligament and exposed the transverse carpal ligament and the flexor digitorum.'

'There was a bottle of pills next to the body,' the DI said. 'Temazepam. And a Stanley knife.'

'Stanley sounds about right. It would have to've been a

mounted blade that made these – there's enough pressure associated here that it would've left cuts on the fingers if it was just a razor . . .'

It took Caffery a moment or two to notice she'd stopped talking. He looked up to find her staring at him. Frowning. She put Lucy Mahoney's hand down, came round the table to him and stopped quite close so she could speak without being heard by the others.

'Jack,' she murmured, 'I've been polite to you, haven't asked you any questions, haven't made a fuss about you crowding my room, but if you're looking for something why don't you just tell me?'

He glanced at the DI, straightened and put his face close to Beatrice's, then spoke in a low voice: 'Comb her hair, will you, Beatrice? Give it a comb and a wash. See if it's been cut.'

'Cut? What sort of cut? Trevor Sorbie cut?'

'Hacked. Clipped, shaved. Anything that looks odd.'

She gave him a long, curious look, then turned to the mortician. 'Fester? Comb her hair through, my love. Rinse it out for me.'

The mortician did as he was told. He drew a comb through Lucy Mahoney's hair and inspected the tiny bits of debris that fell on to the paper he held underneath. Then he placed the paper on the exhibits trolley, and rinsed the hair with the small hose attached to the examination table.

Beatrice and Caffery bent over the head. Cleaned up, Lucy Mahoney's hair was reddish brown. It straggled out in long, damp curls. There were no cuts or shaved areas.

'Not what you were expecting?' she asked.

'Thank you, Beatrice.' Caffery pulled off the gloves and turned towards the door. 'I'll try not to darken your day again.'

11

Small though Flea was, she knew how to use her body. Dressed in her force combats, a neat white T-shirt and dark glasses over her red-rimmed eyes, she was a force to be reckoned with as she stood blocking the entrance to the driveway. The moment he saw her the taxi driver pulled up short. She held up a hand and swung straight into the back seat. No one, she thought darkly, was going to take a car to the front of her house for a while.

It was a warm afternoon and the taxi driver had the air-conditioner on, but they'd only gone a few hundred yards before he began to sniff. Flea, sitting stonily in the back, her arms crossed, her feet planted solidly on the floor, raised her eyes and found him looking at her in the rear-view mirror. He sniffed again, narrowing his eyes suspiciously, trying to look down at her clothing in the reflection. 'Off somewhere nice?' he said steadily. 'Going somewhere nice on this nice day?'

'No.' She opened the window to let the air in. 'I'm not going anywhere nice. I'm going to see my brother.'

She pulled out the phone. She'd called Thom six times

already. Each time he'd dumped her straight into his mailbox. There was no point in calling him again. She could call her dad's oldest friend, Kaiser, but he'd never had sympathy for Thom. Anyway, she'd leant on him too much in the last few days. She dropped the phone into her lap and leant back in the seat. The air coming in was sweet, warm and full of buttercups, bringing with it a sense of the west, a sense of the sea out past Bristol and Wales. She'd known these lanes all her life. She'd grown up here with the views of the seven sacred hills, the Georgian townhouses of Bath cradled between them, with the distant view of Sally-in-the-Wood and beyond it the Avon valley.

She thought about Thom, about how everyone had worried over him as a child. He was underweight, too small for his age. He got infections easily, learnt to walk late, and always seemed to find the fastest way to trouble. Mum and Dad had had to dig deep to keep their patience with him. And sometimes they'd failed.

She remembered coming in from the garden one day. Out of the sunlight, into the cool. It was the school holidays and her parents were in but the house was silent, which made her hesitate and go upstairs quietly. She found her mother first, sitting on the edge of the bed in the big double room. She was dressed in shorts and green Scholl sandals, and was staring at herself in the mirror. Her long white fingers pressed a pair of headphones to her ears and something about her posture, about the tension in her hands, the way her feet were crabbed up in the sandals, told Flea not to approach. Then Jill Marley had looked at her daughter. There was no expression on her face. They held each other's eyes for almost a minute. Then Jill had turned back to the mirror.

The door to Thom's room on the other side of the landing was half open. Flea tiptoed over to it and inside saw an odd tableau. Dad was in the middle of the room, kneeling. Thom, who was about eight at the time, stood a pace away, facing him. They weren't speaking or moving, just staring at each other. Dad's face had the look on it that he sometimes got when he was determined to do something, as if he believed the force of his gaze was enough to cut through mountains. At first Flea thought they were having a conversation. Then she saw it wasn't a conversation they were in the middle of. It was violence.

David Marley took a breath, closed his eyes and slapped his son across the face. It wasn't the first slap that afternoon, Flea knew. She could tell that this had been going on for a long time: Dad staring at Thom, Thom staring back, every few seconds Dad lifting his hand and slapping him. She understood what was happening, too. Dad was trying to make Thom react. But he wouldn't. She could've told Dad he was wasting his time. Thom stood, mouth slightly open, eyes focused in mid-air. He wouldn't react. He wouldn't cry. That was just Thom for you. Irritating, distant and otherworldly. Not quite with it.

And now he was all she had left in the world. With Mum and Dad gone, Thom was all she had left to convince her that their childhood had really happened.

After their parents' accident Thom had refused to move

back into the family home with his sister and now he lived in a thirties semi on the outskirts of Bristol. It was built identically to the others in the street, with tile-hung walls and diamond-shaped leaded panes in the windows. It was tidy. There was an empty milk bottle with a note in it on the immaculately swept doorstep. Thom hadn't been able to find a job in years and recently his energy had gone into tending the tiny house while his girlfriend went out to work. Thom – poor, hopeless Thom, so ill-equipped to deal with the world. And so, so *stupid*.

'You should have called first.' He opened the door a crack, just allowing his face to peer through. '*You should have called. Why didn't you?*'

'*I did call*,' she hissed. '*Your phone was switched off.*' She stepped forward, pushing the door, expecting him to give way. But he didn't. 'Thom. You know why I'm here.'

'*It was an accident*,' he whispered. '*An accident.*'

'Let me in.'

'It was an accident – I didn't mean it to happen. She just stepped out of the trees. It was a fast road. I didn't have a chance.'

'We've got to talk. Let me in.'

'Mandy'll be home soon.' He pulled a handkerchief out of the top pocket of his shirt and rubbed it against his eyes, his mouth. 'She'll be wanting her tea . . .'

Flea pushed open the door, stepped inside and went past him. 'I don't care about Mandy. We've got to talk. Now. Come on.'

She walked into the sitting room with its vase of plastic

flowers, its glass ornaments on the little table, everything neat, dusted and in its place – you could see the reflection in the TV screen, it was so highly polished. Not like Mum and Dad's careless house. Thom wasn't like a Marley at all.

After a while, when he saw she wasn't going to leave, he followed.

'Sit down,' she said.

He sat obediently on the edge of the armchair. 'Well? Are you going to dob me in?'

'No.'

'Why?'

'Because I'm an idiot. A soft touch. Stupid enough to give a crap about you, you useless piece of shit.'

'I deserve that.'

'Yes. You haven't even got the comprehension for the can of shit you've opened.'

He shifted in his chair, not meeting her eyes. He was dressed in his smart corduroy trousers, a chequered shirt under a sensible brown pullover. He was very blond and pale, and his ears stuck out just enough to give him a vaguely nerdish look. It was impossible to imagine he could have killed a woman, even accidentally, and not told someone: that he could coolly have picked her up, put her in the boot and driven all the way back to Flea's house.

'Did you know her?'

'I told you, she stepped out in front of me. I was driving along and the next thing it was all over. I panicked, Flea. I just panicked.'

'But you know who she is, don't you?'

'I've been watching the news. Every second of every day I've been watching it.'

'Then you know they're never going to stop looking for her. Not until hell freezes over.'

'I know.'

She sighed. 'I can't believe I'm having this conversation.'

'I've got no idea, *no idea*, what to do next.'

There was a taste in her mouth she didn't think she'd ever get rid of. She sat on the sofa opposite and, arms folded, looked at him steadily. 'OK. Here it is. Like I said, I won't go to the police.'

'No?'

'No. But you will.'

Thom sat back in his chair. He let all his breath out.

'Listen.' She held up a hand. 'I'm going to remind you of what happened, OK? You've been depressed. Since Mum and Dad died you've been really unwell. We've got doctors' records to prove it.'

'I've been better since I've been with Mandy. Things were getting better.'

'You've been *depressed*. And that night you borrowed my car because everything had got too much. You wanted to drive somewhere, just to get your head together. You weren't drunk but you were crying – you admit that. Hysterical, even. You hit something on the road. At the time you thought it was an animal, but then, when you thought about it, when you saw the headlines, you started wondering if . . .'

'Oh, Christ.'

'Thom. It's the only way. Your papers are all up to date, aren't they? Your driving licence?'

'Yes.'

'My insurance is watertight for you driving and the car was in perfect nick, MOT only a month old. We're in a strong position. We'll get a psychiatric evaluation, plead diminished responsibility or recognized medical condition or whatever they call it these days, and there's not a judge in this country would automatically bang you up. It's more likely they'll hand you a hospital order. Keep you in the psychiatric-evaluation tumble-drier until eventually the sun goes down and someone spits you out of the system.'

Thom lifted his thin hands and massaged his temples. The veins were blue through his skin.

'The first thing we've got to do is return the body.'

'God, please, no. Not that.'

'We return it to the place the accident happened. Then we leave it for a couple of days so the wildlife can get at it. We need to destroy some bits of evidence and create others. In the meantime you go off and get yourself sectioned.'

'Sectioned?'

'We're going to build a psychiatric case. We'll do some research on the best way to go about it. But first we get the body back.' She stood. 'Now. We'll take your car. You've got to show me where.'

He didn't move.

'She has to go back to the same place, Thom. There'll be forensics at the scene proving it was an accident.'

He shook his head and looked at his hands, as if he'd

find an answer in the soft skin on the back. She ran her fingers tiredly down her face. 'Now, listen to me. And you'd better listen really well. I'd do anything for you because you're my little brother. But I can't take away what you're going to have to do.' She leant forward. 'You're going to take me there now. Did you hear me? Do you understand?'

He didn't answer. In the hallway someone was unlocking the front door.

'Mandy,' he hissed. 'Quick.'

Flea sighed. She stood up, arms still folded, while in the hallway Mandy moved around, putting down keys, flicking through the mail on the side table. After a moment or two she came into the living room, stopping when she saw Flea and the pinched look on her face.

Mandy was older than Thom by several years: a short, square woman who dressed in sludge-coloured linen with lots of Indian jewellery. Today she was wearing an olive green jacket and white trousers. She'd had her short hair styled and coloured: a deep dark red, almost purple, cut in a bob against her round face. In one hand she was carrying a half-open rucksack with papers and files peeping out of it. Now she set it on the floor and began slowly to unbutton her jacket, her eyes going carefully from Flea to Thom.

'OK,' she said, at last. 'I've come in at a bad time.'

There was a moment's silence. Thom licked his lips. In spite of his reserve, he'd never been brave – he was terrified of Mandy. And she knew it. She dominated him, never letting him out of her sight, expecting him to cook and clean. She'd spent a lot of the inheritance money too, on supporting a fringe theatre group from Easton. Ordinarily she and Flea didn't have much to say to each other.

'Mandy, I was just leaving. Thom, you give me a call when you've had a think, will you?'

He stared at her, the skin around his mouth faintly blue.

'Thom?' she said, meaningfully.

His trance broke. 'Yes,' he muttered hurriedly. 'I'll call you. Later. I swear.'

12

A man sat near the door in the waiting room outside the mortuary. He raised his hand as Caffery came through. 'Hi.'

'Evening.' Caffery kept walking, pulling out his phone. He wanted to see if Powers had been on with another nag about the Kitson case, but he also wanted to see if Flea had answered the call he'd made earlier. He'd liked the way she'd looked at him earlier. It had made something in him give a little. It was a good feeling – a clean, loose feeling, the same sensation he sometimes got with the first drink of the day.

'Excuse me. I need to talk to you.'

Caffery stopped, turned back. The man was on his feet. He was tall, with big hands, polished shoes and neat brown hair. Too brown. A bit of dye helping him out there.

'Is there any news?'

'Any news?'

'On Lucy. You were in there just now, weren't you?'

'Who are you?'

'Colin Mahoney. That's my wife in there. My ex-wife, but she kept my name. They're saying she killed herself. Is that right? Is that what the doctor thinks?'

'Your FLO will talk you through it. I think she's on her way.'

'My what?'

'Weren't you given an FLO? A family liaison officer to contact when Lucy was missing?'

'Oh. Her.' Colin wiped his forehead. 'Sorry – but I didn't put much faith in her. She hasn't even called me today. And now I suppose Lucy's in there and cut up already.'

'When your liaison officer gets here she can talk to you. It's not my place.'

'Who are you then?'

'DI Caffery.' He flashed his warrant card. Didn't say the words 'major crime unit'.

'OK – DI Caffery. You tell me. Did she kill herself?'

'I can't answer that question.'

'Yes, you can.'

Caffery sighed and put the card back into his pocket. 'It's not my case, but if it was, what I'd probably say to you at this point is the same thing my oppo in there will tell you when he comes out. The same thing your FLO will tell you.'

'And what's that?'

'That we can't say anything definitive until the inquest, but at this point we're not looking for anyone else in connection with her death.'

Mahoney sank into his chair, deflated. He put his

elbows on his knees, dropped his head and stared at the carpet. 'I can't believe this. Just can't believe this is happening.'

Caffery watched him and thought about what it must have been like for his own mother. When he'd been just eight Caffery's older brother Ewan had gone missing from their family home in South London. His body had never been found. It had happened one Saturday afternoon more than thirty years ago, and in those days the Metropolitan Police didn't have family liaison officers. There'd have been no one to sit his mum down and say, 'Look, if you want to talk about it, you can. Here's my number – call any time you want. Would you like a cup of tea, love?'

'The liaison officer should be here anytime.'

'No, see, it can't be right.' Mahoney looked up. His face was a dull, congested red. 'If she's done that to herself, then what happened to Benjy?'

'Benjy?'

'The dog. I told the police specifically about Benjy. It was the first thing I said. Lucy took him with her. She must've had him in the car because they found dog biscuits on the back seat. He's never come back.'

'Mr Mahoney, I really suggest you take this up with your—'

'That's how I know it's wrong. I mean, it was all wrong anyway because if she was planning on doing something to herself she wouldn't have taken him with her. She'd have made sure he was looked after first. So where is he now?'

Caffery thought about a dog. Abandoned. Lost. Living

in the woods. Creeping along the backs of gardens. A wild eye swivelled to take in the human evidence: sheds, hover mowers, strimmers, rusting barbecues, children's swings. He thought about all the creatures living on the fringes of towns and villages. Not his problem. 'I'm sure he'll come back, Mr Mahoney.'

'He'd have done that already. He'd have found someone. He's a smart cookie, that one. Smart and loyal.'

'Mr Mahoney, like I say – this isn't my job. My commiserations, sincerest commiserations, on what's happened to Lucy. And I hope Benjy turns up safe and well. But . . .' He put his hand on Mahoney's shoulder and stood for a moment, looking him in the eye. In this job you had to be careful. You couldn't pull your heart out for every person unfortunate enough to find themselves on the pathologist's table. Even so, you could take one minute to think about them. To mark their life and your short involvement in it. So he stayed like that for a few short moments, then shook his head and turned away. 'But you'll have to take this up with your FLO.'

You took the time to show a little respect. After that you had to move on. Fast.

13

It was eight o'clock in the evening and there was just one message on Flea's phone. From Jack Caffery. She hadn't answered the call. Didn't much feel like talking. When the message icon popped up she dialled her mailbox and listened. Would she give him a call regarding what they'd talked about earlier? He'd like to take it further. He meant her breasts, of course. That was what he wanted to take further. She sat in the living room in her dad's old recliner, a mug of tea at her elbow, her body tired, bones aching, and thought, How odd. How odd that she could have been in such a different world only a few short hours ago. Different hopes. Different fears.

Thom hadn't called. She'd tried to phone him eight times already and always got his mailbox. Mandy did late shifts and would have gone back to work a long time ago, back to the call centre she managed. Which meant what? That he was still avoiding the issue?

Something would have to be done with Misty soon. In this heat it wouldn't be long before it was impossible to handle her. Her body would liquefy. Flea'd seen it happen to a corpse after only a couple of days in hot weather. It would begin to run through the floor of the car. And the longer those fluids leaked the more tricksy it would be to remove the boot-liner fibres from Misty's body and put her on the roadside. They couldn't leave it any longer.

She went upstairs, pulled out an ancient floor fan from one of the junk-filled bedrooms and dragged it down to the garage. She plugged it in, locked the door, double and Chubb, got her keys and her jacket. A little Renault Clio sat on the gravel driveway. She'd hired it when she'd left Thom's. It was a shiny blue and smelt of upholstery cleaner and Turtle Wax. So different from the Focus. It was almost a pleasure to drive.

The offices in Almondsbury were silent. The smell they'd played hide-and-seek with for the last two days had gone. Surprise, surprise. The place smelt like a dentist's surgery. There was a note on her desk from Wellard saying the HSE had picked up the umbilicals and would be in touch when the tests were completed. That meant ages. It also meant they weren't going to question her about the circumstances of the accident – how deep she'd been, for example. Any other day, that would have lifted her spirits.

She worked fast and silently: from the storeroom she got foot covers, gloves and three yellow Tyvek biohazard suits. There were webbed straps in the dead-body recovery locker: she took three, two pieces of plastic sheeting and a handful of zip ties. She shoved it all into a mesh drysuit duffel bag and carried it to the car. With the radio on full blast she drove out on the ring road, stopping at various convenience shops and the Threshers in Longwell Green for bags of ice. At a Smile store in Hanham she found ten pink and green trays that would make ice cubes in the shapes of hearts, diamonds, clubs and spades. She bought all ten. Paid cash.

Thom still wasn't answering his phone.

It was eleven when she got home. She checked for footprints in the gravel – her habit, accustomed as she was to the way the Oscars, her neighbours, would casually wander on to her property as if it was their own. The Marleys' garden had once belonged to the Oscars' house. They made no secret that they wanted to buy it back and reinstate their access to the valley. The garden was huge and stupid and rambling, far too large for her to care for, and somewhere down in its wilderness was a big problem: a folly built by one of the young men of the manor in the nineteenth century. Now it was collapsing. A surveyor in a yellow hard hat had come to inspect it and said it broke all the laws of physics and was dangerous. It needed to be either repaired or demolished. But she wasn't going to give in. The garden had been Mum's pride and joy. It wasn't going to be sold off, no matter how troublesome it got.

There weren't any footprints. The house was exactly as she had left it. She parked the Clio on the gravel and went inside. Even in the hallway the smell coming from the garage hit her immediately. How in Christ's name had she been able to walk back and forth past the Focus for the last couple of days, even *drive* the sodding thing, without noticing it?

She slung the ice bags in the garage, carried everything

else into the living room and stripped down to her underwear. The Tyvek suit was two grades higher than the ones the crime-scene guys used and hot. She dragged it on, knotted her wild hair at the back of her head and pulled on the hood. Then, holding on to the sofa, she lifted her feet, and shoved them into bootees, cross-wise, the way she put on fins. The facemask she left dangling under her chin. From the kitchen she got a bottle of water and, slugging it as she went, traipsed clumsily down to the garage.

'Right.' She slammed the garage door behind her. 'Let's look after you.'

The body needed to be cooled. The nights were still cold and there'd been a couple of chilly days, too, which meant she had to slow down the decomposition process to the level it would be at in the open. She couldn't freeze the body then thaw it: the process left signs a good pathologist would pick up immediately. They would spot the telltale traces of ice crystals in the muscles, particularly the heart. Still, the process had to be reined in somehow.

She plugged in the giant chest freezer in the corner. It hadn't been used for years. Not since the day Dad had brought the family to the electricity meter and made them watch, in awe, the way the little red dials hummed when the freezer was plugged in, and how they slowed when it was off. A power hog, it was switched on only for parties and at the height of summer when Mum made ice cream. Flea filled the ice trays with water and rested them inside on the diamond-pressed aluminium bottom, piling them one on top of another. She closed the freezer, opened the ice bags with her teeth and emptied all the cubes into the old iron bath that stood in the corner among the mowers and diving equipment.

When the boot was open again the smell was overwhelming. With just the mask and no respirator she had to turn away for a few moments and take long, deep breaths to stop the gag reflex overpowering her. Then, when her throat stopped spasming, she got to work, the suit rustling like dry leaves.

She sealed the contents of Misty's handbag in a green plastic bag, took out the Focus's parcel shelf and levered down the back seats into the storage position. She put a sheet of plastic on the floor next to the back wheel and another below the bumper, its top end folded inside the boot and tucked under Misty's left shoulder and left knee. She got into the back seat and leant over to work two webbing straps under Misty's shoulders and hips. Then she crawled out and went back to the boot, finding the trailing ends of the straps, dropping them on the ground on top of the plastic sheeting and placing her feet firmly on them. Leaning over she caught the other ends of the straps and, taking a deep breath, began to pull.

There was a pause. Nothing happened for a moment, then the body gave with a tearing sound as it unstuck itself from the boot liner and rolled sideways so that Misty's face was resting against the lip of the rear bumper. Flea pushed her knees under her to stop her falling on to the ground. She took a few breaths.

The back of Misty's head was matted with blood and now Flea could see what had killed her. There it was: a massive blow to the left side of the head where it had come into contact with the roof of the car. She could see all the details of Misty's ear where it had been torn away from the skull: she could see the folds and crevices and canals – a swift image of them being formed years ago, a dizzying slideshow of a baby taking shape: being born, growing, losing teeth, getting ankle socks and grazed knees. She saw first lipstick, first boyfriend, first heartbreak. She saw the drugs and the drink, the diets. She saw it as clearly as she could see her own past, and although she knew who Misty was, and that if they'd met in life they'd have had nothing to say to one another, something cold and lonely opened inside her.

She turned her head sideways and breathed hard. 'Stop it,' she hissed, clenching her teeth. 'Stop it.' She craned her neck and wiped the sweat off on her shoulder. She'd never lost it on a body recovery and she wasn't going to now.

'OK.' She looked at Misty's torn scalp again, at the thick blonde hair. 'I'm sorry – I'm sorry about the way I'm dealing with this. Please believe that.'

She paused for a second, as if Misty might reply. Then, grunting with the effort, she lowered the body slowly on to the sheeting. She was used to doing this with three other people to help, but Misty was light and rolled easily, her right arm dropping back down at her side so that her face was exposed. Flea stood, hands on her knees, breathing hard, and studied her for a while. Misty was so swollen that even her mother wouldn't recognize her, let alone the tabloids and the fans. How long would it have taken for her to get like this lying next to a roadside? Longer than the four days she'd been in the car.

She folded the plastic sheeting lengthwise over Misty's face, giving it a neat pleat fold along the top, the ends into goosenecks secured with zip ties. With an effort, feeling the strain in her back, she carried the cocoon to the bath and settled it carefully among the ice.

She paused for a second, looking down at Misty, at the smudged outline of a person. Already a faint fog was coming up from the ice, shrouding her, sending iced air past plastic, into skin, muscle and nerve.

'I know right now there isn't any God. But if I'm wrong and he *is* up there somewhere, then for Christ's sake . . .'

She pulled off her gloves, dropped them on the floor. She could feel the weight of everything trying to tug her down.

'For Christ's sake, let him watch over you, Misty. Let him watch over you.'

14

By the time Flea had showered, washed her hair and got dressed – black combats and the black dive-unit polo shirt – the moon was up. Out of the window a bank of clouds had crept over the top of Claverton Down and was marching slowly towards the house. One was the shape of a hand. Claws, extended, reaching down to trail its way through the garden, over the roof. She closed the window. Locked it.

In the garage the smell was still there in spite of the floor fan. She scooped out the ice water with a saucepan, added more cubes and refilled the ice trays in the freezer. The Focus's boot stood open, the inside stripped back to the moulded panels. Earlier she'd carved up the parcel shelf and the ripped-out boot liner using an electric handsaw. The remains were in a black bin bag against the door.

It was easy to imagine what the garage would look like from the outside – new paper shields on the window and, suddenly, the lights on for hours at a time. The Oscar family would notice it. She switched off the overhead lights and found a torch, then used it to hunt for a while along the walls, searching through the remnants of her family's life. Here was an old semi-drysuit her father had abandoned, neoprene flaking at the elbows and knees, there a weight belt, a collection of masks. Dad's first great love had been diving the dangerous and most extreme places the planet had to offer. He'd infected the whole family with it.

She pulled back a wheelbarrow that was leaning against the wall and found what she was looking for. An old container of engine oil, streaked and syrup-coloured with grass cuttings sticking to it. She picked it up, found an empty can at the other side of the garage, a length of rubber tube, gathered up the bin bag and carried it all out to the Clio.

The clawed cloud was still lowering over the house. It hadn't given in to rain yet. She turned the car out of the driveway and took the low road, down through the deserted residential streets at the foot of Solsbury Hill. Up the bypass, she found the tiny single-lane track that led up the side of Charmy Down Hill. The top was flat. In the war it had been used as a night-fighter station for Hurricanes to land. The control tower and the changes in the colour of the grass where the runways had been were still visible.

She pulled the Clio on to the airfield, wedged it next to a wartime bunker so it was completely hidden by insect-heavy buddleia and elderberry, got out and stood for a moment, looking westwards at the underlit clouds closing down on the spires and crescents of Bath. It was strange here, to be able to see everything for miles around. She turned and looked at the deserted airfield, at the clumps of waist-high grass and weed, the disused buildings, the piles of tyres and rusting farm machinery. There wasn't a soul up here – not even a bird, a fox or a cat. It was like crossing into a dead world.

One a.m. It had to be done now. She threw open the boot, pulled out the bin bag containing the boot liner and the chopped-up parcel shelf, threw it on to the ground and went to get the can of oil. With her feet planted on either side of the bag, she opened the can and let the oil gloop in long loops down on to it until it was covered. She gathered up the length of tube from the boot, unscrewed the petrol cap, shoved one end of the tube down into the tank and the other into the empty can. Pinching her nose, using her tongue as a splashguard she closed her lips over the tube and sucked hard, hard, until the oily petrol foamed up from the tank. Quickly she pulled back, thrusting the pipe down into the can and holding it there while the petrol drained.

Keeping her feet spaced and well back to stop them being splashed, she drizzled the petrol over the bin bag. When it was drenched she screwed the cap on the can, put it in the Clio boot with the oil can, replaced the petrol cap and locked the car. There was a box of matches in the bottom pocket of her work combats. She struck one, dropped it into the bin bag and stepped back. The petrol caught instantly, with a blue *woomp*, burning off in a second and leaving a baby flame in the centre – a lone curl of black smoke rising testingly into the air. She walked backwards a hundred paces and stopped next to the car to watch the dark shape of the bag let off a tendril of smoke and oily air, then bloom and thicken into flame. Sure now that it wasn't going to go out she pulled the phone from her pocket and dialled Thom.

The phone rang and rang, then clicked into answerphone. She dialled the home number, watching the incandescence of the fire lighting the undersides of the grass and trees around. When the home phone went to answerphone she dialled his mobile again. This time it rang four times. Then there was a muffled click and the sound of him breathing.

'Thom?'

Silence. She put an elbow on the roof of the Clio. 'Speak to me. Are you there?'

Another beat of silence. Then his voice, thick and nasal, as if he'd been crying. 'Yeah, I'm here. It's really late.'

'And Mandy? Is she still—'

'She's asleep. I don't want to wake her up.'

'OK. Get in your car and meet me somewhere. Saltford. At the pub on the river.'

'No.'

'You've got to show me where it happened.'

'I can't remember.'

'Of course you can.'

'I'm serious. I don't.'

'Then we're going to drive until you *do* remember. I'll see you in half an hour.'

'*No!*' he hissed.

She pressed a finger into the bridge of her nose. 'Look,

if we don't deal with this now it's going to get worse and worse. It'll finish us both.'

'I can't.'

'It happened in Farleigh Park, didn't it? Somewhere near the rehab place?'

'I'm not sure.'

'Well, it must have. She can't have walked far.'

There was silence at the other end of the phone. She pushed herself away from the car and stood with her hand in the small of her back above her hip, where her body armour sometimes gave her gyp. 'Thom, this isn't going to go away – whatever you think or hope it's going to come out somehow. And if you leave it, and if they find out you shovelled her up and put her in the sodding boot of the—' Her voice was rising, speeding. 'Oh, God help you, you'll be up in Long Lartin before you know it. They'll know your sister's a cop. And even if you got vulnerable status that would just put you in with the IPPs.'

'The IPPs? What're they?'

'The ones they keep in for public protection – the nonces, the sex offenders, the real nutters. Not good. Not good at all. Now get in the car and meet me.'

'But Mandy'll know. She'll find out. She suspects anyway. Just from the way you spoke to her she knows something's up.'

'You'll have to tell her eventually.'

'I can't. I just can't.'

'Then I'll do it. Go and wake her up. Give her the phone.'

'No! No, please. Please!'

'*Thom!* Just wise up, will you? *Just wise up*.'

There was a long silence. Embers and black plastic floated into the air. Beyond them the moon, hot and white, glowed faintly through the clouds. Then Thom spoke, his voice thick. Sullen. 'OK. OK – I'll do it. I'll tell her.'

She breathed out. 'Good. You do that. And call me when you have.'

15

The moon comes up fast in Somerset: racing across the lowlands, up the sides of the Mendips, into the Quantocks. It picks out the glittering windows of the cities in the far north of the county, creeps into the car in the mortuary car park where Jack Caffery plugs the key into the ignition. It finds Flea Marley in the north-east, standing on the blade of a hill, watching smoke rise. And ten miles to the east of her, in a quite different setting, it lingers on a lonely grey house. A house set back from a deserted lane, surrounded by fallow farmland, barns and outhouses and a disused swimming-pool. The moonlight fingers the windows of the single-storey extension. It tries but can't reach past the breezeblocks into the specially adapted room.

Inside, the light is a different colour. Here there is only an unearthly blue glow, emanating from seven specialized refrigerator units, all of which have their doors wide open to reveal their contents: stack after stack of carefully inventoried containers, each filled to the brim with formalin.

The man is in the middle of the room on the floor. He is perfectly naked and sits with his legs crossed, almost in a yogic pose, letting the calming light from the units bathe him. He will never see a woman's skin pegged out on his workbench. He understands this. Has understood it for years. That belongs to the realms of fantasy.

But his collection . . . His collection is his reality. It started as a small concession to the fantasy, but it has grown above and beyond that. It is more, much more. It is his life's work. His reason to keep breathing. He'll protect it at any cost. He'll do anything, even kill.

He has a flash – a sudden photographic image of a face on a hospital trolley. The trolley is being wheeled away under fluorescent strip-lights. The patient is anaesthetized but as the gurney disappears something happens – something the hospital porters on either side don't notice. The patient's head tilts back, it twists a little and suddenly, unseen by anyone, her eyes fly open. She is awake. Awake and alert and can see everything. Everything.

He puts his face in his hands and concentrates.

'Sssh.' His voice is soft. A whisper. As if he's soothing a child. 'Sssssh. It's OK. OK now.'

Things have gone wrong, but he's set them right. It's all behind him. All he has to do is keep calm and trust himself.

'Sssssssh . . .'

He sits like this a little longer.

Then, irritably, he gets up. He goes around the room slamming the refrigerator doors.

He hates this life. He hates it.

16

The next morning a low-pressure front nosed in from the Atlantic. Clouds hugged the Mendips, rain fell hard in the cities, flooded the storm drains. Traffic threw up dirty spray on the motorways. At quarry number two, almost at the end of the Elf's Grotto quarries, no light was getting down into the water – it felt as if dusk had come early. Flea had to take the Salvo divelight down with her into the water.

'What is it about you, Sarge?' Wellard's voice was loud in her ear. 'You've got another audience. Traffic guys again. Even a couple of CID, I think.'

She established her jackstay line, got her heading and began to swim.

'I think they fancy you, Sarge. Except no. Probably not you. Me. My eyes are prettier.'

'Give the line a tug.'

'Eh?'

'Give the fucking line a tug.'

'OK, OK.' Wellard pulled the umbilical hurriedly. The line strained at her chest. 'Clear?'

'Clear.'

A pause. Then, 'Bit hormonal again, are we, Sarge?'

'Don't talk to me. I'm concentrating.'

Thom still hadn't called. She'd been up half the night waiting and now she was pissed off. Seriously, seriously pissed off. She was wondering how long she should leave it before she gave up. Threw him to the lions.

'Sure you're OK?'

'Course I'm sure. Now be quiet and give me another bar.'

This was her first time in the water since her accident with the air line and the Health and Safety Executive would self-combust if they knew how many hours' sleep she was doing this on. She kept thinking of the hallucination. This quarry was at the end of the horseshoe and only a quarter of a mile from number eight where she'd narked and nearly drowned. Maybe there were connecting tunnels out here. Old air shafts that were flooded now and had things moving through them.

Bollocks. All bollocks. Narcosis. She'd been narked. That was all. She'd been down at fifty metres. No one could swim at fifty metres.

'Sure you're OK, Sarge?'

'Christ, Wellard. *Yes*.'

'Nothing worrying you?'

'No. I'm just looking forward to the pleasure of seeing who this guy is. That's all. Pulling his body out. Now, will you shut it?'

The job had come in first thing this morning. Three hours ago, at school drop-off time, a Lexus had been carjacked from a small town in north Somerset. A nine-year-old schoolgirl, in a tunic and a grey blazer because it was a top-drawer private school, was sitting in the back. The jacker had driven her for twenty miles, talking to her all the way, before stopping in Wells and ordering her to get out on the roadside, where she'd stood, crying and shaking, for ten minutes, watching the cars go by on their way to work, until a minicab driver had thought to stop. Then the jacker had driven the car another five miles over to the Elf's Grotto cave system where he'd run the Lexus off the road through a disused car-repair garage and straight into quarry number two.

It was a similar MO to another carjacking a year or so ago. That time the victim had been a six-year-old girl. In Flea's opinion it was the same guy. In her opinion he wasn't a carjacker at all but a paedophile. If the jacker today was the same person he wouldn't be the first paedophile to make a try at acting out his fantasies, failed and committed suicide. She hoped he'd kept his windows shut and that they hadn't smashed when he'd entered the water. She hoped he'd taken a while to die.

She got to the end of the first twenty-metre section out into the quarry and turned, wishing it was night-time. Cars were a cinch at night-time – the headlights often stayed on, even in the water, but the jacker's lights probably hadn't been on, in spite of the rain. The team usually looked for 'primary indicators' before they dived, tips as to where the car had gone in, but today there weren't any: no oil floating on the surface or scuffmarks on the edges. Kind of strange. So they'd had to assume the Lexus had come in on the only place leading out of the car park – the slip road on the west side.

She picked up the jackstay weight – the marker they used to delineate their search pattern – and dropped it. Harder than necessary.

'Hey, Sarge? Let's hope it is a body you pull out.'

'Eh?'

'Hope it's not someone wanting a fight with you. You know, freak air pockets 'n' stuff.'

'Jesus, Wellard, you been standing too near your car exhaust again? Just can it, will you?'

The team had been at the office when the call came and they had got to the quarry in under an hour and a half. But the witness who'd seen the Lexus go in didn't have a mobile. He'd driven five miles down the road to a pay-phone so at least two hours had gone by. No. No chance the bastard was still alive.

She finned on, not looking over her shoulder. She didn't think about or picture the yards and yards of dark water back there, but kept her attention focused forward to where the ground dipped away into pitch darkness. A little silt kicked up from the floor. A shape emerged from the darkness below. She realized she was looking at a boat, moss-covered and very old, something to ask the quarry company about. She checked inside. It was empty and thick with weed. Maybe they'd left it as a dive attraction. She put her hand on it and used it to pull herself along, following the compass.

She stopped just a few feet past the boat, sculling lightly to keep her position, peering into the gloom. Something was down there, about three metres below, nestling between the few plants and tree branches at the bottom of the quarry. The silt whirled, cleared.

Something cold went through her – the way water sometimes flushed through a wetsuit. She thought she knew what she was looking at. She kicked her legs up behind her, and swam slowly down. The object was stuck between two boulders. She trained the Salvo on it. Examined it. 'Wellard? Do we know if the Lexus family – did they have a—'

She stopped. No. This couldn't have been thrown free of the car today. It was decomposing – you could tell that from the fine mist of pollutants floating in a miasma around it. It had been in here for longer than a couple of hours.

'Did they have a what, Sarge?'

'Nothing. Just give me a moment here.'

She put her hands under it and lifted it, and then, when she saw what it looked like underneath, she knew it hadn't come here by accident.

'Hey,' she said. 'Send down a body-bag.'

'Have you got the target?'

'No.' She released the object, letting it fall back. A moment's nausea came and went. The cloud of decomposing matter swarmed around her. 'No. But have a word with the CSI guys, will you? Tell them it's a bit off-message. Tell them I haven't got the target, but I still want a body-bag down here. Actually, Wellard, make it two.'

17

A long time had elapsed, too long for the carjacker to have survived, but the ambulance and fire crews had turfed out anyway. They loitered half-heartedly on the quarry edge, peering into the water and watching the various police units come in. As the CSI team took videos and the dive team worked, one by one the emergency services gave up the vigil, trundling off to other calls. The last were going as Sergeant Marley was coming out with the body-bags.

Caffery sat in the heavy afternoon light, car window wound down, and watched the men on the pontoon take the bags from her, disentangle her from the umbilical, and throw an aluminium heat blanket over her. They washed her down and helped peel her out of her drysuit. When the CSI team had gone and she was alone – sitting on the tail plate of the unit van, he approached with a cup of coffee he'd finagled out of the fire crew earlier.

Her face was patchy and swollen and her nose was running. She looked at the coffee dully.

'Hey,' he said. 'Smile now and you've got it over and done with. For the whole day.'

She looked him up and down. 'So they've sent MCIU out. I'm glad. Even if he's not in there I'm glad you're taking an interest this time. I always knew he was going to do it again, the jacker.'

'The unit didn't send me.' Caffery sat down on the tail plate close to her and handed her the coffee. 'It's me. I wanted to speak to you.'

'Yeah?' She didn't sound interested. 'About what?'

'Free-diving. Ever heard of it?'

'Competitive apnoea. I've heard of it.'

'What do you know about it?'

'I know it's the fastest way to kill yourself. That or jumping off Clifton Suspension Bridge. It's a toss-up which is most effective. Why? Been a bit depressed lately?'

'I heard it's possible to dive to more than a hundred metres without breathing apparatus. That's what I'm told.'

She shook her head. 'I'm not getting into this. You forget, in my line of work I do expert witnessing. I've faced down enough smarmy defence briefs in my time to know how not to be led.'

'Well, that's funny. I didn't think I was trying to lead you into anything.'

'Yes, you are. You want me to believe in your Tokoloshe.' She wiggled her hands at him. 'Scary monsters in the water.'

'I just want to know what's possible. I want to know what the Tanzanian we've got in custody is capable of.'

'Then you need to know the facts. Over a hundred metres is a world record – a *world record* – for someone in absolute peak physical condition, using fins, a rope, weighted sleds, a team of helpers, pure oxygen inhalation. The whole nine yards. Your average Joe just can't leap in and do it – he'd be lucky, extremely lucky, to manage ten. So if you're suggesting anyone could have just dived to fifty metres without—'

'I didn't say fifty. I said a hundred. That's what the record is. Why did you think I said fifty?'

'Hundred, then. To go a hundred metres without fins, without swallowing cylinders of oxygen before, then I'm saying get real. Do you know how the professionals manage it?'

'No.'

'They trick their brains.' She tapped the side of her head. 'They override the part of the brain that reminds them to *breathe*. You ever see one of those guys come up from a dive? Trust me, it's not funny. They're basically dead. They need to be slapped around to make them breathe again.'

'And if they were wearing clothes?'

'Clothes?'

'Yes. Or something strapped to them. Plastic or rubber or something. Prosthetics.'

'Anything like that would make it harder. There's no way anyone who wasn't a world-class professional could dive to a hundred metres.'

Caffery was quiet for a while. There were red marks on her face from the mask and her eyes were bloodshot. But it was more. More than just the tiredness of diving. 'You're upset. I've upset you.'

She breathed out. 'Not you.'

'Then what?'

'It's nothing. Seriously. It's . . .' She looked at the still water reflecting back the lowering sky. There was a long silence. Then she rubbed her arms as if she was cold. 'It's just what I found in the quarry. Shook me up a bit. That's all.'

'Something shook *you* up? I thought you were cast iron. Why's today any different?'

'Dunno. Just wasn't expecting an animal.'

'An animal?'

'This jacker character's not in there. Christ knows what the witness saw or thought he saw or where the Lexus is because the damned quarry's empty. But there was a dog. The CSI've got it.'

Caffery looked up at the trees, their new growth dull and unreflective on this leaden morning. That morning Hinton, the vehicle-recovery company, had made a pissy phone call to DS Turnbull. When they'd turned up at quarry number eight there'd been no scooter, red or otherwise. Quarry number eight was beyond those trees. And the lay-by Lucy Mahoney had parked in was only a mile past that. She'd had her dog with her. 'There wasn't a collar, was there?'

'Not that I saw.'

'What kind of dog was it? Could it have been a spaniel?'

'Maybe. It was about the right size. But it's difficult to say after what's been done to it. It's been in there a few days. It would have been another week or so before it floated. You know – enough gases build up and the whole thing just lifts off the floor. Even with what'd been done to it, the stomach membranes were holding in the gases. The whole thing would have come up eventually. In spite of how messed around it is.'

'Messed around?'

'Messed around with. A rat would swim out to eat it if it was floating. But not down to that depth. There's no other wildlife down there could have done it. Some newts, maybe. Nothing else.'

'What're you saying?'

'I've seen quite a few dead dogs kicking around in this job and usually I leave them – you can't bring them all to the surface unless there's, you know, some sort of evidential gain. But then there are one or two you think, Now that isn't right.' She nodded to where the team were assembling the equipment. 'Did you see what they put the dog in?'

'How they put it in two bags?'

'One for the body.'

'And one?'

'For the skin. Whoever dumped it here . . .' She gazed across the water at the lonely quarry. 'Whatever bastard dumped it here, he made sure he'd skinned the poor sod first.'

18

Flea did the paperwork for the dive, packed away the equipment and pulled on a fleece. She checked her phone – nothing from Thom. She helped the boys secure the dive truck, patted it on the back and watched it trundle away through the mud. It was mid-afternoon and the clouds over the quarry were moving now. In the lane the marked traffic BMW was still parked – the cop inside was having coffee out of a Thermos. About twenty feet on the slope above it, Jack Caffery was outlined against the clouds. He seemed to be looking out across the quarry as if he was concentrating on something in the sky.

'You done?' he said, when he saw her scrambling up the slope towards him. 'Bit warmer now?'

'Here.' She handed him a business card. 'It's the CSI's number. For the dog. They're taking it to a vet's to have it scanned, see if there's a chip. Still want it?'

'Sure. Thanks.'

'Jack. I've been meaning to—'

'Yes?'

She hesitated. She still hadn't quite worked him out.

Still hadn't decided which side of the line he was on. 'I've been meaning to ask you. About the Kitson case.'

'The Kitson case?' He frowned. She knew it wasn't what he'd been expecting. 'What about it?'

'Just polite interest. Y'know – I was thinking about the bollocking Pearce gave me. Sounded like maybe I should have been paying more attention.'

'Pearce? The combed-over old twonk?'

She half smiled and rubbed her nose. 'It's just I get accused of being unprofessional and it starts to –' she made a gesture with her shoulders '– make you uncomfortable. That sort of thing.'

'I can't see how you've done anything wrong. Your team searched a lake. You didn't think you'd find her but you still searched the lake. It's not your fault she's gone alien-abduction style.'

A few drops of rain fell and Flea zipped up her fleece. The cop in the traffic car opened the door and tipped the remains of the coffee from the Thermos cup on to the ground.

'You haven't a clue, then. No idea where she went?'

'Ha.' He put his hands into his pockets. Looked at the clouds. 'Nothing. And sorry to sound cynical but the truth is I don't give a stuff what happened to her. She'll probably turn up in some Soho studio coked out of her gourd. Or in a beach hut in Antigua.'

Below them in the lane the traffic cop got out of the car, stood and brushed crumbs off his trousers. Flea watched him suck in his stomach and tuck his shirt into his trousers. 'That's not the official line, is it? That you don't think she's dead.'

'I don't think anything. Never have done. I'm not working her case.'

She was following the cop carefully now. There was something about his appearance, the top of his head, the widow's peak in his tightly shaved hair. Then she got it. It was PC Prody. The traffic cop who'd followed Thom home and breathalysed her. He began to climb the slope towards them. Came four, maybe five, steps. It was enough.

' 'Scuse me,' she muttered. 'Something I forgot to do.'

She pulled out her car keys and slithered down the slope away from him. She got into the Clio, slammed the door and was reaching for the ignition when Caffery caught up with her. He put his head in through the open window. 'You didn't answer my calls.'

'I've been busy.'

'I called three times.'

'I know.' She fumbled with the keys. Her fingers were trembling. 'I've been busy.'

'Too busy to acknowledge a phone call?'

'Yes.'

'I only wanted to ask you something.'

'I told you, I've been busy.'

'Hey!' He leant through the window suddenly. 'Hey. What's the matter with you? What the hell is wrong?'

She stopped fumbling with the keys and looked over at Prody. He'd stopped halfway up the slope and was staring at her, puzzled. She rested her hands on the steering-wheel and fixed her eyes on a point in the windscreen. Took five deep breaths. 'I'm sorry. I've had a lot on my mind.'

There was a pause, then Caffery sighed and pulled back a bit, resting one elbow on the door, running his hand through his hair as if he was tired. 'Christ. Me too. I'm sorry.'

'Truce?'

'Truce.'

He smiled. He looked at the car, at the wheels, the back seats, the upholstery, casually, as if he was thinking of buying it. 'New car?'

'Yes.'

'Very nice. Smells new.'

Twin lines of sweat broke under her arms and ran down her sides. '*Smells* new?'

'Yes. What happened to the old one?'

'The old one?' On the slope Prody had his hand up, smiling uncertainly. As if to say 'Hi. No bad feelings, eh?' The lines of sweat on her back converged and thickened into one. 'I'm thinking of selling it.'

'Shame. A good car, the Focus, so they tell me. More Focuses in the UK than sheep. Or something like that. Not that I know much about cars.'

A couple of drops of rain fell and Prody took a step forward. She turned the keys and put the gear lever into reverse. Caffery held on to the door as if he might be able to stop her leaving. 'When you're ready to talk, you know where I am.'

'When I'm ready.' She glanced again at Prody, released the handbrake and reversed out of the space. She was going so fast that Caffery had to take a step back to avoid getting his feet run over.

19

He watched the Clio spin its wheels. It churned up mud as it climbed out along the coned-off lane and disappeared. When it had gone he walked back up the slope.

The traffic cop was standing a few yards away, hands open, a bewildered expression on his face. 'Maybe she didn't like us watching.' He looked at the assembled cars and vans and shrugged, as if he was thinking that every other bugger in the force had pulled in for a gawp, and why did he get singled out? 'I'm sorry – I heard the call come in and I was just passing. I didn't realize she . . .' He trailed off, dropping his hands, the air gone out of him. 'I thought we were OK. In all honesty I didn't think there was any resentment there.'

'Resentment?'

'No. No – not that kind. We don't know each other. Not really.'

'Then what?'

'It was stupid. I nicked her. The other night – Monday.'

'For?'

'Speeding.'

Caffery almost whistled. He liked this, the idea of Sergeant Marley breaking the law. Suited her somehow.

'It was midnight. I was on duty over near Frome – not usually my patch, but I've had this call to a drunk and when I get there someone else's taken it. So I'm on my way back to Almondsbury when this car goes past – not that one, a Ford.'

'A Focus.'

'Yeah.' He gave Caffery a slow look. 'Yeah. Silver. It's swerving all over the place, trying to take half the tarmac with it. So off I go, blues 'n' twos, tonking down the road, and anyway the car just takes off with me hanging on its tail. You can imagine, can't you, me calling in its plate, thinking I'm on a TWOC chase and giving it that round these corners? And by the time I've got the name back and recognized it's her, she's pulled off the road and is in her house. I knock and she comes to the door with some lame excuse about how she wanted a piss or something.'

'The old bladder defence.'

'The bladder defence. Course, that's where I went wrong. Should've left it, shouldn't I? But she'd got me. Wound me up big-time. So I nailed her all the way I could. Breathalysed her.'

'You didn't?'

'Did. And, fair enough, she was stone cold. So I closed the record after that. But, y'know . . .' The cop paused, scratched his head '. . . obviously she doesn't want an apology off me.'

Caffery looked back at the place where the Clio had disappeared. 'Which day did you say it was?'

'This Monday just gone.'

Monday, Caffery thought. That happened to be the night Misty Kitson had gone walkabout from the clinic. It also happened to be the night before he and Flea had arrested the little Tanzanian and his sick-minded boss. She'd been fine that day considering the circumstances. Still, he thought, as he went to his car and swung inside, she was as guarded as hell most of the time. Christ only knew what Flea Marley got up to in her private world.

He put the key into the ignition and sat there for a moment or two, thinking about what he was going to do when he turned it. He had known just from looking at Flea that pursuing her, or even trying to call her, was a waste of time. He waited a few more moments for his thoughts to settle. Then he turned the key.

He wasn't going to chase her. He was going to chase the CSI guys. He wanted to know more about that dog.

20

Beatrice Foxton lived near Glastonbury Tor, down in the lowland, which only three hundred years ago had been a vast, marshy sea. Caffery met her and her dogs in a field near the house and they stood together in the wet grass, Beatrice smoking cigarettes and throwing sticks for the dogs. It was kind of reassuring to see a woman who cut dead people open for a living smoking. It made him wonder why he was breaking his neck trying to give up.

'Thank you for coming out.'

'That's OK. The dogs needed the walk.'

She had two, a tall sleek setter and a slow, good-natured German shepherd. They wheeled and circled and hunkered in the grass, waiting for a stick. 'She's getting on a bit, the shepherd. She's ex-job, but she had a bad time of it one year at Pilton and they retired her.'

'Pilton' was the locals' name for the Glastonbury Festival. Every year in June a summer city sprang up in the dry valley at the head of the Whitelake river east of the tor. Rainbow tents spread across the hills, flags on medieval castles fluttered in the wind, people came and lived there for four days. They ate and drank, shat and slept, they danced and stole from each other, loved and sang. Some even died there.

'One of the crusties who hang around after the festival – the ones who get paid to clean the site out? You know, ship all the abandoned tents off to Oxfam? Well, one of them, some charming Geordie, I believe, deduced it'd be easier to find any drugs left on the site with a drugs dog so he broke into a police van and took her. Trailed her round the site for two days on a rope and when she didn't find anything he laid into her and broke both her back legs.'

'Christ.'

'Apparently it took two people to pull him off. Hadn't bothered to check if she *was* a drugs dog. As it happens she was a GP. A general-purpose dog. Totally different thing, different training altogether. Course she couldn't work any more, not after that. She's still a beautiful dog, though. Hips holding up too.'

'You like animals.'

'Prefer them to people.'

'A lot of pathologists feel like that.'

'Yeah, well, we tend to live at the sharp end of what humans are capable of.'

The setter came and dropped the stick at Caffery's feet. He picked it up and scratched the dog's head, feeling the silky skin move over hard bone.

'Here's one for you, then. Lucy Mahoney.'

'What about her?'

'They've just found her dog.' He threw the stick. The setter bounded away, tail leaving scars in the air.

'It had been mutilated. Skinned. Slung into a quarry.'

Beatrice was silent for a moment. Then she threw the cigarette into the grass. 'Just when you think you know how low people can go. What sort of dog was it?'

'A spaniel.'

'Gentle dogs.' Her face was bitter. 'Very gentle.'

'I came to Lucy Mahoney's post-mortem because I'm working on another suicide. A boy over at the Elf's Grotto quarries.'

'*Now* he comes clean about why he invaded my mortuary yesterday.'

'This lad had been messed with after he died. Someone had cut his hair, which chimed with the job I was interested in. His body wasn't a million miles from where Lucy Mahoney was found. I was hoping for similarities yesterday at the hospital, hoping to see her hair had been cut, but that drew a blank. Fair enough – except up pops this effing dog of hers. So what I want to ask you is this: were you a hundred per cent that no one got to her after she died? You're sure everything was as it was supposed to be? No misgivings?'

Beatrice picked up the shepherd's stick and slung it. It whirled into the air, throwing out drops of saliva and dew. She watched the dog for a while, then lit another cigarette. 'I hope you've read my report before we talk about this, Jack. I find it irritating to have a long conversation about a job when my report hasn't been read.'

'I've read it. Cover to cover.'

'You're lying. You haven't even seen it. I only emailed it to F District this morning.' She shook her head. 'I'll let it go. Since it's you. And since you look rather nice when you take off your jacket.' She took a lungful of smoke, put her head back and blew it out in a straight line. 'There were a couple of little things. A couple of things felt a bit sticky. Taken in context they don't add up to much.' The setter came back with the stick, tongue lolling. Beatrice took it from him and threw it again. 'There weren't any experimental cuts on her wrists. The majority of suicides I see start off small – they need to decide what hurts, whether they can bear it or not. She hadn't done that.'

'Why not?'

'Christ knows. You can't infer anything from it, not taken in isolation. It's not a hard-and-fast rule.'

Caffery stared at her. She hadn't mentioned this before. It was the last thing he'd expected. 'You're talking about how she died? You mean you're not a hundred per cent it was suicide?'

'The toxicology makes interesting reading.'

'Benzos?'

'They're the obvious choice because there was a bottle of temazepam next to the body. The knife killed her, but when I ladled out her stomach there were seven or eight partially dissolved temazepam tablets. Nothing odd there. People will quite often use both methods. First they get trolleyed on booze and pills until they're numb enough, then do the cutting to make doubly sure everything goes to plan. But I found myself standing there, looking at the stomach contents, looking at the pill bottle, and I'm thinking, Why? Why didn't she take them all?'

'There were some left in the bottle?'

'About five. Why didn't she take those?' Beatrice smiled, took another drag on the cigarette. 'See, just so happens, Jack, that you're not the only detective in town. It just so happens that Mrs Foxton herself is no slouch. Because I looked at the pills in her stomach and I speculated about them. I speculated that those seven or eight pills might not have been for Lucy at all. That they may actually have been for me.'

'For you?'

'A red herring – a false trail. I said to myself, Mrs Foxton, if this young lady on your table didn't take her own life then what did happen? Might you speculate, perhaps, that mystery Person A slipped this young lady a Mickey Finn? In her drink, maybe? He wouldn't be able to slip her temazepam like that because it wouldn't dissolve properly – she'd notice the powder in the bottom of her glass. It would need to be something colourless, tasteless, a street drug, perhaps, because anything on prescription is loaded with Bitrex – you can taste it a mile away. Then when she's good and under, when she's like jelly, mystery Person A could give her a few pills. Pathologist B would find them in her stomach, jump to conclusions, and only test for that breed of benzodiazepines.'

'You'd need to retest.'

'I'm ahead of you. I asked Chepstow to dip for all the street drugs: Rohypnol, GHB, ketamine, clonazepam and Xanax, pretty much everything I could think of. There's a nice little invoice winging its way to F District. I've had several long and rewarding fantasies picturing that miserable git of a DI's face when it lands in his in-tray.'

'What came up?'

She gave him a grim smile. 'That's where it falls down. They all came up negative. Meanwhile the temazepam level was sky high and much, much higher than we'd expect from what she had in her stomach. The only explanation is that those seven in her stomach were the second dose. The first was earlier and had had time to dissolve. So they registered in her bloodstream but were already gone from her stomach.'

Caffery watched the shepherd trying to keep up with the setter and failing. Clement Chipeta may have had the opportunity to kill Lucy, but he wasn't sophisticated enough to have done it like this. And the monster – the Tokoloshe? If he existed, this didn't have his stamp on it either. Neither of them was in a position to convince a healthy, well-adjusted white woman to swallow drugs. 'There were no signs of violence? No signs she'd been forced to swallow anything?'

'Of course not. Do you think I'd've missed that?'

'Then how did he do it?'

'Do you want my SWAG?'

'Your what?'

'My Scientific Wild Ass Guess?'

'Go on.'

'He didn't coerce her. He didn't force her. Because none of this happened. Because we've gone into Fantasy Land, Jack, let our imaginations go walkabout. There was no mystery Person A. No clever plan. Lucy Mahoney decided to kill herself. She printed a suicide note. Signed it. Took something in the region of ten temazepam, got into the car and drove to the quarry with her dog on the back scat, a bottle of brandy and a Stanley knife in the front. Parked, let the dog out because he'd get more chance there than locked in the house. By now she's worried the temazepam hasn't taken effect so she takes some more – the ones I eventually find in her stomach. She walks – staggers, probably, poor thing – the last half-mile to the railway line, sits down and, though I'm surprised at this point she can hold her head up, she finishes the job.'

'A suicide, then.'

'A suicide. And I'm not going to change my judgement because of a feeling. There's no theft, no sexual assault, as far as we could tell – this is just me bringing my suspicious London mind to the gentle folk of the west. If you want to link it to your other suicide – your lad at the quarry – then, please, give it your best. But the two bodies were found a long way apart. They don't have anything much to link them.'

'Except the dog. My target had a history of dealing with body parts. Did you hear about Operation Norway earlier this week? That's why I think he needed the hair from my suicide at the quarry.'

'Hair is one thing – sounds like what Norway was all about. But a dog? A dog's different.'

Caffery didn't answer for a moment. She was right, of course. It *was* different and it *did* feel a bit out of step, that pathetic animal carcass at the bottom of the quarry. If Clement Chipeta or the Tokoloshe had done it, why had they left the skin with the body? The vet they'd taken the dog to had said that, apart from the removed pelt, there was nothing missing from its corpse – no part that could be used for *muti*.

'Anyway,' he said, 'assuming there isn't someone *else* out there sick enough to skin a dog—'

'There are plenty of those, believe me. Little ASBO kids from the Southmead estate, find a spaniel wandering around lost, they'd be capable of something like that.'

'Assuming it's my target who did it, it gives me a serious pain in the butt. I've got to square these two different MOs. Hair removed from the first suicide, and a dog mutilated in the second.' He shrugged. 'Dunno. It's all over the place.'

The dogs brought the sticks back, dropped them and sat like bookends eyeing Beatrice, waiting for her to throw again. The setter had white flecks of saliva on its muzzle.

'Well, Jack Caffery,' Beatrice ignored the sticks, 'if you're not going to seduce me, or try a Lady Chatterley with me up against a tree-trunk, I suppose I'll take my best friends and go home.'

He watched her walk to the car, throw down blankets and whistle to the dogs. When she'd slammed the back door he called to her. 'Beatrice?'

'What?'

'I wish you were serious. I really do. About the Lady Chat stuff.'

She gave a small laugh. The wind blew her grey hair across her face. 'I wish I was too. I wish to God I had the energy to mean it.' She dropped the cigarette and ground it under her sneaker. 'I'll speak to the DI, Jack. I'll tell him I had misgivings about the way Lucy died. But it's verbal.

I'm not rewriting my report. I'm not reversing any decisions.'

Caffery watched her drive away, then looked down at the cigarette butts she'd left. He thought again how great it was to stand in the open air and smoke with someone at your shoulder. He'd like someone at his shoulder for the next part. The part where he had to find out what the Tokoloshe had wanted with a dog. And why, having gone to the trouble of flaying the animal, he hadn't taken away the skin.

21

Ian Mallows had survived the Operation Norway attacks. Or, rather, most of him had. He'd been in intensive care for five nights, but now he was out. They'd put him in a private room, not on the ward, because whatever the staff told him he couldn't stop himself yelling at the other patients, telling them to *stop fucking staring at me*. They couldn't stop staring, of course. Who could, under the circumstances?

When Caffery arrived Mallows was quiet. He was lying on his side facing the door. Fast asleep. The sheet was pulled up to his neck, and the TV on the wall played silently.

Caffery closed the door quietly and placed the chair next to the bed. Put the two hundred Bensons he was carrying on the floor, took off his jacket, draped it on the back of the chair, and settled down to wait, eyes on the TV, hands linked on his lap. His thumbs made loops one over the other.

'Yeah? What is it? What d'you want?'

Caffery looked up. Mallows hadn't moved. His eyes

were still closed, but his mouth was open, a bit of wet red in there. His hair, which he'd kept shaved, was coming back in a blue-black shadow. Over his left ear was a spider-web tattoo, its lines thick and blurry. A sewing needle job done in the slammer. Mallows definitely paddled in the shallow end of the gene pool, Caffery thought – he was never destined to make it in this life. Even without the injuries he'd sustained on Norway. Those were still hidden under the sheets.

'Go on.' He didn't open his eyes. 'Tell me what you want.'

'I'm police.' Caffery reached for his card, but changed his mind. 'I'm Detective Inspector Jack Caffery. Think back. You'll remember me. I was the one who came in and pulled you out.'

Now Mallows opened his eyes. He swivelled them to him. 'You were with that bird? The fit one?'

Caffery crossed his legs, pulling the right foot up and resting it on his knee. 'The doctors wouldn't let me see you until now. You've been critical this week. They thought they were going to lose you.'

'Going to get some stick off my mates on that. Letting ourselves get rescued by a tart. It's been in the papers too.' Mallows rolled on to his back, and pushed himself upright on his elbows. Caffery stopped tapping his feet and stared. Mallows's arms had come out from under the sheets. Where his hands had been removed in the squat, the bandaged arms ended in boluses the size of melons. He moved them slowly, painfully. It was like watching a giant praying mantis moving grotesquely around the bed.

He caught Caffery staring and laughed. 'I know. Pretty fucked up, eh? Doctors reckon they've swollen up three times what they should've.'

'You were operated on yesterday.' He couldn't keep his eyes off the shapes. It was like Mallows had paddles for arms. 'That's what they said.'

'They wouldn't do it before, kept snipping away at the stumps. Bits of skin were still dying and there wasn't a thing they could do about it till they saw what muscles were going to be left behind. Necrotized, that's what they call it. Necrotized. Dead meat.'

Caffery took his eyes off the bandages and fixed them on Mallows's face. 'What's next?'

'They've taken these massive flaps of skin off the back of my legs and slapped them on these.' He studied them, turning them over and over. 'Some time between now and midnight tonight the blood vessels're going to be growing up into the skin. They connect and, with a bit of luck, I'll have normal skin over the stumps.' He dropped his head on to the pillow, stared at the ceiling. 'Wicked, innit?'

'You're doing well, Ian. Really well. I'm pleased to hear it.'

Mallows made a noise in his throat. 'Yeah, but you're not here just to blow sunshine up my arse, are you? What do you want? I've given them a statement already.'

'It wasn't complete. You were out of it when you gave it and you left out some stuff. So now you're on the up we're wanting to come back at you for some more. Find out what you remember.'

'About what?'

'Well, Dundas, to start with. The one who died.'

'What about him?'

'Did you ever see him? Did they introduce you to him?'

'What, like, nice to meet you, mate? Turned out nice again today, hasn't it? What bit are they having off of you, then? I've told you all this before. I never saw him, never even knew he was in the place. It was like a warren in there. You didn't know what was going on from one room to the next.'

'Did you know they cut his hair?'

'I knew his *head* got cut. I knew that part. Don't s'pose he was too worried about the hair going as well, do you?'

'Clement Chipeta – the one who was with you.'

'Oh, that's his real name, is it?'

'When we came in and made the arrests, had he been with you for a while then?'

'What do you mean?'

'He hadn't been out anywhere? In the last few hours, was he with you in the squat?'

'Yes. Why?'

'Just trying to establish his movements.'

Mallows shook his head. 'Nah. See, this is where this conversation stops. I'm not a snout. I'm not giving you my little padmate. He never did me no harm.'

'Funny. From what I remember it was him who introduced you to Uncle in the first place.'

Mallows didn't answer.

'You're protecting him, Ian. There's a word for that.'

'Oh, yeah?'

'Yeah. You're "Stockholming". Happens to people

who've been captive long enough – start to side with their captors. That's what you're doing.'

'He wasn't my *captor*. He never wanted to be involved – he was forced into it. He's an illegal. Didn't have a choice from what I could see.'

'Did you have sex with him too? Is that why you're wanting to protect him?'

'Oh, fuck off.'

'Clement Chipeta tells us he was collecting human hair.' Caffery watched Mallows for a reaction. 'He says it was a tradition. He was using it to make a bracelet. Did he talk to you about that?'

'Look, I just said I ain't in the business of doing your work for you. I ain't a snout.'

Caffery reached under the chair, pulled out the two-hundred carton of Bensons and put it on the bedstand. Mallows stared at it. 'How'm I supposed to smoke them? With my toes?'

'You'd need a friend to help you. As a matter of fact, Ian, I think you're going to need a lot of friends when you eventually come out of here.'

'I keep my mates through not talking to pigs like you.'

'You know what I think? I think there was something in that squat we found you in that you haven't told us about.'

Mallows's eyes flickered. He didn't look at Caffery but the change was there. The smallest dilation of iris, of capillary, to show the words had hit home.

Caffery took a breath, his own pulse picking up. He leant forward and spoke in a low voice: 'I'm right, aren't

I? There was something in that squat you couldn't explain.'

A vein pulsed pale in Mallows's temple.

'Ian,' Caffery murmured, 'did anyone tell you how many people came out of that squat? There was you. One.' He counted them off on his fingers. 'There was the piece of shit who masterminded the whole thing, the one you called Uncle. Two.'

'I ain't listening to this.'

'There was your little friend Clement. Three. And there was a corpse. Dundas. One, two, three and you makes four . . . Ah – that surprises you, doesn't it? You thought I was going to say five.'

'I don't feel well. Get me a nurse.' Mallows lifted both arms and tried to manoeuvre the call button from the bars of the bedstead. 'I need a bedpan.'

Caffery stood and untangled the call console. Held it just out of Mallows's reach.

'Give me that. I need a nurse. Need a crap.'

'It's just withdrawal.'

'I know what it fucking well is. Don't need you giving me a lecture on the agonies, do I?'

'Haven't they got you on something?'

'The green.'

'How often?'

'Twice a day.'

'And that isn't enough?'

'What? You going to hang around and watch me crap myself? Is that your thing? Funny. I never would have labelled you as someone who was into that. You know what I do for a living, don't you? When I get out of here you and I can have a little chat, if you want. I'm reasonable.'

Caffery folded his arms and looked at him patiently. 'You're going to have to talk to me, Ian. Eventually you'll talk.'

'Fuck off.'

Caffery nodded thoughtfully. 'I know where your hands are.'

There was a pause. A long silence. When Mallows had been brought out of the squat, all he'd done was scream about his hands. More than anything, he'd wanted his hands back. Now he turned his cold blue eyes to Caffery. 'You what?'

'I said I know where your hands are. The coroner can't let them go, but I can tell you where they are.'

'Where?'

'When you tell me about what else was in that place.'

'You don't mean it.'

'I do.'

'Take your jacket off.'

'What?'

'I want to see if you're wired.'

'Christ.' Caffery took off his jacket, dropped it on the bed and stood in his shirtsleeves with his hands out at his sides. 'Happy?'

'Open your shirt.'

He unbuttoned it, pulled it off his shoulders and turned in a circle. Mallows watched him steadily. Took in his naked stomach. His chest.

'What? See something you like?'

'I'm never going to repeat this.' Mallows's eyes were hard. 'If it comes up in court I'm going to deny it. I'll say you touched me up. And me all vulnerable in a hospital bed.'

'What was this bracelet he was making?' Caffery pulled his shirt back on and sat down. 'What was the point of it?'

A long pause. Then, 'Protection,' he murmured. 'From evil spirits. He used to brick it over them – really scared.'

'Scared? What did *he* have to be scared of?'

Mallows gave him a look that said police were a mystery that would never, ever be revealed. A different species. And, under that scrutiny, Caffery started to see it from a different perspective. He saw an illegal immigrant, scared of being deported back to a country that would have the skin off his bones in the blink of an eye. He got it and he was embarrassed that it had taken him until now to really get it.

'About Clement,' he said. 'Do you know if he was cruel to animals?'

'Everyone in that place was cruel to everything. That's my understanding of the situation.'

'Ever talk about taking a knife to a dog or anything?'

'Not a dog. They hated dogs in Tanzania, apparently. Thought they were vermin – wouldn't touch them.'

'But the gang he worked for dealt with endangered species back in Tanzania.'

'Not dogs. Dogs aren't endangered.'

What had Beatrice said? *Little ASBO kids from the Southmead estate would be capable of something like that.*

Was she right? Was the dog really not connected here?

'Why'd they go for you, Ian? You're white.'

'I dunno. Clement liked white people.'

'He thought we had more power, didn't he? Thought our bodies made better *muti*?'

'Maybe.'

Caffery shifted in his chair and pretended to be fastening his cuffs. 'The reason I'm asking about who was in the squat, Ian, is that some of my witnesses from this case said they'd seen something they couldn't understand.'

Mallows's Adam's apple moved, but he didn't speak.

'Their imaginations were working overtime, of course, but they talked about seeing a monster. Now your friend Chipeta says it was him. Dressed up.'

'Oh, he does, does he?'

'Yes. Is he telling the truth?'

'Ask him.'

'I'm asking you. Once again. Was there something in that place you couldn't explain?'

No answer.

'Was it there when we came in? Did it escape?'

Silence.

'Did it see me? Was it watching me?'

Silence again.

'Ian, you said you'd speak to me. That was the deal.'

Mallows gave him a fierce look. 'And I've given you all the answers I've got. You want to know anything else you go down City Road. You know City Road, I take it?'

'Yes.'

'Thought you might. Try speaking to the whores down

there. There's one – blonde girl, white jacket. Have a word with her. Ask her opinion on the subject of monsters.'

Caffery stopped buttoning his shirt and stared at Mallows. He thought of his car parked in an alleyway off City Road the night something had slammed on to his bonnet. He'd been with a prostitute that night – not something he had printed on a T-shirt, but it was true. Her name was Keelie. She'd been in the car with him. 'Did you get a name? Of the girl? The hooker?'

'Nah. Just one of the millions. You know how it goes.'

Caffery fumbled in his pocket and pulled out a scrap of paper he'd been carrying for days. It was the disconnected number dialled from Ben Jakes's phone. He'd called it once, on his work phone, not the phone where he stored his personal contacts, but he'd never tried it on his personal line. Now he thumbed the number in. The mobile paused, the screen went blank, then a small flashing icon came up with the words 'calling Keelie City Road mobile'. Someone – the Tokoloshe? – had used Jakes's phone to call Keelie. The prostitute. The ghost of an idea moved through him.

He stood, pulled on his jacket and fastened the buttons. 'Thank you, Ian. I wish you luck until the next dose.'

'Hey.' Mallows sat up hurriedly in bed. 'Where do you think you're going? You made a promise. You said you'd tell me where my hands are. I need to know they're somewhere that bastard uncle can't get at them. Don't want him touching them again.'

'They're safe.' Caffery paused, his hand on the door. 'The pathologist examined them, gave them their own little post-mortem, and now they're under lock and key. Waiting for the coroner to tell him what to do with them.'

'Where?' Mallows sat up, his eyes bulging. The soft light falling on the bed made him look as if he was in some hellish religious painting. Bosch or Goya. 'You said you'd tell me where they are.'

Caffery opened the door and stood in the doorway for a moment. 'They're here. In the hospital mortuary in the basement. In fact, you know what?' He shook his head at the irony. 'They've been here all along. All this time. Just thirty feet under you.'

22

Flea sat in her father's chair, legs pushed out, a glass of Tanqueray and tonic in her hand, and stared at Farleigh Park Hall on the TV. A neo-classical mansion with wraparound porticoes and a sandstone loggia, it had been spruced up by the clinic owners for the programme: the windows had been newly cleaned, the twin fountains at the front were playing and a pair of peacocks wandered near by, pecking idly at the grass. A girl appeared on the screen and walked down the front steps. Her yellow hair was dull – as if it could absorb sunlight. The sandals, Flea thought. They've got those wrong. They were silver, not gold. Silver. But everything else . . . everything else is right on the nail. The neon green dress, the purple velvet coat. In her hand she carried a sequined bag that glinted as she moved. There'd probably be a heart-stamped Nokia in that bag too. Every detail was important.

This morning at eleven, while she'd been in quarry two, MCIU had staged a reconstruction of Misty's last hours at the clinic. When the cameras went to a wide shot of the clinic you could see how many people had turned up for it. Vehicles overflowed the improvised car parks in the fields, live-feed vans bristled with up-link satellite dishes, reporters stood in front of cameras twitching at their hair and ties, crews milled around adjusting tripods, microphones. Groups of cops were standing around, talking in low voices. Up near the fountains a grey-haired man in a dark blue raincoat looked suspiciously like the chief constable.

Pessimism settled down neatly on Flea's shoulders. It would take a miracle for the force to drop this case.

She killed the TV and carried her drink into the kitchen. She couldn't sit there waiting for Thom to call any longer. She had to do something now, had to start looking for the place of the accident. The newest water-cooler intelligence said the forensic lab in Chepstow was testing hairs and fibres lifted from several breached places on the clinic perimeter, just to give them a lead on which way Misty might have left the grounds. She didn't have access to the techniques and budgets the force had. All she had was her brain. She'd have to think harder, faster and neater than the whole force put together.

In the kitchen she took the few things off the table – a pepper grinder and the earthenware mug Mum had always kept cutlery and napkins in – then spread out the paperwork she'd brought home from the office: the photos of Misty's clothes and the Blue 8 map print-offs the unit had used on the Farleigh Park lake search three days ago. She sat in the place she'd sat at all her life, on the left, between where Thom and Dad would have sat opposite Mum, and tried to think.

The police knew which direction Misty had left the clinic. They had a fix on her from her mobile phone. Pearce had been talking to Caffery about it at the Strawberry Line suicide. Phone masts usually had sectored antennae heads that beamed out segments making up 380 degrees. The signal from a particular mobile phone could be placed within one of those sections: some masts had as many as six heads, which narrowed these so-called 'cells' to about 60 degrees, so it was possible to tell at what angle a phone was from a mast, but not how far away. Unless another mast came into the equation. And then, especially if the phone was close to one of the masts, the search segment could be reduced at times almost to a pinpoint.

Misty's phone had been a Nokia flip-open. Flea had studied the mock-up photograph. Its casing had been stainless-steel and it had an LCD screen – a little like her own phone except that Misty had customized hers with stick-on jewels in the shape of a heart. It wasn't in the sequined handbag, it wasn't in the coat pockets and Thom hadn't trousered it, she was sure of that. So where was it?

She hooked her laptop out of its case, fired it up and went into Google Earth. The satellite photos of Farleigh Park Hall had been taken on a summer's evening. The building and surrounding trees cast enormous shadows across the lawns. She found a pencil and paper and pulled the map towards her, comparing it to the satellite photo, running her fingernail over the woodland and the lake. Pearce, the search adviser, had said they'd got a 'ping' from the macrocell phone mast. There it was on the satellite photo, its long shadow lying across the field. On the map it was marked about half a mile away to the north. She loosely sketched pie slices coming from the mast and studied the south-easterly one. There was a tiny white flash of light there. She zoomed in and saw the creamy slash of a track running up to it. The lake. The one she hadn't wanted to search.

She closed the laptop and sat back, holding the map. Just because Misty's phone had given its last signal in that 60-degree cell there was no way of telling if the phone had been a foot from the mast or miles. Which made several square miles to search. If Misty had switched the phone off she could have walked on anywhere, any distance. She could have crossed into an entirely different segment of the macrocell mast. Or crossed into the cell of another mast. She could have left Farleigh Park Hall and walked due south or due east, which meant the accident could have been on three different stretches of road: the A36, the A366 or the B3110. It could have been on one of the myriad C-class roads that laced the fields in that area. Flea scratched her head. There were miles to search. And she'd thought she was ahead of the game. She'd thought that knowing Misty had met her death on a road would give her an advantage over the police.

She must have been there for ten minutes, staring at the map, the ice in the G-and-T melting, when she suddenly thought of something. She thought of Lucy Mahoney. Of her body going into the bag yesterday and of the way her shoes had looked.

She got a freezer bag from the drawer, her latex gloves

from the cloakroom, where she kept her work stuff, and a pair of tweezers from her vanity unit.

Inside the garage it was humid, even though the fan in the corner was whirring silently. Now the body was cooled and the boot liner was disposed of, the smell had subsided to just a faintly unpleasant trace – as if someone had left a bag of rubbish in there. She pulled on gloves and a mask and went to the bath. She'd replaced the ice the moment she'd come in and the plastic shroud was milk-coloured now, as if Misty had breathed on the inside. Her outline was there in places: a piece of green material pressed against the plastic, a dull yellow circle of skin where the back of her wrist made contact: the suggestion somewhere under it all of blonde hair.

'It's me. Just me again. I've got to move you.'

She grasped the bottom end of the cocoon and hauled it along so Misty's feet were leaning on the edge of the bath. Ice water sloshed and slapped on to the floor. Moving quickly, she unsnapped the zip tie and unwrapped the sheeting. The inside of the plastic was smeared with lines of half-frozen brown slush. The feet in the silver sandals were cold and hard.

She cupped one heel in her hand, lifted the shoe into the air and inspected it carefully. Grass and mud were skewered on the high heels along with other vegetation. Very, very carefully she tweezered away a section and dropped it into the freezer bag. Breathing through her mouth, she lifted the other foot and tweezered off a similar section, careful to get as many of the different types of leaf and soil as she could.

'Thank you, Misty.' She wrapped the feet up, slid the body back into the bath. Christ, this was awful. 'I won't disturb you again.'

When she got back to the kitchen the sun was sinking, parting the clouds and sending epic beams of light across the sky. The cabinets and the walls were painted gold, like firelight. She found a piece of kitchen towel and emptied the pieces of grit and soil and leaf on to it. She poured another G-and-T and, using the tweezers, began carefully to sort through the debris.

Most of it was grass, clotted with a reddish soil that might have been clay. She glanced across at the map. Dad had had an amateur love of geology, and even now the shelves in the house were crammed with the stones he'd collected over the years. He'd given her and Thom lessons over breakfast: the Avon Vale, the strip of land running alongside the river, was clay. It gave way to oolite limestone on the higher ground. That could mean Misty had gone east rather than west, towards the river rather than away. Even so, Flea couldn't be sure where the clay soil ended and the limestone began. She separated out the bits of vegetation, pushing the grass aside, until, as if she was uncovering gold, she stopped at what looked like a wrinkled piece of brown paper.

Tongue between her teeth in concentration, she unfolded it, using her fingernail and the tweezers. As it opened she saw it wasn't paper but two conjoined petals – probably yellow before they'd been crushed and half frozen. A scrap of stamen clung at their centre. She looked at them for a long time. It must have needed four petals to complete the flower head. It would have been small. But it wasn't delicate and was too tough for its size. A thought came into her head: Maybe it's part of a bigger flower . . . And the answer came quickly after it.

Rapeseed.

The flower of the canola plant.

She pulled the computer over and Googled rapeseed. Scourge of asthmatics, delight of farmers living on subsidies, for a time in the 1990s there had been too much rapeseed in England. Every hillside, every dale was patch-worked with its distinctive acid-yellow flower. This time of year it was just coming into bloom, the fields were cross-ing from green to yellow, and now, on the screen, there was a petal identical to the one on the table.

Misty Kitson had walked through a rapeseed field to reach the road where Thom had hit her.

Flea switched to Google Earth and zoomed out one click until the screen approximated the search area. Bending closer, she centred the satellite on the clinic, with its leaded roofs and pilasters, then pulled the image back to show the little houses in the hamlets surrounding it – the farmhouses, the petrol stations, the B-and-Bs on the big main road. And the lake.

At the time the photo was taken the rapeseed was at its brightest. But although there was an ochreish field to the west of the clinic, there was nothing that resembled rape-seed. She zoomed out, up a stage, so the whole area was on the screen.

Two rectangular patches of yellow stood out so brilliant with colour they seemed to phosphoresce. They were miles away from the clinic, well out of the area the team had searched. One was to the south, almost two and a half miles away, straddling the edge of the mast segment. The other was to its left, even further away, straddling the other edge. Both were too far away to be in the clever little dick of a search adviser's parameters.

She put the tumbler into the sink, shoved the gloves and the tweezers into her jacket pocket and grabbed more freezer bags. She got a heavy maglite from Dad's study, wellington boots, a long-sleeved T-shirt and a bottle of water. From the recycling bin she pocketed a few squares of stiff paper – advertising inserts from last Sunday's newspaper. She got her old Bergen rucksack from the study.

She came to a halt on her doorstep. A few feet away in the gravel, the late-evening sun making a halo of the hair around her chiselled face, stood Katherine Oscar, dressed in a Musto coat under a sheepskin jerkin that must be very 'country' because it looked so uncomfortable. A copy of the local paper was held loosely in her fingers at her side. She had a look on her face that Flea recognized from years of living next to the Oscars. It said that nothing the Marleys could do would surprise her.

'Phoebe!' She was one of the only people in the world apart from Mandy who used Flea's real name. 'You always fascinate me.'

Flea slammed the door behind her and stepped out on to the gravel. 'Fascinate you? Why? What have I done now?'

Katherine laughed. She touched the sides of her hair, patting them into place. 'Oh, just – you know. The sort of cars you always have. Like this one. Is it new?'

'It is.'

'What is it?' She bobbed down to inspect the badge. 'Ah! A Renault. A sweet little Renault. I suppose it's a kind of city car?'

'A kind of city car?'

'Yes. A runaround. You know.'

'It's not a Land Rover. Is that what you mean?'

'No. No, it's not. Is it?' She smiled, folded her arms and made a show of looking around herself. The garage light was off but the light was on in the hallway, making the brown paper in the windows glow softly. 'I see you've blocked off the windows in the garage. What are you doing in there, so Secret Squirrelly?' She gave a laugh. 'Not cutting up dead bodies, I hope. With your job, my imagination runs riot.'

'You caught me. I admit it. I'm cutting up dead bodies. You know, the people who irritate me. I've got a list. Want to see it?'

'You Marleys, you crack me up.'

'We aim to please.'

She moved past Katherine, pointing the keys at the Clio. It unlocked and blinked its lights at her. Her hand was on the door before Katherine hurried round to the front of the car. 'I'm sorry, Phoebe, we've got off on the wrong foot again. You know, it's only that I'm hoping you'll rethink – about the garden? The press are quite clear about it. Look – it's here in the paper. The credit crunch has taken hold, property prices are sliding. We've made you a good offer. We'd honour it, of course.'

The garden was Flea's headache. It would be the easiest thing in the world to sell it – maybe even half of it, the half with the folly – and let Katherine take on the responsibility. But then Flea thought about Mum, how she used to spend all her time out there. She threw the torch on the Clio's passenger seat and got into the car. 'I don't think so.'

Katherine hesitated for a moment, then hurried round to the window, her face flushed. 'My God, you're as bad as your bloody parents.'

Flea slammed the door. She opened the window and looked down at Katherine's feet. 'I think this conversation's over. Do you want me to drive you back to your place, or will you walk?'

Katherine was still for a moment, then pushed herself back from the car. 'No, thank you. I'd much prefer to walk.'

'Good,' Flea said. 'Then you won't mind if I drive behind you, will you?'

23

The prostitutes had started when Caffery had arrived in Bristol. Back in London there had been girlfriends, women he'd imagined he loved. Women who'd loved him. One or two he'd even lived with, letting them come to share the little terraced house he'd bought from his parents. The house Ewan had gone missing from. But he'd got to a point, with forty staring him in the face, when he'd come to understand that the only real talent he had with women was knowing how to damage them. So he went to girls he would never see again. Girls like Keelie.

The streets around City Road were busy. It wasn't even dark yet and already the girls were out. He saw Keelie straight away – she was easy to spot. She'd made it that way by always wearing the same thing: a white Puffa with silver stripes on the side. It was a street technique so her regular punters would recognize her at a distance. It reassured them. They'd get unsettled, she said, if she changed her clothes and her hair, and would start wondering who she was hiding from and if she'd been ripping punters off. He wasn't going to approach her in the open

– didn't know if the Tokoloshe was sitting out there somewhere in the darkness, watching – and decided to wait in the doorway of a Claire's Accessories shop, loitering with all the girls' gewgaws and pink sparkly things until she noticed him.

They went to a room above a pub. Under the jacket she wore a Spandex mini and a silver T-shirt. She was a tall girl with dense, freckled calves that didn't jiggle as she walked up the stairs in front of him. She'd look like a hockey teacher if it wasn't for her hair, highlighted the colour of cold beer, or the way her heels spread out and hung over the edges of the slingbacks.

She had a new phone. She was proud of the way she took care of herself: never going 'bareback', never faking it – *Most of the girls do. They've got thigh muscles like crowbars. Grease them up and hold on tight. If he's drunk enough he won't know the difference*. Not Keelie. She was a professional. Always used a condom. Always made a safety call on her mobile: repeating the name of the punter, his appearance, the car registration and where she was going to be. She'd done it the night they'd been together in Caffery's car in the alley, but watching her now he doubted she was actually speaking to anyone, standing with her back to him, hip leaning against the sink, one finger holding up the dingy curtain to look out into the street at her colleagues. She probably wouldn't want to spare the price of a phone call. It made him a little sad to think of this token effort to be tough, sensible. Like it would save her somehow.

'Why'd you change your phone number?'

She put the phone in her bag and came over to the chair. 'Why d'you think? I only gave it to repeat clients.' She leant on the word 'clients' as if it would make her sound as if her business was law, or corporate espionage, or interior design. 'But sometimes they take the piss. Start thinking I run a jerk-off phone line or that it's cool to call me at six in the morning while their wife's in the shower or something.' She lifted one foot on to her knee and unbuckled the slingback. 'That, or the wife gets hold of the number and starts having an epi at me down the line. Do you want these on? The heels?'

'No.'

She pulled off the scuffed shoes and kicked them under the chair, then opened her bag and took out a cigarette. Lit it. 'Look at the smoke alarm.' She nodded at the ceiling. The padding of a bra had been gaffer-taped to the sensor. 'That's what most of the girls round here think of no-smoking rooms.' She got up, stepped out of her knickers and kicked them under the chair. They had an Ann Summers label sewn inside. Ann Summers. Respectable sex. High-street stuff now. Not like when he was starting out in London – when you had to go all the way to Berwick Street to be sure of finding a sex shop. 'You're my last tonight. I've done well.'

'You can keep them on.'

'The heels?'

'The knickers.'

'Eh?'

'Just talk.'

She eyed him. 'You've paid me now. Once you've paid

me it's a done deal. You change your mind and you're the one's got to suck it up.'

'Keep the money.'

She took a couple of drags on the cigarette, looked him up and down. 'I can't be here more than fifteen minutes – that's it. Talk isn't cheaper than sex. OK?'

'It's about a punter.'

'Oh, no, you're not doing that. I know you're a cop, Jack.'

'Since when?'

'Always have.'

'How?'

'The way you walk. Like you think you're going to get jumped any second.'

'Is that why you never look me in the eye?'

'No. I don't look you in the eye because you don't want anyone looking you in the eye. I knew that the first time I saw you. Here's someone who doesn't want to be reminded of what he's doing, I thought. Has to be a cop.'

He shifted on the bed. 'Can I have a cigarette?'

She held them out. He took one and let her light it. Her nails were elaborate: each had a snowflake motif in silver glitter. The sort of thing a girl could spend hours on and a guy might never notice in his rush to get the needs of his dick established.

'You'll want to talk about this punter. I just have a feeling you will.'

'Are you threatening me?'

'You're lucky I'm paying for your time. I could take you in for the night. Or throw a Section 60 at the street and no one'll work the whole weekend. That'll make you flavour of the month.'

She sighed, stood up and flicked the line of ash into the sink. She picked up her knickers and pulled them on.

'Go on, then.' She sat in the chair, legs pushed out, toes pointing inwards. Sullen. 'What d'you want?'

'You heard about the arrests.' He lifted a pillow out from under the red quilt and lay back on it, his feet crossed on the bed. 'Over the weekend. The lad with his head half cut off.'

'That wasn't round here. It was the other side of the motorway. Easton.'

'But one of the players was a punter down here. I think you'll remember him. Black guy. African. Really, really short.'

She laughed. 'Chip, you mean? If you'd said it was him you wanted to talk about you wouldn't've never had to threaten me. That sort of thing is free.'

'Chip, you called him? Was that his name?'

'Think so. His second name.'

'Clement Chipeta?'

'No. He was Amos. Amos Chipeta.'

Caffery had the cigarette to his mouth, but now he paused. 'Amos? Are you sure?'

'Yes, the fucking freak. Totally did my head in.'

Caffery lowered the cigarette, staring at her. 'And,' he said, his mouth dry, 'what did *Amos* Chipeta look like?'

'You said you knew.'

'I said he was small. That's all I know.'

'Well, he is – a dwarf, I'd say. But not just your usual

midget. He was a total freak – you know, real Elephant Man freak. He used to have this parka he wore with the hood up over his face so you couldn't see what he looked like and he was always hanging around. Watching us. Then one evening he comes over – he's saved up all this money. Offers me two times my usual and I'm, like, no fucking way! I'm, like, oh, that's so minging, just the thought of it. No way am I sleeping with a mutant. Not even for twice.'

'When did you last see him?'

'Dunno. Couple of weeks ago.' She dragged on the cigarette again. 'So? Are you saying he was connected with the thing in Easton?'

'Maybe.'

She shivered. 'Gross.'

Caffery smoked the cigarette, thinking of the figure in the Norway video, hunched over. There is, he thought, a place where myth and reality merge. Amos Chipeta. Maybe the Tokoloshe had just taken a step out of the shadows.

'Keelie, do you know why he'd have any interest in me?'

'Yeah.' She made the word go up and down. Yeee-aahh. Like: Why're you asking me this Raass question? 'He wants to be like you, hun.' She leant forward, head on one side, smiling too widely at him. 'Wants your mojo, baby. Cos you is cool, Daddy-O.'

'I've got my eye on the clock, Keelie.'

She sighed and slouched back in the chair. 'He just wants what you've got.'

'Why me?'

'Cos I'd been with you. He's jealous.'

'How'd he know I'd been with you?'

'Cos I told him. Duh.'

'You have, what, ten different men a night?'

'That's a good night. A very good night. Try five.'

'Five different men a night. Is he following all of them?'

'No.'

'Then why'd he single me out?'

'Don't you know?'

'No.'

Keelie let the smoke out of her mouth and looked at him for a long time, almost as if she pitied him. Then she struggled, stood up and dropped the cigarette butt into the sink. It made a small hiss.

'You want a BJ?'

'Time's up.' He held his wrist over to her to show his watch. 'Nine o'clock.'

'I'll make more time.'

He looked at the side of her face, her eyelashes lowered. He saw the need there and for a moment he wanted to reach for her. But he didn't.

'That's OK. But thank you, Keelie. Seriously. Thank you.'

'Are we finished, then?'

'We're finished.'

He got up, went to the sink and pulled back the curtain. It was late but the sky through the buildings was a fluorescent blue. Almost indigo. It was worse in the summer, this job the girls did. This thing that men like him did. Somehow it felt worse. In the winter it was OK to live in the dark, to keep chapped skin covered and never look in each other's eyes.

In the summer it felt like an insult.

24

Caffery wasn't sure he would stay in Bristol. Like a boat slipping anchor, the release from what had been holding him in London for years – Penderecki, the paedophile who'd murdered his brother Ewan – had sent him to wander, not to rest. He'd sold his house in Brockley and come west with an inflated bank account and no desire to put down roots. He'd gone into a letting agency and put a deposit on the first place he could move into straight away, without even seeing a picture of it. It had turned out to be a little stone-built cottage just in sight of the ancient and lonely Priddy Circles.

Priddy was a strange place adrift in the damp Mendips. Unpopulated and bleak, the area was pocked with lead mines, sink holes and legends. Local people swore that Jesus himself had once visited the neolithic circles. They said he'd floated in a low boat up from Glastonbury, across what had then been sea, standing proud in the bow. His uncle, Joseph of Arimathea, had been in the stern. And who was to say they were wrong? 'As sure as the Lord walked in Priddy,' Caffery had heard a woman in the local newsagent's say only two days ago. To her it was like saying, 'Is the Pope a Catholic?'

Caffery hadn't settled there. The rooms were too small, and in the morning he had to bend to look out of his bedroom window, it was set so low in the wall. The thatched roof was like the picture on a chocolate box from a distance, but he was woken most mornings by the scratch of squirrels nesting in it and one had already found a way of creeping into the house and crapping on the kitchen table. The cottage hadn't welcomed Caffery so he had agreed to dislike it in return: most of his boxes were still in the garage and even two months along he hadn't unpacked many of his clothes. They lay gathering dust on the spare-room bed in their suit protectors. Maybe girls like Keelie were more than just his way of staying out of relationships. Maybe they were also a way of stopping him coming here. To the emptiness, the smells and the shadows.

He got back to the cottage at nine and went around opening windows to let out the squirrelly smell. He knew he should eat something. Instead he went into the lounge and filled a tumbler with Glenmorangie. He paused to consider the glass, then picked up the bottle of malt and carried it up the narrow, lumpy little staircase, his head bent. The ceilings here were low, the plaster was old and sagging, probably made of horsehair, and he'd learnt not to try to put pictures on the wall. But the bedroom was about OK. There was a satellite hook and a TV on an old box chest near the bed.

He put the bottle on the bedstand, pulled off his shoes

and socks, tie, shirt and trousers, clicked the TV on and lay down in his underwear, his hands behind his head, staring at the screen. There was a programme on about a women's football team from Iceland. One of the players had a harelip that had been badly operated on. Birth was a lottery, he thought. The tiniest mutation in a gene could create a monster. The Icelandic woman. The Tokoloshe. Amos Chipeta.

A check through the *Guardian* database and Interpol had confirmed it: Clement Chipeta had a brother, Amos, who'd left Tanzania at the same time and was still unaccounted for. He'd grown up in the mangroves of the Rufiji delta and, before he'd turned twenty, had found a living with the gangs who operated illegal divers – some without breathing apparatus – to raid the shipwrecks. None of it was covered by local law and there was a lot of money in the operations. For Amos it was just the beginning of the criminal career that had brought him into contact with the trade in body parts and eventually to the UK. Last December someone called Andrew Chipeta had gone to a GP in Southall, London, asking for referral to a specialist. The doctor had looked at the deformed spine, the overlarge ribcage, the gorilla-sized jaw, and was sifting a range of diagnoses in his head, scoliosis, kyphosis, diastrophic dysplasia, but 'Andrew' had left in a hurry when the doctor had asked the formal questions they'd put to any new patient: his address, his circumstances, his age and country of origin.

Amos Chipeta. So who or what was the Tokoloshe? Just a young man crippled by a birth defect? Out there somewhere now, existing God only knew how and trying to find help in a cold, alien country – but still able to find beauty and clarity and maybe even love in the face of a twenty-quid-a-trick prostitute from Hartcliffe? Or was he a monster? A half-human sloping off in mud and dirty water, making a living from raiding graves and cutting the hair from corpses.

Caffery closed one eye and then the other, letting the TV light prism through the liquid gold in his glass. Years ago back in London – he'd have been about fifteen at the time – he was in love with one of the girls at his school. Couldn't remember her name now. But he could remember the name of the guy she was in love with: Tom Cadwall. He could remember, too, breaking into the Cadwalls' garden early one morning. Climbing a tree. Hanging in the branches like a bloody possum. He'd stayed there all day, hoping to see inside Tom Cadwall's bedroom. He wanted to know what Cadwall had that he didn't.

Caffery dozed: right where he was, one hand curled round the glass on his chest. He saw Tom Cadwall. He saw him standing at the bedroom window all those years ago. He saw a woman come into the room and speak to him. She was slight, wiry, a mass of hair bleached by sun and salt water. She crossed the room and leant into Tom. She sniffed his chest, reached her hand to the back of his head, laced her fingers in his hair and began to tear at it.

Caffery woke with a start. The glass rolled off his chest and smashed on the floor. He lay there, heart thudding, the hairs on the back of his neck standing rigid.

Something had woken him. Something was in the room.

Slowly, without moving the rest of his body, he freed one hand and lifted it so it was ready to cannon up and out. Keeping his breathing slow and controlled so that if anyone was watching him he'd seem calm, he scanned the room, trying to place where the bastard was hiding. He thought about the Hardballer – outside in the damned glove compartment of the car.

In one motion he rolled on to his back, snatched up the bottle and held it in front of him, training his eyes into the darkness. 'Right.' He breathed hard. 'Whatever you want, let's do it. Let's get it over with.'

All that came back to him was the flicker of the TV screen. An insurance commercial, a bulldog nodding at the camera. From downstairs he could hear the hum of the refrigerator in the kitchen. He pulled back the duvet and ran his hands lightly across the surface of the sheet. It was bumpy and uneven. Damp. And now he could smell stagnant water. Rivers and quarries. The bastard had been lying in his bed.

He threw the duvet on to the floor. Tucked under the pillow something glinted. Scissors. His own nail scissors from the bathroom cabinet. The sort that had been used to cut Jakes's hair.

He ran his hands across the back of his head. Right at the bottom, at the very nape of his neck, a tiny patch was missing. The size of a penny.

He breathed, long and slow, trying to calm himself.

The little casement windows were open, just the top pane. No one and nothing could have come in through those. What about downstairs? Could someone have opened one of the doors and crept in without him knowing? And the bathroom? He put the scissors on the bedstand and got up, still holding the bottle in front of him.

A noise. Downstairs. The sly sound of the front door opening. Just a tiny creak. It was enough. He got to the top of the stairs just in time to see a shadow, a suggestion of something slightly darker than its surroundings, slip out of the front door.

He launched himself down, two stairs at a time, threw open the door and ran out in his bare feet. There were clouds over the moon and no street-lights this far out in the Mendips, so the garden was dark. He came to a halt in the middle of the driveway and stood with the bottle still thrust out, listening. From the forests to his right came the ghostly calls of two owls, battling it out over territory. Somewhere on the other side of the trees to his left he heard the brook that ran along the bottom of the garden and way, way to the north, the monster whine of a distant jet starting its descent into Bristol. Nothing else. No scooter. No footsteps.

The car keys were in the living room. He went and got them. When he came out again the garden was still silent. He took the 45 Hardballer from the glove compartment. Slammed the door. Listened again. There was something at the end of the driveway he hadn't noticed last time. About ten metres away. A glitch in the darkness. A smudge of light where there shouldn't be any.

He slammed the magazine into the pistol grip and – gun

pointing down away from him because it was only in the movies you held a loaded pistol in the air where it could be easily knocked out of your hands – padded over to the shape. It was a shoe. A rubber Croc. He lifted his eyes and studied the darkness again. The silent trees. The blank walls of the cottage. He picked up the shoe and went inside.

The house was dark. He put the chain on the front door and went into the kitchen. When he switched on the light he saw that two cupboards stood open. A bag of rice lay tipped over on the floor, its contents splayed across the tiles. And inside the cupboards, where there had been the usual blokeish collection of cans, baked beans, soup, stuff he could heat in five minutes, now there was nothing. Just a scattering of dried pasta and the white backboards. He went around and checked what had gone. Food – every bit of food in the house. The CD player on the sideboard was still there. And a portable TV set still in its box on the floor.

He put the Croc on the table next to the gun and sat down, his elbows on the table. The sandal was dark khaki, dusty and very large. He turned it over. Size twelve.

Fucking mutant.

No way am I sleeping with a mutant.

He looked at his hands. They were shaking. This was enough. This was too much on his own. He needed to speak to someone.

25

There had been clay on Misty's feet. It probably didn't mean much but there wasn't anything else to go on. So Flea chose the rapeseed field nearest the river.

If she was right Misty must have headed south-east from the clinic. She would have been lost, confused, and would have walked for hours through difficult terrain, some of it in the dark. Probably, if she had any sense of direction at all, when she hit the road she would have tried to navigate her way back to the clinic, going west. The collision hadn't happened long after she'd come out into the road – the mud, grass and rapeseed hadn't had a chance to be walked off, so her time there had been limited. Flea was going to comb the whole stretch of road from the clinic to a mile past the rapeseed field. If she found nothing she would turn around, go to the other field and do the same thing there.

She left the car in a pub car park in Norton St Philip – it would be less conspicuous there than in a lay-by – and walked the half-mile down to the lane using a footpath, keeping the lights of the road to her right and reaching the south-westerly end of the lane before ten p.m. She dropped the rucksack and rummaged in it until she found the squares of paper and the Maglite. Using a rubber band she lashed the paper to the top of the torch, adding a second piece to block off the open side. She held the torch at arm's length, turned it from side to side and adjusted it until no light was leaking around the edges. The beam was focused white and thin. It wouldn't be bright enough to spot from a distance unless someone was actively looking for it.

Keeping the torch pointed down, she moved slowly along the lane, hugging the southern side, counting her steps in her head. One. Two. Three. Four. She kept her attention on the road, monitoring the few buildings she passed out of the corner of her eye for signs of life. Some were close, others were distant, homely flashes of lights in the trees. No traffic went by. There were just a few shadowy cows in the fields, the slap of her feet on the tarmac and her own breathing for company.

A hundred and ten, a hundred and eleven, a hundred and twelve, a hundred and thirteen.

The moon came up and the road glowed silver, winding away in front of her like a stream. In this light the plants had no colours; the crops, the trees and the grasses were the same uniform grey as the shadows they threw at her feet.

A hundred and twenty-one, a hundred and twenty-two, a hundred and twenty-three . . .

She stopped, the hairs on the back of her neck standing on end. There had been a sound, almost indecipherable above the jingling of the Bergen on her back. A shifting in the hedgerow. She turned cautiously, the torch held out like a weapon, and scanned the lane. It had been on the other side of the hedge, about two yards behind. She was sure, without quite understanding why, that it had come from about waist height.

'Hello?'

Her voice was hollow, flat in the cold air. She blinked at the silvery fretwork of hedge and tree. It could be livestock in there. A fox or a bird. Definitely an animal. She thought of quarry number eight. She thought of a house she'd visited on Operation Norway: a house with dark rooms. A place that had made her feel that wherever she went a small shadow was moving behind her at waist height.

'Let's get it over with,' she hissed. 'I'm in a hurry.'

Silence again. The distant sound of an aeroplane slipping into the Bristol air corridor, the faintest movement of a light breeze in the hedgerows to her left. She went back a few steps to the place the sound had come from and kicked into the hedge. Her foot hit twigs. Nothing moved. She went a few yards along and did it again. A couple of yards further still. No response.

She took a few deep breaths, then shook herself. Jack Caffery and his fantasies were getting to her. She stuck a finger up at the hedge, pissed off now, and turned away, picking up the search where she'd left off. The lane was on an incline, marked with passing spaces, with entrances to fields, and she walked close to the edge, training the torch down, searching for anomalies. By now the moon was high and after about a hundred yards she turned a corner and found the land had levelled out, the lane opening into a wide, flat road with central markings. You could see almost a quarter of a mile along it. If you were in a car you'd be able to get your speed up here. You could accelerate, drive fast enough that if you hit someone you'd kill them instantly.

The field was on the left. The flowers were greyed out by the moon. But it was unmistakable. Rapeseed. It sloped down to the road to her left. Further along on the right, where the land rose up, a few lights twinkled among the trees. A tiny hamlet nestled against the hillside, the moon picking out tiled roofs, a chimney, two thatched roofs. Anyone in those houses wouldn't see the torch from this distance but they might spot her, stark and unprotected on the road. She moved to the side of the road where a line of poplars stood straight and ordered, as they did on the Roman roads in France. Keeping in the tree shadows, she moved along, scuffing her feet on the ground, moving the torch from side to side, checking the trunks, the grass, the tarmac.

And then she stopped.

About twenty feet to her right there was a set of very clear, very distinct skidmarks on the road.

She stared at them, her pulse picking up. They were so perfect it made her want to turn around and check it wasn't a set-up. That someone wasn't watching her, smiling slyly at her reaction.

She approached slowly, shining the torch up and down them. They bent gently towards the centre of the road as if someone had swerved to avoid something. She walked the length of them, pacing carefully, about forty feet from start to finish, a yard or so into the oncoming lane.

She was breathing hard now. Whatever wheelbase had made these tracks it wasn't too wide, or too narrow, and if she'd had to bet she would say they came from a family saloon car. A Focus, maybe. If Thom had made these marks he must have been coming from the east. Misty must have been in this lane, on the opposite side of the road from the rapeseed. He would have seen her almost two hundred feet away. Reaction time would have been slow – he'd drunk two bottles of red wine that night. He'd slammed on the brakes and hit her somewhere around here, on the central road markings. Misty had gone over the roof, and probably, since the dent had been above the driver's side, fallen off the car and come to rest somewhere in the oncoming lane or on the verge opposite.

Flea shone the torch around the ground, inspecting the tarmac – a piece of glass glinting at her here, a scrap of chewing-gum paper there. Just where the grasses from the verge overhung the road, slightly countersunk where the tarmac had softened in the sun, she could see a hair slide. A pink one. It might have belonged to a small child. A little girl who had mourned its loss from the open window of a car. Or it might have belonged to Misty Kitson.

She took off her rucksack and pulled out gloves and a plastic freezer bag. Quickly, because she didn't know when a car might come, she crouched at the side of the road and carefully prised the hair slide out of the tarmac with a nail. It was more like a child's clip now she could see it properly. She pushed it into the freezer bag anyway. Then something to her left caught her eye.

About a yard away a hole had been made in the grass on the verge. Whatever made it must have been big, heavy. Not as large as a deer, bigger than a badger. The grass stems had been broken in an almost circular shape, as if it had lain down there to sleep for a while. Above the hole, between the verge and the rapeseed field, there was a low dry-stone wall. Four stones at the top had been dislodged. One hung precariously over the field. It looked as if it might fall at any moment.

She crouched, swept the Maglite around. The cow parsley against the wall had been snapped, and the heads hung down limply. Something dark coated them. Careful not to touch the flattened area she plucked a stem and sat back on her haunches, inspecting it. In this light it wasn't easy to see exactly what she was holding, but when she put down the torch, took off her glove with her teeth and pushed her fingernail along the stem, the dark stuff flaked and fell into her cupped hand.

Blood. She knew its properties and behaviour too well. It was caked blood. So this, this unremarkable stretch of road, was where Misty's life had ended.

An image came: Thom leaping out of the car, his face drawn with shock. His panic – because that was what he would have done, panicked – when he saw the broken body in the hedge. Crying as he scooped Misty up, shovelled her into the boot. Her handbag must have been lying somewhere on the road, somewhere around here, its sequins glinting at him; he must have picked that up too and—

Crouching there on the verge with one hand holding the cow parsley, the other cupping the flakes of blood, the latex glove dangling from between her teeth, Flea became very still. Something lay in the vegetation to the left. Something small. Reflecting a low metallic glow from the moon. If it had been a dark night, if you weren't crouched at this level, you wouldn't have noticed it, she thought. Quickly she rested the cow parsley across her knees. Felt in the Bergen for the freezer bag. She emptied the flakes of blood into it, followed by the cow parsley, which she broke in two. She shuffled forward on her haunches, pulling on the spare glove. Gingerly, she pushed her hand through the grass, the roots of elder and hawthorn.

Misty's phone.

She manoeuvred it out of the undergrowth and held it cupped in both hands. A Nokia, stainless-steel casing with diamonds encrusted, just like on the intelligence mock-up photos. But where was the on-off switch? On her own phone you needed to hold down the end-call button and it would spring to life, but on this phone there was a small button at the top of the casing, sunk low. And three more on the sides. Any one of those buttons could switch it on. Instantly it would send another signal to the phone masts.

She couldn't drop it. She couldn't leave it. The battery. Take out the battery. She remembered something about how certain phones carry GPS technology that stays active even with the battery out. Or was it just active with the phone switched off? She couldn't remember. No. If it had GPS technology the police would have found it ages ago. It was safe to take the battery out. It had to be.

She turned it over. Eased her fingernail under the battery casing. From the forest behind her she heard a car. Going fast.

She snatched up the Maglite. Crawl-walked into the shadow of a large sycamore. Already the car's headlights had hit the undercanopy of the trees at the far end of the road. She pulled herself into a tight ball around the torch, her knees hard into the verge.

The headlights fell on the hedge next to her. She put her face down into her chest, the phone and the torch jammed hard against each other. The car swept past and disappeared until all that was left was the residual sound of tappets and music in the silent night.

When it had rounded the bend she dropped forward on to her knees and looked at the phone. Dark and silent, she hadn't switched it on accidentally. She let out all her breath at once, put her head back against the tree-trunk and stared at where, hovering in the air above the tyre tracks, like a feather caught in the airstream of the car, a single hair caught the moonlight as it seesawed down. White and kinked, it yawed and pitched through the air currents.

She knew the head it had come from. Misty Kitson's. Not alive and open-eyed, tottering down the silent lane clutching her handbag and mobile phone, but silent, finished. Caked in body fluid and lying secretly in a bath ten miles from here.

26

It was gone midnight. Caffery found two flagons of cider in the pantry, pulled on his RAB jacket, locked all the doors and got into the car. He put the radio on loud and drove without a plan, not thinking where he was going, letting instinct take over. He was drawn to minor roads, the ones that laced around the Mendips and out east almost as far as Wiltshire. Every field he passed, every lane entry, he let the car slow, craning his neck to see over the hedgerows. Nothing – no red firelight, no flicker of flame in the dusk.

When Caffery had left the Met he'd chosen Bristol for one reason: to track down the person they called the Walking Man. The Walking Man had been convicted of torturing a paedophile named Craig Evans, who had killed his daughter. In Caffery's head this detail teamed himself and the Walking Man, because if Caffery knew one thing it was how to live with revenge in your heart. Ivan Penderecki, the ageing Polish paedophile who'd lived on the other side of the railway track from the Cafferys, had got away with Ewan Caffery's murder, and with concealing his body, and this had rotted Jack's spirit for years. Then, when Penderecki died, the revenge he'd never taken took over rotting his spirit.

So he'd come here to meet someone who had taken revenge, the sort of revenge he should have taken on Penderecki. What Caffery hadn't expected was the strange, limping friendship that seemed to be starting between him and the Walking Man.

He found himself on the B-road running straight through the area that had been covered by the team searching for Misty Kitson. It ran along the bottom of the hill, straight past the entrance to the Farleigh Park Hall clinic: a vast lit-up mansion, with sparkling colonnades and imposing steps. He slowed, trying to imagine Misty coming out of that building, turning right, or was it left? Ironic, he thought, looking at the sign at the foot of the driveway glinting in his headlights. How ironic that Lucy Mahoney had been missing about the same length of time as Kitson and that while the force had thrown all their horses at the Kitson case, the whole of the high-powered MCIU engine, Lucy Mahoney had just one fashion-plate model of a DI, who hadn't even stayed for the post-mortem, and a family liaison officer too lazy to let her relatives know she'd been found until she'd had every piece of her insides hauled out by Beatrice Foxton, weighed, sliced, tested and crammed back inside her ribcage.

Caffery drove slowly, past a rapeseed field that led up the hill and to the lake Flea Marley's team had searched. The lights of a small hamlet opposite twinkled in the trees.

He was out of the search radius now. He hit a road lined with poplars, like a European road, and speeded up. Got to the main crossroads and did a left. Drove another five miles then saw a lane he recognized on his left. He'd been there at the beginning of the week with the Walking Man.

He locked the car, climbed over a farm gate and, using the little flashlight on his key-ring, walked up the long hill, his bluish torchlight small and insignificant in the weight of the darkness. In the distance Bristol threw a halo of sodium orange into the sky. He stopped at the place the Walking Man's campfire had been a few nights ago, buttoned his jacket, knelt on the cold ground and sniffed the faint residue of charred earth. It was cold.

'Hey,' he murmured into the dark. 'Are you there?'

Nothing came back, just the distant movement of wind weaving through the trees. No Walking Man.

He went back to the car and reversed it along the rutted track. Retracing his steps, he turned left on the A36, then after half a mile took a right on to a small, meandering lane and drove for almost ten minutes. He caught glimpses of his own eyes in the rear-view mirror. Blue. Dark-fringed. His mother's eyes. She had been a good Catholic girl from Toxteth. He hadn't seen her for more than twenty years, not since she'd last given up on Ewan and left London – putting it all behind her. Even choosing to forget her younger son, Jack. Now he didn't know if she was dead or alive. But he knew one thing for sure: if she was dead she'd gone to her grave with the rosary wrapped round her fingers and no one would have thought anything of it. He pictured a bracelet made of human hair to ward away bad spirits. 'Crude beliefs', had been Powers's words. There are lots of paths to God, Caffery thought, fingering the back of his head where the hair was missing. A whole world of different routes.

He slammed on the brakes. It had been such a small glow that he'd nearly missed it. Somewhere in the fields down to his right, down where the riverbanks were thick with mud and bulrushes, there was a fire. He reversed the car up the silent lane, levering himself up in the seat to see over the hedge, put the car into a three-point turn and nosed it down the first farm track he saw, letting it bump on to a field, the exhaust banging on the furrowed earth. He turned off the engine and the lights, and for a moment he was still, looking out at the fire.

The Walking Man.

He'd heard Caffery's car but he didn't look up, just sat nonchalantly next to the fire, scratching his oily beard and staring into the flames as if they'd been telling him a story and now he was giving it some thought. His belongings were arranged around him, lit red by the crackling fire: his sleeping-bags, his all-weather gear, his plastic bottles of cider. Two plates sat ready for the food he was cooking in the pot. Two plates, Caffery noticed. Not one. He was expected. This was the way with the Walking Man. It wasn't possible to just *find* the Walking Man: *he* decided when the time was right, then – as if their shared histories chimed on some element – exerted a casual magnetism on Caffery. He threw out an invisible lariat and drew him in.

He got out of the car, taking the two-litre flagons of cider with him

'Took a long time to find me,' said the Walking Man, as Caffery approached. He took good care of his feet and his clothing was expensive outdoors gear, but to look at him you'd think he'd been soaked in tar: he was black from head to toe as if he slept in the charcoal of his campfires. 'You've been looking for me for two hours now.'

'How do you know that?' Caffery said, though it didn't surprise him.

The Walking Man didn't answer. He stoked the fire and edged the tin plates closer to the flames. Caffery set down the cider. The Walking Man had more than two million pounds tucked away in a savings account somewhere yet he drank scrumpy cider, the worst the local apple presses could cough out. And he never, ever slept under a roof. It was just his way.

'I've plotted your routes on a map.' Caffery unrolled the piece of bed foam the Walking Man had waiting for him, warming next to the fire. 'I can see the beginnings of a pattern.'

The Walking Man snorted. 'Yes. Of course you'd feel the need to study me. You're a policeman.'

'I've got an intelligence database to help me. When people see you they call in the sighting.'

'Because they're scared of me.'

'They know what you're capable of.'

Craig Evans, the killer of the Walking Man's daughter, had been only half alive at the end of the torture. They had him down as DOA in the ambulance. And when they'd patched him up and seen what the Walking Man had removed from him, most of the professionals thought privately he'd have been better off dead. With no eyes, no genitals, it wasn't going to be the best of lives. It would have been better for Penderecki to end like that. But he hadn't. Instead he'd stolen the chance and killed himself by hanging from a ceiling beam in his bathroom. The lost opportunity stung Caffery even now.

'I gave you some crocus bulbs the other night. Been asking myself about them. What's going to happen to them?'

'They're here.' The Walking Man patted his breast pocket. A small rustling noise came through the night. 'Safe in here.'

'When are you going to plant them?'

The Walking Man looked up. His eyes were the same colour as Caffery's: dark blue ringed with dark eyelashes. 'When the time is right. And how do you know I haven't already planted some? I won't be asked about it by you again. Jack Caffery. Policeman.'

Caffery gave a wry half-smile. He was used to this from the Walking Man. He was starting to understand how it worked, that things would be explained in their time. While the Walking Man attended to the food Caffery uncorked the cider, poured for them both in tin cups and leant back on the bedroll, one hand drifting up to finger the gap in his hair. The night settled around them. The sounds of the river gurgling and rolling its way through the fields, the clicking of his car engine cooling. The faint electronic buzz of a weir further downstream. About fifty feet away someone, some kids maybe, had hooked a tyre on a rope from a tree that leant out over the river. It hung motionless in the starlight, the ghosts of all the children who had swung from it over the years, the yells and the laughter and the crashes of water, swarming silently around it.

'You saw it, didn't you?' Caffery said, after a while. 'The last time I came to you it was there. It wasn't my imagination – there was something watching me from the trees.'

The Walking Man grunted. 'Yes. There was.'

'You weren't scared of it.'

'Why would I be? It wasn't coming for me.'

'And if it was? If you were me? Would you be scared then?'

The Walking Man was quiet for a while, thinking about this. He spooned the food on to the tin plates and added fresh herbs collected during the day, maybe from private gardens he'd crept into. The food next to this campfire was some of the best Caffery'd ever had, straightforward, always steaming hot. The Walking Man distributed it between them and added forks, pushing one plate to him.

Caffery took the plate, and repeated, 'Would you be scared?'

'I don't know.' He sat down and paused for a moment, letting the steam from the food come into his nose, holding his mouth open like a dog tasting a scent. 'Are you?'

'I don't know what it – he – wants. I don't know what he's capable of.'

The Walking Man took a forkful of food and looked slyly at Caffery, half smiling.

'What? Why're you smiling?'

The Walking Man pointed his knife at him. 'I'm smiling at you. And at the way you can't let anything go. The way you treat your job as your penance.'

'My *penance*? My penance for what?'

'You know.'

'Are you talking about Ewan again?'

'Of course I'm talking about your brother. You're still paying penance for the way he died and you didn't. The penance your mother always wanted from you. And this is the main way you find to stay dead.'

Only a few days ago the Walking Man had told Caffery he had a chance to choose between living and dying. He'd said he could continue to pursue Ewan, the child who had gone, by continuing to pour everything into his work. Or he could pursue 'the child that could be'. *The child that could be.* Caffery had pondered those words over and over again in the last few days. There were no kids in his life and never would be. It was stamped on his heart. Better to never have them than to risk losing them.

'When you've got a child there is a line from you to the child that exists for ever and cannot be broken. At the moment the only child Jack Caffery has a line to is a dead one. Therefore your link is to death. But you know and I know – we both know – for you there could be a child who lives. Stop looking at death, Jack Caffery.' The Walking Man wiped the plate with his finger and licked it carefully. He put it down and looked first up at the stars, then thoughtfully into the trees as if something was there, something come to watch them both. 'If you stop looking at death, death will stop sending out its handmaidens to find you.'

27

The room is warm so the man is naked. It's easier this way. Not so much mess. He stands at a workbench, busily dismantling a rabbit. He pulls the skin away from the flesh until it is attached only at the feet, the tail and the head. Then, using a heavy Damascus-steel cleaver, he takes off its paws and tail.

Skinning an animal takes less effort than skinning a human. It's to do with the fact that there's so little fat in the subcutaneous layer of the animal.

He cuts into the rabbit's neck until the vertebrae are revealed, like small, smeared teeth. Then he uses a quick twist to snap the backbone and the head free, and pulls away the tiny coat with its weighted ends. Poking it with a finger he rubs it so the outer and inner silvery fascias slip up and down against each other. Then he bends over and sniffs, letting the smell rise through his nostrils and lodge in the back of his throat. It's a simple smell, woody and tart. It's nothing, nothing, like the smell of human skin.

He straightens and lifts the skin on his finger, dangles it for a moment over the bin, then drops it.

Animal skin is always like this. A disappointment. Even soaked in lye water, dehaired and mounted it is never the same as the real thing. Anyway, he's not interested in the skin. It's not that but the process he craves. The tearing feel of the lower layer separating from the underlying muscle.

He skins an animal at least once a week. More when he's particularly anxious.

This week he's done five.

28

Early the next morning the lanes around the rapeseed field were silent. Sunlight caught at the diamond points of dew in the grass. Flea stopped the Clio on the tarmac, got out and walked along the road in her trainers, casually passing the place Misty had been killed. Stopping a hundred yards past it, she turned and retraced her steps.

It was only seven a.m. but she knew it was going to be a warm day. The line of thaw in the grass was a few inches behind the shadow of the sun creeping up over the hill. A few cows stood watching her, breathing heavily, clouds of breath and steam wreathing them. Back at the car she stood for a moment, looking about, listening, checking nothing was coming. The lane was silent. This place wasn't just a long way from the clinic: it was also outside the base station cell. In range of a different mast, in fact. Misty had switched off the phone a long time before the impact. MCIU would never have thought to search out here.

But – she turned to look up the hill – if the case went on any longer they might turn their attention to places this far afield. Maybe not to search but for house-to-house enquiries. Like in the hamlet up there. The sleepy roofs and chimneys of a short row of Victorian houses and five or six older cottages scattered above the terrace. Some were thatched, some reminded her of her parents' home, their tiled roofs mossed and dank. Below the cottages, on the lower slope nearer the road, sat a modern bungalow. Out of whack with its surroundings, it had a side gabled roof and PVC windows.

Something, a light or a reflection, flashed from the back of it.

Slowly she raised a hand, shielded her eyes and stared. The flash came again. A brief square of white light. Then nothing. Maybe it was a window opening and closing. Someone in the bungalow was moving around. They might be watching her.

She dropped her hand, shrugged the collar of the jacket up around her neck, went back to the car and drove half a mile along the lane into the trees at the bottom of the hamlet. There was a small ingress on the right. She pulled into it and parked the car deep in the trees where no one would pass, deadlocked it, got out and followed a small footpath that led away from the ingress in the direction of the bungalow. The path was overgrown and choked with nettles, but it climbed steadily towards the hamlet. She stopped when the trees cleared and she found herself at a low brick wall, looking at the bungalow's back garden.

It was large and unkempt, spreading away across the hillside: grass and the first dandelions were coming up through the brown skeletons of last year's bindweed.

Brambles had strewn themselves across the lawn like tentacles, and everywhere fibrestone lawn ornaments nestled in the wet grass: cats and dolphins, a Pegasus with a broken wing, a donkey next to a manger. Plastic bird feeders, in faded sherbet shades of pink, orange and yellow, hung in the trees and saplings. A Siamese cat, a real one, the colour of *crème brûlée*, sat under one, blinking sleepily at Flea.

The house was as shabby as the garden. The paint on the window frames had once been a deep red but had faded with years of sun and rain. It, too, was studded with animal statuary: chipped and peeling butterflies flew up the walls; three cast-concrete cats squared off at each other on the roof ridge and another appeared to be crawling head first into the chimney. No windows were open. But she could see where the sun's reflection had come from – not a window. On the patio, next to french windows, a telescope was mounted on a tripod. Next to it, also on a tripod, was a camera.

She climbed stealthily over the wall. She walked quickly to the side of the house and the sun-cracked hard standing where a faded old Volkswagen sat, covered with white bird shit. The house was almost silent – just the faint sound of a TV playing inside, a high-octane voice, shrill, rising. She took a step nearer the french windows. Listened again. No one was moving in there. The telescope was just feet away. She stared at it, trying to work out what it was focused on. She looked down at the road. You could see the tyre tracks from here. They were like a beacon. You couldn't miss them.

Enough. This was enough. Someone here might have seen the accident.

She went back down the garden the way she'd come. She got to the ingress and, sitting on the Clio's warm bonnet where she couldn't be seen from the road or the house, pulled out her phone and plugged in the force communications number.

She and Thom had to be very, very careful. Any risk, however small, had to be taken care of.

29

In the bottom of Flea's navy Bergen there was an ID card for a dive conference she'd attended last month. Now she slung it round her neck, pushed all her hair up into a peaked baseball cap, and headed back up the path to the bungalow. The communications department held logs on every address in the jurisdiction. Called STORM logs, they recorded details of residents and their contacts with the police. The logs said the name of the bungalow's owner was Mrs Ruth Lindermilk, and that there had been only one incident in the last ten years to which the police had been called: an assault by a middle-aged female on a male. An airgun had been voluntarily surrendered and taken to the armoury at HQ, but no one was nicked.

The doorbell didn't work and there was no knocker, so she banged the letterbox two or three times. No answer. She knocked again, then stepped back off the doorstep and peered up at the eaves. From there she could see that the cat's tail sticking out of the chimney was faded and cracked.

She looked back at the rest of the hamlet. This was the

only cottage that had the vantage-point of the road. 'Stunning views of the Westbury white horse', it would say, in an estate agent's blurb. She was turning to go back to the terrace when the sound of a chain being pulled came from the front door.

'Yeah? What?'

The front door had been opened a crack, through which a pair of baggy eyes peered out from beneath a sailor's cap. They belonged to a woman, you could see that from her size and the soft quality of her eyes. A wary, mistrustful woman. She was very tanned and her nose was flattened, as if she'd lived a man's hard life outdoors and still bore the scars.

'Hi.'

The eyes studied her suspiciously. 'What are you? Jehovah's Witness? Better get off my land.'

'No.'

'If you're selling something you can eff off too. Don't like fuckin' salesmen knocking on my door.'

'No. I just want a word.'

'You have to be joking. Better get off my land now.'

'Are you Ruth?'

There was a pause.

'Ruth Lindermilk?'

'Who are you?'

Flea took off her cap and rubbed a hand through her hair, showing herself as plainly as she could. 'My name's Phoebe.'

'Yeah – but who *are* you?'

'I'm from the . . .'

'The?'

'Highways Agency.' She flashed the ID, her finger over the bit that said 'ACPO Delegate'.

'The council, you mean?'

'Yup.'

Something in Ruth Lindermilk's face changed. 'About the letters?'

'The . . . ? Yes. Can I come in?'

Ruth Lindermilk glanced up and down the lane to see if they were being watched. 'Are you on your own? No one else with you?'

'No one else. Just me. Can I come in?'

She hesitated. She gave Flea another once-over, taking in the T-shirt, the combats. Then, with a grunt, she let the door swing open. Flea stepped inside. Mrs Lindermilk slammed the door and headed away down the narrow little corridor. It was dark here. Flea followed the ghostly white blob of the woman's cap, keeping her neck slightly bent because she sensed the ceilings might get suddenly low, like at home. There was a smell in the house, a mixture of dinners cooked long ago and alcohol. Not whisky. Something sweeter than that. Rum with mixers, maybe.

'I'm like a snake.' Mrs Lindermilk stopped in the dark, breathing harshly. A faint light filtered from under a door ahead. 'A fuckin' snake.'

'Sorry?'

'Like a snake in an aquarium. They'd all come and peer at me if they could. Peer and point. The wankers. Only interested in making my life difficult. Now, you never made no appointment so you take me as you find me. OK?'

'Fine.'

Ruth Lindermilk opened the door to reveal a large, dishevelled room. The french windows at the far end were hung with vertical blinds, but they stood slightly ajar and a small fan of sunlight came through, illuminating the crowded furniture: chairs, small tables and lumpy armchairs. Magazines, paperbacks and miniatures crammed the shelves – bad copies of Dresden shepherdesses, fat children in bonnets kissing, horses rearing, cats sleeping. Every piece of wall space was covered with framed photographs of different shapes and sizes. In the corner the TV flickered: QVC. A hefty blonde girl in hotpants was struggling to balance on a gym ball. Through the small gap in the blinds Flea could see the shiny eyepiece of the telescope on the patio outside.

'That's it. Feast your eyes. This is how I am and I ain't making any apologies.' Mrs Lindermilk pottered around, switching on lights, shooing cats off chairs. 'Sit down. Sit down.' She indicated a sofa at the other end of the room. Now Flea could see her better she saw she was stout. Dressed in white shorts and a pink polo shirt with an anchor insignia on the breast, she had short, muscular legs jammed into stiletto sandals, with narrow ankles and hardened calves like a man's. Her thin hair under the jaunty cap was worn short and dyed an anaemic ochre red. 'Push the cats off. Sit down or die standing. It's your choice.'

Flea looked at the sofa. Two long-haired tabbies were

curled among a pile of stuffed toys. Under them the leather was dry and split with a salty stain across it that looked like sweat or sea water. She moved the toys and sat next to the cats. One made a small grunt and wriggled closer into its partner. She felt the warmth against her leg and liked the comfort of it.

'A drink? S'pose you want a drink?'

A black glass and chrome bar stood in the corner, coloured tumblers balanced on their rims, a gold ice bucket, mixers lined up. Flea took stock of the bottles of spirits at the back. 'Yes.' She put her cap on the arm of the chair. 'I'll have what you're having.'

Mrs Lindermilk wiped her hands on her shirt and went to the bar. She upended two tumblers, put her hand on a bottle of Bacardi, stopped and gave Flea a sickly smile, as if to say, *You almost caught me. Almost. Not quite*. 'Coke, then,' she said. She got two cans from under the bar, snapped off the ring pulls and poured. Gave one to Flea.

'Mrs Lindermilk—'

'Ruth. You can call me Ruth, if you want.'

'OK, Ruth. Is there a Mr Lindermilk?'

'Was.' She took her drink and settled into a worn recliner next to a rickety occasional table on which lay a remote control and an ashtray. Her bare legs in the heels were tanned, and sinewy, blackish clusters of spider veins dotted up and down them. 'It's just me and Stevie now.'

'Your son?'

'Yeah – that's him.' She nodded to the walls. Some of the framed photographs were of boats. One or two showed a much younger Ruth at the helm, wearing her jaunty cap next to a grey-haired man in a Hawaiian shirt. Another showed a younger man, in a white wife-beater and baseball cap with an anchor insignia, at the helm of a small boat, gazing straight into the camera. His hair was thick and blond, and he was very tanned, but there was something closed about his mouth that stopped him being good-looking. 'Got his own business now. Doing well for himself, our Stevie.'

'Ruth, the police came a few years back. You and one of the neighbours?'

'How the hell do you know about that?'

'We have access to that sort of thing.'

'It wasn't me who started it. Have you got access to that part? Eh?'

'It didn't say.'

'Well, it was his fault. He was poisoning the squirrels. He *knew* my cats might eat the poison, *knew* it would wind me up. And it did. He got what was coming.'

'You pulled a gun on him?'

'A BB gun. Not exactly an AK47, is it?'

'It's still a gun. Could do a lot of harm.'

Ruth Lindermilk held up her hand. 'No. You're not going to discredit me. No effing way are you going to come in here without an appointment and try to discredit *me*.'

'OK, OK.' Flea kept her voice level. She wanted to look up at the telescope but she focused her eyes on Ruth. 'I'm not trying to discredit you. I'm really not. I'm trying to build a picture of your situation.'

'How much more of a picture do you want? You've got the letters I wrote you, haven't you?'

'Yes. I . . . Do you spend a lot of time watching the road?'

'Most nights.'

'What time do you go to bed?'

'Late.'

'When you say late?'

She shifted in her chair. 'Are you here to help me or not?' She raised her eyebrows challengingly. 'Hmmm?'

Flea's eyes went to the glass she was holding. Ruth Lindermilk was absently sloshing the Coke around in it with a circular motion. The way you would if there was booze in it. This was going to be uphill all the way. But the drink. She definitely had a drink problem. It might be useful for them. 'Can I have a look through the camera?' she asked. 'The telescope?'

Lindermilk didn't answer. She went on studying Flea thoughtfully. Her eyes went to the combats again. To the ID tucked inside her T-shirt.

'Ruth? The camera?'

She smiled. 'Of course you can have a look.'

She stood and opened the french windows. They stepped out into a day that had exploded into light. Sun was bouncing off the dew in the grass, the trees. One or two cats followed them, dropped on to the drying patio and lay blinking. Flea stood on tiptoe and squinted into the camera viewfinder. It was trained on the road below. Not on the site of the accident, but further up nearer where she'd left the car. She clicked the button on to 'quick view' and scrolled. There were only twenty or so photos, showing cats, a sunset, a badger eating cat food, all of which looked to have been taken in the back garden. There were no pictures of her just now, standing next to the Clio on the road.

Flea switched the camera back to photo mode, stepped sideways and put her eye to the telescope. It was trained on the road too.

'Know how to use it?' Ruth Lindermilk said.

'Yes. The focus is here, right?'

'It's a good one. A nautical one. The neighbours hate me using it.'

Flea made a show of getting the adjustments right. She moved the telescope, letting it scan the hillside above the rapeseed field, down the track that went up the side, along the edge of the road. She moved it slightly to the right. Hit something pink.

She looked up. Ruth Lindermilk had walked a few paces on to the lawn and was standing with her hands on her hips, grinning at the telescope. There was a chipped tooth at the top of her mouth, next to the canine. 'Get a good look?'

'Yes.'

'Notice anything?'

'Just you. In the way.'

'But anything special about me? Go on – tell me what you noticed.'

That you're mad? That you're an alcoholic? 'What am I supposed to notice?'

'That I'm not fuckin' stupid.' She came back to the telescope and pulled it away from Flea, snapping on the lens cover. 'That's what you're supposed to notice.'

'I'm just trying to do my job, Mrs Lindermilk.'

'No, you're not. You're not trying to do your job because you're not from the fuckin' *council*. You're not from the Highways Agency and not from the council, either.'

'Of course I am.'

'Do you think I was born yesterday? It's them's sent you, isn't it?' She turned, gesturing at the hamlet. 'Neighbours ganging up on me, wanting to get a spy of my house. Go on – say it. Say, "Yes, they sent me." '

'I told you. I'm from the council.'

'Well, if you are, you're not from the department that wants to help me. You're from bleedin' environmental health, aren't you?'

'No.'

'Then tell me about the letters I sent. When was the last one? What was the date?'

'I handle several cases like this a week. I can't remember exact dates.'

'Then tell me what the letters are about.'

'The road.'

'*What* about the road?'

Flea put her hands in her pockets, stood on tiptoe and looked at the horizon.

'If you're really from the council you'll tell me why I'm interested in the road.'

Flea dropped back on to her heels, and turned her eyes to meet the other woman's. 'I don't know,' she admitted. 'Just don't know.'

'Jesus fuckin' wept.'

'Tell me what you've seen down there. That's what I want to know.'

Ruth Lindermilk grabbed the tripod, collapsed it, tucked the bits under her arm, took them to the french windows and put them inside the room. 'Go on, get out of here. Want to see your hiney heading down that path right now.'

'Just tell me what you've been watching.'

But Ruth Lindermilk had crossed over. 'No. No fuckin' way. Now get the hell out of here before I call the police.'

30

When Caffery woke, stiff and cold, to find the campsite deserted, just a mottled dead fire to prove the Walking Man had been there, the first thing that came into his head was Benjy: that damned dog of Lucy Mahoney's. It had been in his dreams: a skinless dog in a body-bag on a vet's table. The smell, and the shelled-egg stare of its eyes. Mallows said the Tanzanian brothers hated dogs: wouldn't go near them. In Africa the dog was often considered a pest. There was plenty in the literature about *muti* using parts from endangered species, but nothing about dogs. So, had it been kids who skinned the dog? Or Amos Chipeta? And, if it was Chipeta, then, why? As Caffery tinkered around, rolling up the mattress and sluicing his mouth out with water from a bottle, he decided he wanted to know more about what had happened the night of Lucy Mahoney's suicide.

He called Wells police station and when he arrived an hour later the property clerk was already waiting for him, pen in hand for him to sign out item eight, three mortise keys and a Yale, from the detained-property register.

Beatrice Foxton had pronounced Lucy Mahoney a suicide and so, technically speaking, all the personal effects from the post-mortem were under the auspices of the coroner's office. But the clerk agreed no one would miss any of them for a few hours.

Lucy had lived in a new development on the edge of Westbury-sub-Mendip. Caffery drove past row upon row of brick-built starter flats and maisonettes, tiny front lawns, empty driveways that, by night, would fill with Mazdas and low-end Peugeots, because this was a place for workers, not families. Lucy's was a downstairs maisonette. Two dustbins and a recycling wheelie with '32' painted on it in white stood outside a little porch. As he put the key into the lock he could see through the pane the takeaway food circulars on the floor. Domino's, Chilli's Curry, the Thai House.

He glanced over his shoulders, then stepped inside, not switching on the light. He stood behind the door and pulled on blue plastic bootees, and a pair of nitrile gloves. He closed the door, opened the inner one and padded through.

The living room was dark and cluttered. Not what you'd expect when you were looking at the place from the outside. A new Dell LCD monitor, a scanner and a digital camera stood on a desk in the corner, but everything else was worn, a little battered. A threadbare Turkish rug on the floor, embroidered cushions scattered around, furniture painted with flowers and vines. Every surface was crammed with wood carvings, aromatherapy bottles, Nepalese painted papier-mâché, a faded sculpture of a wading bird that looked Asian. Tacked on to the living room was a little dining area and beyond that a kitchen with hand-painted tiles above the sink. The curtains were pulled back from the large window to show distant hills. Glastonbury Tor was out there – a little blip on the horizon.

He went around the few rooms, peering at things, trying to get a feel for the place. Lucy was the collecting type. Paperweights seemed to be her thing. Paperweights with flowers in them. Paperweights with volcano bursts of red and orange. Paperweights with tiny, almost translucent shells set at angles. The place was clean, though – cleaner than it had a right to be. Weird, he told himself, looking at the kitchen. Weirdly clean. Nothing to start a parade over – sometimes suicides spring-cleaned the place before downing the co-proxamol. Even so, this cleanliness felt odd, out of whack. Suddenly, out of nowhere, he remembered something Stuart Pearce the search adviser had said: *Lucy Mahoney's suicide had broken all the rules.*

He went upstairs and switched on a light. Three doors opened on to the landing. One was a bathroom tiled in dark blue, a resin toilet seat embedded with seashells, and two pairs of thick striped tights hanging from the shower-curtain rail to dry. The dog team would have left those behind because there'd be no scent on them. They'd have gone instead for pyjamas, underwear: stuff taken out of the laundry basket. The second door was locked. He rattled it. It wasn't moving. He went downstairs and ferreted through the drawers for keys, then checked the coat rack in the hallway. Nothing. He went back upstairs and lay on the landing carpet with his face close to the gap. Closed his mouth and breathed in the air coming from under the door.

Perfume. Perfume and joss-sticks. And something else. Turps, maybe. The room would have been unlocked by the search teams when they came through here looking for her when she first went missing. Someone must have come and locked it since. Lucy's ex, maybe. He'd been listed as next of kin because her parents were dead.

The last door was the bedroom. Green velvet curtains, crystals and doeskin dream-catchers hung in the windows, and sequined belly-dance shawls had been draped over lamps – as if she'd had a lover recently. He went to the window and studied the photo in the frame on the sill: a little girl at a fête, wearing a wide-brimmed black straw hat, her arms around an old-fashioned rag doll. This would be Daisy, the daughter. The property clerk at Wells had said the Mahoneys had had a daughter – that she was staying somewhere near Gloucester with the ex-husband and mother-in-law.

There was a noise at the bottom of thc stairs, a faint clunk and a shuffling. Caffery picked up the heaviest paperweight he could find and went out on to the landing. He stood in the doorway, weighing it in his hand and counting in his head.

A light went on in the porch. The door opened and a face appeared at the bottom of the stairs. It was the ex-husband, rumpled in a suit that looked as if it belonged on an insurance salesman. He blinked up at Caffery, at his hands in the nitrile gloves and the paperweight. Then he looked down at Caffery's booteed feet. 'And who are you again?'

'DI Caffery.' He came down the stairs. 'We spoke yesterday at the hospital. I can't remember your name either.'

'Colin Mahoney.'

'What're you doing here?'

'Picking up the post.'

'You're divorced.'

'We were still friends. Didn't know there was a law against being friends with your ex. They told me I wasn't going to hear anything else until the inquest.'

'No one's been in touch, then? No one from F District?'

'No. Should they?'

'Have they told you about the dog yet?'

'Yes. He fell in the quarry. Apparently.'

'That must have been hard. Hard to take.'

'Yeah. Well, sometimes life kicks you in the face. And when it does your teeth fall out.'

Mahoney walked into the sitting room and sat down. He put his hands on his knees and looked around, as if there might be an answer to something in the walls of the crowded room. Caffery followed him in and stood in front of him.

'Here.' He handed him some gloves. 'Try not to touch anything.

Mahoney took them. 'Which unit did you say you worked for again?'

'I didn't. Major Crime Investigation Unit.'

'Major Crime? That's the murder unit?'

'That's the one.'

'On Friday you told me it wasn't your case. And now it is.' He stared at the gloves. 'I didn't think Benjy *fell* in the quarry. Not for a second. He wasn't stupid. They wouldn't let me see his body and that didn't sound right either.' He raised his eyes. 'Well? Is it a murder? Is that what you're here to tell me?'

'No.' He set the paperweight on the coffee-table next to the two A5 'Searched Premises' forms the search team had left. 'We do random checks – just reviews on suicides, here and there. It's something the Home Office are testing in Avon and Somerset. Then they'll roll it out nationwide.'

'Is that true?'

Caffery held his eyes.

'Is it?'

Caffery cleared his throat and nodded at the gloves. 'Can you put those on?'

'Why? The place has been searched. Has something changed?'

'Put them on, please.'

Mahoney did what he was told. Caffery sat down opposite him. 'Mr Mahoney, I've got some more questions for you.'

'I gathered.'

'Do you think Lucy was the sort to kill herself?'

'Of course not. I've been saying it all along. Haven't you got this in your notes?'

'Like I said, I'm reviewing the case. It's come to me cold. First thing I knew about it was Friday morning. Did she know the Strawberry Line? Did she know the area well?'

'She knew it was there, but I've never known her go over there.'

'Didn't have any friends in the area?'

'Not that I know of.'

'What about the quarries over at Elf's Grotto? Quarry number eight? They call it the suicide quarry.'

'I'm not even sure why you searched it.'

'Her car was found near by. Half a mile away. But you're telling me she never went to the quarries?'

'No. Odd, isn't it, that she parked up near them? And she definitely would never have taken Benjy there either. She never took him near water. Didn't like him getting wet.'

'There was a Stanley knife.'

'So they tell me.'

'Do you know where it came from?'

'Upstairs. Her studio. She used it for her framing work.'

'That's the door that's locked.'

'Yes.'

'Why locked?'

He shrugged. 'She didn't like people in there. It's got all her paintings in it. She was sensitive about them. She didn't mind me seeing them but hated anyone else in the studio. Once the search team had come through I locked it.'

'Can we get into it?'

'The key's at my mother's. It's an hour's drive there and back.'

'But the knife's definitely missing?'

'Yes. I checked the other night, after they'd found her.'

Caffery looked around the room. At the paperweights catching the light. All clean and sparkling. 'You last saw Lucy on Sunday?'

'I was here. We had coffee together. I left at five thirty.'

'And she seemed OK to you then?'

'Absolutely fine. Very relaxed.'

'She didn't tell you she was anxious about anything? Depressed?'

'Not at all.'

'Any of her friends say anything about her being depressed?'

'No. The police went through her address book and interviewed them all and no one could come up with anything. Everyone feels the same way I do. Everyone feels . . .' He trailed off and Caffery saw the look in his eye. He saw it and he saw his mother again – saw her screaming in the kitchen, holding on to a police officer in the hallway, begging him, 'Find my little boy. Just do it – go out there now and find my little boy.'

Caffery closed his eyes. Then he opened them. 'It's clean in here. Did you clean it?'

'No. This is how she left it.'

'Was it normal for the house to be this clean?'

'No. To be this clean was unusual. Lucy had . . .' he hesitated '. . . priorities. And, as you can see, she had tastes. Some I don't share.'

Caffery picked up the paperweight on the coffee-table and turned it over, idly studying the bottom. 'The Emporium' was printed on a gold lozenge-shaped sticker. 'We never found her phone.' He replaced the paperweight and picked up another. The same sticker on the bottom. 'I was at Wells and I went through all the possessions she had on her. I was looking for bills but the officer in charge tells me he left them here. He said it was a bugger of a job because most of the bank statements and bills were missing. In fact, he said there were hardly any records of any sort in the house.'

'I know. I was told they'd got a warrant out. I was told Orange were supposed to be releasing the missing bills.'

Mahoney was right. But here again the system had favoured people like Misty Kitson whose phone records had come back in hours. When Caffery'd checked he'd found Lucy Mahoney's records had never arrived. They were jammed in the system somewhere and now her body had turned up no one would bother to chase them. Caffery had Turnbull chasing another warrant to track them down, but it'd be days before they had access to them, days before they learnt what had really happened to Lucy Mahoney in her last hours.

'Didn't she have somewhere she kept her paperwork?'

Mahoney pointed to a box file next to the computer. 'Over there.'

Caffery put down the paperweight, went to the desk and opened the box. It contained four phone bills, mostly from last year. Only one from this year – January. There were twelve electricity bills, two council-tax bills and ten bank statements, all dating from more than two years ago. He turned round and held out the file to Mahoney. 'Like this, was it? When you first came in.'

'Exactly like this.'

'Do you know why she'd keep statements for these months and not for others?'

'She was secretive, that's all I can say. When the police questioned her friends they couldn't find out anything about her. It was like that even when we were married. I never knew what she was thinking.'

Caffery gazed around at the walls, the higgledy-piggledy furniture. 'I can see how she lived, but I've got no idea what she looked like. No photos.'

Mahoney got up. He went to the computer, switched it on, pulled out a small stool and held out his hand. 'Help yourself. It's all in here.'

Caffery sat down. The computer was the newest thing in the place. It was good, fast, a 2.9-gig processor. He took a quick look through her documents. Nothing of interest. The search team would have gone through them with a fine-tooth comb. He opened her email account – two new emails. Both junk. Clicked on to Explorer and dropped down the search-history file. The terms were Pot Plants, *Hollyoaks*, Mascara, Body Toning, Crystals. Nothing very interesting. He opened her video folder and chose one at random.

The clip opened in a field. It was some time in the summer because the grass was green, the trees thick with leaves. A tall, heavy woman in a calf-length black dress stood in the middle distance. Her arms were stretched out, trying to catch the legs of a slight girl in pink shorts who was hopping around throwing wobbly handstands. The woman was laughing. She had very short auburn hair. Her face was ruddy, heavy-boned. It was a jump to link her to the blackened pile on the table in the mortuary.

'I filmed that one.' Mahoney came to stand behind him. 'That was three summers ago. The year Daisy decided Nastia Liukin had competition.'

'Daisy? Your daughter?'

'She's staying with my mum. Broken-hearted, of course.'

Daisy threw another handstand. This time Lucy caught her legs. There was a long, precarious moment while Daisy tried to hold the position. Then her arms buckled. Lucy tried to maintain it but Daisy rolled on to the ground and lay on her back, her hands on her stomach, giggling. The camera zoomed in on Lucy. She was laughing too, but when she saw she was being filmed, the smile faded. 'Oh, no!' She shook her head and held up a hand to block the camera's view. 'Don't. Please. You're making me blush now. Leave me alone.'

The camera swung away. There were a few frames of a lawn and the fumbling noise of the camera being switched off. The screen went blank.

' "Don't make me blush." ' Mahoney went back and sat on the sofa. 'Yes. That was Lucy all over. Everything embarrassed her.'

'She loved Daisy.'

'Everyone loves Daisy.'

Caffery opened another file. This one was dated just three months ago. It showed a small room, dull daylight coming through the window. A woman was standing side on to the camera, looking at an easel with a canvas on it. Lucy. Her red hair straggled down her back – it was much longer – and her clothes were different, colourful. She wore a red waistcoat over a sapphire blue shirt with a flowered bandanna tied in a knot at the front of her head. She was holding a paintbrush in one hand; the other fiddled with the shirt. She was thinner here. Much thinner. In three years she'd developed a waistline.

'Who shot this one?'

'I don't know. A friend, maybe. I wasn't there.'

The camera came in close. Lucy turned and looked steadily at the lens. She didn't blush. She didn't try to turn away. She smiled ironically, held up the paintbrush and spoke in a mock-French accent: 'Welcome to my atelier, little one. This is where the magic is made.'

The video stopped and for a moment the room was silent. Caffery tapped his finger on the mouse pad. *This is where the magic is made*. Something was here, in this video. Something important. He played it again, looking carefully at her face, at the way her hand fiddled with the shirt, self-consciously touching her stomach. *This is where the magic is made*. What are you trying to tell me, Lucy? What are you trying to say?

A noise behind him made him turn. Mahoney was sitting forward, peering at the table. 'That's odd,' he murmured. 'That's very odd.'

Caffery pushed back the chair. 'What is?'

'Those.'

He looked to where Mahoney pointed and saw nothing out of the ordinary: just the search forms, the paperweight and Lucy's door keys where he'd left them earlier.

'Her keys? I booked them out from the station at Wells.'

Mahoney leant over. Picked them up. 'Was this how you found them?'

'They were in her pocket. Yes.'

'Just these two. The Chubb and the Yale?'

'They fit the front door.'

'But one's missing. There should be a back-door key. Usually it's up there, on that nail.'

Caffery turned. The nail was empty. He glanced at the front door, then the back door. For a moment he felt a small chill. As if something had just come into the room and settled down with them.

'And . . .' He gave a small cough. 'And I take it you haven't got it?'

Mahoney turned his eyes to him. The pupils had shrunk to pinpoints. 'No. And if you haven't got it,' he said, 'then who the hell has?'

31

The residential roads around Hanham were quiet at lunchtime, and as Flea came round the corner she saw Thom's black Escort pull away from the kerb. It raced to the end of the road, indicators flashing. Hitting the T-junction, it turned right. She kept close behind it, fumbling on the front seat for her phone.

Mandy was driving, of course. She would be. Flea knew what the guys in the unit would say about Mandy. It'd be: 'Well, there goes a girl with a nine-inch clit.' Or words to that effect. The Escort stopped at traffic-lights, and Flea pulled in behind it, jabbing out Thom's number with her thumb. Up ahead she saw Mandy turn her face and watch Thom rummage in his coat pockets. He said something to her as he got the phone out, but in Flea's ear the call was bumped to answerphone and she saw him lean sideways to return it to his pocket. He rested his forehead against the side window and stared out.

Flea floored the Clio, leaning on the horn, flashing the lights. Mandy raised her chin: a glimpse of startled eyes in the rear-view mirror. Flea put her hand out of the window, gesturing for the car to pull over.

There was a moment's hiatus while the two cars rolled along the road almost bumper to bumper, Mandy taking time to register what was happening. Then the entrance to a cemetery came up and the Escort jerked left into it and stopped just inside the gates. Flea slammed the Clio in behind, jumped out and went fast to the driver's side, making a circular motion with her fingers telling Mandy to roll down the window.

But for a moment, her white face just stared back through the glass. On the passenger side Thom had slid down until his chin was almost on his chest. His face was canted over, resting on his splayed hand so no one could see his expression.

'Open the window.'

Mandy did. 'You frightened the life out of me. What's going on?'

'We need to talk.'

'I'm on my way to work.'

'Now, Mandy. Now.'

'Riiiiight,' she said cautiously. 'You're upset.'

'Get out of the car.'

She did as she was told: slowly, hands raised, as if Flea had a gun to her head.

Thom unbuckled and got out, too, his face appearing on the other side of the car roof. He was flustered. 'Flea, there's no need for this. I'm going to tell her.'

'Going to tell me what?'

'Mandy, don't listen to her. Please. I swear I was just about to tell you.'

Flea held up her hand. 'Get back in the car, Thom.'

'Let me tell her.'

'*Get in the car.*'

He stared at his sister, his hands on the roof, his face drained of colour now. A vein in the side of his neck pulsed blue.

'Do what she's telling you,' Mandy said. 'Go on – sit down.'

Thom might have been able to ignore his sister, but he didn't know how to defy his girlfriend. He got into the car and sat, slouched in the seat. Mandy turned to Flea, her arms folded under her huge breasts. 'What on earth's going on?'

'There's been an accident. Thom's had . . . an accident.'

Mandy bent very slowly to look across the driver's seat at Thom. His face was in his hands again. 'He doesn't look as if he's had an accident.'

'It wasn't him who got hurt.'

'Then who?'

'It was a woman.'

'A woman?' Mandy raised her eyebrows questioningly, as if the idea of Thom having anything to do with a woman was preposterous. Even through an accident.

'He was driving. The other night. He was drunk and she stepped out in front of him. He didn't have a chance to stop.'

'What happened to her?'

Flea shook her head. No way of sugar-coating it. 'I'm sorry.'

Mandy closed her eyes very slowly. 'Killed?' She opened them, looked at Flea, unblinking. 'You mean he *killed* her?'

'Yes.'

'When?'

'Last Monday.'

'The night he came over to you?'

'Yes.'

'He can't have had an accident. He stayed at yours all evening. The car's fine.'

'He didn't stay at mine. He was lying to you. He didn't want you to know he was going to a business meeting because he didn't want you thinking he was getting into another cock-up deal, so he came to mine and used my car – he left his outside in case you drove by to check up on him.'

Mandy turned away and gazed distantly at the graves, at the plastic containers under the standpipe, the silk flowers made grey by the car fumes from the road. Seeing them but not absorbing them. 'I can't believe this. No one told me anything about it.'

'Because no one knew. It wasn't reported.'

'Not *reported*? Then what happened to . . .' This new dimension hit home with a bang. She put her elbows on the car roof and dropped her face into her hands. 'My God. My God. My God.'

'There's something we can do.'

'This will be the end of everything.'

'Mandy, calm down. Thom and I have talked about it

and there *is* something we can do. We've got to get him into hospital. We've got to build a case. There isn't much time.'

'Build a case? You mean you're going to lie? *Why?* Why would you do that?'

'Because he's my brother. Because I'm totally fucking furious with him and I'd like to pull his eyes out right now. But he's still my brother and I love him.'

Mandy rested her finger against her throat as if there was a small lump there. Then she pulled back her sleeve and checked her watch – as if knowing the time would somehow keep everything in place and stop the world tilting. In the distance thunder rolled. A bird – a rook, maybe – took off from the line of pencil cypresses edging the cemetery. 'We need some time to think about this,' she said eventually.

'OK.'

'Alone, I mean.'

'I'll go and sit in the car.'

'No. Longer than that. We need to go home and think about it. Sleep on it. I'll call you.'

'When?'

'Tomorrow morning. Maybe in the afternoon. I've got to work in the morning.'

'It can't wait that long. Things are . . . changing. Things with the body are changing.'

'Things with the . . . ? Christ.' Mandy shook her head. 'Oh, Christ.'

'Call me first thing in the morning.'

'Some time in the morning.'

'If I haven't heard by midday I'll be at your front door. And if we don't start doing something about it then, I'm going to have to—'

'Going to have to what?'

'Midday. I'll see you at midday.'

32

Four o'clock in the afternoon, and Ruth feels good. A drink in her hand and the music's on loud. She'd like to open all the windows so the neighbours know she's here. Because their little trick today – sending that slag to spy on her – hasn't got to her. Not at all. In fact, it's made things even clearer. If before she wasn't sure of the changes she's decided to make, she's a thousand per cent now. It's time to get out of here. Time to go back to where she belongs. To the sun. Her and the cats and maybe Stevie, somewhere better than this shit-hole.

She carries the drink up to her room and rests it on the bedside table. Slops some of it, so she takes off her T-shirt to blot up the mess. When she's straightening she catches her reflection in the mirror on the big old wardrobe. She gives herself a long, hard look, unbuttons her shorts, slides them off and steps out of them. Now she's in underwear, her bra and knickers, and her high heels. She stands straight and appraises her reflection.

She's got good legs. Always has had. Short, a bit muscular, but shaped well with good knees and ankles.

Legs that look good in heels. Good knockers, too. She pushes her breasts together and bends towards the mirror. Makes a kissy face. A bit of help with the boobies: East European help. But a nod's as good as a wink to a blind horse, and she's always had a way with certain types of men. A little promise, a little excitement. It's a two way-street. They get what they want . . . and she gets what she wants. Which, right now, is a ticket out of here. Away from the snoops and the rain and all the people who want to hurt the cats with their poisons and fast cars.

There's a new shopping centre going up between the hamlet and Trowbridge. It brings all sorts of lonely men down, a project like that – architects, engineers, investors. One or two of them have already started appearing at the pubs in Rode. One bought her a drink the other night, and that's a move in the right direction. Not that she's naïve: it's not going to be bleeding Pierce Brosnan, for the love of God. There'll be compromises.

She takes a gulp of the rum and Coke. Puts it down and turns back to the mirror. She gathers up the spare flesh that pushes over the top of her knickers. Squishes it together and watches it pucker. Folds of tanned flesh all indented and lumpy. Stevie. He did that. Not that she resents it, but that's Stevie's belly right there. She jiggles it around, then flattens it back against her hipbones and turns half in profile. Turns to the other side. Admires the change in her shape with it pulled tight like that.

It's only a tiny bit of work. A tiny scar. From all the reading she's done she'll be able to pass it off as a hysterectomy. A movie star or a jet-setter wouldn't think twice about it. They'd call it maintenance. They wouldn't worry like this, or spend time thinking about it. They'd just crap or get off the pot.

Ruth drains her drink. She goes downstairs and stands at the bar in her underwear and high heels, a little unsteady, scoops ice into the glass and fills it. She carries it over to the computer table and begins pulling things out of drawers. There are stacks and stacks of photographs, and she has to rummage through them to find the folders of bank and credit-card statements. She dumps them on the table and sits down, sorting them into piles.

After a while she realizes there's a problem. She lays them out in date order and starts again, making notes this time, adding things up. It's not good. Two glasses of rum and Coke go by and she still can't work out how it got so bad. She pours another and sits, head propped up on one finger, trying to work it out.

She's got an appointment for the day after tomorrow. Little Sue made it. A good girl, Sue, stays in touch despite the divorce. Weird face, though: pushed in. Like there's a touch of the manta ray in Lindermilk genes. Basically she's a good girl, though, and she's spoken to the clinic about getting a staff discount for Aunty Ruth's tummy tuck. Twenty-five per cent apparently.

But even with the discount there isn't going to be enough. Ruth can see that now.

What's she supposed to do? Get another mortgage on the house? That would take for ever, and with the way things are going in this country no one can get a mortgage, not even the doctors and lawyers. She looks up and catches sight of herself in the mirror. Thinks about the money. Thinks about her bank account. And, suddenly, it's all wrong. Suddenly it doesn't matter how she looks at it, everything looks awful. She looks awful. Her stomach looks awful. Her face looks awful. And there's that chipped tooth at the front. Christ only knows how much that'll cost to fix. Needs an implant probably.

'Fuck,' she tells the little black cat curled up at her feet. 'Fuck.'

She goes back to the bar. Opens the rum again and pours another couple of fingers. Spills a bit on the bar top. She looks at it. Wonders whether to lick it up. Changes her mind and puts down a paper napkin. One from the Puente Romano hotel in Marbella. They'd moored in the Cabopino marina once and had a drink in the bar. Stevie stole about a hundred napkins that night. She's still using them. A good boy, Stevie.

She picks up her mobile and flicks through the numbers. Stops at Stevie's and stares at it for a long time. He's got a good little business in Swindon, selling white goods. Built it up from nothing. He wouldn't like to see his mum want for anything. Her thumb hovers over the call button.

'No,' she tells the cat, putting the phone down. 'I won't take the bread out of my baby's mouth. I won't do it. I'm not that sort of mother.'

She pours in the Coke and drops in a swizzle stick for fun. There was something in a magazine the other day, talking about how a woman had gone to her doctor and said her flat chest was making her depressed. *Depressed.* The doctor referred her and she got a new set done on the

National Health. Cost her nothing. What is the world coming to?

She looks at the phone again. At Stevie's number, then the clock. It's almost five. He'll be on his way to the pub. She dials and gets his voicemail. 'Stevie, darling, it's Mum. Sweetheart, give Mummy a call, will you, darling? Come and see me, will you? There's a little something I need to discuss with you.'

33

Caffery hung out of the window of the MCIU offices at Kingswood and smoked a guilty roll-up. He watched the guy in the halal butcher's close up shop. The story one of the DCs in the office liked to tell was how, a year or so ago, the dumbfucks in the Chinese supermarket two doors down had got jealous of the trade the butcher was doing. They'd decided it was all to do with that word: halal. They'd copied it down really carefully and stuck it on a sign in the window. Halal beef for sale. Halal chicken for sale. Halal pork for sale. Halal *pork*. The butcher had lost it at the pork insult and really dropped the hammer on the Chinese for that. For a while it was like gang warfare out there. At the window now Caffery smoked slowly, looking at the butcher's. He was a Londoner. He didn't see why the DC had thought it was worth mentioning. That sort of thing happened all the time in Lewisham.

He dropped the butt out of the window and went to his desk. He had to speak to Powers but the superintendent wasn't there. He was in Glyndebourne, of all places, with his phone switched off. He'd been working sixteen-hour days since the Misty Kitson case had come to them, but today his wife had tickets for the opening performance of *La Cenerentola*, and considering what she'd put up with over the years he wasn't stupid. After the morning press conference he'd got straight into his car, driven home and got the DJ and picnic hamper out of mothballs. He'd left Caffery a little message, though: pictures of the actress who'd played Misty Kitson at the reconstruction had been carefully taped over the PM photos of Ben Jakes and Jonah Dundas.

He unstuck the tape and carefully peeled them away. Then he put the photographs together and shovelled them into an envelope. He paused for a moment over the one of Misty's coat. Purple – made of velvet. Something about the fabric pulled at his mind a moment. It was something about a car – something that made him think of a car and the coat. Car, coat. Car, coat. He tried to superimpose the two images one over the other, but each time they slipped and frittered away.

Nothing had come of the reconstruction yet. No suspect caught in the bushes with his dick in his hands, like the shrinks had said would happen. It made the whole team insane to think how little they had to go on with the case: just the witness statements from the rehab clinic of the last sightings and a statement from the boyfriend. All they knew for sure was that one of the other patients had smuggled in some goodies and they'd been partying. A little after two Kitson had left the building by the front entrance. She'd called the boyfriend as she left the clinic grounds. It had been a tearful conversation: she'd told him she was leaving for a walk because she needed time to think, that she couldn't stand the place one more second. She'd said she'd be back at the clinic before five. The boyfriend had already been pissed off with her – he admitted it in the interview: it was his hard pennies earned in the midfield that were paying for the clinic. There was an argument. She hung up. He didn't call back. It was only when the clinic telephoned hours later that he realized anything was wrong.

Caffery's mobile rang. It was Powers. He put the photos into the top drawer and pulled the chair tight up to the desk. Time to talk.

'Evening, boss. You still down in Sussex?'

'Don't. *Ceneren*bloody*tola*. Had to wait for the interval to get my phone out – she's giving me the evils even as we speak.'

'How's the weather?'

'Place is a mudbath. She keeps saying her Jimmy Choos are ruined. I mean, who is this character? You ever heard of him? Jimmy Choo?'

Jimmy Choo, fuck-me shoes. Not what Powers would want to hear about his wife of thirty years. 'Saw you on telly this morning,' Caffery said. 'The Kitson press call. You looked very empathetic. Thought you might cry.'

'Good, wasn't it? Spent years working on it. Did you spot the lie?'

'That the force is confident of finding her?'

'No. When I said I was throwing all the manpower I had at it. When I said the whole team were committed one hundred per cent?'

'Yeah. Well. We need to talk. It's bad news.'

There was a pause. 'Oka-ay. Do I need my Bolly livened up before we go on?'

'Maybe.'

'I don't like this.'

'I've been wondering how many murders we're filing as suicides. Makes your head ache thinking about it.'

'You're talking about Ben Jakes, I suppose. He wasn't a suicide?'

'No. That's the sweetness to this. Jakes was a suicide that looked like a murder. But I've got something else: a murder that looks like a suicide. Her name's Mahoney. Lucy Mahoney. Found up near the Strawberry Line on Friday.'

'What does the pathologist say?'

'Well, she's sticking to suicide. But she's wrong. Look, boss, something's way out of whack here. I've got this woman's cx going on at me about how the dog's missing – the dog was with her when she went misper – and what turns up yesterday in the quarry?'

'Don't tell me. Her dog.'

'It was mutilated. The CSI lads said it looked like someone was trying to make a coat out of the damned thing. Then the ex says one of her door keys is missing.'

'And how does she fit with what you've been doing on Norway?'

'She doesn't.'

'Then, what the hell are you doing worrying about it?'

'The time you gave me to tidy up the Norway problem? I want to spend it on this instead. I want to speak to the coroner.'

'Oh, for fuck's sake.' Powers gave a deep sigh. Caffery could picture his face. He knew he'd be struggling not to climb down the phone line and chew him out for this. 'Let me get this straight. You're telling me you've dropped Norway and instead of coming back into the team on Kitson you've decided you're off chasing another rabbit? I can't believe I'm hearing this. I'm starting to think you've got something against the Kitson girl. It's like you want to avoid the damned case. Like anything's better than this. I can't believe it.'

Caffery drummed his fingers on the table. 'So? Is that a yes, then?'

'Oh, brilliant. Very funny.' He took some time, breathing carefully. Maybe he'd been to one of those alternative therapists to learn how to breathe his way through stress. 'Look, if F District want to investigate this woman and her dog as something other than a suicide that's their business. And if that happens, and if at the twenty-eight-day review they think it should come to us, then that's the review team's business. And I won't argue with them. Because by then we'll have found Misty Kitson and she'll be safe and well and being photographed with her scum footie boyfriend and their horrible lapdogs in her kitchen in Chislehurst or Chingford or wherever it is these people come from. I'm sorry, Jack.'

'Am I really that difficult?'

'No. Just need you to pull with me. Pull with me.'

Misty's case was so resource-heavy you could hear the cartwheels squealing. The force had thrown everything at it. Everything. Her phone records had come back in forty-eight hours. Lucy's had gone missing and no one had even noticed.

'You know what?' Caffery said. 'You're right. I'm going to get in early tomorrow and sit in with the HOLMES girls. Get up to speed with what's going on. How about that?'

'Yeah, well,' Powers said gruffly.

'I'll help divvy up the day's "Actions" for you, if you want. I can be there, let you have a lie-in.'

'I'd settle for you telling me that when I get into the office in the morning my DI will be there. I don't think that's too much to ask.'

'I will,' Caffery said. 'Have a good evening. Hope the rain stops for you.'

He hung up and stood for a minute, staring out at the butcher's. It was starting to rain. He went to the desk and ran down the extension list, looking for Wells police station. He checked his watch. Six thirty. There was time. He was going to find out if the DI on the Lucy Mahoney case was still on duty, get all the witness statements from when she was a misper, take them home and read every one from cover to cover.

The Walking Man was right. This was his downfall. He just couldn't let go.

34

All around the world scientists are growing skin. They're using skin removed during cosmetic surgery, harvesting the cells and feeding them in a petri dish with agarose, glutamine, hydrocortisone and insulin. They add melanocytes to give pigment, dry off the top layer, and expose it to UV light to age it. Then they use it to test cosmetics, or sell it to order over the Internet to patch up burns and wounds.

The man has ordered some of this synthetic skin from its American manufacturers. It's been shipped to him in injection-moulded polystyrene blocks: five flabby discs about the size of his palm, suspended in an agar nutrient medium and sealed in a high-grade polythene bag. As evening falls across the farmland that surrounds his lonely house he is examining the skin. He smells it, rests it on his hand and holds it up to the light. He screws his eyes shut and presses it to his face. Clenches his teeth and waits to feel better.

He's been caught. Again.

Again.

'Sssssssh.' He rocks slightly. Lets the skin settle into the shape of his jaw. The problem is taken care of. He's sure it's taken care of. Nothing to get upset about. 'Sssssssh.'

He pulls the artificial skin away from his face. Stares at it angrily. It has no hair, no pigment and none of the Langerhans cells that allow real skin to fight infection. It has no blood and no sweat glands. It's no better than rabbit or dog skin. In disgust he flicks it off his fingers into the bin, where it hits the side and clings. He watches it and then, when it shows no sign that it will drop, he gets up and uses a long tanning awl to push it into the bottom.

Nothing, *nothing*, is fair in this world.

35

The gastro pub was at the top of a steep city road in Clifton. It had red-brick floors, squashy sofas, a Swedish wood stove, and racks of vintage wines behind glass. Caffery and Colin Mahoney ordered J20s, 'sharing bread' and a sandwich each. They sat in one of the huge bay windows where they could see office workers hurrying to lunch.

'How's Daisy?' Caffery asked. 'How's she coping?'

'How do you think she's coping? There just isn't the vocabulary.'

'Have you told her about the dog?'

'Thought I'd save that one.' Mahoney was dressed in his grey suit, a white shirt and an old-fashioned Paisley tie. He looked tired. 'No one's been in touch since you came over yesterday. Haven't heard a thing. Nothing. Not even a card or a bunch of flowers from the FLO.'

'Those liaison officers. They're just scared of commitment.'

'I was at least expecting someone to call to tell me it had been reclassified. You know, as a murder.'

'Yeah, well.' Caffery patted his pocket, felt the tobacco wallet and thought about having to go outside to smoke. He'd been into the office this morning and gone through the day's HOLMES 'actions' for Powers. As he'd promised. He was entitled to do what he wanted with his lunch-hour. 'I'm working on that. I really am. I've spoken to the pathologist.'

'And?'

'She's having problems reversing the suicide decision. Standing pretty firm on it. The only wobbly place is the temazepam. If she's got any knot at all, it's that. When Lucy died she was full of benzodiazepines.'

'Her GP used to tell her she'd get addicted, that she should have a nice G-and-T instead. But she knew how to work him. Bathroom cupboard used to rattle with them. It scared me, with Daisy around. So? Am I going to get an answer? Are you treating it as a murder?'

'Not officially. But, for the sake of argument, say you and I work on the assumption we are?'

'Not an assumption for me. It's a fact.'

'Then we move on to whodunit territory. Like suspects and motives.'

Mahoney held out his hands to show he was clueless.

'We think someone used that missing key to come into her house. Maybe after it happened, right? To clean up. Or was there something else they wanted? You've checked nothing's missing?'

'Nothing, as far as I can tell. Only the Stanley knife and the key.'

'Whoever's got it could still come in and out.'

'No, they couldn't. I've changed the lock. I did it myself, this morning.'

For starters came Haloumi bread, warm and shiny with oil, lumps of cheese and caraway seeds pressing up through the crust like tiny black veins. The men ate, looking out at the suspension bridge. The sun glinted on the chocolaty river below.

'I spent the night reading the witness statements from when she was a misper,' Caffery said. 'Talk to me a bit more about how it happened. She went missing at five thirty on the Sunday?'

'That was the last time I saw her.'

'And you called the police on the Monday?'

'Yes.'

'That was nearly twenty-four hours later. Why did you wait?'

'I didn't think it was appropriate. Until she didn't turn up to get Daisy from school.'

'Appropriate? But she was missing.'

'I didn't know she was. Not at that point. She just wasn't answering my calls. If she chooses to stay out all night it's not my business any more.'

'How long have you been divorced?'

'A year. Separated two.'

'You were still close?'

'Not at first. Daisy came with me to my mother's, that was agreed right from the start, and at the beginning Lucy'd wait until I was at work to visit her. I didn't see her for a year – we managed to avoid each other. Then things mellowed a bit, around the time the divorce was finalized.

We settled some old arguments, started talking again, for Daisy's sake. Lucy had changed in that time. You saw that, didn't you, in the video?'

'Why did you separate in the first place? What were the circumstances?'

'I left. We'd run out of things to enjoy together. We were growing apart.'

'Growing apart – that sounds like the sort of excuse people come up with for something else.'

Mahoney smiled nervously. 'I don't know, but the way you're speaking to me here, it sounds as if I'm on trial.'

'No. I'm just trying to get a picture. Something you tell me might have the key to all this. Even if you don't realize it. Did Lucy have a boyfriend? She was an attractive woman.'

Mahoney folded a napkin on to his lap. The rest of the meal was already on its way, but he picked up the menu and studied it anyway.

'Colin? I asked if Lucy had a boyfriend.'

He coughed. 'I'm wondering if I should have chosen the roast-pork sandwich instead. Wednesdays, in the summer, they do a hog roast here on the street for people coming out of the office. Whole pig on a spit. Hand it out in napkins. Nice with Somerset apple sauce.'

Caffery sat back in his seat and watched him. He thought again about his mother, wondering what she looked like now, wondering if she was in pain, if now the pain was physical, from joints getting tired of rubbing together, from muscles aching with hard work, or if there was still pain from losing Ewan. He wondered if time had changed the pain – mutated or softened it. 'Colin? You left her. Why's this difficult for you?'

'Does it matter *why*?'

'I'm trying to pull with you, mate, not against. Did she have a boyfriend?'

Mahoney rubbed his eyes and put down the menu. 'You should know the answer to that. It'll be in those statements her friends made.'

'I want to hear it from you.'

'Yes. She had a boyfriend. OK?'

'A name?'

'No. And her friends didn't give you one. They don't know either, do they?'

'Weird . . . that she didn't tell her friends her boyfriend's name.'

'Not that weird. She was the most private person I knew. And she was protecting him. He was married.'

'Well, *that*'s interesting.'

'Not really. They were sort of . . . lukewarm together. She liked him but there was nothing serious. Oh, don't worry, I've thought about it, whether or not he had something to do with her . . . You know.'

'And?'

He shook his head. 'No. Doesn't seem right. She didn't feel threatened by him.'

'He's still interesting to me.'

'I can think of something that's more interesting.'

Caffery raised an eyebrow.

'The money.'

'The *money*?' Caffery sat forward. 'Well, you've got me by the goolies with *that*. Go on.'

Mahoney didn't smile. 'When we split up I gave Lucy some money, not a lot, just enough for a deposit on the house and a bit extra. She used to work for a company in Filton that made Christmas decorations. Designed bits and pieces for them, worked in the office, that sort of thing. But one day she announced she was giving it up. I didn't give it much thought at the time but, with hindsight, her lifestyle didn't change even when she stopped working. She still went shopping every weekend and came home loaded with things – oddments, paperweights. A proper pack rat. Well, you saw her house.'

'A loan, maybe?'

'Against what? Property prices didn't go up much in that area and she had a ninety per cent mortgage anyway. But she went on four holidays last year.'

'Did he pay for them? The boyfriend?'

'No. He didn't contribute, and that's from the horse's mouth. His wife would find out if he did. And he didn't go abroad with Lucy. She was either on her own – I should know, I took her to the airport – or with Daisy. And then . . .' Mahoney reached into his inside pocket and took out a folded piece of paper, pushed it across the table '. . . there's this. In the post this morning.'

Caffery opened it. It was property particulars from an estate agent: a stone cottage with white-painted windows and a clematis climbing over the doorway. 'Everything but the white picket fence.'

'Look at the price on it,' Mahoney said.

'Six hundred K.'

'The maisonette is worth almost two hundred now. But there was a hundred-and-forty-thousand-pound mortgage on it.'

Caffery turned the letter over to look at the back. Nothing.

'Goland and Bulley.' Mahoney nodded towards the window. 'That's them. Other side of the road. What do you think?'

'I think . . .' Caffery put down the letter and signalled for the waitress '. . . I think we'll take those sandwiches to go.'

36

The girl in the estate agent's was a bit like Keelie. Or, rather, a bit the way Keelie might have looked if she hadn't, at some point in her teenage years, stumbled on the delights of crack cocaine. This girl had powerful swimmer's shoulders and her body seemed too tanned and muscular for the navy suit she'd squeezed it into.

'Mrs Mahoney?' She typed in the reference number from the letter. 'Obviously I can't tell you very much about our correspondence. It's confidential. But I can tell you whether she's a client.'

Caffery put his warrant card on the table.

She peered at it. 'Police?'

'Police.'

A nervous laugh. And then, in the knee-jerk way honest people often did, suddenly she was spilling out facts like water. 'Yes, well, I *do* remember her, of course. She was wanting something in the region of, uh, five to eight hundred. There's a property to sell – we're due to value it on, um . . .' she searched the screen '. . . tomorrow.'

'You may as well cancel that.'

'I see.'

Caffery was sure she didn't. Didn't see at all.

'Well, if I . . .' She turned the computer screen to face him. 'Is there anything here that could help you?'

The two men leant closer. The screen was filled with email correspondence. Nothing out of the ordinary: Lucy's requests for information on property. The agent's replies.

'What's the date on that one?'

'Last Sunday.'

It was the day Lucy had gone missing. She'd been arranging house viewings on the day she was planning to kill herself?

'Are we the first to visit? No other calls from the police about Ms Mahoney?'

'Not that I know of.'

'They wouldn't have come here,' Mahoney's voice was subdued, 'because none of these were in her mailbox. I should know. I spent hours going through her emails. She must have deleted them.'

Caffery didn't answer. He was thinking about the search history on Lucy's computer. *Hollyoaks*. Pot Plants. Body Toning. Now he thought about it, those searches had never fitted with his impression of Lucy. They sounded more like the sort you'd invent for a woman you didn't know much about. To disguise the fact that the cache had been emptied.

And then it came to him. An idea, hard and complete, the way ideas often did. The suicide note Lucy had been found with hadn't been handwritten. It had come from a computer. It hadn't occurred to anyone to wonder why it wasn't on her computer at home.

'Come on.' Caffery pushed back his chair and got to his feet. 'Let's have another look at Lucy's computer.'

37

Mandy called Flea at midday on the dot. She and Thom had had a long talk. They were calmer now. They'd meet her in Keynsham tonight after work to discuss the 'way forward'.

'Where are you now?' she wanted to know. 'You sound distant.'

'I'm outside the district council offices.'

'Where?'

'Trowbridge.'

'What are you doing there?'

'Something important. Someone we need to think about. I'll explain later.'

It didn't take Flea long to find the department she wanted: down a prefab corridor with dirty windows and a fireproof carpet underfoot. The head of the department was harried, careless: he didn't namby around asking for warrants – a flash of her card was enough as he took her down to the desk where he thought Ruth Lindermilk's correspondence would be held.

The clerk dealing with it was a bubbly blonde, in her

fifties with an out-of-season lamp tan and lots of gold jewellery, busily working her way through letters that overflowed from three plastic letter trays. 'We call this CYA corner,' she told Flea. 'I work on CYA corner – great, isn't it?'

'CYA?'

'Cover Your Arse. I get all the stuff the other departments want to put in the bin. You know, old ladies complaining the local post office is closing and how the council really wants to deal with the UFOs over Salisbury Plain.' She indicated a pile. 'I've sent answers to these already. Don't expect to hear back but I've got to file them, keep them for a while just in case.' She pulled one of the baskets towards her. 'You said this letter was sent last week?'

'I think so, yes.'

'And the name?'

'Ruth Lindermilk.'

A small smile twitched at the corner of the secretary's mouth. 'Lindermilk?'

'Yes?'

'I know that name. It's distinctive.' She took two stacks of letters in rubber bands and put them to one side. She flicked through the next pile and came up very quickly with a letter on council headed paper, stapled to a piece of flowered notepaper. 'This covering one is the reply we send them all. Just standard, you know, "we're dealing with your complaint". Yackety-yackety.' She folded the reply letter to the back, ironing it flat with her palms, and scanned the notepaper underneath. 'Yes, this is her. Ruth the snitch, I call her, because she's always trying to get these motorists into trouble.' She passed Flea the letter. 'Obsessed with wildlife – feeds the hedgehogs and the badgers, and if someone hits so much as a wood louse on the road Ruth the snitch is on to it. Thinks we should be doing something about every frog, mouse and worm that gets squished.'

Flea took the letter and sat on the low plastic bucket chair. The letter was handwritten, bordered with roses and sparrows. It was dated 18 May. The morning after Misty was killed.

To whom it may concern.
Since my last communication to you of 3 January I haven't heard hide nor hair from you and I've now got four more incidents to report. It seems to me like absolutely nothing is being done. One of these last night is a really serious incident where a deer got hit. You will ignore me at your peril.

Date	Time	Incident	Car make and plate	Other comments
15 January	22.06	Badger got hit. Crawled to edge with broken pelvis. Later died there in pain.	Black or blue Vauxhall	Did not stop.

Date	Time	Incident	Car make and plate	Other comments
22 January	12.00 noon	Rabbit got hit and killed.	Silver Land Rover NO7 XWT	DRIVER WAS AWARE!!! (Stopped and stared at dead rabbit so knows EXACTLY what he did)
3 March	19.45	Badger got hit. Killed instantly.	Not sure of make. Dark car. First letters of number plate S58.	Driver did not bother to stop.
17 May	23.11	Deer(?) got hit. Or large animal. Crawled away. Driver was AWARE !!!	Silver Ford Focus. Last letters of numberplate GBR	Driver was aware.

As I've said on numerous times, I am of the opinion that all of these drivers should be brought in and really hit where it hurts. If these were human casualties you would of solved them no doubt a long time ago. They would be called hit-and-run and the police would be involved. I've got evidence I can produce in court if you can get it that far.

Once again, I call for you to chase these wrongdoers and hit them where it hurts. IT IS ONLY A MATTER OF TIME BEFORE ANOTHER OF MY CATS IS KILLED. This worry is causing me sleepless nights and has shortened my life. You can be sued for that too.

Ruth Lindermilk

The secretary had got up from her seat and was bending over a filing cabinet, pulling out sheets of paper from a low drawer. Flea watched her, seeing her but not really seeing her. May 17. Ten past eleven. A silver Ford Focus with the last letters GBR. A 'deer' hit on the road at the bottom of the hamlet.

'Here are the others.' The secretary came back to the desk and dumped the letters next to the piles from the in-tray. 'These are all from Ruth Lindermilk.'

Flea pushed them around with her fingers, looking at dates going back to 2001. They were written in the same feverish hand, tabulated with the same columns in which Ruth had carefully entered dates, times, licence plates.

'Been sending us letters for years. She's obsessive.'

Flea stacked the old letters up and pushed them towards the secretary. 'You're right. She's mad as a box of frogs. Obviously.'

The secretary took them back to the filing cabinet and dropped them into their slots. Flea folded Ruth's May letter and slid it into the back pocket of her jeans before the secretary noticed. From the in-tray piles on the desk, she pulled out another letter at random and folded the council's reply back over it, to conceal that it wasn't Ruth's letter. She held this letter up and got the woman's attention.

'Thank you for this.' She pushed it carefully back to the bottom of the pile, where it would take the secretary a few days to deal with. 'You've been very helpful.'

38

In the maisonette Caffery peered up the silent stairwell. 'Don't suppose you've got that key on you? To the studio?'

'I wasn't expecting this visit. Give me some notice next time.'

They went into the living room. Caffery put on gloves, switched on the computer and got into the cache folders, where all the cookies should be stored. There were just ten. For a while he sat at the desk, face close to the blank white space where the files should be. The recycling bin was empty too. Sometimes what is missing is the most crucial evidence of all, a CID trainer had once told him. Sometimes it's not what you see but what you *don't* see.

In the kitchen Mahoney put the sandwiches they'd bought in the pub on to a plate and brought it through. He stuck it on the table and stood behind Caffery, his eyes on the screen. Caffery knew he should wait. He should pass the PC to the hi-tech unit at Portishead, but he wanted this now. He scrolled around the free data-recovery sites and chose a shareware programme – Restoration – downloading it from a fast European site.

'What're you doing?'

'Unless someone ran a wipe utility, like Killdisc, the files'll still be on the hard drive somewhere. As long as no one's wiped the partitions, and as long as a system file hasn't been allocated over those spaces, it should all still be here.'

They ate the sandwiches and waited for the download to finish. Then Caffery hit 'set up' and watched the programme unpack itself. He chose C drive to search, ticked 'include used clusters by other files', configured it to display the date the file was created, and set it in motion. The numbers in the 'files found' box spun round dizzyingly. In seconds the window had filled with folders, files of every extension, doc, xls, ppt. Near the top of the list a Word file had been created on 6 May, 9.30 p.m. Last Sunday. The day she'd gone missing. Titled 'Goodbye'.

Caffery opened it and let all his breath out at once. The suicide note. He'd read it several times already at Wells and there wasn't anything unusual in it: the same depressing stuff he'd seen too many times – too much pain to go on, life not worth living, no one who understands. Others killed themselves out of cowardice, or from the strain of living with the knowledge of what they'd done. People like Penderecki. But he'd never known anyone write a suicide note, print and delete it.

'She didn't write that,' Mahoney said. 'No way she wrote it. That's not Lucy's language.'

'Someone else did, though. Wrote it and wiped it. If it had been on here, the search adviser would have found it.'

He scrolled through the list. 'There are emails to the

estate agent, all deleted, but he's left others on the desktop. He's only hiding specific things.'

Mahoney pointed to a folder halfway down the list. 'Is that something?'

'NatWest statements.' Caffery restored it to its original location and opened it. It contained twenty-four jpegs, each titled by a month in the last two years. He opened one from January two years back. It was a scanned image of a bank statement. He gave a low whistle. 'The missing statements.'

'She was scanning them into the computer? To save space?'

'Looks like it.'

Caffery opened the most recent one, dated this April. For a moment he and Mahoney stared at the screen, neither speaking.

Lucy Mahoney had died with the mortgage on her £200,000 house at just seven thousand pounds. There was another £190,000 in her savings account.

'Je-*sus*,' Mahoney muttered. 'What the hell was she up to?'

'All coming in in cash.' Caffery clicked into the other months. 'Two thousand here, another eight thousand in December.'

'Jesus.'

'And look.' He tapped the screen. 'This is where it started. Almost two years ago.'

Both of them peered at the bank statement. Twenty-six months ago Lucy had been receiving a regular wage from her job at the Christmas-decorations factory. Then, in the

May after she and Mahoney had separated, she'd made a one-off payment of £7,121. It had been a cheque – no indication of who the payee was. Two weeks after the debit the cash deposits had started.

'Any idea what that seven grand payment was for?'

Mahoney shook his head. Wearily, as if he'd come to the end of anything like rational thought, he picked up the plate. He trudged into the kitchen, leaving Caffery at the computer, clicking through the scanned statements. There was a lot of money here. If it wasn't from a rich boyfriend, if she hadn't got a job and she hadn't got a loan, where the hell was it coming from?

'Blackmail.' Mahoney had come back from the kitchen. He was holding out a steaming mug of coffee to Caffery. His eyes were cold and hard. 'That's it, isn't it?'

'I don't know,' Caffery said. 'It's one explanation.'

'It's the only explanation. She was blackmailing someone. They got fed up with it. Decided to put a stop to it.'

Caffery took the mug. 'Tell you what, let's start slowly, sensibly. Let's start by getting the case reclassified.'

39

Caffery drove slowly back towards Kingswood, thinking about how he'd get Powers to authorize a warrant on the £7,121 cheque so the banks would go back into their records. It would take days. But the cheque was important. The more he thought about it, the more he thought Colin was right – Lucy had been blackmailing someone. And that seven grand was pivotal to the whole thing. She'd bought something – something expensive – and someone she'd encountered in the process was the one she had started blackmailing. Whoever it was had got fed up. Maybe her demands had become too much. They'd killed her and worked hard to cover the paper trail. He didn't have much doubt that that was how it had happened.

Mahoney said she hadn't felt threatened by the boyfriend. Caffery believed that. But the boyfriend was the key to all this. Not because he'd killed Lucy, not necessarily that, but somehow, somehow, he held a key. Whether he knew it or not.

Caffery slammed on the brakes. Behind him, a lorry had

to swerve to avoid going into the back of his car, and the driver leant on the horn. Caffery pulled his unmarked Mondeo on to the kerb and came to a stop next to a bus shelter. Unsnapping the seat-belt he swivelled round, elbow on the back of the seat, and looked out through the back window. On the other side of the road, a sign was mounted on the roof of an electrical superstore. He must have driven past it a hundred times and never noticed it. Now it made things pop in the back of his head.

It was a golden oval set on its side. In black letters tooled into the middle was the word 'EMPORIUM'. He waited for the pedestrian lights behind him to go red, then pulled out, did a U-turn into the opposite lane, and slipped into the turning that ran behind the superstore.

Something of an industrial estate had grown up down there, unplanned and piecemeal. Various businesses were dotted around in a hodgepodge of buildings overlooking a central car park that must have once been a farmyard. The Emporium was housed in what might have been an old farm building. As long and high-ceilinged as a hangar, with daylight and breeze coming in from both ends, it had the feel of a scrapyard under a tin roof. Everywhere reclamation pieces were piled high, vague walkways meandering around them.

A customer stood in the middle of the building, head down, concentrating on untangling the wire attachments on a crystal-drop chandelier. She wore a tribal-print dress tied with a belt and had very pale skin, her dark hair was backcombed and tied with a printed scarf. Her features in profile were beautiful, unusual, but closer he saw that the dark eyeshadow and plum lipstick were smudged. She didn't look up or acknowledge him as he passed.

He skirted crumbling sash windows stacked in rows, a set of merry-go-round horses, a ship's figurehead hanging from the ceiling. He went past the innards of a cider press, a row of knives in a worn leather tool-belt, and a low oak breaking bench, polished by years of use. The office was a square glass and wood-sided construction at the far corner. Inside, every shelf and surface was covered with oddments: old shell casings, dust-coated chandeliers, a cracked 1930s Betty Boop mannequin, a yellowing wedding cake in the shape of a church with a tiny dusty bride and groom in the doorway. Paperweights were wedged into the spaces – and for a moment he wandered around studying them, thinking he was alone. Then he noticed a man staring at him from the corner, standing half bent over the open drawer of a filing cabinet, so motionless that for a moment Caffery thought he was one of the fairground curios. 'Hello.'

'Yes?' The man closed the drawer and straightened. 'Can I help?'

'You are?'

'James Pooley. Who wants to know?'

Caffery opened his warrant card. 'Got a moment?'

Pooley closed the cabinet, came forward and looked at the card. He was slim and vaguely feminine, his brown turtleneck expensive and finely woven, the thin leather jacket worn open, cuffs and collar turned up. There was more jewellery on his hands than a man should wear. His thick hair lay down to his collar.

'Oops,' he said, giving a thin smile, showing neat teeth. 'Does this mean I've caught something again? Accidentally downloaded a virus? A few non-kosher pieces lurking in the recesses?' He gestured out of the office window at the huge amount of merchandise on display. 'It's so difficult, these days – the fences get better and better, more and more sophisticated. Couldn't tell some of them apart from a Christie's clerk, they know their game so well.'

'It's about a customer.'

'OK,' he said slowly, eyeing Caffery. 'OK. Why don't you sit down?'

Caffery sat opposite Pooley in a vintage desk chair, its wooden arms worn thin and smooth by years of traffic. In his pocket he had a copy of the misper poster, which he unfolded and put on the desk. Pooley studied it, his nose very close to the photograph. There was a long, long silence while all Caffery could see was the top of his well-conditioned hair. Then at last he looked up. 'Yes. I know her. Lucy Mahoney. She's a customer.'

'Was.'

'Was?' Pooley gave a nervous laugh. 'Not a nice sound, the past tense. Never have liked using it when talking about a customer.'

'She's dead.'

'Dead? How?'

'We don't know yet.'

There was a pause, then Pooley's face lost a little of its control, as if it was crumbling at the edges. 'Good God, good God.' He shook his head. 'What a tragedy. What a waste. She was young.'

'Very.'

'How terrible. Tell me – her family? Are they taking it very badly?'

'About as well as can be expected. She had a daughter.'

'Yes, of course. Well, if there's anything we can do, here at the Emporium, any condolences we can extend . . . She was a valued customer.' He looked at his hands on the table. He moved a stray rubber band and put it into a desk tidy. He had very fair eyelashes – almost non-existent – and his skin was very smooth. The hands moving the rubber band were nice too, sort of manicured. 'And I . . . I suppose you think it was a sex killing?'

'What?'

'A sex killing. I suppose that's what it was?'

Caffery folded his arms and eyed Pooley. 'Are you having a laugh?'

'No. Good God, no. It's just that . . .' He paused, tilted his head. 'You do know about her? Don't you?'

' "*Know*" about her? No, I don't.'

Pooley eyed Caffery, the way he was sitting comfortably, as if he was settling in for the duration. He glanced out of the window at the dark-haired woman in the scarf, who was still fiddling with the chandelier crystals, her head bent. Then, with a brief smile, he pushed his chair back, got up, went to a glass cabinet at the far side of the office and unlocked it. He brought out a velvet-lined case and set it on the table. Caffery leant over.

Several lumps of stainless steel were set into the green velvet. It took him a few seconds to realize what he was looking at. Sex toys. Beautifully carved instruments.

Dildos. Butt plugs. Nipple clamps. In ivory, jade, glass. A human-hair scourge with a gold-embossed handle. Some were engraved with Chinese characters. The prices on the tags started in the low hundreds.

'She bought this sort of stuff from you?'

'She did.'

'How long has she been coming here?'

'Eighteen months? More. I couldn't say for sure.'

Lucy, Caffery thought, you're not the girl I thought you were. There's another side to you. Did you play sex games? Maybe that was when someone gave you the pills. Did he tell you they'd help the sex?

'When she visited, would she always be on her own?'

'I believe so.'

'And she never seemed anxious?'

'No.'

'Never said anything about feeling she was in danger?'

There was a pause. Then Pooley said, in a careful voice, 'She bought things from me. I don't think she ever came here expecting to share her secrets. I only knew her well enough to exchange pleasantries. I knew what she liked to collect and sometimes I acquired things with her in mind, but our connection was purely aesthetic.'

Caffery looked at the human-hair whip. At the butt plugs. 'Aesthetic?'

Pooley curled a nostril, as if Caffery smelt bad. 'I shared her taste in collectibles, Mr Caffery.' He snapped the box shut. 'Her taste in the bedroom? Well, please – she was a customer.'

'She bought paperweights from you too.'

'That was her other interest.' He went back to the cabinet, replaced the box and took out a pair of paperweights, both a deep, cerulean blue, holding them in his palms like two fat plums. 'Pretty, aren't they? I got them from a shop in Andover – these parochial outlets, they haven't a clue what they've got half the time. These are French. From the Clichy factory. Quite old. I got them with her in mind. I thought she'd like the colour especially.' He put them on the desk. Then, tongue between his teeth, he returned to the cabinet, walked his hands delicately over the other objects in it, selected a few and brought them across. 'I had her in mind with these too.'

He put out three paperweights, two filled with a riot of oranges and reds, the third a plain white, its top surface nipped and stretched upwards as if the glass was reaching for the sky. 'They're not my thing, to be honest, too contemporary, but I think Ms Mahoney liked them. I always meant to suggest to her she took them. See? You could line them up like this. Maybe on a windowsill.' He sat down and steepled his hands, making a tall, narrow shape with them. 'If there was something out of the window you wanted to draw attention to, for example.'

'The items she bought from you?' Caffery wondered what it was about the one in the centre that was making his head tick. 'Would you have a record of that somewhere? Sales dockets?'

'Sales dockets. Yes, I . . .' Pooley paused. He collected himself and gave a calm smile. 'I keep most of my invoices at home. Can I get back to you on that? I could bring them to you.'

Caffery reached into his pocket for his wallet, taking time to do it because he was thinking, trying to decide if there was something else, something more he should have asked. But just as the answer was about to pop into his head, his phone rang in his pocket. He pulled it out. Beatrice Foxton's number was flashing on the screen.

'What're you doing?' Her voice was echoey. He guessed she was in the mortuary. 'Where are you?'

'Brislington.' Caffery pushed back the chair and stood. He fumbled a business card out and put in on the desk in front of Pooley. 'Call me,' he mouthed. 'Why, Beatrice? Where do you want me to be?'

'Southmead Hospital. Like now.'

40

Fester and Lurch, the morticians, were tidying up the body when Caffery arrived. He left his coat in the office and was pulling on the little white wellies the mortuary provided when Beatrice met him in the doorway, mask below her chin, a glass laboratory beaker in her hand. 'Hello, Jack.' She shook the beaker in his face, sloshing the contents around. He got a sharp whiff of vomit. 'Glad you could make it.'

'Thanks.' He turned his head away, felt in his pockets for the Airwaves gum and squinted sideways at the beaker. 'Stomach contents?'

'Coca-Cola, salad, bits of something I think must have been a pizza, coffee and about eight half-digested temazepam tablets. Like Lucy Mahoney.'

'Oh, Christ,' Caffery said dully, putting his hand on the beaker and pushing it away from his face. 'This is *not* what I need to hear.' He looked over her shoulder into the dissection room where Lurch, in mask and a sunny yellow tunic, was stitching up the long Y incision in the body on the table. 'What've you got, then?'

'A suicide. Or, rather, a death that's supposed to look like suicide. Come on.'

Tipping two gum lozenges into his mouth Caffery followed her into the room. The woman lying on the block in life had been plump, with pale skin and fair pubic hair. She had a tattoo of a swallow on her right breast, but her face and hair weren't visible. A second mortician stood at her head and was using both gloved hands to peel her face gently up and over the skull. Beatrice would have made an incision at the back of the skull and pulled the skin and hair down over the front of the head, letting it gather in folds under the chin. Now the autopsy was over it was Lurch's job to peel it back up, flatten it and make it presentable for the relatives. Beyond him a man wearing a navy blue raincoat stood with his side to them, a mobile glued to his ear. A divisional DI, Caffery guessed.

'She's not long dead?' Caffery walked around the table, studying the body, the dark stitching burrowing deep into her flesh. The Y cut had circumvented the navel so it was attached to the left flap of stomach wall – Lurch stitched the little lump of gristle back to the opposite flap of skin. 'Not in rigor yet.'

'We think it probably happened yesterday evening some time before midnight. Her name's Susan Hopkins.'

Beatrice put her hand out to the CSI man, who passed her a sheaf of photos. She gave them to Caffery. They showed Susan Hopkins in belted jeans and a black-and-white floral-print blouse, lying on the floor of a garage, a dark pool of blood around her. She was young, quite pretty, with a flat face and a small nose.

Her blonde hair was worn short. Neat, not showy.

'She was a nurse in a private clinic out near Yate. She'd done an early shift and was supposed to be meeting her friend at seven for a drink – they were going to celebrate because her boyfriend was coming off the rigs in Aberdeen after three weeks apart. She never showed for the drink. The police found her this morning at three in her own garage. No sexual assault, no underwear disturbed. No robbery. The parents – poor bastards – are on holiday in Croatia. Someone's trying to find them now.'

'And you're not convinced she pulled the plug because . . . ?'

Beatrice glanced at the DI to make sure he wasn't listening. 'She was lying down,' she murmured. 'On her back. Just as you see her now. The same way Mahoney was.'

'And?'

'Most suicides are in a sitting position. Or half propped up. You never seen that? If they arrive when they're still in rigor it's like trying to fit a chair on the table – legs sticking out everywhere. But no. I don't break bones to get them to lie flat in case that's what you've heard. I have other methods.'

'So she lay down to die. That's suspicious?'

'All right, all right.' Beatrice sighed. 'Give an old lady a chance here. Of *course* if a suicide comes to me lying flat on their back, hands at their sides, it means nothing. It's a little unusual, that's all. But you add it to the big picture and . . . I don't know. Maybe I'm just getting bored out here in the wilderness with the woollies. Looking for murder on every corner, eh?'

She lifted Susan's right hand and showed Jack the inside of her wrist. It was a clumsy cut, made in the same longitudinal direction as Mahoney's had been.

'No experimental nicks?'

'Just like Mahoney. They both went straight in there for the biggie. Same as the lying-down thing. You take it in isolation and it means nothing. But there are other things.'

'What other things?'

'She did it the same way Mahoney did. Benzos and the knife. And, just like with Mahoney, the temazepam is only half digested.'

'Where does this leave us, then?'

Beatrice rubbed her forehead with the tip of her finger. 'You tell me. Lucy Mahoney had temazepam on prescription for an operation, but Hopkins . . .' She looked up at him. 'So far no one can work out how she got her hands on those tablets.'

Caffery peered at the cut on Hopkins's wrist. He could see past the skin right down into the mechanics of the arm: the dun-coloured tendons, the slippery fascia of muscle. 'I don't know. Feels a little like you're stretching it a bit.'

Beatrice pushed a stray strand of grey hair off her forehead and gave an exasperated sigh. 'You know, I didn't expect you to propose marriage to me over this, but I have to say I'd hoped for a different reaction, Jack. I'd kind of hoped for some sort of appreciation. Even just a nod. A smile that I bothered to call you, maybe.'

Caffery glanced across at the DI, who hadn't looked up and was still muttering into the phone, one finger in his ear to block out the roar of the air-conditioning unit. 'It's just that if you're *right*,' he muttered, leaning into her, 'then all I can say is, God help me.'

'And all *I* can say is, I hear the clink and clank of God ponying up right now – because I *am* right. You just haven't heard everything yet.'

Caffery turned his eyes sideways and held hers.

'Yes,' she murmured, her eyebrows raised. 'Oh, yes.'

She gestured to Fester and Lurch. Like Mahoney, Hopkins had been a big girl – it took two of them to roll her over. And when they did Caffery stopped chewing the gum. He stood quite still, his hands in his pockets.

'See what I mean?' Beatrice said. 'Do you see why I don't think she killed herself?'

On the backs of Hopkins's heels an area of skin had been sloughed away. Little pinpoints of black showed gravel embedded in the grazes.

'She was dragged? You're telling me she was dragged into the garage?'

Beatrice gave a low, humourless laugh. 'At last,' she murmured. 'At last we're reading from the same hymn sheet.'

41

Flea parked in the shaded trees, just out of sight of the road, and walked up the path to Ruth Lindermilk's bungalow. The heat of the day was just leaving the air. The hamlet was quiet, the only sound a dog barking furiously inside one of the cottages. Flea didn't go up the path to the door. She opened the gate and went around the side of the building to where the land dropped away sharply towards the road.

Ruth was about ten feet away, her back turned. Hatless, dressed in a short white skirt and a denim jacket, she was busy dropping birdseed into one of the feeders.

'Hello.'

Ruth looked round, saw Flea, put the seed on the ground and began walking towards the house.

'Ruth – please.'

'Eff off. I'm going to get my gun.'

'You haven't got a gun. The police took it.'

'Got another one. Going to get it.'

'Christ, Ruth, this isn't *The Beverly* shagging *Hillbillies*.'

She stopped in her tracks and turned slowly to Flea. Without the cap she seemed older. Her badly dyed hair was cut short and greying at the back. Her makeup was caked in the corners of her eyes. She was sweating, breathing hard. 'You've got some fuckin' neck, showing your face round here.'

'I'm sorry about last time, but the neighbours didn't send me. You should at least believe that.'

Ruth shook her head. 'Then who are you? With your combats and your hat. Hasn't no one never told you those are boys' clothes? You look a right wanker.'

'I'm a private investigator.'

'A private . . . ? How comes you told me you were from the Highways Agency?'

'It was the first thing that came to mind.'

'I should've known you weren't from the council straight away. Council'd never come out to see me. Now, if I was on the social it'd be different – if I was on the soash they'd have been straight round . . .' She trailed off. 'A private investigator? What do you want out of me?'

'Can we talk? Inside? Don't want to give your neighbours a show, do we?'

Ruth's mouth twitched. Her foxy little brain was working on the situation. She glanced at the road – at the other houses in the hamlet. Behind the puffy skin her eyes were grey and hard. Uncompromising. 'You've got five minutes. Then I'm calling the police.'

They went into the living room. It seemed bigger with the french windows wide open, and it smelt of cleaning fluid and burnt toast. Flea pushed some cats away and sat down on the sofa. 'I'll be absolutely honest.'

'It's not in your nature.'

'I'll be absolutely *honest*. Even though I shouldn't, I'm telling you the truth. I'm in trouble.'

'So what? Don't confuse me with someone who gives a shit.'

'This case is my last hope. If I don't get it right I'm basically going to lose my job. That's why I lied to you. I was desperate.'

'Desperate?' Ruth licked her lips. 'How terrible for you. What? Down to your last million, are you?'

'It's a difficult case. My client's husband's been having an affair. He came home drunk last week. He'd had an accident. The front grille of their car was dented. He told my client he was parked in Bristol at a work do and that someone had driven into it in the car park.'

'And?'

'My client didn't believe him. She thought he'd been seeing his girlfriend over at Tellisford. If he'd been in Tellisford he'd've had to drive along this road to get home. I think whatever happened to his car happened down there on the road. There are skidmarks. When I was looking at them yesterday I saw your telescope from the road. That's why I came up.'

She held Ruth's eyes steadily. 'My client's accident was last Monday. Some time before midnight. Do you know anything about it?'

'Course I do. He hit a deer.'

'How do you know it was a deer?'

'I could tell from the noise of the collision.'

'You didn't see it, then?'

'I heard it. That was enough. The deer must have limped off because when I went down there later with the camera there was nothing. It probably died in one of the fields, the poor—' She broke off, eyeing Flea suspiciously. And then she grinned. A gap-toothed beery smile. 'Oh,' she said. 'There you go again – taking me for an idiot.'

Flea looked at her stonily. 'Are you going to talk to me or not?'

'Depends.'

'Depends on what?'

'On what you can give me in return.'

'I don't know what I have to give you in return. What were you thinking?'

'What do you think I was thinking?'

'Money, I suppose. But you won't get far with that. It's against the ethics to pay for information.'

'Ethics? Whose *ethics*?'

'Mine. My company's. My client's.'

'Oh, I'm sure you could find something. Ten K. That's all I want. It's not a lot. Not to someone like you.'

'You'd be surprised what's a lot to people like me.'

'That's fine.' Ruth went to the bar and picked up a cracked glass with a drink in it. She raised it to Flea. 'If it's interesting enough for you, then it'll be interesting enough for someone else.'

Flea got to her feet.

'Where're you going?'

'There's no money. I'm going home.'

Ruth shrugged. She put down the glass and went to the

computer table. Pulled a cellophane envelope from the top drawer and slid out a black-and-white print. 'My evidence.' She came across the room and held it out. 'I never got all his registration, only the last three letters. Otherwise I'd have called the police on him.'

Flea looked at the photo, her heart thumping low and hard in her chest. Taken from the patio, it showed the road at night. A double set of tyre tracks ran down the centre and at the head of them, where it had come to rest, a car was parked, the driver's door open. A man was standing at the back, as if he'd just slammed the boot. He had turned away from the camera, and although he was too far away for Flea to see what he looked like, if you knew Thom you'd know it was him standing there.

The numbers on the plate were illegible because of the lighting, but the letters were clear: GBR. And just peeping out above the numberplate a tiny slip of something dark. Unless you were close to it, you wouldn't notice it was there. But Flea noticed. And knew it was a section of velvet coat. *He'd already put her in the boot and was leaving . . . So you didn't see the whole thing. You heard the collision, but you didn't know it was a person he'd hit. You didn't see him put Misty in the boot. That's why you thought it was a deer . . .*

She reached for the photo, but Ruth was quick. She shovelled it back into the cellophane, went to a small bureau in the corner, pushed it inside and turned the key. She looked back at Flea, smiling, something sly crossing her expression. 'No, no, no,' she said. 'It would be too easy, wouldn't it?'

'Lend me the photo, Ruth. It would prove my client's husband was there.'

'No.' She dropped the key down the front of her bra. Winked. 'I don't think I'll do that.'

'I'll make a copy of it. It'll take me a few minutes just to run it down to a copy shop. Then my case'll be over and I can leave you be.'

'The price has just gone up. Fifteen grand. That's what it'll cost you.'

Flea opened her mouth. Closed it. What did the photograph prove? That Thom had stopped. That he'd got out of the car to check what he'd hit. They'd have to work that into his story. They'd position Misty far enough into the field for it to be believable that she'd been thrown through the hedgerow and that when he'd got out to check he hadn't been able to see her from the road. Then he'd say he'd assumed it was a deer that had limped off. Just the way Ruth had told it.

'I don't think so.' She checked her watch. It was six thirty. She was meeting Mandy and Thom in Keynsham in forty-five minutes. 'I'm sorry but I really don't think that's going to happen.'

42

A modern cider pub had been built where the old lock-keeper's house in Keynsham used to be. Flea, Thom and Mandy went down to the rickety fishing platform so the roar of the weir would blunt their voices and tried to look normal. They'd ordered long pints of thick orangy cider, but none of them felt like drinking. Thom rested his glass on a supporting post and stood with his arms folded, looking down at his toe, which he moved in circles as if he was writing something with it. He wouldn't look either woman in the eye.

Flea stood shoulder to shoulder with Mandy, gazing morosely into the river. She'd pulled a body out of there once. A seventy-year-old man with throat cancer. While his wife was at Somerfields he'd taken a mallet and bolster to part of the garden wall, chipped out seven bricks, zipped them into a rucksack, which he'd padlocked round his chest, then come out here and stepped straight into the water. A wedding party in the pub grounds opposite watched him do it. His body had been pulled under and held against the weir by the current. It had taken the underwater search unit six hours to get him out, and when they did, his face, some of which had already been removed during his treatment, had slammed into the weir so many times it was like uncooked hamburger.

'We need to come up with a plan.' Mandy was wearing a black linen dress that stopped mid-calf, and fading blue Birkenstocks. The heavy tops of her arms had small reddish pimples scattered over them. 'For everyone's sake, we need a plan. We need to decide the best way out of this for all of us.'

Flea glanced up at the pub. A few people stood on the terrace. Some wore business suits; some, shorts and T-shirts. No one was paying them any attention. She took a step closer to Mandy anyway, lowering her voice. 'Look, it'll be easier than you think. There's a huge shake-up going on at the moment in the forensic system and most investigative teams don't have big forensic budgets to start with. The autopsy will show she was hit by a car. With a confession from Thom they won't look at it too closely. There'd be no reason to order extra tests.'

'What sort of extra tests?'

'Tests that would show she hadn't been out in the open for all that time. That's the only hot button. If they ever find out she was put in the car . . .'

'You've thought it all through.'

'The car has to look right because they'll test the point of impact. I've burnt the boot lining and you're going to have to take a trip somewhere – London, maybe – to buy a new one. You'll need to pay cash. I'll take care of her clothes, get rid of fibres from the boot. The only other thing is her body.'

Mandy winced. 'Yes. That.'

'She'd have decomposed differently in the boot than if she'd been in the open. On the roadside there'd've been animal artefacts. Rats, mice, foxes. They're not discerning about what meat's on the menu.'

'Jesus Christ,' Thom muttered. 'This is a nightmare.'

Mandy gave him a sharp look. 'Be quiet.'

'So, this is the crucial part. We've got to hide her somewhere it's plausible she landed, but where she won't be seen from the road. She needs to lie out there for a night or longer – as long as possible, really, so the animals can do their thing. Move her around. Destroy some evidence, make it believable.' She took a sip of her drink and wiped her mouth with the back of her hand. 'And that's where it gets tricky.'

'What?'

'It's in a remote place but someone's got a view of it. A good view. That's where you come in, Mandy. I'm going to ask you to distract someone.'

'How am I going to do that?'

'I don't know yet. You like animals, don't you? Maybe you tell her your cat's gone missing and you're searching the neighbourhood.'

'I'm not an actress.'

'You might not have to be. This woman's a drunk. If we time it right you won't have to work hard to convince her.'

She took another sip of cider, put the glass down and got a pellet of chewing-gum from the packet in her pocket.

Easy on the booze – the last thing she needed was to get pissed. 'And it's tonight. We're going to get started tonight.'

Mandy and Thom didn't speak. They both stared at her.

'I know, I know. But it's got to be done. When it's done we'll all feel better.'

'OK.' Mandy scratched her head. 'One last thing.'

'What?'

'Take me through what really happened again. That night. Because at the time you told me he was in the back garden. I phoned you three times and you told me each time he was in the back garden.'

'We've gone through this.'

'Just so it's clear in my head.'

Flea sighed. 'OK. Like I said, I was covering for him. He went to meet some people about importing chandeliers from the Czech Republic, didn't you, Thom? He thought you'd lose it if you knew. So we lied. Simple as that.'

'It's just that, on the night when I called, you told me, over and over again, he was down at the bottom of the terraces. You said he was pruning some tree or something.'

'Mandy.' Flea kept her voice patient. 'Concentrate. Read my lips. I. Was. Lying. Thom was out. He had a drink with his business contacts and came home drunk. Come on, Thom? Haven't you explained all this? She's not listening to me.'

'I . . .' he began hesitantly. 'I – I don't know what to say.'

'Just explain, for Christ's sake. We're wasting time.'

He glanced at Mandy, then away. He had exactly the

same distant expression he'd get as a kid when Dad would try to pin him down over something. 'I – I can't remember,' he muttered. 'You know, it's a bit of a haze.'

'A bit of a haze? A bit of a *haze*? Wake up, Thom. This is serious.'

Mandy put her hands into the air. 'Let's calm down. Phoebe. We're only trying to get to the truth of what happened.'

'The truth? I've told you the truth.'

'Yes, but do you see our point? That's what you said to me on the night of the accident. You said you were telling the truth then. But you weren't. You were lying *then*, so how do I know you're not lying *now*?'

'I'm not fucking *lying*, Mandy.'

'No need to shout.'

'*But I'm not lying. Why the hell would I be lying?*'

Mandy's face became calm. 'To save yourself? Maybe?'

Flea put her hand up to shade her eyes from the lights in the pub and studied Mandy's face. 'Are you being funny?'

'It *was* you driving the car, wasn't it?'

'*What?*'

'I said, it *was* you driving the car. You swore to the cop it was you driving.'

'Swore because I was protecting Thom. He was off his tits.'

'Says who?'

Flea let all the air out of her lungs. 'This is fucking insane. Insane. I can't believe this is coming out of your mouth.'

'You were so high-strung that night – you know how you get. You were upset with work – upset about your parents.' Mandy's tone was pained, uncomprehending, as if it was not the sort of thing she'd understand but she was willing to be flexible about what others did. 'You drove when you were upset and got followed home by the policeman. He breathalysed you. There'll be a record of it somewhere.'

'Tell me you're not serious. Tell me you're not trying to turn this on to me.'

Mandy didn't answer.

Flea gave a low, disbelieving whistle. 'You fucking bitch.'

'Be careful what you say.'

'Right.' She put her glass down on the platform. 'We're going to the police.'

Mandy didn't move. 'I don't think so. It's your word against Thom's. Mine. And the cop's.'

'That's not going to work, Mandy. You take the gloves off, mate, and *you* lose. I've got proof I wasn't driving the car.'

'Really?'

'A photo. Showing Thom hit Misty.'

Mandy sighed. 'What is it about you, Phoebe, that always makes whatever you say sound so unfeasible? Where is this photo? Shall we have a look at it?'

'It exists.'

'Then show us.'

'It *exists*, Mandy. You'd better believe it.'

Mandy smiled and put a reassuring hand on her arm.

'I'm sure it does. Somewhere – maybe in your imagination. But there's no need for you to invent things because we're not going to tell anyone anyway. No, you've got nothing to worry about from us. We'll protect you. We're not going to say a *thing*.'

Flea snatched her arm away. 'Don't fucking touch me.'

She went to the car. Sat inside, windows closed. Turned up the Snow Patrol album as loud as it would go and tapped out the music hard on the dashboard. From the pub balcony one or two people were staring at the little Clio. On the fishing platform Mandy and Thom stood facing her, shoulder to shoulder. Their faces were in shadow but she could tell they weren't speaking. They were doing nothing. Just watching her.

She thought of Ruth Lindermilk. Remembered the key going down her T-shirt. She imagined how she'd react if she ever found out the real reason the photo was important. Not a woman who'd be scared by the police into giving up a bit of evidence. Especially not to help Flea. She'd sooner destroy it.

Thom and Mandy. Still over there. Watching her like dummies from the jetty. She tapped harder.

PC Prody's testimony would be that he'd chased her. Not Thom. It'd be that she'd sworn over and again she'd been driving the Focus. Pearce: well, Pearce she didn't want to think about. He'd tell everyone that Sergeant Marley had been bouncing around some very confident theories about where Misty would and wouldn't be found. Not in the lake, she'd said. We definitely won't find her in the lake. Like she knew. Big fat mouth. She'd only said it because she didn't think someone as groomed as Misty would commit suicide by drowning. It had been a stupid thought – off the top of her head.

She looked at the jetty.

Thom: *It's a bit of a haze.*

Mandy: *We'll protect you.*

She turned the music off. Got out and came back to the jetty.

'Flea.' Mandy's hand went out warningly. 'Let's have a talk about this and—'

Too late. Flea was on Thom. Had him by the shoulders. Slammed him against the post. '*Tell the truth!*' she yelled.

'*Let go of me.*'

She dragged him forward. Slammed him back again. His arms flew out. The pint glass toppled, shattered. '*Say it now.*'

Winded, he slithered down the post to a sitting position. On the balcony people turned in amazement. She got him under the arms and pulled him forward, throwing him down on his face, put her feet astride his back and dropped her weight on his buttocks. Got his hair in her hands. '*Take some responsibility.*'

'Stop it.' Mandy scrabbled at her hands. 'Stop it now.'

Flea wasn't listening. She was seeing Dad, a million years ago, slapping Thom. The flatness in Thom's face. The way he didn't react. '*Tell the truth!*' she screamed.

He groped blindly behind him. '*Leave me alone.*' He got his fingernails into her hands and tried to pull them out of his hair.

She clenched her teeth. Leant back and hauled his head up. '*Tell the fucking truth—*'

He threw himself sideways, his bony hips twisting, until he was on his back, facing her. She tried to slam his head down but he stopped her, grabbing her wrists. While she struggled, he lifted his knee swiftly, twice, three times, catching her in the groin. And now Mandy was squatting next to her. Not screaming. Silent. Face screwed up in concentration, her meaty arms grappling around Flea.

'*Get off me, you bitch.*' Flea rammed her elbow out sideways. Missed. A muscle jarred in her shoulder. '*Get off.*'

She flung her weight sideways, hair flying. Back again, trying to break Mandy's grip. But she was twice Flea's weight and strong, and she kept her face against Flea's shoulder, held the armlock grimly, going with the movement. They rolled on to the jetty. She felt a fragment of glass slice into her cheek, felt Thom wriggle out from under them, heard him stand as she struggled with Mandy.

'Let go of me, Mandy,' she spat. 'Because I will kill you.'

'Get her hands!' Thom yelled suddenly. 'Get her.'

Flea kicked blindly as his hands scrabbled for hers. She felt spiteful fingernails in her wrists. Felt herself being lifted. He was strong too. Stronger than she'd ever guessed. Blood was running down her chin. Vague ghosts of people were coming from the bar, shouting.

'*I'll kill you.*'

A kick. Or a punch. In her stomach. Up high, under the diaphragm. She didn't see who it came from, but it pushed all the air out of her – finished her in one. Mandy released her and she fell forward and lay there, not moving. The cop trained to stand up in a riot was on the jetty with blood coming out of her face, thinking the only important thing was to get another breath into her body.

'Phoebe.' Mandy's voice was just a whisper close to her face. Flea could smell the tang of her sweat. The sweetness of laundry detergent. 'Phoebe, Thom and I love you very much. Very much indeed. That is why we are going to help you. We're going to help you sort out your problems, your issues, and together – *together* – we'll find a way of not taking you to the police.'

43

Caffery broke all the rules and took alcohol into the unit meeting that evening. He got a can of Coke from on top of the filing cabinet, drank half of it, then uncapped a bottle of Bell's and filled the can to the top. The Bell's was there because, compared to a good malt, Glenmorangie maybe, he hated the taste. The idea was to stop himself necking the whole bottle. Sometimes the trick worked, sometimes it didn't.

Every force he'd ever known called the daily meeting with a senior investigating officer 'prayers'. Some SIOs held prayers once a day to collate what the team had done the previous day. Some held it twice: morning and afternoon prayers. Some held it whenever the wind changed direction. Like Powers. He was a nightmare.

Today's prayers was mostly about Kitson's phone records and how well Powers had come across on TV at the press conference. Caffery stood against the wall, drinking the whisky and Coke and thinking not about Kitson but about Susan Hopkins. Susan Hopkins and Lucy Mahoney, he'd worked out, probably hadn't known each other. There was no mention of Mahoney in Hopkins's address book or paperwork and vice versa. Nor had Hopkins's family and friends heard the name, though the boyfriend from the rigs thought 'Lucy Mahoney' sounded like a porn star, if Caffery wanted the honest truth. And yet there *was* a link between the women. Somewhere, something connected them, he was sure of it. Which left a nasty truth, a truth that felt like a dark and limitless hole opening in the air close to his face: not Amos Chipeta, but someone else. Someone cold and slick, who could disguise a killing as suicide. Who had reasons for wanting to pull the skin off a dog.

'Quiet in there, weren't you?' After the meeting Powers caught up with Caffery in the corridor. 'Not seen you so quiet before.'

Caffery stopped at the door of his office. He was still holding the Coke can. He didn't try to hide it, not with what he knew Powers kept in his filing cabinet. 'There wasn't much to say.'

'You weren't in the office this morning. Like I hoped you'd be.'

'I was. Early. I divvied up the actions like I said I would. Then I went for lunch.'

Powers looked at him thoughtfully, then at the Coke can. 'Jack, let me tell you how it is. I drink on duty. That's just what I do. As long as the job gets done, and one of the traffic guys at Almondsbury doesn't net me going the wrong way down the M4, it doesn't make a difference. In twenty years no one has said a thing about it.' He raised his eyes. 'And do you know why?'

'Why?'

'Because I do my job and I don't get in people's faces. I don't get in people's faces and I toe the line so they don't find ways to hurt me. But if I *did*, if I *was* the sort of person who made people angry, who didn't pull with the team . . .' he paused '. . . I'd be shit on toast. No time at all, it'd take them. Shit on toast.'

Caffery gave him a long look. He pushed open the door to his office and went inside. Put the can down, sat, unbuttoned his jacket and arranged it loosely around his torso. He beckoned to Powers. As if he was inviting a body blow. 'Go on, then. Give me it if you have to.'

Powers eyed him carefully, then, with reluctance, came in. He closed the door behind him and sat down. 'I heard you were out for lunch in Clifton.'

'News travels.'

'Turnbull's very faithful.'

'That's nice. And there was I thinking he and I had something special going on.'

'And then I heard you went to a post-mortem.'

'Yes.'

Powers put a mild, puzzled look on his face. 'You see, Jack, I'm having problems figuring out what a senior MCIU detective was doing at a routine PM when he's supposed to be working on the Kitson case with the rest of us. District brought it in as a suicide.'

'But the pathologist didn't agree. She thinks it's a murder. And I think it's connected to the other "suicide" I told you about. Lucy Mahoney. I want to bring them both into the unit as linked murders.'

'You *what*?'

'They're linked. Lucy Mahoney wasn't a suicide at all, and here the pathologist is starting to agree with me. I want to bring them both in, and the first thing I want is for you to authorize a warrant. I need to open Mahoney's bank records.'

Powers sighed and ran a hand over his scalp. He didn't look happy, not happy at all. But he took the time to master himself, did the calming breathing technique again. He got his composure and when he spoke his voice was softer. 'It's almost a week into the Kitson case now. Nothing came out of the reconstruction, morale's at tipping point out there.' He nodded in the direction of the briefing room. 'I can just smell it on them. And you, Jack, you mean something to them. They *look* at you. They might not admit it but they all know what you did in London – you're poster-boy material to them. One of our CID trainers has got a whole powerpoint presentation of your Brixton paedophile case. Did you know that?'

'Great,' he muttered. 'Great.'

'But just because you worked some high-profile cases doesn't mean you do whatever the hell you want. You go off on that Norway wild-goose chase, giving me the old maverick line, but the moment that gets dropped you're off chasing another hare. So something, *something*, is stopping you pulling with us on the Kitson case. Come on – look me in the eye. Tell me what it is.'

Caffery did what he was asked. Looked him in the eye. He concentrated on not blinking, and said the first thing that came into his head. 'It's because I can't be seen working on it publicly.'

'*What?*' Powers's eyes narrowed. He searched Caffery's face. 'Are you saying you've got a snout?'

'Yes.' It was a lie. But it might get Powers off his back for a day or two. 'That's exactly what I'm saying.'

'You've been here five minutes and already you've got a snout? On something like this? No. You're sticking one on me here, aren't you, Jack? You're taking the piss.'

'Look, there's a whole stack of dealers connected with the clinic. There always is with any of these rehab places. Some local yob gagging to cater to the needs of the inmates. For Farleigh Hall they come from Bath and Trowbridge.'

'Kitson was going to meet a dealer?'

'That conversation with the boyfriend? What did you think when she said she wanted "time to think"?'

'That she wanted time to think?'

'You don't think it sounded like whitewash? He said, "Where are you going?" and she said, "I'm just going to wander around a bit." Does that sound right? In the highest-heeled shoes known to man and – here Jimmy Choo *would* be impressed – she's going to have a wander around? Visit the local cowpats? And how come she was so specific about when she'd be back?'

'She wanted to be back for something? I don't know. Dinner?'

'Or she knew that what she had to do would only take that long.'

Powers gave a soft whistle. 'I *knew* you were hiding

something about this case. I knew you had something up your sleeve.'

'It's one thing having intel. It's another making it stand up in court, as we all know. That's why I'm waiting. I need another piece of the puzzle. Can't be seen to push it.'

'You're as closed as an arsehole, Caffery. What'm I supposed to do with you?'

'Let me bring in both these cases as a murder.' He drained the Coke can, crumpled it and chucked it into the bin. 'I need to let some time go by with Kitson, let it evolve naturally. Let me just ferret away for a bit on the Hopkins and Mahoney murders. I'll keep the Kitson thing on the back burner, low level, and the moment I get anything on it, I'll come back to you. What d'you think? Just give me some rope and let me work on it?'

Powers held Caffery's eyes for a long time. Then he sighed, opening his hands resignedly. 'I want an update every day on your snout. By Thursday I want to know what's happening. OK?'

'Thursday?'

'That's right.'

'OK. It's a deal. Just one thing. I'm not getting Turnbull this time, am I? I've gone off him.'

'You're not getting Turnbull this time.'

'Good. Who am I getting?'

Powers held his eyes, repeated in a monotone: 'You're not getting Turnbull this time.'

44

At nine thirty the next morning in the Almondsbury offices the nine members of the underwater search team sat in a horseshoe shape watching a trainer apply heart pumps to a dummy. Flea and her team were all trained in basic life support – what used to be called CPR – and had annual refresher courses because skills faded and recommendations changed. For example, the board didn't want fifteen compressions to two breaths any more, explained the trainer, now they wanted thirty to two.

Flea sat at the end of the horseshoe, bolt upright in her chair. Arms folded, back stiff, knee jittering unconsciously up and down. Her eyes were locked on the trainer but she wasn't seeing what he was doing. She'd drunk four cups of coffee and taken 600 mg of Cuprofen – enough to bring on an instant ulcer – and all she'd got was the jitters. Her face still hurt and she had a headache that wouldn't shift – tight and stretched, like there was a fist in her head.

'Boss? *Boss?*' Wellard was next to her, leaning forward, frowning.

'What?' she said. Everyone in the room had stopped

watching the trainer. They were staring at her. 'What is it?'

'Uh – the phone? You know – the one in your pocket?'

And then she got it. Her mobile was ringing and she hadn't even noticed. She fished in her pocket. 'Private Number' flashed on the screen. A work call. She held up her hand to the instructor, pushed back the chair and left the room. 'Yeah, this is Sergeant Marley. How may I help?'

It was a search adviser. Not Stuart Pearce but the dedicated MCIU search adviser.

'I want to talk to you about Misty Kitson.'

'Hang on a second.' She went into her office and shut the door tight, scratched her head for a moment or two until her heart stopped banging. 'OK,' she said slowly. 'You want to talk about Misty Kitson. What about her?'

'The chief's pouring some more money our way. I'm widening the search parameters. Have you got a map there?'

'I'm looking at it now.'

'Our radius was two miles. I'm extending that to four. No fingertip searching, but some door-to-door. You usually do some door-to-door for us, don't you?'

Flea looked at the map on the wall. She didn't need a compass or measuring gear to show her how far a four-mile radius would reach. It would take in Ruth's hamlet, which was slap bang in the middle of the new radius.

'You still there?'

'Yes.'

'I said your team's usually available for some door-to-door, isn't it? I was going to suggest you took the south-east quadrant. I've got some serials out of Taunton to cover the remainder.'

South-east. Ruth's hamlet. 'When do we start?'

'Tomorrow?'

'My team's on lates.'

'Then we'll start in the afternoon. Say, two o'clock.'

'Two o'clock?'

'Is there a problem with that?'

'No. Why should there be?'

'You sound odd.'

'I'm fine, thank you. Absolutely fine. Tomorrow, then.'

She hung up and dropped into the chair, her head in her hands, staring at the desk – at the knot patterns in the cheap laminate. This was clever – so clever. The way the world had got her face down in a trap. Thom, her own brother, dancing around on the jetty yelling, '*Get her*.'

Get her. Fucking incredible.

She picked up the work phone and fiddled with the panel. Unlike her mobile, the number was automatically hidden on outgoing calls – so Thom might just pick up instead of dropping her into mailbox. And this phone had a conversation record feature. She hit the record button and plugged in her number.

He answered after four rings. 'Hello?'

'Thom. Please don't hang up.'

There was a pause, then vague shuffling at the end of the phone. Silence.

'Are you there?'

Again that shuffling, as if he was moving the phone, breaking up the signal a bit.

'Are you there, Thom? Can you hear me?'

'Yes, I can hear you.' Mandy. Not Thom. 'I can hear what you're saying, Phoebe.'

'Put Thom back on. I was talking to Thom.'

'Well, you're talking to me now.'

'But I don't like you, Mandy.'

'And I don't like you.'

'Put my brother on the phone.'

'He's very upset, Phoebe, and he doesn't want to talk to you for a while. I don't think you can keep up this harassment. Why are you calling?'

You know why I'm calling. You fucking bitch.

'I want to get things straight.'

'Well, Phoebe, I know you've got some serious issues.' Mandy's voice was soothing. 'And you know how much we care about you. Both of us. Thom and I both care desperately about you and we'll do anything we can to help you with whatever problems you've got. But for now I think a little distance might be a good idea.'

Flea looked at the red LED blinking on the phone. 'I want to get this thing with Misty's body sorted.'

'Phoebe, I—' There was a pause. The line hissed. The light blinked. On, off, on, off.

Say it, you bitch. Go on – say it.

But when Mandy spoke again it was in a stage-whisper as if she was artificially enunciating the words. 'This thing with *what*? With *whom*? Do you mean the girl who's missing? What's she got to do with you?'

Flea sat back and rubbed her face wearily.

'Are you still talking about the night you had that problem, Phoebe? Are you still going on about that?'

'The night *you* had the problem. Do you remember? Your phone records will show it all. You called me over and over from the house that night.'

'You know what? You're right. I did. I did call – I remember now. I remember speaking to Thom. I remember how terrified he was something had happened to you. You were out, driving all over the place.'

'Mandy, you'd better believe me when I say there *is* a photo. And it *does* show that Thom hit her. Thom hit Misty Kitson in my car.'

Mandy sighed. 'I wish you'd go and see someone, Phoebe.'

'It's true.'

'Bring it to us then. We're at home. You could be here in half an hour. Tell you what, I'll put the kettle on.'

'This conversation's going nowhere.'

'Then let me put you out of your misery and tell you how we're going to finish it. Not only are you going to drop this thing – stop these hurtful fantasies about your younger brother – you're also going to come up with a plan to cover up whatever it is you've done—'

'What Thom's done—'

'Whatever *you've* done. Your deadline is midnight tomorrow.'

'Deadline? What planet are you on, Mandy?'

'You can live with a *fucking* deadline, can't you, *Sergeant*? Isn't that all you do in your job? Stick to deadlines? Midnight tomorrow night. Our house.' Mandy's breathing was harsh. 'I want you to turn up and tell me that *you*'ve dealt with *your* problem. I want to hear that you've put it all to bed or I'm going to have to push the button on this and go to the police.'

'Stop right there. I am not having this conversation.'

'Fair enough.'

There was another shuffling sound, then silence. It took her a moment or two to realize that Mandy'd hung up. She pressed play and leant in to the speaker, listening to their voices. '*I want this thing with Misty's body sorted.*'

'*This thing with* what? *With* whom?'

Mandy was clever. One clever bitch.

A knock at the door. Wellard was there. Worried.

'You OK?'

She quickly hit erase on the phone and swivelled the chair to face him. 'Why wouldn't I be?'

He shrugged. 'Just your – you know.'

She touched her face gingerly. 'This?'

'Uh-huh.'

'It's nothing. Cut myself shaving.'

He tried to smile. Failed. 'No banana bread? Thought maybe we'd upset you?'

She looked at him for a long time. Dear, dear Wellard. The dear men who worked for her and never questioned what she said. Decent, decent people.

She got up and found her sunglasses and keys in the top drawer. 'Hold the fort for me, will you? Just hold it for a couple of hours?'

'Where you going?'

'I'm going to the bank, Wellard. I've got to see a man about a dog.'

45

Mahoney had agreed to bring the studio key to Lucy's home. He said it would take him two hours to get there and not to come any earlier. Caffery wasn't surprised to find him already at the maisonette when he arrived ten minutes early.

He met Caffery at the front door. They didn't waste time with greetings.

'Is the studio open?'

'Yes.'

He led Caffery inside and went up the stairs, his footsteps heavy. He stopped at the studio door. 'I've left it just as it was. Haven't touched a thing.'

'I'm sure you haven't.'

'Anything in here is Lucy's choice. Things she chose. You see?'

Mahoney unlocked the door and held it open. He didn't make eye-contact as Caffery passed but followed him in and stood in the corner, arms folded, not speaking.

The room was large – it must have been intended as the master bedroom. Caffery recognized it as the place Lucy had been filmed in on the second video. The walls were painted in metallics and canvases hung everywhere. She'd divided the area into two with a painted Oriental screen. The half of the room nearest the door was full: almost twenty canvases leant against the wall, four more on easels facing the window. He went to the other side of the screen, away from the window, and stood for a while with his hands in his pockets, looking at what was there.

Pooley had been right. Lucy'd had unusual tastes. Dominating the room was a three-quarter life-sized bronze of a naked woman. She was bending over, buttocks in the air, showing every inch and fold of flesh between her legs. Beyond her, a row of smaller wooden sculptures were probably modelled from the *Kama Sutra* or something like it. On the wall there were several paintings of nudes, men and women, some alone, some together. Those looked amateur so Lucy had probably done them. On a small table in the corner there was a box like the one at the Emporium. A velvet-lined display case with crystal penises and pewter nipple clamps. It was just as Pooley had said.

He didn't say a word. He walked calmly back to the other side of the screen. Went into the area where the other paintings were lined up. He didn't look at Mahoney, but peered into a stack of paintbrushes nose down in a jar of turps. Idly he pushed them around with his fingertips as if there was nothing much on his mind, then wandered around the canvases. They were mostly skyscapes: clouds, birds, a kite. All were painted in a shade of blue that reminded him of something. One of his exes in London had been an artist and she used to talk in terms of colours being saturated or clean, and of hues being at the blue or red end of the spectrum. Caffery had never fully understood, and he didn't have the words to describe this blue. Or to explain why it felt familiar to him.

'They're all the same colour,' he said levelly.

'She loved it.' Mahoney still hadn't made eye-contact. He was looking at his feet. 'Mixed it herself. Said it was her signature.'

Caffery was still for a moment. He stood among the paintings and studied Mahoney's grey suit.

'Colin, I never asked. What do you do? For a living?'

'Me? I'm a certified financial planner.'

'What? Like an insurance salesman?'

'I advise on indemnities.'

'You're an insurance salesman, then?'

'These days, we're more likely to call it a liabilities consultant. Or a risk-management agent.'

'But you're an insurance salesman.'

Mahoney raised his eyes and looked at him. Then he pulled out a canvas and held it up. It was only about two feet square and it showed a girl's face, very close. She wore a ribbon in her blonde hair. The same blue again. 'This was the first painting she did of Daisy.'

'Nice.' Caffery pulled out the photo of Susan Hopkins, held it up to Mahoney's face. 'Do you know who that is?'

Mahoney turned his head away from the photo as if it had a bad smell. 'There's no need to hold it so close.'

'I said, do you know who she is?'

'No, I've never seen her.'

'Know the name Susan Hopkins?'

'You already asked me on the phone, remember? I said no.'

'This is serious now. Really serious. Look at it.'

Mahoney put down the canvas, took the photo and peered at it. He shook his head and handed it back. 'No. Seriously. What's this about?'

Caffery put the photo in his jacket pocket. 'The case has been reclassified. I've been back to Lucy's friends. I know what they say about her past. About you.'

'I don't know what you're talking about. What on earth have they been saying?'

'That you've got a stick up your arse so high it'll choke you. That you left her. But not because you didn't love her any more. Because you couldn't handle what she was doing. Collecting all that stuff in there. Doing those paintings. Why didn't you tell me about it?'

'I didn't think it was appropriate.'

'Not appropriate – not *appropriate*? Stop using that expression, you pompous git. Don't you know how important something like this could be?'

'How could it be important? It was just her hobby. Just another of the things she collected. Frankly, it's embarrassing.'

'She could have been a prostitute. Don't you know how often hookers get killed?

Mahoney's face went a hard red. 'She wasn't a prostitute. She wasn't like that. This is just a hobby.'

Caffery put his hands on the windowsill and stood for a moment, getting his temper back. Out of the window the clouds and mists swirled around the base of Glastonbury

Tor, a lonely island on the drained Somerset levels, like an upturned pudding on the horizon. 'You're right. She wasn't a hooker. But that's not the point. You should have told me. She could have got involved with someone and they might be the one she was blackmailing.' He gestured to the other side of the screen. 'Is that why you got custody of Daisy? Did you use all that against her? See, I look at you and I can just picture the words "gross moral turpitude, your honour" coming out of your mouth. You're the type.'

'Don't be ridiculous. There was never any argument about where Daisy would go. None whatsoever.'

'Seems strange for the mother not to get custody.'

'It's not strange at all. I'm her father. I let Lucy see her, but she had no legal rights. She'd never adopted Daisy. Lucy was completely reasonable about it.'

Caffery glanced sharply at Mahoney. 'What did you say?'

'Lucy was completely reasonable about it.'

'No – before that. That she didn't adopt her.'

'Well, she didn't. Not officially.'

'She wasn't her real mother?'

'She was her stepmother. Daisy's real mother's dead.'

Caffery stared at him hard. 'No one mentioned she was her stepdaughter.'

'We didn't advertise it. For Daisy more than anything. She always thought of Lucy as her mum.'

'So what happened to . . .' He hesitated. He was thinking about the Caesarean scar – the botched one. Something was missing here. 'What about Lucy's other child?'

'Lucy's other child? There wasn't one.'

'Are you sure?'

'Perfectly sure. She never had children. Never wanted them.'

'And never lost a child?'

'No. I just said, there were no children. Only Daisy.'

Caffery opened his mouth to say something, then thought better of it. He could see from Mahoney's face that he really didn't know there had been a child. He returned to the window and stood for a while, pinching his nose, his eyes on the tor, letting his thoughts settle in the right places. If Lucy's Caesarean hadn't been for Daisy, it must have been *after* they'd separated. There *was* a child. But Mahoney didn't know anything about it.

'When you separated . . .' he said, eventually, 'Lucy wasn't pregnant, was she?'

'*Pregnant?* Good God, what are you saying?'

'I'm not "saying", I'm *wondering*. Just wondering. That's all. Did you tell me you didn't see her for a long time after the separation? Almost a year?'

Mahoney put his thumb to his right eye and pressed in the corner. He did the same with the left. 'I don't know what you're trying to tell me.'

Caffery didn't answer. He looked out of the window at the tor, his mind floating away. He wasn't sure. He wasn't sure it was the right way through this, but it was something. Something big. Lucy had had a child that no one knew about – none of the friends, and not even her ex-husband. She'd had a child. It had disappeared. And maybe, just maybe, that was why she was blackmailing someone.

Now all he had to do was find out who she was seeing after she'd left Mahoney.

46

The bank had carved itself offices out of a listed Georgian building in the centre of Bath. Frosted glass and fibreboard cubicles were crammed against the walls, a gap of almost eight feet between their tops and the corniced ceilings. At eleven a.m. the bank assistant found Flea a cubicle and they sat at opposite sides of a modern laminate desk, a computer screen between them, trading inconsequentials for a while and filling in forms.

'So you're police?' He looked at the badge on her polo shirt. 'Underwater search? What's that? Like the coast-guard?'

'Not really.' She'd learnt a long time ago there were only two responses to what she did for a living. Either a fascination that bordered on weird, or disgust. And usually the first thing anyone did was look at her hands and her clothing. In some countries jobs that connected you with death – undertaker, slaughterhouse worker – made you untouchable. As if death could rub off on you. 'What's that thing for?' she said.

'Hmmm? Oh, that. Panic button.'

'In case what?'

'You know.' He moved his tie knot. 'Sometimes customers get upset.'

'About?'

'Whether we'll give them a loan or not.'

'Do you think that's going to happen to me?'

He coughed and tapped a few more keys, studying the screen. Then he got to his feet and held up the folder he'd started. 'Will you excuse me? I'm going to have a word with my line manager.'

When he was gone Flea got up and went to his side of the desk to look at the computer screen. He'd logged out. The words 'Just 8% APR' flashed in blue on the screensaver and when she shook the mouse a log-on box came up. She wandered around the room, looking at the leaflets, the lifestyles you could buy for just eight per cent APR. Her head still ached. The polymer Elastoplast itched where it held together the edges of the wound on her cheek. She went to the frosted-glass doors and peered out at the people coming and going. At the door he'd gone through. He was taking a long time. She went to sit down again and tried not to fidget. Put her fingers to her temples and pressed hard to hold the headache in.

'Hello.'

He was standing in the doorway. He gave her a brief smile and shut the door behind him. Not so friendly now. He put down the folder, sat at the desk, got himself comfortable and logged on. The computer came to life, lighting up his face. He began tapping in numbers.

'You going to torture me?'

He glanced up. 'I beg your pardon?'

'Please don't torture me. If the answer's no, just say it. Have I got the loan?'

'Of course you have.'

'Of course I have?'

'In spite of the horror stories, we do still give out loans, you know. And you've got good collateral in your property, a good job, you've been a customer for twelve years. In fact, there was never any question you would get it.'

'You mean you always knew I'd get it?'

He squinted at her over his spectacles, as if he hadn't properly looked at her before, then went back to the computer: hitting a button, firing off a sheet on the printer. He made a couple of crosses on the paper and passed it to her. 'Sign here and here.'

She signed, pushed it back.

'Simple as that.' He recapped the pen. 'The funds will be ready for withdrawal in twenty-four hours.'

'Twenty-four—'

'Yes.'

'But that's a day.'

He looked at his watch. 'Tomorrow lunchtime.'

'That's no good. I need to be able to walk out with the cash.' She paused. 'OK, let's go for a different loan. One I can take out now. We can do the forms quickly.'

'There isn't a loan on offer you can walk out with today.'

'There has to be. Look at all these products. I don't care what interest you charge – I just don't care. Like you said,

I've been a customer for twelve years. I've got good collateral. There must be a loan I can . . .' She trailed off. He was looking at her pointedly, his eyes going from the scar on her cheek, to her police badge, to her hands. She realized she was half standing, hands on the arms of her chair. He raised his eyebrows, then glanced down at the panic button.

'Just testing.' She sighed and sat down. Forced a tired smile. 'Just testing.'

47

'Well?' Steve Lindermilk is sitting on the sofa. The french windows are open. It's a nice afternoon, and in the garden the pink azaleas are out. There's a rum and Coke at his elbow but he hasn't touched it. 'What did you want to see me about?'

Ruth smiles at her son. He's wearing jeans and trainers. An Umbro top with piping down the sleeves. He's got her legs: strong. And her nose. Not too much of the Lindermilk side in Stevie. None of that pushed-in face like with Sue. 'There was a question, darling. But there isn't any more. I just wanted to see you.' She raises her glass to him. Like it's his christening or a special event and she wants to toast how wonderful he is. She's feeling good this afternoon: only an hour ago she put the phone down to Little Miss PI. Little Miss PI who might not know how to dress like a girl but at least has a sensible head on her shoulders. She's come up with the money. It'll be delivered tomorrow afternoon. 'I just wanted to see my lovely boy. My lovely, lovely boy.'

He gives a weak smile. Crosses and uncrosses his legs.

Looks at the drink in her hand. Looks at the calico cat lying on its back at her feet.

'See you've got another cat.'

'Two, darling.'

Steve sighs. 'Two more?'

'Don't be like that. They were going into a rescue centre. What was I supposed to do?'

'You could always say no.'

'*You* might be able to harden your heart, Stevie, but I can't. Not ever.' She taps her glass. 'You don't want to start sounding like them out there, do you? Don't want to be one of those who hassles me?'

'Mum, there's a simple way round this. Put the telescope away. That's what's pissing them off.'

'No. I'm not taking it in. If they know I'm watching they might drive a bit slower.'

'Give it to me. I'll keep it safe.'

'It's not worth anything, Stevie.'

'I'm not interested in what it's worth, I'm interested in what they think. And for God's sake, Mum, stop taking photos. We don't want a repeat of what happened last time.' His eyes run over the photos of the seagulls and the cats and the guillemots. The dolphins. The beautiful creatures of this planet. He gets up and goes to the computer table. Leafs through the pictures she's taken of the neighbours in their cars in the mornings. 'I mean, look at this. They think you're spying on them.'

'Well, I am. And I need to. These are the innocents of the world I'm trying to protect, Stevie. The ones that never did anyone any harm. Whose side are you on, anyway?'

'Yours. Of course I'm on your side, always will be. But, Mum, the place looks nuts. And the more photos you take, the more rubbish you pile up, the more people think you're tapped. Just do me a favour. Stop taking photos, Mum. Bring the telescope in. And those stone cats on the roof have got to come down. They're embarrassing.'

'I like them.'

'*You* do but the rest of the village doesn't, does it? Looks like Hansel and fuckin' Gretel's gingerbread house. Just stop taking the photos. And get rid of the ones you've got.'

Ruth taps her tooth. The chipped one. Regards him thoughtfully. 'Do I embarrass you too, Stevie? Do I?'

Steve pushes away his drink. He looks uncomfortable. 'Of course you don't,' he mumbles.

'What's wrong with your drink, poppet? Don't you want it?'

'Nah. I'm driving.'

'One little drink won't do any harm. When your uncle got stopped he had three pints and half a bottle of wine down his throat and he still came up negative.'

'Thanks, Mum, but no.'

'You're a good boy, Stevie. A good boy.'

'Yeah.'

She chews her nails. Looks at the TV. *EastEnders*. Sound down. The drinks are making her warm. It's interesting how the private investigator found the money so quickly, she thinks. No quibbles. The full amount. It makes her wonder who the client is, because she's sure she can smell a little more money loitering around that particular honey-pot. Her appointment with the consultant is tomorrow morning. First thing. If he wants the money for the operation up front she'll take the fifteen K off the private eye and be happy with it. If he's prepared to wait for it, she'll have time to move the goalposts. Refuse the fifteen K when Little Miss PI comes at lunchtime. Ask for a bit more.

She studies her nails where she's chewed them. Pushes back the cuticle on one and holds out her hand to check the light bouncing off the varnish. 'Stevie? Do you want to know why I asked you here today?'

'I didn't think it was just because you wanted to see me.'

'You're right. I asked you here cos I wanted to give you a really nice present.' She smiles coyly at him. 'Something beautiful, Stevie. Very soon. I'm going to get you a – a Porsche. No – how much does a Porsche cost? Maybe something . . .' She blinks. 'How much does a Porsche cost?'

'Dunno. Eighty grand, should think. If you get it new.'

'Something like a Porsche. As good as a Porsche. Something black. Tinted windows. One of those SUVs you like.'

'Nah. You're all right, Mum. You save your money. Spend it on yourself.'

She leans across and presses her fingernails lightly into his arm. 'I'm in a comfortable position with money. You're going to see me, Stevie, one day not very far away, you're going to see me and you're going to be very, very proud.'

48

It was a cool evening with no hint of the heat from earlier in the day. Flea wore a Powerlite tank and shorts set and ran a two-hour circuit along the lanes that meandered lazily through the hills north of Bath. Years ago, before Mum and Dad's accident, she'd had boyfriends. Lots of them. One had been an ex-marine who'd trained in Quantico – they used to run together. He taught her the Fartlek technique, and she still used it: two-kilometre sprint, five-minute walk, then a long, loping run, extended stride, comfortable pace, interspersed every three hundred metres with sixty-metre sprints. Every ten sprints she checked her heart rate: average 173. Way further into the cardio range than usual. But it was what she needed today.

After ninety minutes she calculated she'd already gone over the lactate threshold twenty times. She should ease off into cool-down, drop back a little and come home on a jog. But she didn't. She kept pushing it to the wall, pounding the lanes until the sun dropped behind Bristol, until the shadows were long in the fields, until her legs were shaking. Until she was calm. She ran until the only thing she felt was a residual sadness – an ache located somewhere near her lungs – to remind her of her brother.

On the homeward leg, a narrow stretch of tree-lined road with a small stile and horse fields on her right, she thought she saw something at the entrance to the house. Something small like an animal. A large dog, maybe, standing on its hind legs, looking back down the dark lane towards her. She slowed to a jog. Narrowed her eyes. Whatever it was had gone. Must have been the shadows playing tricks with her eyes. There was nothing. Just the long straight trunk of the neighbour's eucalyptus tree at the edge of her drive.

She trotted on to the point and did a short circuit of the area, looking for anything out of the ordinary. The place was empty. The garden was silent. It was almost dark now and just a vague yellowish light came from the Oscars' windows high in the wall.

She began to unlock the door but stopped for a moment or two, sweat streaming off her, her mind working. Then she took the key out of the door and went about two yards along the wall to a place where the wisteria hung in heavy fronds.

For years it had been the family's habit to leave a spare door key on a nail under the wisteria. For emergencies. It was hidden behind the thickened stem so even in the winter it would only be visible to the initiated. She pulled aside the leaves and scrutinized it. It hung there just as it had for years: a little rusted, completely hidden. There was nothing different about it. She was sure. Nothing wrong. Nothing amiss.

She turned slowly, watching the stillness of the trees, the cold disc of the moon coming up, a Hallowe'en filigree of branches splayed in front of it. She thought about human feet disappearing above her in the bubbles. About Caffery: *Have you ever asked yourself if we missed someone that day? When we came to the squat?*

After the raid on the squat in Operation Norway, Wellard had complained he'd 'felt watched' when he was coming out of the building. 'Watched' was the word. They'd all felt it. And that night, when it was all over and she was at home, she'd had a moment of feeling something had been wrong about the arrest.

She unhooked the key from the wall, put it into her pocket and went inside. The empty hallway was cool, with just a moth battering the ceiling light. 'Hello?' she said. 'Hello?'

She switched on lamps in all the downstairs rooms, went into the garage and stood for a long time staring at the shape in the bath, at the places where the plastic showed over the rim. She'd been in here before the jog. Had scooped out the water earlier and refilled the ice. Nothing had moved since. Nothing.

She went into the kitchen and looked at the things on the shelf: her mother's pots and pans, her father's old safe, which no one could open and contained God only knew what. She took the key out of her pocket and put it on the mantelpiece. There were only two people who knew where the key was kept. One was Kaiser, her father's friend, and one . . . Well, one was Thom.

From somewhere above her in one of the bedrooms she

heard a small creak. She turned her face to the ceiling, her eyes watering a little. The hot water came on at six every night. Sometimes the pipes had a life of their own. They made the old house creak and complain.

She went into the hallway. The moon had come up and its light came through the half-glazed back door, giving everything fizzy, metallic outlines: the runner carpet, the polished floorboards on either side, the umbrella stand and the old carved mirror at the foot of the stairs. Her wellington boots stood patiently at the back door as if someone had just stepped out of them. They seemed a million miles away. As if the hallway had lengthened itself stealthily while she'd been in the kitchen.

The umbrella stand contained no umbrellas, but was full of bric-à-brac – a hunting stick, an old dog leash from a pet long dead, a malacca sword cane Dad had brought back from Poland years ago. Eyes on the staircase, on the dark gulf of the landing above, she went to the stand and silently fumbled the sword out of its sheath. She held it in front of her and went up the stairs. The boards squeaked underfoot.

The landing was dark. She went along the corridor with its lumpy floor and low ceilings. Into the bedrooms, quickly and quietly, following her professional search-and-clear training: her own room, Mum and Dad's room – their bedding in piles on the floor because she still hadn't found the heart to put it away. The room where Dad had slapped Thom that day. Two spare rooms at the end. Empty. There was no one here except herself and the hot-water pump.

She sat down on the top step, fished her phone out of her pocket and dialled Jack Caffery.

'I'm driving,' he said. 'I'll put you on speaker.' There was a pause and a clunk. Then she could hear the muffled thud and vibration of the car travelling at seventy m.p.h. somewhere out there in the night. 'What's on your mind?'

'Did you ever find him?'

'Find who?'

She rubbed her legs, trying to smooth down the goose-bumps that had broken out. 'The thing you were looking for, the Tokoloshe.'

'You thought I was mad. But it turns out I wasn't. There *was* someone else in the squat that day. Someone who escaped. His name is Amos Chipeta. He's an illegal immigrant.'

'How old is he? He can't be an adult. An adult would never have got out of that window.'

'But someone with a birth defect might. Ever heard of bone dysplasia?'

She massaged her temples, a slideshow of images starting in her head. There'd been an illustration of the Tokoloshe in a book on African superstition she'd read during Norway, and when she mentally superimposed it over the sort of images she'd seen occasionally in medical textbooks, she could see what Caffery was talking about. 'No,' she murmured. 'But I suppose I can imagine.'

'And you'll like this. Remember the free-diving stuff? Amos started his life like that, wreck-diving. Ends up dealing in *muti* and graduates to teaching our local thugs how to cut up bodies. Nice CV.'

'Jesus,' she murmured, thinking about the feet in the water. She'd been so cynical about those fifty metres, but some of the world's best free divers had started life wreck-diving. And then she thought about the spare key on the mantelpiece downstairs. Amos Chipeta taught the people on Operation Norway to cut up dead bodies. What might he do with what was in the garage? 'What's MCIU doing about him? Where is he?'

A pause. 'We don't know.'

'You mean he's out there?'

'Yes. He's hiding somewhere. Probably living rough. We don't know.'

'Is he . . . When you say cutting up dead bodies, you don't mean he's still dangerous?'

'Dangerous?' Another pause. The low throb of the car hurtling through the night. 'I don't know that either. But I think—' Caffery broke off.

'Yes,' she whispered, her arms very cold now. 'You think—?'

'The tor,' he said distantly. 'The bloody tor.'

'What?'

'Nothing,' he muttered. 'Nothing.'

And before she could answer he'd hung up. She was left holding the phone, the screen light dying, the noise of his car still vibrating in her ears.

She sat there for a long time, staring at the phone in her hand, her body cold. An illegal immigrant? Out there in the night somewhere? Creeping through hedgerows and forests?

She got to her feet, steeling herself to go back into the garage and check Misty Kitson's body again.

And that was when the knocking started at the back door.

49

The last few encounters Caffery'd had with Flea hadn't been exactly knockdown dragout fights, but they hadn't been exactly friendly either. So it was a surprise, an uncomfortable surprise, to hear her voice. Under different circumstances he might have used the opportunity as a springboard and dug a little deeper into why she'd been acting so bloody *odd*, but then the image of the tor slipped into his mind and a stark blast of light stopped that train of thought dead. He was in the fast lane of the M5, a boy racer in a Golf GTi right up his backside, when it happened. He cancelled the call and slowed the car so quickly the boy racer gave him the finger.

It was nearly ten at night. He'd spent half the evening trying to catch the thread of a lead into who Lucy had been seeing – who had fathered that baby and what had happened to the child. He'd got the warrant for the bank, to be served in the morning, and first light he'd be out re-interviewing the friends, Lucy's GP, and getting a second warrant signed by the magistrate for all the local labour wards to open their records for the last twenty months.

He'd done everything in his power. At half past ten, feeling beaten and running on empty, he'd left the office.

Now he dropped the phone and pulled across the carriageway into the middle lane, ignoring the Audi and the F signs. Glastonbury Tor. The shape, like a tall pudding, had been somewhere in his mind for the last couple of days, lingering on the edges. But it was only now that it made sense. He steadied the car in the middle lane, keeping the needle at a level seventy-five, gripping the wheel. He was seeing the reclamation-yard owner, James Pooley, looking down at the paperweights, making the shape of the tor with his hands.

You could line them up like this. Maybe on a windowsill, he'd said. *If there was something out of the window you wanted to draw attention to.*

That was why Pooley didn't have any sales dockets. Lucy hadn't paid him for those pieces. And the other paperweights Pooley had produced, bought because Lucy would have liked the colour, were exactly the same shade of blue as her paintings. How did Pooley know she'd like the colour if he'd never been inside her bedroom and seen the paintings? How did he know she had a view of the tor out of that studio window? Especially when she was so defensive about the room. Were they things that came up in natural conversation? He didn't think so. He thought it was Pooley who'd made that video of Lucy in the studio.

He called the crime-scene manager who'd searched Susan Hopkins's flat, but his phone was switched off so he left a message: 'Just wondering if there were any antiques in Hopkins's flat, or paperweights. Did the name "The

Emporium" come up at any time? Call me. ASAP, if you can, mate. Even if you get this at two a.m.'

Then he called someone at Control to check on James Pooley but the guy was clean. An electoral search brought up three James Pooleys – two in Wiltshire and one in Somerset. All three were at least an hour and a half's drive away. And then, as he was making up his mind which to hit first, he noticed he was passing the ring-road exit to Brislington. He indicated left and swerved off the motorway, swinging the car up over the bridge and pulling hard on the steering-wheel so the car headed south on the empty road.

The little industrial estate had a security guard in a booth at the entrance. He was fast asleep, a copy of the *Mirror* spread over his stomach, a yellow milk skin floating on his cold coffee. Caffery had to hammer on the booth to wake him up. He couldn't have been gagging to keep his job because he let Caffery in without a murmur, and even though he'd seen the warrant card and knew it was police business, once Caffery had driven through the barrier he didn't bother to watch, just went back to sleep.

At the back of the lot the first thing Caffery noticed was that the big twin sliding hangar doors of the Emporium stood open. Odd at this time of night – even with the guard on site. He killed the engine and wound down the window. There was no artificial illumination, only the milky light of the Bristol cityscape spilling down from the clouds, dimly bathing everything a uniform smoky grey. He could just make out the spectral outlines of the bric-à-brac stacked against the walls inside the hangar.

There were two cars parked about twenty feet away, their noses facing him. He was wondering about calling Control again and checking their indexes when a sound came out of the hangar. A sound that made the hairs go up on his skin.

He leant across and opened the glove compartment. The bling gun was in there, tucked behind a map and two packets of tobacco. Not to be used. He looked at them for a moment or two, then closed the glove compartment and checked his suit pocket for the ASP baton and the pepper spray. He got out of the car, closed the door silently, and walked quickly and quietly to the doors, stopping a little to the side so he couldn't be seen from within. The noise was louder here, and although he screwed up his face in concentration, he couldn't identify it. It might have been an animal, an injured fox panting. Or a child whimpering.

He opened his mouth to speak, because that was how it was supposed to be. You were supposed to warn people you were police and you were coming in. Give them a chance. A chance to do what? A chance not to panic? Not to shoot? Or just give them a chance to run? He flipped his jacket away from the radio clipped into his breast pocket so he could hit the red emergency button if he had to, then slipped inside the hangar.

The space was taller than he remembered, and higher. In the semi-darkness he sensed huge cavities arching above his head. The faint illumination from the city came behind him, and from ahead the dusty blue light of a computer or a fax machine filtered through the windows of the glass office cubicle. At the point he remembered seeing the customer pulling at the chandelier crystals he stopped.

Standing next to a low oak bench, one hand on the CS gas, the other resting on the bench to steady himself, he put his head back to concentrate on the sound. It seemed to be coming from everywhere and nowhere: as if it was ricocheting across the roof girders. What *was* it? It made his skin crawl because he was sure of one thing. It was made by something living.

There was a smell too. Old and unnameable, but familiar. He waited a beat, trying to place it, then realized it was coming from the bench he was leaning on. He turned, slowly, half of him not wanting to see what he had leant against. He raised his fingers. Rubbed them together. They were coated with something. He put them to his nose and sniffed. The smell made a cold line of suspicion move down his back. This was fat. Animal fat.

He remembered the bench from yesterday. A worn breaking bench with a vertical blade, about four foot high, gimballed at the head. Tanners would have used it to 'break' animal skin. To soften it. They would sit on it, working the skin against the blade. The skin would be from something as big as a deer or an elk. Or something as small as a dog.

The noise stopped.

He turned, his fingers lightly brushing the ASP, to face into the darkness. *Let's go outside*, he wanted to say. *Let's go out where there's a bit more light and where my car's waiting and I know I can get a signal on this piece of shit radio*. But instead he kept his voice low and level. 'I think we should talk,' he murmured. 'I suggest we switch the light on and talk.'

Silence. A group of bats wheeled through the overhead struts, the fragile *crack crack crack* of their lower-frequency chatter circling down to him.

'Are you there?'

He thought of the mad customer, endlessly sorting her chandelier crystals. He recalled the blunt, defeated expression in her eyes. He thought of the gun, sitting in the glove compartment.

'I said, are you there?'

A click behind him and a loud boom. He wheeled around as the huge double doors slid closed, cutting out the night, leaving him in the darkness with just the blue light of the computer and his thudding heart for company.

He pulled out the CS gas. Held it in front of him, arm rigid. Good job the gun was in the glove compartment because it could easily have been that. 'Don't fuck with me,' he said. 'I mean it. Don't fuck with me.'

The darkness lay hard up against his eyes as he moved the spray in an arc, ready to unlatch the safety button if something came hurtling at him. Every inch of his skin crackled, and his ears yawned open to pick up the smallest sound, the tiniest shift of air.

'I'm moving now,' he said. 'I'm coming towards the door.'

He took a few short steps, then stopped. His foot had connected with an object at knee height. As he pulled his leg back, he became aware that something was standing a few feet to his left. Something pale, spectral – something at head height, watching him. He didn't turn to it. He kept facing forward, the hairs all over his face and neck standing up stiff, trying to study the shape out of the corner of his eye.

A face, a pale, oval face, stared at him steadily from the darkness. About three feet away. Tall. Tall and big.

'I can hurt you,' he murmured. 'I'm trained and you're not. I can make you very uncomfortable. So step away from me.'

The face didn't move. Just went on looking at him.

'Step away from me, I said.'

Still no movement. Heart hammering, Caffery went through the move in his head, thinking of reaction distances and the effect of the spray – not just on the creep staring at him but on his own respiratory system.

One, two, three, he counted to himself. *One, two, three – and good to go.*

'Step back!' He held his left hand against his face, right hand forward. Protect your own eyes first. 'I said, step back, dickhead. *Step the fuck back*.'

Three seconds of spray, then he released the nozzle and dropped his hand, taking a clumsy pace back, knocking something over, the other arm across his face, squinting through the cloud of chemical. The shape hadn't moved. He lifted his hand slightly, his eyes watering from the chemical's kickback, his heart thrumming low and deep in his chest. It was still there. A motionless, smooth face, the gas running slowly down it, forming at the chin into a rivulet and dripping away into nothing. Eyes open and glassy, none of the coughing or vomiting he'd expected.

'*Shit*.' He dropped his head. Spat on the ground. '*Shit*.'

It was a fairground effigy, its brittle doll's face

impassive. He turned, breathing hard, to the doors. So where the hell was Pooley? Which avenue had he slid down? Which pile of furniture was he hiding behind? The doors, he thought. Start for the doors. He took a step forward. Felt his chest collide with something. Felt an arm lock around his neck, and a hand come up into his groin, immobilizing him and pulling him down.

50

Katherine Oscar stood on the back doorstep, hand raised ready to knock again.

'For Christ's sake.' Flea let the sword clatter down and leant back against the wall, her hand to her forehead. 'Christ's sake. Don't do that again.'

Katherine examined Flea's worn face. The way her hair hung in a shambles all over her shoulders. 'Good heavens. What's the matter?'

'I'm tired.' She shook her head. 'It's been a long day.'

Katherine answered with a brief, efficient smile, as if she hadn't heard. She seemed to enjoy catching Flea at her worst, stealing little victories from her every day: unwashed hair, out-of-date coats, no invitations to Ascot or Cheltenham. These were Katherine's scoring points. 'How are you, Phoebe? How is that bloody awful job treating you?'

Not waiting for an answer she stepped forward, craning her neck to peer round the front door and into the hall-way. Flea took an answering step sideways to block her view. Katherine was always trying to edge her way into the house and get a glimpse of the antique hoard she'd convinced herself the Marleys had amassed during their trips. There were a few things lying around in the upstairs rooms – African masks and Russian dolls and boxes of shells her father had pulled to the surface in Palau, the sword cane. But otherwise, Katherine was wrong: there was nothing of any real value.

There was a moment's silence. Then what Flea was doing seemed to sink in and Katherine took a step back. 'I'm *sooo* sorry. So sorry – I'm so rude. My mother always said I've got no manners.'

'How long have you been outside?'

'How long? Only a minute. Why?'

'You sure you haven't been looking through my window?'

'What a stupid idea. Of course I haven't.'

'Well, then.' Flea put her hand on the door, indicating the end of the conversation. 'I'll say goodnight.'

'The electricity-meter man was here today,' Katherine said. 'I showed him where yours is.'

Flea frowned. It was in the shed at the top of the driveway. 'You went into my shed?'

'Yes.'

'I never said you could go in there.'

'You weren't here. The poor man was ringing the doorbell for ages.'

'I could have phoned in the reading myself.'

'I was only trying to help.'

'Next time just leave it. I'll deal with it.' She inclined her head politely, and began to close the door. 'Goodnight, Katherine.'

'He was amazed when he read the meter. Said it was sky high.'

'Goodnight, Katherine.'

'He said you must have got lots of things running off the power. More things than usual.'

Flea stopped, the door half closed. Katherine's sculpted face was made into concentric circles by the half-glazed glass door. There was a moment or two's silence. Then she opened the door again. She knew her face had frozen. She could feel the blood stop under the skin, stop and go blue from cold. 'I beg your pardon?'

'He says . . .' Katherine glanced over her shoulder at the empty gravel drive, at the ornamental shrubs casting their shaggy shadows on the grass, as if she, too, suspected them of being watched. 'He says something in your house is eating electricity. He says he's never seen anything like it.' She let her gaze wander to the garage with the brown paper in the windows. 'He says you should have it checked out.'

Flea closed her eyes, then opened them slowly. The cold tick of fear was back. Somewhere down in her bowels. 'What are you implying?' she said slowly.

'Nothing. I only came over to tell you what had happened. And to ask if you've thought any more about—'

'No,' Flea said coldly. 'I haven't. My mind hasn't changed and it won't change. Now, goodnight.'

Katherine took a breath to reply, but apparently

thought better of it. She shrugged, turned on one foot and walked sweetly away, a little hand held up, the fingers wriggling.

Flea stood on the doorstep and watched until she turned the corner. Then she slammed the door, locked it and went into the garage. Everything was as she'd left it, nothing out of place. She checked the paper in the windows and that the bolts were run on the garage doors. She checked Misty's corpse hadn't been touched. When she was sure no one could have been in there or seen inside, she went back into the house and locked the inner door.

In the living room she took a decanter from her father's old oak bureau and uncorked it. This port had been open five years. It was crusted with sugar around the top and when the stopper came out the rich Christmas scent nearly floored her, with all the memories it brought of her dad, home from university in his outdoor coat and smelling of rain and cigarette smoke from the station platform, tipsy in a party hat on Boxing Day, sitting on the sofa asleep and smiling. Or standing in the study on a dry Saturday morning, his old Oxford shirt on, his glasses at the end of his nose, ponderously picking through the stones, occasionally calling into the kitchen, 'Jill, the granite – is this from the karst window in Telford or is it from Castleton?'

She found a crystal glass and filled it to the top, knocking back the liquid in one. She refilled it and drank again. Sat on the floor, her arms around herself.

If she was someone like Caffery's Tanzanian, Amos Chipeta, she wouldn't be shaken by Misty's body in the garage. She'd know what to do with it – it would be commonplace to her. But this situation wasn't commonplace. And she couldn't be controlled or sensible or easy about it. Not any longer. Not since Thom had betrayed her.

She looked at the clock. Eleven p.m. In thirteen hours she'd have the money. She'd have the photo of Thom.

And what she did then was anyone's guess.

51

'*I almost fucking killed you!*' Pooley shook Caffery furiously, forcing the blood into his brain, making his face bulge. They were on the floor where they'd both fallen, their heads up against a steamer trunk. Pooley's hands were on Caffery's collar. His breath was stale on his face. 'Did you hear me? *I could have killed you.*'

Caffery's guts screamed where Pooley had grabbed his balls to take him down. He could hardly breathe, but he groped blindly in his pocket for the ASP. Just as he was sliding it back, ready to crack it down, Pooley thrust him back against the trunk, then crawled away a small distance and collapsed in a sitting position, his back to a stack of Victorian stained-glass doors. Caffery curled up in a ball, gulping air.

'What are you doing here?' Pooley spat on the ground. 'How did you get past Security?'

Caffery fumbled the ASP back into his pocket and took a moment or two to recover. Slowly he sat up, loosening his shirt and tie. There were raw, raised areas around his neck where the fabric had dug into his flesh. When he swallowed, his Adam's apple was hard and sore. 'That.' He nodded to where his warrant card had fallen out of his shirt pocket and lay about three feet away on the polished concrete floor. 'My get-out-of-jail-free card.' He swallowed again, rubbed his throat. 'Why the vigilante stuff?'

'I thought you were a burglar. There was a break-in last week.'

'And what about that – that torture bench you've got over there? What've you been doing with it?'

Pooley glanced in the direction he was pointing. 'The tanner's bench?'

'Where did you get it?'

Pooley opened his hands wearily as if this was all irrelevant. 'From a tannery. Why?' He moved his head slightly and now Caffery saw, in the blue light from the computer in the office, that his face was wet. He'd been crying. The creepy noise like an animal panting.

Caffery pulled the warrant-card holder back, pocketing it. 'Why're you crying? Is it Lucy? You knew her more than you said, didn't you?'

Pooley shook his head. 'Christ, oh, Christ.'

'I'm right. Aren't I?'

'I miss her . . . I miss her so much . . . I never did the best for her, never. It would have pushed Jane over the edge if I'd left.'

'Jane? Your wife?'

'You saw her.'

'Your wife? Yesterday? With the chandelier?'

'She's not well.'

Caffery blew a little air out of his nose. Too bloody right

she's not, he thought. He felt in his pockets for the bag of tobacco he carried everywhere. Sod the Nicorette chewing-gum, but there were times, he thought, when you had to stick your good intentions and hotline nicotine into your system. 'How long had you been seeing Lucy?'

'Two years. Since she left *him*. Colin. Bastard.'

Caffery rolled the cigarette, using the tip of his tongue to moisten the gummed strip on the inside of the paper. 'How often were you with her?'

'Once or twice a week.'

'When your wife wasn't around?'

'On the days she goes to her family.'

'And the sex toys?'

'Purely aesthetic.'

'Really?'

'Really. She just thought they looked nice, that was all. Her ex, though, Colin, he never came to terms with it. Never.'

'Yeah. I know.' Caffery twisted the end of the rollie. Felt in his pocket for the lighter. 'So. Were you the only one? For Lucy?'

Pooley lifted his chin and stared at him, his eyes hard.

'No need to look at me like that – you see a woman once or twice a week and you don't expect her to hang around waiting for you while you're at home playing happy families.' He lit the cigarette and studied Pooley, squinting through the smoke. 'I'm just trying to make sure you were the baby's father.'

'The b—?' Pooley retracted his head, taken aback, frowning. 'What *baby*?'

'Don't give me that. Some time in the last two years Lucy Mahoney had a baby. What happened to it?'

Pooley dropped his arms limply. 'No,' he murmured, his voice a little scared, a little puzzled. 'No. You've got that wrong. There was no child.'

Caffery studied him. The guy was doing a bomb-ass acting job. 'Nah. I'm not falling for this. You can't magic a child away, no matter how hard you try.'

'I'm not,' Pooley said. 'Seriously I'm not. I don't know who you're talking about, but Lucy, *my* Lucy, she never had a *baby*.'

52

The call came through just before morning prayers. One of the nurses who'd worked with Susan Hopkins at the Rothersfield clinic had been with her boyfriend all night, her mobile switched off. The first she'd heard about Hopkins's death was when she'd arrived at work in the morning. She'd dialled 999 because she thought she knew something that the police didn't – something that none of the staff who'd been interviewed yesterday would know. Control told her to wait at the clinic. Someone would be right there.

Beatrice Foxton lived only a few miles away from the Rothersfield clinic. When Caffery called and told her they needed to talk she said it was time to walk the dogs anyway. There were fields surrounding the clinic, so why didn't they meet there before he went in?

They stood talking in the morning sun watching the two dogs run great loping circles around them. Caffery was smoking again, his shoulders slightly hunched, tension in his arms and neck.

'Lucy Mahoney.'

'What about her?' Beatrice was dressed for the summer in a white linen blouse, trousers and canvas espadrilles. Incongruously she wore a battered gardening glove on her right hand to throw the tennis ball for the dogs.

'She had an abdomectomy.' He looked up the driveway to the clinic, at the neatly cut lawns, the box hedges, the colonnades and the expensive cars in the car park. This was where Lucy's seven grand must have gone. James Pooley hadn't liked talking about the operation. Lucy hadn't wanted people to know about it, he said, and he didn't see why he shouldn't protect her privacy even though she was dead. But he did tell Caffery where she'd had it done. Up here at the Rothersfield clinic. The same place Hopkins had been working when she'd died. Whatever connected Mahoney to Hopkins had happened at the end of this driveway. Caffery just didn't know what yet. 'A tummy tuck. Two years ago, her boyfriend says.'

'I know.'

He sighed. 'I thought you might.'

'It was the scar that looked like a Caesarean. Remember? After you left I opened her up and her uterus hadn't been touched. She was G zero.'

'G zero?'

'Gravida zero. Never gave birth and had never been pregnant. The incision didn't go into the deeper aspects.'

'You said it was a mess. What did you mean?'

'Not untidy – there was a lot of skill there. And I mean a lot. But I got the feeling the surgeon cut far too low – lower than he needed. Cut away half her pubis. And she had a sympathectomy. It must have happened at the same time, judging by the healing.'

'A what?'

'She had the sympathetic nerve cut. It's the nerve that controls blushing and sweating in the face. Remember those nicks under her arms?'

He remembered them. Two scars in the armpits.

'It's the sort of thing you'd see if someone had had a lung biopsy done through a video-assisted feed. You insert a thin tube into the chest cavity and push the blade down through it. But in this case he was going for the nerves, not the lungs. Lots of people have it done. Usually it's a bloody disaster – they have to have it reversed. And that fails too. Surgeons in the States are waking up to it. They clamp the nerve now in case the patient changes their mind. We're a bit behind, though.'

Caffery saw Lucy's face on the video – *Welcome to my atelier* – remembered her hands fidgeting around her stomach. The way she wasn't blushing. It hadn't been something spiritual or a rise in confidence that had made the difference. It had been an operation. And somehow he'd missed it. He pulled hard on the cigarette. Everything – *everything* – he'd thought he knew about Lucy Mahoney before her death was wrong.

'Why didn't you—'

Beatrice held up a hand warningly. 'I know what you're going to say and you know what I'm going to say . . .'

'That it's all in your report? That I should've read it?'

'Did you?'

'We've been talking about nothing else for the last

couple of days. There must have been a moment you thought to say something.'

'I just asked, did you read my report?'

'You could have told me. That's all. You could have said something.'

'I could have told you lots of things.' She threw a tennis ball to the setter and it leapt away in the grass, its hindquarters bucking like a horse's. 'I could have told you she'd broken her ribs when she was, I don't know, about twelve. Or that she had bad teeth – four crowns and five root canals. I could have told you the colour of her toenail polish and the brand of her bra. None of those seemed relevant so I put them in the report and didn't talk to you about them. Cosmetic surgery two years ago not related to the cause of death isn't something I'd have flagged up. It's my job to think about cause of death, not ante-mortem behaviour, especially from two years ago.' She whistled at the dog, beckoning it to come back. 'That part, I'm afraid to say . . .'

Caffery sighed. 'Yeah, yeah. I know.' He pinched out the cigarette and put it back in his tobacco wallet.

That part was his job.

53

'I'm going to make an incision here – I'll go in through your Caesarean scar – then pull this part back.'

Ruth is sitting on an examination table. She's wearing her bra and her underpants. Her high heels are still on and she's resting her feet delicately, so as not to go through the strip of paper towel and mark the leather underneath. The room is well lit, airy and wood-panelled, with the surgeon's degrees framed and mounted. Outside a gardener is cutting the grass. No doubt about it, the clinic is top drawer. Not the sort of place that asks for money up front.

'We need to expose the muscles under here.' The surgeon lifts up the flesh around her abdomen. 'Then I'll pull them together like this. Remove a little of this fat and skin here. When you come round there'll be a couple of drains – one on either side. Just for the first forty-eight hours. Sometimes with an abdomectomy this muscle here, your rectus muscle,' he drew his finger down the front of her belly, 'can get a bit sore afterwards. It might make you feel nauseous too so I'll inject into it while you're under. OK?'

'OK.'

'You know there'll be a bit of discomfort?'

A bit of discomfort here? In the Rothersfield clinic with its fancy landscaped gardens and bellboys in smart little hats? With satellite telly in all the rooms and champagne cocktails on the menu if you're feeling well enough? She can deal with that. She pulls on her T-shirt and watches him squirt Spirigel on his hands, wipe them with a starched towel and go back to the big leather-topped desk. He's not good-looking. Not really. A bit dowdy. But he'll be loaded probably. Just the sort she needs.

He opens her notes and scribbles a few words with a scratchy Montblanc. Makes circles around the stomach of an outlined diagram. Pulls out a sheet of pink paper and starts filling in boxes.

'Do you smoke?'

Ruth wriggles into her skirt. 'No.'

'Drink?'

'Only if you're having one.'

He gives a small, pained smile. 'How many units do you drink each week?'

'I don't know. I'm a social drinker.'

'So, ten to twenty-one drinks a week?'

'That'll do it.'

'Live alone?'

'Now it sounds like you're asking me for a date.'

'It's a serious question. We need to know if you'll have someone to care for you on your discharge from the clinic.'

'Yes. I mean – I do. I live on my own. But I could

arrange for my son to come. He'd be happy to be there.' She buttons her skirt. This guy might be minted but he's got no sense of humour. She gets off the table and takes the seat opposite him, crossing her legs and tensing the muscles so her calves look nice. She rests her fingernails on her knee.

'My, uh, my niece works here. She recommended you.'

'Did she?' He doesn't look up. 'Kind of her.'

'She and I are very close. She tells me everything. She confided in me.'

'Confided?'

Still writing. Still not interested.

'Said she thought you were one of the best surgeons around.'

He looks up at this. 'Thank you. Always nice to hear.'

'I think she spoke to you about . . .'

'About a discount?'

She breathes out, relieved. 'That's right. A discount. She did speak to you.'

'Yes, she did. Marsha will deal with it. My secretary. When you make the appointment she'll take you through all that. I've got some spaces late June.'

Ruth narrows her eyes. 'When do I pay?'

'Marsha will invoice you.'

Her heart jumps. Invoices take days. Weeks. Time to milk Little Miss PI a bit more. 'When?' she says.

The surgeon looks up. 'Don't worry about that,' he says. 'We'll be in touch after the procedure.'

54

Rothersfield clinic wasn't dissimilar from the Farleigh Park Hall clinic to look at, Caffery thought, with its oak-panelled waiting rooms, marble staircase and rooms with sliding glass doors that led out on to sweeping lawns. But there the similarities ended. Here, there was a porter service, five-course meals chosen from handwritten menus, and no one expected you to clean the toilets as part of your treatment. Chauffeurs waited in the driveway in their Mercedes and Bentleys for their rich employers to recover from their facelifts.

In a little office at the back of the building overlooking a knot garden, where one or two patients were wandering in their towelling robes, the nurse, Darcy Lytton, was waiting for him. Not yet changed for work, she looked the part of the girl rumpled from a night with a boyfriend: she wore scruffy Atticus skinny jeans, a studded belt and a black T-shirt with the words 'Don't make me kill you' slashed across the chest. Her eye makeup was last night's too: it was smudged into the folds under her brown eyes. She sat with her hands jammed between her knees, biting her lip. She'd been crying.

'What's happening?' She'd got up as he came in. 'Did she kill herself? Did she leave a note?'

'Darcy?'

'Yeah.'

'I'm Jack. Jack Caffery.'

She shook the hand he held out. Her palm was damp, cold. 'Did she say why? In the note?'

'Sit down.'

She did so and he sat next to her, his feet set slightly apart, his knee not far from hers, his head bent down a little so he could look up into her face.

'It's hit you hard, hasn't it?'

'It's not exactly what I was, y'know, expecting when I came into work this morning.'

'You up to talking?'

'I've said a lot of it already – I've told them how I . . .' She turned smudgy eyes to Caffery. 'I keep thinking there was something I should've done.'

He put a hand on her shoulder. Stupid thing to do, maybe, because strictly speaking he shouldn't even be here on his own with her. You never knew what accusations people were capable of. The East European girls in the Dover pens had developed a habit of waiting until they were on their own with a cop, shoving their hands inside their panties, then wiping their fingers on the cop's hands before he knew what was happening. Screaming assault – and who was going to deny it when the DNA popped up from the swabs? Cops were taught to travel in pairs these days. But this girl looked like she hadn't the resources left to go to the toilet on her own, let alone accuse him of assault.

'I'm police too,' he said. 'But the questions I've got might be different from the ones they asked you on the phone. Is that OK?'

'What was in the note?' Darcy pressed a balled-up handkerchief to her nose. 'The suicide note?'

'She was unhappy. Said she felt abandoned.'

'Not abandoned. I just can't believe it. She had loads of friends. Her parents are great, really cool – for parents, y'know. And Paul was coming off the rigs. It was all she could talk about. She'd spent most of the week getting ready.'

'You knew her well?'

'Years ago, we used to do everything together. We had a bit of a – I don't know – a bust-up about six months ago and since then we've kind of avoided each other, but not seriously, you know. We kept it light after that so we didn't have to talk about the argument. But we'd still socialize at work – laugh and gossip and that.'

'Control tells me you last saw her yesterday lunchtime.'

'In the locker room. I was getting changed, ready to meet my date. She was going to the loo. I'm standing there looking in the mirror and I've seen her come out and wash her hands and . . . and that's why I'm sort of . . .' She bit her lip. 'That's why I'm sort of screwed up by it all because I think she wanted to tell me something and I was in a hurry so I didn't listen. I thought about calling her later, but when I did her phone was switched off. I didn't leave a message.'

'Her phone was off when she was found and the log was wiped. Was she in the habit of wiping the log?'

'I don't think so. One thing I *do* know is she would never switch her mobile off. Never.'

'So tell me again – what happened in the changing room?'

'It was her face. She . . .' Darcy paused, clearly trying to think how to explain it. 'You know if someone has just seen something but they can't believe *what* they've seen? They get this sort of look on their face, like they think someone's having a laugh or something, but they're not sure.' She wiped her eyes again. 'I was in a hurry so I looked in the mirror and I go, "What's up, Suse?" and she shakes her head and she's like, "Do you know any of the recovery nurses?" And I go, "No, why?" And she's like, "I think they're all a bit thick – not to see what's going on under their noses." '

Caffery raised his eyebrows. Darcy nodded. 'I know. But I'm the thick one cos I was only half listening, thinking she's getting into some bitching session about the other nurses, and then she goes: "I'm going a bit mad. I think I've just seen one of the surgeons stealing something." '

'Stealing what?'

'She didn't say. I don't think it was money or valuables. It was the way she used the word "*stealing*". Like it wasn't quite the right word. Like it was the nearest she could come to it. And later, when I'm thinking about it, I'm convinced whatever she wanted to tell me was well weird. It was written all over her face, like she'd seen something really horrible.'

'Where had she come from?'

'The operating theatre.'

'Did she say which surgeon it was?'

'No. She'd have worked with a few yesterday, I think.'

There was a moment's silence. She looked back at Caffery, not understanding the impact of what she had said. 'God, I'm sorry,' she said. 'I'm not much help, am I?'

'Don't be sorry,' Caffery said. He had to avoid the instinct to pat her shoulder again. 'Don't be sorry at all. You've been very helpful.'

55

The manager of the clinic couldn't think what Susan Hopkins had meant by 'stealing'. The patients shouldn't have anything of value in the recovery room: everything would have been placed in the clinic's central safe upon admission. Signed for. She showed Caffery the register as proof. Her day wasn't exactly working out as she'd planned it, and Caffery could sympathize with that, but he didn't think it excused her rudeness. She was as tight-lipped as a camel's backside in a sandstorm. And when he asked for the details of all the surgeons Susan Hopkins had been working with yesterday, that really tore the lid off for her. The clinic rented the space and facilities to the surgeons, she insisted, that was all. She'd happily give him the names of the three surgeons Susan Hopkins had been rostered with, but absolutely no details of the operations performed and under no circumstances details of the patients. He was welcome to take his chances with the surgeons' secretaries, but medical secretaries were notoriously hidebound about things like this, and, she explained, looking down her nose at him, she didn't fancy his odds without a warrant.

But she was wrong, as it turned out. The secretary who managed the books for two of the surgeons, Davidson and Hunt, was sweet-faced. She knew Susan Hopkins and had heard what had happened. The whole clinic was talking about it.

'I want to look into their records.'

'I'm not supposed to tell you anything.' She stood at the door of her office anxiously, her back to it as if she was guarding a treasure. 'You know that, don't you? I'm supposed to wait for a warrant.'

'Susan didn't commit suicide. Has that part of the news reached you?'

'That's what some of them have been saying.'

'There might be other cases we're linking her death to. Can you see what I mean?'

She didn't answer. She was so pale even her mouth had lost its colour.

'A serial killer.' He leant in to hiss the words. The silver bullet. The most frightening words a woman could hear. 'I'm saying we might be talking about a serial killer.'

The secretary bit her lip. Looked down the corridor to check they weren't being watched. 'Oh, Christ.' She stood back to let him in. 'I could get the sack for this. Quickly. Close the door.'

She went to the other side of the desk and leant over the computer, shook the mouse and the screen came to life.

'We've been having trouble with the server. The men are due this morning, but it's still . . . Ah – there. Now, what am I looking for?'

'Both surgeons' lists for the beginning of May two years

ago.' Caffery came to stand next to her and watched her scrolling through. 'Specifically a tummy tuck and a sympathectomy in the same op.'

'We keep records going back five years. You never know what claims people are going to cook up. I'm pretty meticulous about it. There.' She stopped scrolling. 'Mr Davidson did an abdomectomy on the fifth – that's about it. After that it was mostly rhinoplasties. Mr Hunt did three corrective operations on the fourth – that's one of his specialities, scar revision. You know, they come in with some other surgeon's botches. He's good, Mr Hunt. Really good. No sympathectomies.'

'Who did you say did the abdomectomy?'

'Mr Davidson. Paul.'

'Patient's name?'

'Karen Cooper.'

'Nothing under the name Mahoney?'

'No.' She tapped her pen. Looked at the screen. 'That's all. The names might be fake – people get embarrassed: we can't control that – but the ops in the system aren't. That was the only abdomectomy in those three days. And nothing on the sympathetic nerve. Not for Mr Hunt or Mr Davidson. I don't think I've ever known either of them do that operation anyway. I'm sorry.'

Caffery got up and put his business card on the desk. 'Where's Mr Gerber's secretary?'

'At the end of the corridor. There are three secretaries in there. You need Marsha. If you get lost just follow the cold air.'

'The cold air?'

'That's me being bitchy. I'm just saying, good luck walking into Marsha's domain without a warrant and asking for a peep at her surgeon's records. If you know what I mean.'

'Not very amenable?'

'The words "blood" and "stone" come to mind. Or "Cruella".'

'Thanks,' Caffery said. 'Thanks for the tip.'

56

There were three work stations in the office but it was coffee break and only one was occupied. By Marsha. The indomitable Marsha. She was tall and stately with perfectly black hair cut in a blunt line at her shoulders, rather orange skin and oval, black-lined eyes. If she knew about the Cruella tag she was playing up to it. She was dressed in a long pencil skirt, killer stilettos and a bat-winged purple blouse. Her lips were done in dark, heart-attack magenta. Not one to be messed with.

'Hi.' Caffery looked round the office, found a chair and sat, his hand in his pocket, fingers on the mobile-phone number pad. 'Are you Mr Gerber's secretary?'

'Who wants to know?'

Good start, Cruella. With his free hand he fished out another of his business cards and put it on the desk. 'Is Mr Gerber here?'

'No.'

Marsha studied the card. The computer screen was turned away from everything – from the window, from the door. She'd made sure no one would be sidling up behind her and looking at the screen.

'Is he due in today?'

'No. He's already been in. Not coming back until Friday. What's this about, please?'

In his pocket he hit the phone keypad. The ring-tone sang out.

' 'Scuse me.' He stood, went to the door, pulled out the phone, his finger still on the ring-tone button, looked at the display then took his finger off. The noise stopped.

'Hello?'

Marsha watched him stonily from the desk.

'Gotta take this call,' he mouthed. 'I'll be right back.'

He slid away, pretending to talk, stopping at the bottom of the corridor, out of earshot from the offices. He dialled Reception.

'UPS here. I've got a delivery for a Mr Gerber. Have I got the right number?'

'Yes.'

'I'm coming off the A432. I'm only a few minutes away.'

'Come down the second track on the right. It's signposted.'

'I'm tight on time. Need to just drop and fly. Can you get someone to come out and meet me at the front?'

'I don't know. This is getting to be a habit with you guys.'

'Yeah – I'm sorry about that.'

'I can't always do this, you know.'

'You'd be helping me out.'

'Oh, ho ho. Now *there*'s an incentive.' The receptionist

sighed. 'Leave it with me. I'll get his secretary to wait for you. But just this once.'

'Good girl.'

By the time he got back to the office the phone call had already come from Reception. Marsha was on her feet, replacing the handset. 'I've got to go. I won't be long.'

'That's OK.' He sat down. 'I'll wait.'

She looked at him, looked at the chair he was sitting on. Then she looked at the computer. She bent over and, very coolly, very deliberately, logged out of the session. Taking her handbag off the back of the chair, she gave him a tight smile. Caffery smiled back and held up his hand. If you can't trust a cop who can you trust? That was what his mother used to say. It had always made his dad laugh.

When she'd gone he went to the window and waited for her to appear on the gravel driveway. She came out with her chin held high. Taut and controlled, arms crossed, looking off down the driveway. In his thirty-nine years' experience he'd learnt that girls who dressed and behaved like Marsha never followed it up in the bedroom. Guys would get fantasies about whips and leather and being sat on, but girls like Marsha wanted more gentleness between the sheets than the ones who wore angora cardigans. Out of the bedroom, though, the Marshas of the world could be true predators. She'd got him – nailed him with logging out like that. This was going to end up with a sodding warrant. More time wasted.

He looked back at the computer. No, he thought. Not a chance he could get into it. Not a chance in hell. But then, he reasoned, it would be rude not to try. He went to her chair and sat in it, staring at the log-in screen. Two empty spaces – USERNAME and PASSWORD. The choke point – and in the movies it'd always be on the third try that the hero got the password. He searched the desk for clues. Nothing. Ran his hands over the computer, opened the drawers and felt up under them for taped pieces of paper. Nothing. He turned Marsha's nameplate to face him. Marsha Wingett. Typed 'm.wingett'. Thought, What the fuck? and typed 'Cruella' into the password box. Hit enter. The message flashed up. *Oops! Have you forgotten your password?*

He deleted Cruella. Typed in: 'Cruella1'. Hit enter.

Oops! Have you forgotten your password?

It was like being heckled. And he knew there wasn't long. Marsha wasn't going to stand out on the gravel all morning waiting for a non-existent parcel.

'Cold bitch'?

Oops! Have you forgotten your password?

'Five eight seven QU zero.'

A woman stood in the doorway, watching him expressionlessly. Sandy blonde hair tied at her neck, a handbag over her shoulder and – who'd believe it? – a pink angora over her shoulders. She was holding a cardboard Starbucks carry-out tray with a coffee on it. Car keys dangled from her fingers.

'I beg your pardon?'

'I said, "five eight seven QU zero".'

'Her password?'

'Yes.'

He typed in the sequence. Hit enter.

Have you forgotten your password?

He looked at the woman. She looked back at him.

'Uh?' he said, waiting for her to speak.

She made an impatient noise in her throat, tipped sideways a little and studied the screen. She had little white pearls in her ears. 'The username's wrong. No dot after the initial.'

'I should have known that.'

'Yes. *You* should.'

'Server's acting like a mule. Everything's going snail's pace.'

She looked at him as if he'd just changed colour right in front of her eyes. 'I know. I was the one who reported it to you.'

Caffery closed his eyes. Opened them. What were the chances? 'Yes. Of course you did. Thank you for that.'

'That's OK. What time will you get to mine?'

'Twenty minutes. As soon as this is done.'

She went to the desk in the far corner, set down the coffee, took off her angora and hung it carefully on the back of the chair. Baby pink. She'd be the one who'd walk over you in stilettos, he thought, deleting the dot. He hit enter and the screen lit up in front of him. All of Gerber's consultations today.

It was the same system the other secretary had used and, having seen it in action once, it was easy for him to hop-skip backwards even though the database was working slowly, the diseased server grinding its cogs like a dray horse. He went back through the timeline two years and found the days in question. The name Lucy Mahoney came out at him like a bolt. At ten o'clock on the morning of 4 May she'd been given an abdomectomy and a sympathectomy by Georges Gerber FRCS.

Georges Gerber FRCS.

One hundred and eighty. Got you, you bastard.

He closed the database, logged out and stood up just as Marsha appeared in the doorway.

'Hello.'

She gave him a courteous smile. 'Are you leaving?'

'I'm going to talk to Mr Gerber.'

'He's not here.' She looked beyond him to the chair he'd been sitting in. 'I think I mentioned that earlier.'

'Do you know where he is?'

'At home?' She came past him, and stood for a moment looking at the chair again. Then she hung her handbag over the back and sat on it – tentatively, as if she thought it might burn her or give way. 'Probably at home, I don't know. I tried to call him a few minutes ago. He didn't answer his phone.'

'Thank you, Marsha. You've been a great help.'

He was at the door when she said his name. He waited. Hand on the door. Turned back slowly. From the other desk the pink angora girl had stopped what she was doing and was watching over the top of the monitor.

'Yes?'

'I just saw the other secretaries. They said you were looking for patient records.'

'That's right.'

'The database is a bit slow but it's still working.' She pulled the keyboard towards her. Logged on and the screen came up. 'I can go through Mr Gerber's records, if you'd like?'

Caffery stood half in, half out of the door, and looked at her black hair, her little curranty eyes. Wanted to laugh for a moment. He thought, Marsha, bless every hair on your head, I take it all back. You're an angel, a Samaritan. And probably a vixen in the sack. 'Thank you,' he said. 'But I'll speak to Mr Gerber directly.'

'In that case I'll print out his home address for you.'

57

Home and Away's just finished and Ruth's pouring her third rum and Coke when someone knocks at the door. She checks the clock. Only one p.m. Little Miss PI said later in the afternoon. It annoys her to think she might be early. She's been trying to work out how to approach the subject, how to go about upping the amount. Maybe it's the rum but she hasn't got it sorted in her head yet, and that annoys her.

Another knock. Irritated, she sets her drink down, goes into the hallway and puts on the safety chain.

'Yeah, what?'

But when she looks out she finds Mr Gerber, the surgeon from the clinic, standing on the doorstep. The last person she was expecting. He's wearing something strange. Like a tunic made out of denim, but there's a bottle of champagne in one hand and a sheepish smile on his face.

'Ruth?'

'Yeah?'

'I'm sorry.'

'Sorry about what?'

'I shouldn't be here.'

'Why not?'

'It's not ethical. If I wore a hat,' he gives a rueful laugh, 'I'd have it in my hands now.'

She opens the door a crack more, puzzled. He looks odd out here in the sunlight. He's got very fine bones, a tiny nose and a thatch of wiry hair shot with grey threads, which he keeps running his fingers through nervously.

'When I asked if you lived alone, Ruth, it wasn't my place to do that. That's the clinic staff's job.'

'Eh?'

He bites his lip and glances up and down the road. Looks back at her again and something dawns on her. She thinks about the Mercedes and the Aston Martins she saw in the staff car park at the clinic that morning. She thinks about sitting down at the pub, waiting for someone to speak to her. And then she thinks about the way she'd arranged her legs sitting opposite him earlier on.

'My first name is Georges,' he says.

'Hello, Georges.'

'Can I come in? I won't stay long. Not if you don't want me to.'

She opens the door, lets him in and he walks down the corridor, looking from left to right. She follows, stopping for a moment in front of the hall mirror to dig out clumps of mascara from the corners of her eyes. Quickly she puts the wad of gum she was chewing in an ashtray, cups her hands round her mouth and checks her breath.

When she gets to the living room he's standing in the middle of the carpet.

'Nice place.'

She adjusts the strap on her bra and makes sure her breasts are sitting up high. Noticeable. 'Would you like a drink?'

'That'd be nice. If it's not too much trouble. What're you having?'

'I'm . . .' She indicates the drink sitting on the bar. 'Rum and Coke. But I can get you something else.'

'Rum and Coke.' He smiles. He really isn't all that bad-looking. Just needs a bit of grooming. 'Sounds perfect.'

He sits politely on the sofa, his feet together, and watches her mix the drink. When she turns to hand him the glass, she finds he's holding out the champagne in both hands. 'I think this needs to be chilled.'

'Oh, yes.' Veuve Clicquot. Stevie loves Veuve. She puts the glass on the table next to him and takes the bottle. It is a little warm. She carries it into the kitchen and puts it in the freezer, packs a bag of ice round it. When she comes back into the room Georges is standing next to the bar, looking at the photos. In the middle there is a picture of a dolphin in Greece. She stands shoulder to shoulder with him.

'Lovely animal.' She picks up her drink from the bar and takes a sip. 'Isn't it?'

Gerber turns and looks steadily at her. 'I can think of something lovelier.'

She wants to giggle, but stops herself short. Georges isn't the sort to appreciate giggling. He's serious. Classy. So she smiles and points at another photo.

'My ex-husband. And my son. He lives near by. Drops

in from time to time. But otherwise I'm on my own. Like I said.'

'I'm sorry I quizzed you like that. I'm sorry about all of today. You made me nervous. That's all.' He sits down on the sofa. 'I made a mess of the whole thing.'

'No, you didn't. You were lovely, just lovely.'

He gestures at the wall. 'Tell me about the dolphins, then. You're quite a sailor, I take it.'

Gratified by his interest she sits on the recliner and arranges her skirt nicely. She starts to talk about the animals, the dolphins in Greece, the guillemots she saw flying over a harbour near Sitges once. He lets her lead the conversation. Asks her lots of questions: what's it like living on a boat? Is she happier on land? Do the cats prefer it here? He supposes it's nice that she can keep so many animals. He really is quite lovely, she decides. Appearances can be deceptive.

'You've finished your drink.'

She looks at the glass in her hand and sees he's right – it's empty. They've been talking a long time. His drink is still untouched on the table next to him. He twists in the chair and looks towards the kitchen. 'What about that champagne? Do you think it's cold yet?'

She gets up and goes into the kitchen. She takes the champagne out of the freezer and pulls down two crystal bowl glasses Stevie stole from a restaurant in Sardinia. While she's uncorking it she has a moment of dizziness. She puts the bottle down and leans on the work surface to steady herself. This isn't like her. A few rums can't put her on her back usually. She scoops a little water straight out of the tap into her mouth, dries her mouth on the tea-towel and continues with the champagne. It's open and both glasses are poured when she feels strange again. She puts down the bottle noisily and within seconds Gerber is at her side.

'Are you OK?'

'Fine.' She smiles. 'Feel great. Just a little—'

She puts out a hand and he takes her under the arms, then leads her through into the living room. Helps her into the armchair.

'Do you feel faint?'

'Feel strange.'

'I know why. When I took your blood pressure earlier, I thought then it needed to come down.'

'My blood . . . What did you say?'

'Don't move. I've got some tablets for it.'

'Tablets? My blood pressure's always OK. The doctor says it's good for my age.'

She looks down. He has taken a small brown bottle out of a pocket and is shaking white tablets into his palm. The pills seem huge and very white in his hand.

'What are they?'

'They'll bring the pressure down. Make you feel better straight away.' He nods to the computer. 'What's the password?'

'My password?' She puts a finger to her head. The room seems smaller than she remembers it. 'Why do you want to . . . ?'

'I need to check a dosage. What's the password?'

'Stevie21.'

'And how much do you weigh?'

'How much do I . . . ? I don't know.'

He goes to the computer and she hears him tapping keys. Her head's too heavy to turn and look. She rests it on her hand and imagines for a moment that it's made of stone, like a statue's, and will crack if she moves it. Gerber comes back and drops loads of tablets into her hand.

'So many?'

'They're homeopathic.'

Homeopathic. She's heard of that. She puts them into her mouth and takes the glass of Coke he's holding out. The tablets are bitter and scratch her throat but she swallows them in two gulps.

'I think you need to go for a drive. Get some fresh air. Where's your car?'

'Outside,' she mutters. Her mouth seems full of dust. 'Outside in the . . .' She tilts her head back. Tries to focus on him. 'Over there next to the patio.'

She tries to push herself to her feet but she can't. And instead of it worrying her, she finds she couldn't care less. Her feet are a long, long way away. Her legs are just fuzzy poles of light. She looks at her shoes and thinks: Beautiful, beautiful shoes. Red and shiny like rubies. Thank you, God, for lovely shoes.

'Your keys.'

Gerber is next to her. Shaking her. She lifts her heavy eyes.

'Where are your keys?'

'I think I need something to eat.'

'No, you don't. Just tell me where your keys are.'

'In the hallway. Hanging up.'

'The front-door keys too?'

'Yes. But why do you need my door keys?'

Instead of an answer all she hears is the distant sound of birdsong. And when she tries to see where he is she realizes he's left the room. She drops back into the chair and her eyes roll upwards into the lids. She sees constellations of light and electricity. She sees dolphins jumping and ruby red shoes. 'There's no place like home,' she murmurs, smiling. 'No place like home.' She floats to the stars and Stevie's there next to her, holding her hand.

Mum, I think you'd better get up now. Come on. Get up.

Hello, Stevie, darling. You're a good boy. A good boy.

Listen to me. Get out of your fucking chair. Bitch.

Stevie – what're you talking about?

Shut up about him now and—

Her eyes open. The light is too bright. Georges is there, his face close up. He's smiling.

'Get out of your chair,' he says encouragingly. 'Get out now.'

She pushes herself up. He's wearing gloves, she thinks. Didn't notice that before. He's wearing latex gloves. But, then, everything today is strange, really strange, like a dream.

He puts his hand under her elbow and she lets him lead her to the door.

58

Years ago a trainer had told Caffery that if he ever felt faint on parade he should look at something green: a lawn, a tree. Colours had an effect on the brain – stopped it freezing and giving up – so when he got out of the car in the quiet country lane outside Georges Gerber's house he stopped for a moment and rested his eyes on the grassy bank. His head was sluggish and staticky from lack of sleep. He needed it to be clear.

Darcy said Susan Hopkins had caught Gerber stealing. Lucy had been blackmailing him: maybe she'd threatened to take him to the GMC over the abdomectomy. Maybe she'd also witnessed the stealing, or whatever had been happening in the recovery room. It had taken him two years to get fed up with the blackmail and kill Lucy. With Susan Hopkins it had been quicker. Maybe she'd confronted him. Maybe he'd already been stirred up enough by Lucy's murder to have killed again in quick succession.

An early butterfly flapped its lonely way across the lawn, then over the hedge that grew alongside the house, attracted by the blue of a disused swimming-pool. It was very clean – no slime growing on the painted blue walls. He stood on tiptoe and looked past it. About twenty feet on was the distinctive sand mound and manhole inspection cover of a septic system. The house itself was to the right: square and grey, set a long way back from the quiet lane. Everything was tidy, very well kept. Tidy but wrong, Caffery thought, dropping back on to his heels. In spite of the tidiness something felt out of kilter.

He licked his palm, pushed it through his hair and buttoned his jacket. The house had two entrances, one a blue-painted front door to the left, which looked as if it went into the main house. No one answered when he rang this bell so he went to the other entrance, where the house had been extended into a low-roofed building running out at an angle. The stone extension had shuttered casement windows, a narrow portico, and a small porch with an antique foot-scraper built at the left-hand side. He rang the bell. Waited, looking at the brass sign screwed to the front door: Georges Gerber FRCS (Plast) engraved in ornate script.

No answer. He went along the side of the house, glancing into the windows as he went. At the end he stopped. The shutters were closed. He got his Swiss Army Hiker from his pocket and prised off the catch. Pulled the shutter wide.

About ten centimetres into the room, a breezeblock wall had been constructed. He put his nose to the glass. The wall stretched up as far as he could see, and out to the sides as far as he could see. There was an airbrick about six blocks to his right.

Oh, goody, he thought, smiling against the pane. Oh, goody, Mr Gerber, I smell your blood.

59

In South-east London there had been long, complex issues around stop-and-search laws. When Caffery was a PC, his inspector had adopted a head-in-the-sand solution to the problem and thrown most of his manpower into meeting quotas on other crime. Breaking and entering fell to Caffery. In two short months he'd learnt a lot about the clever ways people had of getting into other folk's houses.

He drove six miles down the road to a village iron-monger's and got some of the things he needed. The rest Gerber had generously provided: in the unlocked maintenance shed near the pool. Didn't people know about locking sheds? Hadn't it sunk in yet? You were just as likely to have your shed burgled as your house. Hey, Georges, he thought, it's difficult to comprehend this slack attitude to security. He carried the stepladder and the power drill to the side of the house so that he was hidden from the road. He would hear a car on that lane from miles away. There'd be time to hide the tools if anyone appeared.

Whatever Gerber was getting up to in that strong-room

he wouldn't be wanting a key-holder or the police rolling in if the alarm ever went off. Which meant that the system probably wouldn't be connected to a control centre, and was probably designed just to unnerve an intruder. Even so, Caffery chose a point about ten metres from the house and snipped the telephone wire. He carried the ladder back to the house, fitted a 9 mm bit in the drill chuck, climbed to the alarm box and made a hole in the 'T' of the company name, right where the print was at its darkest so it wouldn't be visible from a distance. He shook a canister of expanding foam, eased the nozzle into the hole and filled the interior of the box until the face plate made a low noise and popped out a little. He placed a square of black gaffer tape across the strobe unit, climbed back down and returned the stepladder to the shed.

The house and the grounds were silent. Not a single car or truck or motorbike had passed on the lane the whole time he'd been there. Things could happen out here and no one would know. To the left of the front door there was a small window with pebbled glass that looked as if it belonged to a toilet. He gaffer-taped the top vent and smashed it with the butt of the drill. Reached in, undid the latch on the big window. Climbed through, on to the toilet lid, jumped down and went out into a flagstoned corridor.

Somewhere in here would be the internal box. When it let go, the noise would be mind-numbing. He had maybe ten seconds left.

He came to what looked like an office, oak-panelled with plush carpets and tasselled, floor-length curtains. The furniture was classic but not especially elegant: an ornately tooled mahogany desk with a green-leather inset, a button-tufted Queen Anne sofa, large gilt-framed oil landscapes adorning the walls. The windows looked out towards the swimming-pool. No alarm box. He carried on, passing a kitchenette, a boot room with wellingtons lined up and Barbours hanging on pegs. He came to a second corridor, sunlight falling through the windows on to an expensive walnut floor. More than ten seconds had passed and there hadn't been a noise. But now he could see the box at the end of the corridor, mounted above a padlocked solid oak door.

The light unit wasn't flashing. No klaxon either. Infrared eyes blinked at him from both sides of the ceiling and the door had two contact sensors, one on either side. He realized the klaxon wasn't sounding because the alarm wasn't designed to go off at an intrusion into the house. It was designed to protect the breezeblock room and only that room.

He went to the box. Broke the infrared beams and instantly the strobe unit began to blink. The circuit board usually sat just behind and above the battery – it was best to destroy them both. He put the drill bit against the box and leant into it. Curled swarf flew everywhere as the bit popped easily through the door, deeper into the workings. The drill jumped in his hands, clattering around in the box, causing havoc. The klaxon started and wailed deafeningly for two seconds before the drill bit found circuitry. It leapt around some more, doing its work, then the wailing died abruptly.

Silence. Ears ringing, he jiggled the chain and tried the

door. It wasn't only protected by the padlock – there were four more deadbolts in the door. He went back into the office and opened all the drawers on the desk. The top one was locked so he used the drill again. He didn't much care what Powers would think about the damages Gerber might claim – he was already in a world of trouble and disciplinaries with what he'd done to the alarm box. In for a penny, in for a pound.

The keys were in the drawer and they fitted the four locks. Another lecture in effective security coming your way, Mr Gerber. The padlock came off easily – a thirty-second squirt of pipe freeze, a crowbar inserted, given the right torque, and it shattered into four pieces. He opened the door.

As soon as he stepped inside the darkened room he smelt something bad. Something he knew from the mortuary and from undertakers. Something that made his throat close. Formalin.

He closed the door behind him, locking it for good measure. He could make out shapes in the half-light: a bank of floor-to-ceiling refrigerators to his left, a massive workbench to his right, like in an old-fashioned school laboratory. In the far wall a door stood slightly ajar. He went to it and peered round. It led to a small enclosed stairwell twisting up into daylight. He listened, heard nothing above him, so he pulled the door closed, locked that too, and switched on the overhead light.

It was a fluorescent strip and too bright for the size of the room, as if work went on in here that you'd need good visibility for. The refrigerators lined the wall to his right.

In front of him the wall was decorated with medical diagrams, all showing the skin in varying styles: one depicted the body's sweat glands, representing them in red on a black-and-grey genderless outlined human. Another showed skin lifted up on a hook to reveal its interior, the dermis, epidermis, the subcutaneous fat, hair erector muscles and blood vessels.

But it was what was on the work station in his peripheral vision that really sent a line of adrenalin through him.

Tools and racks laid out on the bench in a clear pattern as if they were expecting something. Some he recognized as a tanner's – skinning and fleshing knives, a small gambrel – others he'd never seen before. They looked like specialized surgeon's tools. In the centre there was a series of blocks with pegs in them. The sort of thing you'd stretch out an animal skin on.

Animal skin.

The skinned dog in the quarry definitely hadn't been Amos Chipeta.

I'm getting near you now, my friend. I can feel you. I'm not far now.

He took a few steps forward and opened a refrigerator. It gave with a gentle vacuumy hiss, cold air coming out at him. He peered inside. Every shelf was crammed with vacuutainers: like the Tupperware sandwich boxes his mum used to put his and Ewan's lunch in when they were kids. Each was labelled and through the sides he could see brown liquid, rocking lightly from the movement of his opening the door.

He pulled one out. It was cold, slightly sticky, the smell of formalin coming from it. Taped to the top was a photo of a young woman. First off he thought she was dead. She was lying on her back – the camera had shot her from above, the way they sometimes shot corpses in the mortuary – and she wore a mask strapped over her mouth and nose. She was naked, except for a bandage across her breasts and a tangle of flower-sprigged cotton bunched at her knees. Her eyes were closed, but she had too much colour to be dead. He looked at the fabric: an operating-theatre gown. The bed was a hospital bed. She wasn't dead: she was under anaesthetic. Maybe just coming out because that wasn't a laryngeal mask on her face.

Under the photograph was a printed box, intricate lines of text in it: 'Name: Pauline Weir. DOB: 4.5.81. Op date: 15.7.08. Op: Breast reduction.' Below the text was a diagram of a female – a little like the one on the wall. Two semicircles in red pen were sketched on the undersides of the breasts.

Caffery carried the container to the table and opened it carefully. Seven or eight slivers of skin in the clear brown fluid floated. Like an exhibit in a medical museum.

He clicked the lid shut, went back to the fridge, pulled out another. Another photograph of a woman on a bed, naked except for the gown that had been pulled down to her knees, and a bandage across her stomach. No anaesthetist would leave a patient's side while they were unconscious, but they wouldn't supervise the recovery period past a certain point: that would be left to trained recovery nurses who might be persuaded to leave the room. If they were instructed to by the surgeon. Was that what Susan Hopkins had meant by *They're all a bit thick, the recovery nurses, not to see what's going on under their noses*?

He opened the container. In it he found a single elliptical piece of skin, bleached and puckered by the formalin. He returned it, ran his fingers down the list of containers until he came to the M section. Mahoney, Lucy. He carried it to the table, opened it, and there he saw the last piece of the puzzle.

A piece of Lucy that hadn't made it to the autopsy table. A piece of her pubis. The hairs were still attached.

For years and years and years this had been Gerber's secret.

For years, by a series of crafty moves, in ways that would never be detected, he had been stealing the skin of the women he operated on.

60

Caffery heard the car coming from a distance. He shut the vacuutainers away and left the room silently, clicking the door closed behind him. He kicked aside the metal swarf and was stepping out of the front door as an immaculate blue Mercedes swept up the drive. A 500 AMG with all the bells and whistles.

He didn't know if he'd been seen coming out so he stepped away from the building into the sunlight. The Mercedes came to a halt. There were a few moments' pause, then the door opened and a small man with greying hair got out. He was about fifty, unremarkable, except for the odd tunic he wore. Yoked and made of brushed denim, it was the sort of thing an artist might have worn in the 1970s. There were damp spots on the front.

'Georges Gerber?'

He glanced towards the road, then back at Caffery. 'Who wants to know?'

He held up his card. 'Inspector Jack Caffery.'

There was a slight pause. Gerber closed his eyes. And opened them. As if he was taking a picture of Jack. Then his face cleared abruptly. 'Where are my manners?' He pushed his hair back from his face with a chalk-white hand. '*Do* come in.' He slammed the car door and took out a key, came forward and opened the front door wide. Smiled. 'I'll make you some coffee.'

Caffery pocketed his card and followed. While Gerber went to the corner of his office and busied himself with a coffee-maker Caffery stood next to a winged armchair, shifting it slightly so he could keep three things in plain view: Gerber, who had pressed two sachets into the machine and was now filling the cups, and the two doors – the one he'd come through and the other, which led to the refrigerator room where the padlock lay snapped on the floor.

'So,' Gerber said pleasantly, as he turned with the coffee, 'you found me easily enough. How long have you been here?'

'I just arrived.' Caffery gave him a cool smile. 'Why?'

'A polite enquiry,' he said lightly. 'Simply making conversation.'

He put a coaster on to a little occasional table next to the chair and set the coffee on it. When he straightened Caffery noticed he was sweating. Nothing too obvious, just a faint sheen across his forehead. 'My father was in the force. A chief inspector – Hampshire.'

'Really?'

Why haven't you asked me why I'm here yet? When are you going to ask?

'I feel I've got an affinity with the police.' Gerber pulled up a small table next to the sofa and put down his own cup. He went back to the coffee-maker and stood for a moment with his back to Caffery, opening a packet of biscuits. Something with a royal crest on the box. He shook them out on to a plate. 'Fixing things. You know. Making the world a better place. Biscuit?'

'No, thank you.'

'Drink your coffee.'

'When I'm ready.'

The last thing Caffery was going to do was eat or drink anything in this place. No other incapacitants had come up on the tox results because Gerber was a doctor and had access to the liquid form of temazepam. He could have slipped it to the women in a drink – they wouldn't have noticed. Knowing it would come up on toxicology, and that using a liquid temazepam that Lucy hadn't been prescribed might point to murder and maybe to someone in the medical profession, he'd fed them pills later to account for the tranquillizer in the blood result.

'Is there something wrong with your coffee?'

'You tell me, Mr Gerber. Is there something wrong with it?'

Gerber went still. He turned swiftly to Caffery. Something off centre had crept into his eyes. The spots on his smock were still dark. If they were water, Caffery thought, they'd be dry by now. 'S-sorry,' he murmured. 'Is that a riddle?'

'No. It's a straightforward question. Is there something in my coffee? Liquid benzos, for example.'

'What?' Gerber put his hand to his forehead. 'Goodness – this is confusing. You're confusing me.'

'I haven't just arrived, Georges. I've been here for a long time. Enough time to go into your room. See what you've been up to.'

Gerber dropped the biscuits. They scattered on the table, some on the floor. He stood with his hands limp at his sides, making no attempt to pick the biscuits up. 'There's an explanation,' he said woodenly. 'I can explain everything you've seen.'

'I can explain too. Lucy Mahoney caught you, didn't she? She saw what you were doing. Saw what you'd taken from her. Or did she remember being photographed? Was that it?'

'This is a fantasy you're having. Some sort of fantasy. If you let me explain I'll—'

'She was blackmailing you. And then what happened? My guess is she asked for too much. She wanted to buy herself a house – her demands got too big. There was no way out for you. You're a thief. For years, by the looks of things, you've been stealing skin, like a serial killer who takes a part of his victims. These women have been your victims.'

'Victims?' He raised his eyes to Caffery. 'That's a harsh word. I didn't hurt one of them. They left my surgery better than they came in.'

'They are victims. They didn't consent.'

'The skin – it's part of my life's work. I s-study skin. I'm trying to build synthetic skin.'

'Building synthetic skin?' Caffery laughed. 'Oh, good one, Dr Frankenstein.'

'It's the truth. Have another look in that room. You'll see the boxes. From other manufacturers.'

'I'm not stupid, Mr Gerber. From the limited knowledge I have, I'd say what you're doing is nothing about building synthetic skin or whatever bullshit you're asking me to swallow. I'd say it's nothing to do with that and everything to do with sex.'

Gerber's face went blank for a moment. He blinked.

'I'd say that, whatever it looks like on the surface, this sort of behaviour always has a sexual motivation. Where's your problem, Georges? You can't get it up? Or did your mother make you give her bedbaths when you were six?'

Gerber blinked again. Once, twice. Three times in succession.

'You photographed those women naked. God only knows what else you did to them while they were still half under. And you kept trophies to remind you. I looked at those – those *specimens* – and I couldn't help asking myself: If I tested them would I find traces of your semen on them?'

Gerber stopped blinking. His left hand opened and closed as if he wanted to touch something. He came towards the table where he'd put the cup of coffee. 'No wonder you're not drinking your coffee. The table's too far away.'

'It's fine where it is.'

'Here.' He bent to pick it up. 'Let me just move it along.'

'I said it's fine where it—'

A spasm hit the back of Caffery's calf and bolted up his body. He rolled away, a shout coming out of his mouth, scrambling across the sofa, fumbling for the back of his leg. He got clumsily to his feet, knocking over a chair, and turned, panting, to see Gerber, half bent over next to the table, his head at a slight angle, watching him. There was a weapon in his hand. It looked like a small pick or an awl – the sort of thing you'd use to work leather. A piece of material clung to it, from Caffery's trousers, and long loops of blood lay across the cushions where he'd just scrambled over the sofa.

'Why didn't you drink my coffee, you fucking shithead?'

'Hey,' Caffery panted, reaching down to hold his leg, finding ripped fabric and something else – shredded calf muscle. 'You are so *fucked* you just don't have a clue.'

With his free hand he grabbed the chair and took a limping step forward, swinging it at Gerber, who side-stepped, nimble as a dancer, and landed the heel of the awl across Caffery's temple. The pain pushed something black into his head. He fell forward, grabbing at things as he went, seeing the legs of the sofa fly up to meet him.

What's happened to the sofa? he thought dimly, as he hit the floor. *Why is the sofa on the fucking ceiling?*

61

The bank kept Flea waiting. It was almost two o'clock when she left for Ruth's, the money stashed in a banded petty-cash envelope in the glove compartment. The weather was patchy, the sun playing tag behind the clouds, but it was warm and she opened the windows in the Clio. The dusty, new-bloom scent of the hedgerow filled the car.

One of the units from Taunton was parked at the junction with the A36, a Lexus and an old Peugeot next to it. She pulled down the sun-visor, drove past calmly, eyes ahead. She was on the sick today and not supposed to be here. Wellard was acting sergeant – he had his instructions: no matter what the inspector told them he was to keep the team to the north of the search area and leave the south until last. Until after five. By which time she'd have the photograph. And have found a way to get Ruth out of the house.

Round the next corner an oncoming motorcycle flashed his lights, jerked his thumb back down the road and sawed his hand across his neck. The sign that there was a hazard, an accident. She slowed as she came round the corner and saw it about quarter of a mile up the road. A traffic car was parked sideways blocking half of the road, a PC in a fluorescent hi-vis jacket in front of it.

Her foot came off the gas and the Clio cruised forward a bit, slowing gradually until it came to a halt. Beyond the traffic BMW she saw her own unit's Sprinter van parked nose to tail with the coroner's. Shit. What the hell were they doing here? Wellard had *promised*.

Her car dawdled for a moment, the PC's eyes on her face. Before she could gather herself and do a U-turn away, a face appeared from behind the Sprinter, looking at her in mild curiosity. It was Wellard. Eyebrows raised to see her there.

She was had. No getting away. She pulled the car to the side of the road.

'Hi.' Wellard put his elbow on the roof and smiled through the window at her. 'Job-pissed, are we, Sarge? Coming in even though you're on the sick?'

She turned off the engine and kept her eyes on the steering-wheel. 'I thought I told you not to come over here until the end of the day.'

'This job came up. The officer in charge wanted someone quickly. The inspector was cool about it – I didn't think you'd—'

'OK. OK.' She looked past him. Behind the screens a car was parked in the secret little alcove she'd once parked in to walk up to Ruth's. She could just see its roof. 'The CSI's here. What is it?'

'Suicide.'

'Past its sell-by? That's why they've got you, is it?'

'No, it's recent. Still warm. Like I said, we only took it cos we were in the area.'

The roof of the car was sun-bleached and covered with bird droppings. Seeing it now made something cold walk across her heart. 'That's the car I can see, is it?'

'That's the car.'

'A VW?'

Wellard blinked. 'A VW? Yeah – I mean, yeah, it is. You can tell from here?'

She pressed her fingers into her temples.

'Sarge – you OK?'

'I'm . . . fine.'

She got out of the car, leaving her keys in the ignition, and began to walk, back straight, legs stiff. Flashing her card automatically at the loggist on the cordon, she ducked under it and passed the van. The two coroner's men stood in their grey suits outside the inner cordon, just as they always did, smoking and chatting in low voices. She went past, not speaking.

The first thing she saw was the body-bag on the road, the orange stretcher next to it in the sunshine. Then she saw her own men gathered around the opened car door, bending to look inside. They glanced up when she approached. Smiled. Called something in greeting. A joke, maybe. She didn't hear it. She was looking at the place between their legs where she could see a woman's calf. The foot crammed into a green stiletto. A graze on the ankle. She could see the hem of the short black dress above it. To the right she could see the offside window, moss growing in the seals.

She turned away and stood with her hands pressed into the small of her back. Lifted her face to the sky and breathed in. Out. The sun had broken through the clouds for one last try at warming the world, but she couldn't see it. She couldn't see the way it was picking out the different greens of the newly budded trees in the distance, the way it was lighting the distant hills.

What she could see, on that pretty May morning, was the way the sky could suffocate her. The way the sky and the world and all the people in it could push her down so low that eventually they simply stopped her breathing.

62

Must've let it slip a bit on the Scotch last night, Caffery thought. His head was banging like a bastard and any movement sent pressure waves galloping from one ear to the other. He passed a hand across his face, thinking something must be draped over it because the light was so dim. But there was nothing. He reached out in front of him, expecting to feel sheets. Instead he hit something hard and rough. He pushed his hands backwards and behind him met the same hard, immovable barrier.

He lay there, breathing fast. He wasn't in bed. This was an enclosed space, a vault or a box, about eight foot by eight. Somewhere echoey with a stale, foul smell. About ten feet above him there was a single hazy blob of light.

Think now. Push it.

Vague images came back: a tanner's awl, blood draped across fabric. He fingered his face. Blood was crusted over his top lip, his nose was tender and a lump had swollen on his gum. He ran his hands over his body. He was dressed, in his suit, but it was crusted and hard on the legs. Behind his knee the flesh was tender, swollen and hot to the touch. He reached a little further down and found a ripped, pulpy area, meat and fabric mixed.

Shit shit shit. He pulled his hands away and dropped his head back, panting hard. The awl. Gerber looking at him calmly. The plate of biscuits. The crack of the handle to his temple. Blood on the sofa.

He fumbled down his torso. The radio was gone. No phone either. No phone, no ASP, no wallet, no CS gas, no Swiss Army knife, no quick-cuffs. All that was left him was his watch. He squinted at it in the gloom. Two thirty p.m. He'd been out for three hours. With his erratic appearances at the office probably no one would even wonder where he was until the end of the day.

His head stopped spinning and the blurred light began to take form and perspective. He tried to listen to what was happening outside. At first he couldn't pick up anything, just silence and the echo of his own breathing. Then he heard a bird singing and the distant grumble of a tractor. He sniffed again. A pungent, old scent, almost sweet above the tang of blood and his sweat.

And then he knew where he was.

He was in Gerber's cesspit.

Wincing, he raised himself on to his elbows and squinted around. The pit was empty and probably hadn't been used for years, but the evidence of its function was still here. He could smell it. The hazy light above him was daylight filtering through the cracks in the access cover – a ladder ran up the side of the wall to it. To its right was a large pipe hung at right angles to the ceiling, the baffles to carry the waste up to the sandbank drainfield. At head height a yellowish layer of grease about a foot deep coated the walls. Caffery lay for a few minutes, ignoring his thumping head, eyeing the cover the way he'd eye up an opponent.

He counted to three, then pushed himself up on to his good leg. Shakily, not putting weight on his right foot, he limped to the ladder and climbed up a few steps. He looped the good leg into the ladder rung, wiped his mouth with the back of his hand and, gritting his teeth, reached up and jammed both hands against the manhole cover. It made a small creaking noise. And stopped. He gave it another shove. Rigid. Another. Nothing.

He clung to the ladder, breathing hard. Most inspection-chamber covers like this rusted up and needed a sledgehammer to open them, but this was the only way into the cesspit. It was the only way Gerber could have got him down here so it must have been opened recently. He ran his hands around it, trying to work out the secret. He found a lump – a triangular piece of metal, the apex of the triangle at the dead centre of the lock. This was the sort of cover that locked with a slip bolt. Ordinarily the mechanism would be underneath, but Gerber had inverted the cover and locked it from above. The bastard. There was no way anyone down here could release the lock without tools.

He disentangled his leg, came down the ladder and felt around underfoot. The floor was an uneven mix of unfinished sharpstone and ballast, covered with a hardened layer of grease and toilet paper. Moss and a few weeds were growing in it, making it smooth to the touch. He let his fingers skim the surface and found a couple of rusting old bolts, a food wrapper of some sort, blown in here maybe when the pit was decommissioned. And a long slim tube. Hard plastic or Perspex. It was wider than a needle but slimmer than a rose stem.

A Perspex tube?

He found another one. And another. They were gathered in the place he'd been lying. Clinking together like wind chimes. He sat down and held his wrist canted over so the dim fluorescent green of his watch face illuminated them. The ends were dark and sticky with blood. He turned them over and over, trying to guess their function. The blood was fresh. Still tacky. His blood. Had to be. But why?

He rested the tubes against the wall in the corner, where he'd be able to find them again, stood and gave the baffle pipe at the edge of the pit a sharp thump with the heel of his hand. There was a faint sound of rust flakes falling to the floor, a creak of old metal, but the pipe was solid. It had been set into the mortar of the bricks and nothing short of a sledgehammer would move it. He turned to the ladder and tugged at that. Again, solid. It was designed to hold the weight of a man and there was no way he'd be able to pull it off. He gave in to a moment's anger and booted it. Something soft gave in the back of his leg. He felt the wound reopen, begin to leak.

He bent over and locked his hand around his calf. The pain was so bad his teeth felt metallic, but he kept his head up and back. Couldn't afford to faint.

When he'd got hold of himself he examined his leg. He took his hand away, and as he did, a strip of flesh about the width of a piece of tape flopped from the top of his calf almost to his ankle. It was still attached at the bottom where it hung like a piece of stripped bark, twisted inside out so the fleshy underneath was open to the air. Bits of brick dust, wood and things he didn't want to give much thought to clung to the flesh. Blood came out new and warm, soaking into his socks.

He tore off a strip of trouser leg and used his teeth to rip it in half. Clumsily he pressed the strip of flesh back into the wound hole, smoothing it into place. The debris would have to be cleaned out later. For now it was enough to stop the bleeding. He wrapped the trouser material around his calf, laying his leg back hard on the floor to get the pressure, and, wincing at the pain, tied the material against his shinbone. The blood pumped on for a few seconds, trickling through his fingers. Then it slowed until it was just running out of the edges of the wound.

He thought of the spots on Gerber's tunic. Lucy and Susan would have bled a lot. He wondered what their last thoughts had been. He recalled their wrists. The way Gerber had sliced them. Up and down. Not left to right.

And then he got it. He let out all his breath and slumped back against the wall. He'd just figured out what the Perspex tubes were. And it wasn't good. Not good at all.

It meant Gerber would be back before long.

63

Flea's team were trained in MOE – method-of-entry techniques. A smart name for the time-honoured skill of kicking in doors, except that when the police did it, it was with specialist equipment and the blessing of the law. The unit went back each year for a day's requalification training. The last session had been only a month ago and Flea knew that the forced-entry tool-bag – which Wellard called the Bag of Bollocks – was still to hand in the office.

She drove back fast, using roads the traffic units didn't bother with, grabbed the bag and the heavy cylinder of the thermal lance the team used to cut through metal, put them both in the car and headed back towards Farleigh Park Hall. She didn't have very long.

She was pissed off with herself. It was brainless to have dealt directly with Ruth Lindermilk. She shouldn't have tinkered around. She should have treated her like an object, should have got in there, taken the first opportunity she had, kicked the door down and grabbed the photo of Thom. Time had just been slipping out of her hands. And all the time Misty had been decomposing.

She parked further up the road, careful not to go anywhere near the body-recovery scene. There might still be police there. Hiking the bag on her shoulder, she headed up through the undergrowth.

As always the hamlet was hushed – deserted. It was only the one or two cars parked down the lane that told her anyone was at home. Someone somewhere was watching sport – she could hear crowds cheering as she passed a window. At the bungalow she took a moment to go to the top of the garden and peer out over the wall, just to satisfy herself that no one was watching, then went to the back of the house and set to work.

First she tried all the doors and windows: no point pulling out the heavy artillery if Ruth had simply left a door unlocked. Everything was tightly closed, about what you'd expect with Ruth's paranoia. The bungalow had quarter-lights in the lower windows, which were small and easy to break. She went to the kitchen ones and studied them. If she remembered rightly the sink and the dishwasher were under them. She recalled a butler sink. Solid. It would hold her weight.

She pulled on gloves and fumbled in the bag, past all the big equipment, for the smallest in the arsenal of tools: the tiny spring-loaded centre punch. They called it the Glasgow key. It took no effort at all, and now she gave just the smallest of taps against the pane. A sharp *crack* and a spider-web break zigged out into the float glass. It was the tiniest sound, but even so she held her breath and checked over her shoulder. The garden stood motionless – not a breath of air, not a sound of wildlife moving, only the distant hum of the television in the still air.

Tongue between her teeth she pulled out the pieces of glass, cleaning off the edges with a cloth. The last thing she needed was blood, forensic evidence that would link her to this break-in. When it was clean she pulled her sweatshirt sleeve all the way down over her hand and pushed her arm inside, feeling for the latch. She found it, tugged at it. It was locked, so, groping around, she found the other. That was locked too, with no key in it. She stood back, swearing to herself. It'd have to be the little wrecking bar, then. This time it worked like a dream. It fitted perfectly under the locks. The first came out after two or three wrenches and the second with no effort at all, splinters scattering everywhere.

Very carefully she opened the window and lifted the bag of tools through it. The curtains were closed as usual and when she peeped through there were no lights on, only the illumination of the green light on the boiler and the little pilot flame flickering blue. She could smell cats and food, lasagne or something – maybe what Ruth had eaten last night. Did she know, as she put the food into the microwave, that it was the last thing she'd ever eat in her life? It didn't feel right, this suicide. Not at all right. Yesterday on the phone Ruth had sounded fine. Happy, even.

Not now. Don't think about it now. She pulled her sleeves back and hoisted herself up into the window, arms trembling. Even though she worked at it – going into the office gym and doing high-weight, low-rep lifting whenever she found a spare moment – she didn't really have the upper-body strength for her job at the best of times. And recently, with no time for the gym and not enough food, it had got worse. She had to fight now just to lift her own weight up into the kitchen.

She fell inside, into the half-gloom, knocking over a bottle of washing-up liquid, landing among the dirty crockery in the sink – something smashing as she went. She dropped down on to the kitchen floor and found that her trousers were soaked. Water dripped on to the earth on her shoes, clinging to the tiles and leaving a perfect print. She scuffed it with her heel. Cleaned off the worst of the mud with a kitchen towel. In the cupboard under the sink she found plastic freezer bags – should have thought of this before – and pulled two on over her trainers.

The living room was ghostly. Just the light from the broken kitchen window behind her filtered through on to Ruth's possessions, the books and photos, the piles of paperwork and the empty glasses. A large glass of Coke was on an occasional table, an opened bottle of champagne next to it. Cats' eyes blinked in every corner.

She went to the bureau where Ruth had put the photo and tested the drawer. Still locked – no key. She gave the rest of the bureau a cursory search for the key, checking inside a small papier-mâché cup, fingering her way through a desk tidy full of paper clips. She dropped some in her hurry, leaving them where they fell – it didn't matter. There was no concealing there'd been a break-in.

She found the small pry bar in the bag and inserted the head into the gap in the drawer. From the wall Ruth

Lindermilk and her son stared down impassively at her. Someone says, 'I'll take a photo,' and you let them, she thought. You let them whether you want it or not, and before you know it that moment – that unthought-out, unplanned and out-of-control moment – is all you have left to mark a life. And then you're dead.

She turned away from the photos and jemmied the lock in one hit. It caved with a loud splintering. She let the jemmy clatter down and wrenched open the drawer.

It was empty.

She stood there for a moment, staring stupidly at it.

'Shit, Ruth. *Shit.*'

The cats shrank away, cowering nervously behind chairs and sofas. She slammed the drawer on to the floor and stood in the middle of the room, her hands out, staring at the rows and rows of books. If Ruth hadn't left the photo in the drawer, where *had* she left it?

'Come on, Ruth. What the hell did you do with it? What were you thinking?'

She turned. Ruth had got the photos from here – she remembered her taking them from the computer table. She opened the top drawer, pulling things out, rummaging through the contents. All that was in here was magazine cuttings and old clothes brochures. She pushed aside the sofa, swept a whole shelf of haphazardly piled chick-lit and romance stories off the bookshelves on to the floor and squatted next to the pile, scrabbling through the books, shaking the big ones, throwing them aside. She moved on to the next shelf, scattering everything. Within five minutes all the bookcases were clear and she was standing calf deep in books.

No photo.

She widened the search, going fast. The house was small – the only thing she found on the ground floor was a tea chest filled with framed photographs: wedding shots of Mr and Mrs Lindermilk, black-and-white shots of a baby. Not the photo she was looking for. She went up the stairs two at a time, hauling herself along on the banister to the small landing. There was a chest pushed up against the wall. She threw it open and pulled out everything inside: clothes, hats scarves. Nothing. Sweating now, she went into each bedroom and rummaged through divan drawers, under pillows, even in the pockets of coats hanging in wardrobes. She had got to the fourth one – had just emptied four shopping bags out on to the bed – when it caught her eye.

It was on the wall above the bed and it was what she should have been looking for all along. Sepia-coloured, about the size of a vinyl LP. A small wall-mounted safe.

'Oh, Ruth,' she murmured. 'You couldn't have, could you?'

The answer came back instantly: *Of course she did, of course she would have put it here. She knew how precious it was to you, knew you might try something like this.*

She straightened, went to the safe and gave it a tug. It was locked tight. Nothing in the Bag of Bollocks would open this number. Only the thermal lance would help her here. And it was still in the car down on the road. She threw the dial from side to side, hit it with the crowbar in her frustration. Hit it again. Then stopped and stood still, listening hard. There was a noise. Coming from the front of the house.

Someone outside had just opened Ruth's front gate.

She went silently to the top of the stairs and peered over.

A second passed. Another.

Footsteps came around the side of the house, heading for the back. Suddenly panicked, Flea went quickly down the stairs and into the kitchen where the curtains were still drawn. The footsteps had stopped.

Whoever it was must be on the patio. She collected all the gear off the counter, counting it quickly: one, two, three, four, five. After cramming it into the bag, she zipped it up, threw it over her shoulder and headed for the hallway.

Someone put a key in the front door. There was a brief metallic clink as it turned, then the shush-shush of the draft excluder moving on the mat.

She turned back into the kitchen and stood for a second or two sizing it up. Opposite, behind curtains, the broken window stood open. No. It would take too much time to climb up there and drop through. In the hallway the door closed. She opened the oven and pushed the bag inside. Went to the tall fridge. Turned her face sideways, raised her hands and squeezed herself into the gap between it and the wall. She bent her arms at the elbows so her hands wouldn't be visible and stood there trembling, breathing in shallow pants through her mouth because her ribs were constrained.

Someone came in. A man – she could hear him

breathing as he surveyed the mess. He moved around, his feet crunching the glass underfoot, then stopped about a yard away. She could see his foot now, in a clean white trainer, 'Nike' written on it. There was a long silence while she listened to his breathing. It was fast, heavy, as if he was excited by what he saw. Or distressed.

He left the kitchen. In the living room she heard him kick his way through the mess. He went back into the hallway and the moment she knew he was at the front of the house she eased her way out from beside the fridge, got the bag from the oven and closed it without a sound. She skirted the broken glass, lifted the bag on to the work surface and hauled herself up.

The footsteps stopped. He'd heard her moving.

'Hello?'

She pulled the curtain wide and dropped the bag through the window.

'Hello? Who's there?'

She looked at the drop. Looked back at the hall. Took a breath. And jumped.

64

Caffery shifted where he sat. His bones were cold, aching. He'd given up searching for a way to get out. How long would it take Turnbull or Powers to notice he was missing and not just AWOL again? How long would it be before the trail led to Beatrice Foxton – the only professional apart from a telephone operator at Control who knew he'd been to the Rothersfield clinic that morning? A day? Maybe more because they didn't have his phone to go by. And when they arrived, his car wouldn't be anywhere to be seen. Gerber had taken his keys and would have moved it. Which meant he had probably found the gun too.

But he didn't intend to use it. Caffery knew Gerber was too clever for that, knew he wanted Caffery to die in the slowest possible way. Maybe for the sake of self-preservation: he could argue that Caffery had fallen into the cesspit and bled to death. Or sadism: the need to imagine a drawn-out death in the cold and dark of the pit. He was a skilled doctor and knew the arteries of the leg would spring back on themselves where they'd been severed, that the blood would clot and Caffery's leg would heal itself.

So he'd inserted those Perspex tubes into the arteries to keep it flowing. He'd wanted to bleed him to death.

Caffery was lucky – the tubes had fallen out – but Gerber would be back eventually. Just to check.

There was a noise overhead. A footstep. The sound of weight on the roof of the tank. Caffery stiffened. Bit down on the instinct to scream at the fucker. He knew what he had to do: he had to let Gerber think he was dead. He got to his feet and moved to the edge of the tank where the ladder was, keeping his breathing shallow and quiet.

There was a pause, a long silence when nothing happened. Maybe he'd imagined that sound. He was about to sit down again, when he heard another footfall. A clunk. Followed by a metallic bang. The sound of the lock on the manhole being tested.

He grabbed the ladder and climbed one or two steps until his neck and shoulders were pressed against the ceiling, his head inches from the cover. Wedging his bad leg back he held himself there, teeth gritted. One hand out and ready. He couldn't wait at the bottom of the tank for the bastard to come in – it would be shooting fish in a barrel for Gerber: there was one chance and one chance only. Caffery had to go out and take it on the nose. Then, if he caught Gerber in time, he could throw the manhole cover at him. Catch him off balance.

The lock on the cover opened. He waited, trembling in his bat position, hands up hard in front of his face. Adrenalin bolted around his body. He was ready. *Come and get it. Come and get it.*

But nothing happened. Nobody came. The manhole cover didn't open.

There were a few moments of silence, then another footfall. This time Gerber was retreating. He had unlocked the cover but not opened it. Caffery let his jaw stay slack, tried to keep his breathing slow and steady as he tracked Gerber's movements in his head. What was he planning?

Silence again. He counted to a hundred, listening. The stillness stretched on and on, out of the cesspit, down past the swimming-pool, out into the lane. He counted to a hundred again then relaxed his ribcage, breathed normally.

He dropped off the ladder on to his good leg. Checked his watch. Looked back up at the cover.

What's he doing? What's he wanting me to do?

Maybe Gerber had changed his mind about finishing him, knowing the weight of shit that would descend on his head if he added cop-killer to his list. Maybe he was waiting outside to apologize. No. Of course he wasn't. Caffery knew what was going on: he was being flushed. Gerber had a gun and was waiting for him.

If that was the way it was going to be, then that was the way it was going to be. Simple as that.

He let the second hand move round his watch five times, then pulled himself back up the ladder. On a deep breath he gave the lid a hard shove.

It flew open and rolled away with a deafening clang. Light flooded in. He clung to the ladder, breathing hard, good foot coiled into the rungs, one hand up, ready for whatever came flying at him.

High above him the sky was blue, completely cloudless. He waited, making calculations. The swimming-pool was about a hundred yards from here. There was a pump-house at the deep end, if he remembered rightly. And the maintenance shed with the stepladder in it. There'd be something in there. A hacksaw. An axe, maybe.

Three minutes passed. Then, using his good leg as the dynamo, he vaulted clumsily up and out of the hole, and rolled quickly away. He scrambled head first across the lawn, threw himself down behind the pump-house, where he crouched, hands pressed hard against his leg to stop the wound opening and bleeding again.

It was as hot as an August day: the trees, the hedges, even the grass stood motionless, their outlines a little hazy in the heat. When the pain stopped he raised himself cautiously and looked out at the grounds. Gerber's car sat in the driveway soaking up the sunshine. Caffery's own car, as he'd expected, wasn't there. It had been hidden from anyone standing at the entrance to the house, but from here it was easy to spot: covered with a tarpaulin, its nose pointed up against the doors of a derelict barn about a hundred yards away.

He limped quickly to the car, threw back the tarp and rattled the doors. All locked. He could see through the window that the glove compartment was open, so he'd been right: the bastard had taken the gun.

It felt better to hold his bad leg as he walked, so he gripped it in both hands and half carried it across the lawn, past the swimming-pool to the shed. He found a chisel and a screwdriver on the magnetic tool rack. No axe.

He continued up to the house. The front door was ajar. Using the tip of his finger he pushed it. It swung open soundlessly to reveal the office where the attack had happened. It was empty. The curtains had been half closed, the biscuits swept to one side, and he could see where the great ribbons of blood on the floor and sofa had been hastily scrubbed. He went inside and stood for a while, looking around. Where was Gerber hiding?

He limped to the desk, pulled open the drawers, riffled through the contents, seeing paper clips and pens, old business cards. He straightened and looked at the glass bookcases. In one there was a tooled-leather keepsake box. He took it out and opened it. Inside a plaque read: 'To Georges, with much love and respect from the staff and patients of St Hilda's clinic, 1998'. Set into the moulded blue velveteen were six gold-plated surgeon's instruments – haemostats, tweezers, scissors and three scalpels. Caffery pocketed the scalpels with the chisel, replaced the box and went back to the corridor.

The door to the refrigerator room was closed. He put his ear to it, took a breath, then lightly turned the handle. Just once. Listened.

Nothing. Just the vague electronic hum of a fridge, the tick of a clock.

He rested the scalpel hard and snug in his palm. The chisel was ready too, its handle sticking out of his left pocket. He gave the door a shove so it flew wide open, banging against the interior wall, then shrank back into the corridor, flattening himself against the wall, scalpel at the ready.

Again, nothing. He took a deep breath and swung into the opening, doing a quick 360-degree sweep, checking the ceiling too – he'd been caught out on that one before – then stepped neatly inside, his back to the wall.

The light was off, the room was empty. But the door opposite was ajar. He could hear the distant sound of birds floating down the steps into the room. He went to it and opened it, waiting to see if the sound drew any movement from above. It didn't. Gerber wanted him here. Wanted him to see the things he'd done. But where was he? Maybe he wasn't in the building at all. Maybe this was just the beginning of an elaborate game.

Caffery moved around the room, gathering weapons: a long fleshing knife and the awl Gerber had used. It still had a scrap of grey fabric on it. His trouser leg. He put the awl in his sleeve, the knife in his pocket. Feeling as armed as an Apache attack helicopter, he went quietly up the stairs, concentrating on not making them creak. His leg had almost stopped bleeding, yet, even so, when he got to the top of the stairs and looked back he could see one or two dark blood spots. The CSIs would thank him for that – if he survived and they ever got to find out about this place.

A door shut off the top of the staircase, this one also open a crack. He put the tip of the fleshing knife on it and pushed. It swung open with a slow creak. The moment he saw what was ahead he took a step back, letting the fleshing knife come up in front of him.

It was a corridor, a replica of the one below except for one detail. About eight yards away, nearly at the far door, with his back against the wall, sat Gerber.

He was turned slightly away from Caffery, half in profile, one leg crossed over the other. He had changed and was wearing a white shirt and a beige travel coat pulled down off his shoulders. His right hand, nearest to Caffery, was stuffed into the pocket. The other was out of sight, resting near his thigh. That'd be where the gun was. When the door opened he didn't turn immediately. He continued to stare out of the window, almost vacantly. That was his way, thought Caffery. He was content to sit and wait for his prey, a half-smile on his face. Snake in a hole. He had been clever enough to kill Lucy Mahoney. And Susan Hopkins. Clever enough to almost get away with it.

Caffery kept his back against the wall, out of range. 'Show me your hands.'

Gerber didn't react.

'You heard me. Show me your fucking hands.'

Gerber allowed his right hand to flop out of his pocket, palm up. It was empty. Then he lifted the left about five inches above his thigh. It was holding the Hardballer. But it wasn't pointed at Caffery. It drooped, hung limply for a second, then fell, clattering across the floor and landing up against the wall, only a foot away from Caffery.

Gerber's eyes followed the gun but he didn't make any attempt to pick it up.

Caffery scanned the corridor, the windows and the door at the far end. What was supposed to happen here? That door beyond – was it locked? He looked at the gun. 'Whatever you think you've set up it ain't going to work,' he told Gerber. 'You're not going to dictate how this ends. *I* am.'

Gerber breathed out noisily. He turned his head a fraction and stared at Caffery. His face was pale, his lips painfully swollen.

Caffery frowned, puzzled. Something was very wrong here. He took a step forward and swiped up the gun, pointing it at Gerber's head. Still Gerber didn't move. If anything his chin hung a little lower, as if it was difficult to keep his head up.

Caffery took another step forward. Then another. Gerber stared at him with his heavy eyes, a drop of saliva gathering on his bottom lip.

Caffery stopped just out of arm's reach and stood with the gun held out, contemplating the strange little man, with his wiry hair and his pale, flaky-skinned face. Now he was close he could see Gerber was trembling. He waved the gun in his face. Gerber's eyes followed the barrel dully, but he didn't move – didn't try to grab it. The saliva grew into a long string, then broke and dropped on to the floor. Caffery peered at the glob on the walnut floor. There was blood in the saliva. He was beginning to get the first wave of understanding. He raised his eyes to Gerber's face. 'What've you done?'

'Fuck off,' Gerber muttered. He was shaking hard now. Perspiration stood out on his forehead. 'Fuck off and die.'

His hand lifted slightly, as if to swipe at Caffery, but the effort proved too much and he dropped it on his lap, breathing hard.

And now Caffery could see why. His shirt on the left side, the side that was hidden from the staircase, had a long stain of blood from the collar to the waistband.

Caffery leant forward, not so close that Gerber could spit at him or grab him, but close enough to see the wound in his neck.

'Shit,' he muttered. 'Look at that.'

The tear in the flesh began at the front, then moved diagonally up and finished at the back of his neck inside the hairline. Caffery could see all the way into the wound, could see the tell-tale dull glint of a bullet lodged in the bone behind the ear.

Gerber's teeth were chattering.

'Shot yourself, you cowardly dog turd. You shouldn't do bad things if you can't face the consequences. Don't you know that? Shouldn't mess with—'

He broke off. He looked at the gun on the floor. Back at the wound. Looked out of the window to the empty swimming-pool, dull and blue in the sun. No. That couldn't be what had happened. Gerber hadn't had time to open the cesspit, come back here and attempt suicide. From the cesspit the gunshot might have been inaudible, but from the swimming-pool, where Caffery would have been at the time, he'd have heard it clearly. Especially with the window open. And the blood on the shirt – some of it was dark and crusted. As if it had been there a long time.

He looked out of the window again. Back at Gerber.

'This is all wrong,' he murmured, fascinated. 'All wrong.'

Then, as if in answer, from the front of the house, he heard a thin whine. The noise of a two-stroke engine. A lawnmower. No. It was more contained than that, more like a small scooter.

And then he got it. All at once. Gerber hadn't opened the inspection cover – he hadn't been able to. He'd been here all along. Leaking blood on the floor.

Caffery limped as fast as he could back down the steps through the refrigerator room and out into the gravel driveway. In the middle of the lane he stopped and stared south to where the sound was fading. The lane was empty from here to about a hundred yards down where it took an abrupt turn out of sight. The sound of the scooter dwindled in the still air, then was gone, and all he could hear were the birds in the trees.

The Tokoloshe. Amos Chipeta.

Caffery stood in the dappled sunlight, staring at the point where the lane vanished. *What the hell am I supposed to think about you? What the hell do you want?*

For no apparent reason, he'd saved Caffery's life. And in doing so he'd opened a can of shit for himself that might take for ever to shovel away. The hair taken from the corpses was one thing – he'd probably have got away with that – but shooting Gerber? He'd go down just as fast as Gerber would. Even if he'd saved a cop.

But, as life will sometimes have it, when Caffery turned from the quiet lane and limped back inside, up to Gerber's corridor where the afternoon sun was bathing the floor in a syrupy glow, he found that the tables had turned again.

He found that another door in the story had just opened. And this time it was one both he and Amos Chipeta could slip through like ghosts.

65

Prosecution lawyers sometimes talked to Caffery about the '*CSI* effect' – the way the American TV programme made people, specifically juries, believe forensic science was omnipotent. That there was a test for everything. That if the clue was there the crime-scene officers would automatically find it. The truth, as every law-keeper knew, was that the best forensic scientist was only as good as the investigating officer. All forensic science was intelligence-led, so it was exquisitely easy to manipulate.

Gerber was dead. In the few moments Caffery had been outside, his heart had pumped out the last of its sticky heat and was now motionless and grey, sunk in on itself. Which gave Caffery a chance to change the course of history. He limped around the house recovering his belongings: his phone, his quick-cuffs and pepper spray. Then he spent forty minutes orchestrating the scene: wiping prints, scrubbing at bloodstains, positioning Gerber's body, so that when the teams arrived he would treat the place as if he was the investigating officer, not the victim, taking the CSI people around and selling them his own very feasible version of events.

The scenario: Gerber had known the net was tightening. He'd dumped Caffery in the cesspit, thinking he was dead, and had ended his own life with the illegal gun he'd kept wrapped in a tea towel in his desk. When Caffery had regained consciousness, he'd found enough of a signal at the top of the ladder in the cesspit to fire off a text to Turnbull. There was no mention of a gun in the text, Caffery didn't know anything about a gun, he said he'd heard nothing down in the cesspit. It was all a terrible surprise when the teams arrived and released him to see what Gerber had done to himself.

He watched them take Gerber's body away. When his fingers were tested there'd be gunpowder residue on them. There'd be a stray bullet found in the ceiling of the corridor that must have been fired off reflexively by Gerber after the initial suicide bullet. The only fingerprints on the 45 Hardballer and on the rounds still in it would be Gerber's. Otherwise it would be clean. The only fibres they'd find on it would come from a tea towel they'd recover from a drawer in his office where he must have been storing it for years. There'd be none of Caffery's blood or footsteps or fingerprints anywhere above the ground floor, only what he'd left in the break-in – a misdemeanour he'd put his hands up to straight away. There'd be no mention of Amos Chipeta.

Caffery stayed long enough to see the ballistics officers recover the Hardballer from the floor of the corridor. Seven hundred nicker down the drain. Shame. It was an effective gun: ugly, but effective. Given time, it might even find its way back out on to the street. Then he'd have to buy it all over again. Outside he stopped for a moment in the evening sun and looked back at the place, at the manhole cover and the swimming-pool. He thought about Tanzania. What it would be like to grow up deformed and in poverty. What England would look like through Chipeta's eyes.

Two paramedics stood in the front doorway watching him. They'd been trailing him around the place all afternoon, patiently trying to coax him into the ambulance. Now he gave them a friendly smile and, before they could stop him, got into the Mondeo, lifted the bad leg into the driver's footwell and started the car. The hospital was twenty miles away. He didn't need an ambulance. He gave the paramedics a small wave as he pulled out of the driveway. If he could survive what he'd survived today he figured he could manage twenty miles on his own.

66

The call came at half past eight in the evening when Caffery was lying on the bed in A and E, face down, head on his arms, his ripped trousers on the chair next to the bed. He was a cop so they'd triaged and assessed him double-quick. It was a superficial wound, no nerves, ligaments or bones involved, but even so if he wanted his leg to look near-presentable in a year's time he'd need specialized surgery. He should be admitted. He'd refused. He just wanted to be patched up and get out. So now he had a junior doctor who looked like a surly male catalogue model sitting on the bed behind him, jacking Naropin and sutures into the back of his leg and sniffing loudly at the foul clothes Caffery was still wearing. When the phone rang Caffery had to push himself up on his elbows to get at it in his breast pocket.

'Yeah – DI Caffery,' he mumbled.

'There's another.' It was Turnbull. 'Came in this afternoon. First attending thought it was a suicide and sent it over to the Royal United, but someone in the call centre got thinking about it after work and – bright spark – put it together with our job, did a Crimesnitch number and picked up the phone. It's the same MO. They found her in her car – pills, knife, same shit as before.'

For a moment Caffery didn't answer. The doctor had stopped his work and was standing at the head of the bed, arms folded, eyebrows raised at the sign on the wall – a picture of a phone with a line through it. Caffery held up his thumb, giving him a bear-with-me-I-won't-be-a-minute look, and stuck his finger in his left ear.

'Yeah, go on. Who is it?'

'Woman called Lindermilk.'

'Lindermilk? I've seen that name somewhere.'

'Ruth Lindermilk? Lives out near Farleigh Hall in one of those hamlets we were searching. She was kind of a recluse. You're going to love who her niece is. *Was*, mind.'

'Let me guess. It was Mahoney.'

'No. It was Hopkins.'

'Christ.'

'Yes, and Lindermilk had an appointment at the Rothersfield clinic this morning. Surgeon's name?'

'Gerber. That's where I saw her name – in his records.'

'And meantime,' said Turnbull, 'while they're giving it duhs at the site they found her, another call comes in. Lindermilk's house has been screwed. Place is trashed.'

'From when Gerber killed her?'

'Don't think so. From her body it seems like she went without a struggle. We're thinking this happened *afterwards*. He did her, then went back and screwed her house. Just like with Mahoney, 'cept not as discreet.'

'Who found it?'

'Lindermilk's son. He hears what's happened to his mother and – get this for the calibre of human being we're dealing with here – because she's got some property or other he wants before the police seal the place off, he goes straight over and lets himself into the place. He's got a key apparently. Except when he gets there, someone's beaten him to it. Nearly catches them too. He hears them jumping out of a window at the back. That's how close he came.'

'What time was this?'

'Two or three hours ago.'

'Then it can't have been Gerber.'

'Lindermilk's got some history of pissing off the neighbours. Couple of disputes there. Maybe it was one of them.'

The doctor, apparently at the end of his tether, walked out of the cubicle, leaving only a half-stitched wound, a few syringes in the kidney bowl, a blood-soaked sheet and a little sway of the curtain to prove he'd been there.

'What do you want me to do?' Turnbull said.

A huge wave of tiredness came over Caffery. He didn't think he had it in him to get up and keep going. He wanted to eat, drink and sleep. Nothing else. 'Dunno,' he muttered thickly. 'Where's the body?'

'Up at the mortuary. We're waiting to hear when the PM's going to be. The CSI are heading down to the house now. Do you want to have a look at it?'

Caffery inched his legs around, easing them carefully off the bed. He waited a moment or two for his head to stop spinning, then looked around for the call button. 'I'll be there, just as soon as I can find a doctor in this place.'

67

The first thing Caffery noticed was how near to Farleigh Park Hall Ruth Lindermilk's place was. In fact, now he thought about it, he remembered driving past the hamlet only a few days ago. He got a rush of adrenalin as he pulled off the road and parked behind the marked police cruiser outside the bungalow. No way Misty Kitson could have been on Gerber's list too? No. That would be too, too neat. Wouldn't it?

First things first. Check out the burglary. Then think about Misty. He looked around. The scene-of-crime guys' cars were lined up by the bottom of the road and one or two neighbours were standing in the dark lane, arms folded, coats over their shoulders, trying to get a glimpse of what was going on inside. Someone had put screens outside Lindermilk's front door. Maybe that was why the rest of the village were so interested.

He'd been given an antibiotic shot, packets of hospital pharmacy tramadol and codeine. They'd send him to sleep so for now he was sticking to ibuprofen 400s and a top-up of paracetamol. Giving into a rare burst of professionalism, he'd stopped at his cottage to dump his suit in a bag for the CSI guys. Now he was in black jeans and a black nylon warm-up jacket, but the limp still gave it away. That, and the swollen nose and the way his face creased every time he put weight on his foot. The district officer waiting for him in the house came forward, hands out instinctively to help him along the path.

''S OK.' He shook his head. 'It's OK.'

Pulling on the gloves the CSIs gave him, Caffery followed the officer along the tread plates into the little lighted dining room where a stubby, thick-bodied man dressed in a grey polo neck sat at the polished oak table. He was in profile, his chin resting on his fist, his mouth pursed. In front of him on the table was a brass telescope.

'Mrs Lindermilk's son,' the officer muttered. 'Steve. I think the reality's just hitting him now.'

'You coping there, mate?' Caffery stood in the doorway. 'You all right?'

Steve Lindermilk's face was very red. 'Not really. I should've done something – I never saw it coming.'

'You've been asked if you want to speak to a family liaison officer?'

'Yeah, I have. Don't need it.'

'They've been assigned already. You can change your mind.'

'No, thank you. But could you have someone speak to the neighbours? The ones gawking at us?'

'Sure.'

Caffery glanced down the hallway at the yellow crime-scene tape slung across the entrance to the living room, then back at Lindermilk. 'You know why I'm here?'

'To ask me questions?'

'And to look at the house. We need to find out if the break-in was connected to her death.' Caffery's head and leg were hurting like hell, in spite of the painkillers. 'Do you understand?'

Lindermilk nodded.

'Are you OK about that?'

'I'm OK.' He got up and followed Caffery along the tread plates. They stopped in the living-room doorway, leant over the tape and peered inside like visitors to a stately home. It looked to Caffery as if Ruth Lindermilk hadn't been a good housekeeper to start with, but this was something else again: every cupboard, every shelf, had been emptied in a pile on the floor. An angry break-in? With those they usually took time out to shit on the floor. Or on the beds. This one looked more as if they had been searching for something. In the kitchen a window stood open, the locks prised off. It looked professional. A cat jumped on to the window ledge, paused when it saw the visitors and balanced for a moment, all four paws tight together, staring at them.

'Look at that,' Lindermilk grunted. 'My mum encouraged that behaviour. Didn't have much in the way of boundaries.'

'When was the last time you were here?'

'Couple of days ago.'

'And the place didn't look like this, I take it, the last time you were here?'

'No, it bloody well did not,' Lindermilk said. 'Those

pictures on the wall – the ones of the animals – that's what was pissing people off round here. I'm surprised they never took those, if it was one of them did this.'

'We're looking at every possibility.'

Lindermilk shrugged. 'Tell you what, when you're done here can I have them photos? I'm going to burn them all.'

'Speak to the CSI men. It shouldn't be a problem.'

'There's some stuff on the outside I want to take too. Those things on the roof. I don't want the neighbours coming through here and making a laughing-stock of us.'

Caffery turned to the staircase. Silver aluminium oxide dust clung to the banisters, crisscrossed with rectangular gaps where the fingerprints had been lifted by tape. 'You didn't see anyone hanging around last time? No cars you didn't recognize?'

'Never saw a thing.'

'Would you know if something was missing? Anything of value she kept around? No cash on the premises? Jewellery? Credit cards?'

'Only the computer. And the TV. And the telescope. She did have a bit of jewellery, though, rings and that.'

'Where would she put them?'

'In the safe.'

Caffery raised his eyebrows questioningly at the CSI man standing next to the front door. 'Safe's not damaged, sir.' He lifted a finger and pointed to the next floor. 'It's in the bedroom. They've given it a whack, but haven't got into it.'

The three men went upstairs, Caffery pulling himself up on the banister, not putting any weight on the damaged leg. Another CSI guy, in blue forensic overalls, crouched at a chest on the landing, eye level with its handle, brushing it with black powder. As they came past he gave a long sigh.

'Only getting one set of fingerprints at the moment. And they're hers. I'm thinking the guy wore gloves.'

Lindermilk took them into a bedroom, a small, low-ceilinged, room with an under-eaves window and exposed beams. There was a bed with a quilted headboard in the corner and above it a wall safe, a small one, just big enough for paperwork and jewellery. It was covered with fingerprint dust. Lindermilk went to the safe. He was about to turn the dial, when Caffery coughed.

'Just a moment.' He limped back into the hall and bent to fish a pair of gloves out of the CSI's kit. He tossed them to Lindermilk, who caught them and pulled them on.

'Know the combination, then?'

Lindermilk peered at the lock. 'Used to. Unless she's changed it.' He twirled the knob experimentally, muttering the numbers under his breath. The lock clicked, turned, and he opened the door, standing back, hand up to indicate what was inside.

Caffery stepped forward. The safe was full. He could see two plastic envelopes of paperwork with pale blue backing, and a small black enamel box.

'The jewellery.' Lindermilk pulled it out. He opened the box and looked inside, poking through the contents with a fingertip.

'Anything missing?'

'Don't think so.' He held it out to Caffery.

Nothing remarkable was in there: a solitaire diamond on a chain, a pair of cufflinks, a few rings and a diamanté brooch in the shape of an anchor.

Lindermilk put the box down and turned back to the safe. He took out the top envelope, tipped the contents into the palm of his hand and looked through them. 'Legal stuff. Her will, house deeds, stuff from her solicitors.'

He unpicked the rubber band of the second folder. It contained photographs, all the same size, A4, but from the different print quality and paper they must have been taken over a span of thirty years or more.

'What're they?

'Photographs of animals. God knows why she kept them, the silly cow. She used to like taking photos of dolphins and stuff. I'll burn these too.'

'Let me see.'

Lindermilk fanned them. Some were in colour. A few showed a wedding, probably in the late seventies: a couple smiling outside a churchyard, the bride, a fair-skinned blonde in a long blue-and-white flower-sprigged dress and straw hat. Others showed dead animals: badgers splayed across roads, their hindquarters and heads smeared into the road markings, dead rabbits, dead squirrels. A deer with its neck broken so its head was turned back to face its hindquarters. 'Just about every piece of roadkill in the country.' Lindermilk sounded weary. 'She wanted to get up a campaign to have speed controls on the road down there. That's what had the neighbours so pissed off.'

But Caffery had stopped listening. Out in the garden, where the trees made sharp black cut-outs against the night sky, something had moved. He went to the window and peered out, careful not to touch the glass even when his breath steamed it. He'd caught the movement out of just the corner of his eye. It hadn't been the reflection of one of them in the room but something else. Something was in the garden.

He stood for a moment, thinking how dark it was out there, thinking of the miles and miles of countryside that anything could crawl through, thinking of the road that led down to the clinic, of the place he and the Walking Man had sat, watching shapes move in the trees. He thought of that tinny little scooter phut-phutting on the country lane. And then he thought of what he, Caffery, might look like from outside, standing at the window, his serious face lit from the back and the side.

'Sir,' Lindermilk said, 'can I ask you a question?'

He turned, distracted. 'What?'

Lindermilk was holding out the photos. 'I'll take these too, then? Along with the ones on the walls downstairs?'

Caffery's eyes went back to the window. What had been out there? It hadn't been much more than a smear of light, but somehow he'd had the impression of eyes.

'Sir?'

'Yeah.' He didn't glance back. 'Whatever.'

He came away from the window and limped for the door, holding a hand out to the district officer. 'Thanks for your help, mate. I'm done now. Get the CSI guys to bag everything up, and when they're finished, close up, will you?'

His leg hurt more than he liked but he went fast down

the stairs, out of a side door into the night, which was cool and muffled, a scent of something like lemon in the air. The back of the house was silent and dark. The lawn was terraced for about a hundred yards: he could see bird-feeders standing skeletal and ghostly in the gloom. Beyond that the road and the hills and the rapeseed field he'd driven past the other night when he'd been looking for the Walking Man.

He stopped at the trees and spoke in a low, clear voice. 'Are you there? Is that you?'

He could hear his heart thudding. Nothing else.

'If you're there, you don't have to worry. I'm not going to say anything. I won't give you away.'

He held his breath and listened, but all that came back was a cold, soundless breeze. In his mouth he tasted metal. He thought of the way the breeze had come across the fields, thought of the scents and sounds it must carry. He glanced at the house, at the windows. No one was listening. No CSI guys having a fag on the country lane. He took a few steps into the trees and crouched, his leg sending blue pulses of pain. He put his fingertips on the cold ground and held himself there, staring into the trees.

'I know what you've done.' He hesitated, not sure how to continue. This was nuts, talking to trees and thin air. 'You've got away with it. But listen.' His voice got softer. 'I can't help you any more. From here you're on your own. That's just the way it is.'

He stopped and waited for something to come back. Long minutes passed until his leg ached so much he had to straighten. He put his hands into his pockets and listened again. He wasn't sure what he was expecting: a movement or a breath. A rustle of leaves or cool clear words, spoken in the darkness.

Nothing came. Nothing. Just the sound of the blood pounding in his head.

68

I'm not going to say anything. I won't give you away . . .

Half frozen in the trees, crouched behind the cylinder of the thermal lance she'd dragged up from the car, Flea stared at Caffery in disbelief.

You've got away with it. But I can't help you any more.

She didn't move. Just squatted there with her mouth half open, his words freezing her to the spot. What the hell was he talking about? What the hell did he know?

From here you're on your own. That's just the way it is . . .

Something hollow opened inside her. She felt colder and lonelier and more scared than she ever had in her life. She remembered what Mum had said in the quarry. Look after *yourself*. It hadn't been a bland imprecation, a throwaway line telling her to be careful. It had been something starker than that. It had meant: you're on your own, so put yourself first. In front of others. Now she saw clearly what she had to do: saw that the only important thing left was to protect herself. She had to fight for her life.

Caffery stayed there for a long time and gradually,

watching his face, the moonlight glancing off his eyes, it dawned on her that maybe he couldn't see her. She raised a hand in front of her face, moved it back and forward. He didn't react. Tongue between her teeth she leant forward a little, scrutinizing his eyes. He wasn't focused on her. She stayed there, weight resting on her knuckles, head lifted, trying to work out what the hell was going on.

When he sighed and straightened, she was sure of it: he didn't know she was there. The words hadn't been meant for her at all: whoever he thought he was talking to it wasn't her, and if the words had meant something it had been a coincidence. But that didn't change her resolve. As he turned and walked to the front gate, as she let all her breath out and sank back on her haunches, she was resolute, focused and completely calm. At midnight tonight Mandy and Thom were going to get the surprise of their lives. They were going to get the photo, and they were going to get something more, much more. They were going to get Misty's body. On their front lawn, if necessary. Flea wasn't going to listen to any arguments or reasoning: from here on it was their mess to clear up.

By ten the CSI team had gone and the house was empty, just a copper on the gate, his back to her, waiting for the maintenance crew to arrive. After ten minutes he got bored of waiting, as she had known he would, and went to sit in his car, from which he could see the front of the cottage, not thinking there was someone round the back, sitting silently in the trees. Neither did he know that Caffery had left the back door open.

So cold her bones were aching, she straightened, the

muscles in her legs stiff, gathered up the thermal lance and went painfully across the lawn to the house, then inched her way through the back door. The copper might be lazy but he'd notice light seeping out of the windows, so inside she fumbled the Maglite from her jacket pocket, pointed it at her feet and crept along the hallway in the half-darkness, her ankles brushing against cats as she went. The house was smeared with fingerprint dust from the CSI team, strange pocked light filtering from the broken window, sending shadows across the walls. At the foot of the stairs she caught a glimpse of herself in the mirror, dressed in the pale blue shirt and jeans she'd thrown on a million hours ago, the cylinder of the lance hiked up on her back, her eyes watering. Her face seemed strangely smooth and young, as if stress had airbrushed it.

The backpack was heavy and the tendons in her knees still hurt from jumping out of the kitchen window so she went slowly up the stairs, careful not to rub against the walls. She wasn't thinking about fate or twists of destiny. She wasn't thinking about what Caffery had been doing up here in the bedroom when her movements in the trees had distracted him. She was only thinking that she was cold. And there were less than two hours left to get the photograph over to Thom's. Which was when everything would begin to change.

Then she shone the torch along the wall to the bed, up to the safe, and found it not closed, but open. Open and completely empty. Yawning, wide and cold. And saw that things might well change in the next two hours. But not in the way she'd expected.

69

Ten minutes to midnight. Ten minutes to go. Flea slammed on the brakes and came to a halt in the dark street. She switched off the engine and eyed Mandy and Thom's house. It was dark. The curtains were closed. Just the porch light on.

She went fast up the path and banged on the door. Mandy was in her nightdress when she answered. Her naked calves were white and veined, her eyes puffy without makeup. Her hair stuck out in all directions. She stood in the doorway with her arms folded against her chest, shivering in the cold night, squinting at Flea.

'I've got her in the car, Mandy. She's in the boot.'

'Who's in the car? Who've you got?'

'You can relax. No recording equipment.'

Mandy gave her a puzzled look. 'What equipment?'

Flea sighed, went back to the car and opened the boot. The body was covered with a blanket, a few flattened cardboard boxes crammed around it. Already water was soaking into the cardboard. She raised her eyes to Mandy. 'Have a look.'

Mandy came a few paces down the path in her bare feet and stared at the shape in the boot. In the orangy sodium street-light her expression was blank. Almost a minute passed. Then something vital in her face – something structural – seemed to slip. She glanced up at the neighbours' windows. Swallowed. 'Close it, please.'

Flea slammed the boot and came back to the gate. She took a breath and looked up at the sky. Clouds again. Always clouds. 'I've come to tell you you've got what you wanted. You've won.'

'Won what?'

'I'm going to take care of the problem.'

There was a pause. Mandy glanced out at the street to make sure no one was there, then looked back at Flea. 'Good. That's good.'

'Is Thom there?'

'He's asleep. It's been hard on him. I don't want to wake him up.'

Flea stared at Mandy. 'Tell me something.'

'Do I have to?'

'The truth, please. The truth. It's all I'm going to ask of you, and then I'll be gone.'

'What?'

'Thom. Did he put you up to this? Or was it your idea?'

Mandy's eyes glittered. She shot the car boot a glance. She was shivering now.

'Well? Was it your idea or his?'

'For everyone's sake.' Her voice was quiet. Almost inaudible. 'It's better you never know the answer to that question.'

And she went back up the path and closed the door, leaving Flea in the empty street, lonely and cold under the lamppost.

70

The countryside was deserted. The clouds had wrapped themselves across the fields, trapping everything, every leaf and branch, in an eerie, chalky light. Flea drove slowly, determinedly, taking the Focus down the small routes, the places she knew weren't going to be monitored by the traffic guys at this time of night. Just a handful of other cars were out. She wondered what she'd look like to the oncoming drivers. Her face set and hard in their headlights. Gripping the wheel, eyes boring through the windscreen. Half possessed.

She pulled off the road. The Focus bumped along the rutted drive to quarry number eight. In the boot the body shifted against the cardboard. She found a weak place in the surrounding bushes, swung the steering-wheel, gunned the engine, and forced the car deep into the undergrowth. It came to a halt, the axle hard against a fallen tree-trunk. She got out, crunched her way back to the quarry edge. Stood on the deserted track, listening hard, peering back along the route she'd come. She hadn't been followed. Elf's Grotto was so remote, so isolated, no one ever came up here. Still, she watched the road for almost five minutes until she was satisfied.

About fifteen years ago, when she and Thom were still kids, a woman had gone missing from a nightclub in Bath. One minute she'd been there, the next she was gone. In the playground at school they used to scare each other: they'd say whoever had got the woman would go after kids next. It was only when Flea grew up and entered the police that she learnt the truth. The woman hadn't been killed by a bogeyman but by the one-night-stand she'd left the club with. He'd reversed his car at her. Probably never meant to kill her, but did. He'd dumped her on a pig farm and Flea had spent three weeks one stifling summer pulling animal bones out of a pit there, steam-cleaning them, then passing them to an anthropologist. They never found the body and, without it, the CPS couldn't bring the case. Even though everyone knew the truth.

It showed what you could get away with if a body was well enough hidden. The most sensible thing Flea could do right now was to hire a chainsaw and cut Misty into a thousand pieces. Scatter them in rivers and fields. But even this new, cold imperative of hers couldn't look that solution in the eye. So she'd come to another frantic but rational conclusion – the only one she could think of.

She dragged her dive kit from the back seat, dumped it a few feet away and set about covering the car with sticks and branches. Then she pulled off her shoes, got into the drysuit, hauled on the buoyancy jacket and the cylinders, and gave the regulator three short breaths – one, two, three. She secured all the harness straps, deadlocked the car doors – checked again that it couldn't be seen from the slip road – and carried her fins down to the edge of the quarry. She pulled them on, then the mask, and climbed down the rusting ladder that led into the quarry. At 1.13 a.m. exactly she slipped silently out of sight, into the dark waters of quarry number eight

The Marley family had always dived. Mum and Dad had taught the children. They'd put them in junior Solar suits aged eleven. Most family holidays revolved around scuba- and wreck-diving: the Red Sea, Cyprus, once into Truk Lagoon half bankrupting themselves. It was how they had come together, the place they found comfort, the place they settled into something easier. Even the accident hadn't changed that. But diving here now, alone and in the dark? It broke all the rules of danger and common sense. It was a dumb, stark invitation to death.

She sank slowly, letting out small amounts of air from the suit as she descended to fifteen metres. The divelight she held pointed downwards, its membranous beam picking out swirling particles in the pitch darkness below. The light pierced a long way down, maybe another fifteen metres, but it didn't reach the bottom. She was in the deepest part of the quarry. There was still twenty-five metres – almost seventy-five feet – of unlit water beneath her.

Down another fifteen metres. She found the net from memory, its weed-coloured webbing faint and furred in the torchbeam. She handheld herself along it twenty feet until she could see the warning sign. The hole she'd made last week was still there, the frayed edges moving slowly like wafting sea anemones. She ducked through, twisting over as she did to stop the cylinders snagging – she didn't want a repeat of last time. A few feet inside the net, at the place where the accident had happened, she stopped, turned around and around in the water, pointing the torchbeam into the swirling darkness.

Usually, when she did decompression stops, she'd clip herself to a rope with a carabiner and rest on her front, horizontal in the water. Tonight she wanted to stay vertical. Wanted to be able to turn, to see 360 degrees. Upping the buoyancy in her jacket, releasing a little air from her drysuit so it didn't shoot up and gather round the neck seal, she found her neutral buoyancy, then let her arms drift out sideways. The divelight shone off to the side and she bobbed peacefully. Like a spaceman in the blackness.

She rested to start with. Eyes closed. Concentrated on emptying her head so there was nothing, no thought, no sound, just the in-out-in-out of her breathing. She'd heard once, years ago, that some seabirds have an internal compass that they use to navigate across oceans, around half the world, and always come back to the same breeding ground. The birds don't have to think about it, they give themselves up to something ancient and miraculous – the fact that their bodies know what their heads can't: which is north and which is south.

She tried to imagine herself as a seabird. Put her head back. Turned her face to the surface. She wanted to be told a direction. She wanted to be like a seabird and be told which way to go.

The minutes passed. Between each noisy breath her pressurized ears played tricks on her. From everywhere she was being pulled by imaginary sounds, her attention drawn first right, then left. She let them wash over her, waiting to feel where her body wanted to lean, what it wanted to do.

'*You've got to look after yourself . . .*'

Her eyes flew open. The torch beam came up in front of her, seesawing against the black. She gripped it. Steadied it. Turned it from side to side, hunting out the sound.

'Mum?'

No answer.

'Mum?'

She sculled with her free hand, turning herself in the water. The beam of light yawed around her. It was a hallucination.

'*Mum?* Are you there?'

A movement. To her left. Just outside the beam of her torch. She swung the light across. About twenty yards away she saw feet. Human feet. Swimming away from her, fast.

Amos Chipeta.

She pushed her arms out into the darkness, the Salvo divelight clenched in both hands. The beam danced crazily across nothing. The feet had gone. All the light picked up was emptiness.

Heart huge in her chest she tipped the top half of her body down and began to swim towards where the feet had been. Her instinct was to switch off the light, not wanting to give herself away to whatever was disappearing ahead of her into the darkness, but without it she was blind. Shielding it with her hand, letting a pinkish half-light filter through her fingers, she moved carefully through the water.

According to the compass whatever it was had been travelling west and slightly upwards. She reached the underwater rockface of the quarry edge, shone the torch along it and saw nothing. The other way. Nothing. She checked the depth gauge. She was still a hundred feet below the surface. Turning the light above her head, she moved it in an arc. Even going fast Chipeta should still be within the beam. When she shone it down and swung it from side to side, covering every angle, there was still nothing to see. Just the plant life on the side of the rock. Moving lazily.

Something occurred to her. It was rumoured that the quarry connected with local caves left behind by the Roman lead miners. That there were tunnels here. Wedging the torch in her buoyancy jacket she moved her hands along the slimed surface.

It jumped at her, almost as soon as she'd started looking. A cavity. A place darker than the rest of the rock. It wasn't on the quarry schematic – she was almost sure of that. She pushed her hand into it and shone the light around the edges, then into its depths to get the measure of it. There was no end to it. The beam shone into blackness. The diameter of the hole was big too: you could fit three men through here, even if they were wearing full diving gear.

Even in diving gear. She screwed up her face. No excuses, then.

One kick propelled her up and into the opening. She kept her hands on the walls, walked her fingers along, knowing how easy it would be to come into a narrowing so fast that the ceiling ripped the cylinders off her back. People had died like that, in places like the Eagle's Nest sinkhole, or the Yucatan cave systems, not like her parents, in a fatal freefall to the bottom, but tangled in guide lines, lodged between unforgiving rocks, trapped in water-filled sumps and crawl spaces. She thought of them struggling on and on in the lonely darkness. Until the air gauge hit critical. Until the pony cylinder was dead and lungs sucked at a vacuum. Clangtanking, they called it. The worst way to die.

The floor sloped upwards. She was entering a chimney: a narrow tube about four feet wide heading vertically. Undeviating. The beam showed it was one straight ascent, the sides smooth, almost as if they'd been machine cut. She forced herself to take a brief decompression stop – breathing slowly, picturing the nitrogen fizzing out of her muscles. The clock numbers tumbled round. Six minutes. It would have to do. She filled her jacket with air and entered, one hand raised above her.

The expanding gas in the system lifted her fast. The walls whirred past, streaks of black limestone. Up and up and up, the long bore sucking the circle of light ahead of her, like a dream, *look after yourself* thudding in her ears with every heartbeat. Until at last, unexpectedly, she surged out of the top. Into air.

It was dark. She fumbled one elbow over the side of the chimney, breathing hard. Held herself level, only her face at the surface. Her legs she wedged in place, keeping her shoulder near the edge. If anything came at her she'd ram the dump valve against the rock, offload the air from her suit and drop straight back down the chimney. She concentrated on her breathing. In and out. In and out.

Almost a minute passed. No hands grabbed her head. No face appeared in front of her mask. Tentatively she lifted the light out of the water and aimed it in front of her. The beam floundered in the darkness and hit rock about twenty feet away – a mossed, dripping rockface. She moved the beam to her left: more rock. No mist, no moon, no trees. Instead, when she turned it skywards, the light found a roof almost forty feet above. The rumours had been true. She'd come out in one of the old lead caves.

There'd been accidental deaths in other UK dive units and after those it had been drummed into her in training: never take the mask off. Not until you know what the air's like. She inched herself up with her feet, pulling herself out so she was kneeling astride the hole, sitting on her heels, tensed, the torch rammed out in front of her like a weapon, all the time ready to drop straight back into the chimney. Slowly, with her free hand, she lifted the mask webbing away from her ear, tipped her head to one side, held her breath and listened.

Something was breathing. Somewhere in the darkness. Hiding in the rocks.

She lifted the mask. Sniffed. Tasted the air. Waited. It was clean. Damp and full of the smells of water and rotting leaves. But clean. She looped the mask on one wrist so it was ready to pull back on, and put the fingers of her right hand on the floor. Leg muscles screaming, she tipped forward a bit and trained the flashlight on the sound.

The beam hit black rock and slithered around. Then, wedged between a crevice, something glinted. Eyes. Elliptical, set straight and level about three feet above the ground. Human eyes, but yellow and polluted. Staring at her. They blinked in the light and then, for a second, a large hand came up to shield them. Now she could judge the size of his head. It was anvil-shaped, the jaw too big, the neck squashed, almost non-existent. She could see the protruding tops of the ribcage, the way the bones looked too big. Could hear laboured breathing. Not an elf. Not a troll or a pixie or a gnome. Not a Tokoloshe. This was a human being. Wearing a threadbare sweatshirt and shorts, mashed-up flip-flops on his feet. She held herself steady. Held herself calm.

'I'm police. Don't move. Don't come near me.'

The eyes blinked.

'You take one step towards me and you'll find yourself in the biggest shit fight you could imagine. OK?'

A hesitation. Then he nodded.

She pushed herself upright. Faced him squarely.

'Amos. You're Amos. Have you been following me?'

He shook his head.

'What about that day in the squat last week? The day we broke in?' She ran the back of her wrist across her mouth to clean away the taste of the quarry. 'There was me and another officer. A man. In plain clothes.'

Silence. The eyes regarded her carefully, and now she glimpsed something else in the torchlight. A glimmer of plastic – storage containers, white plastic. The sort of thing you'd see in a teenager's bedroom. Four, maybe five, stacked one on top of another. Then she saw more belongings. Smelt something burning. Saw a battered sleeping-bag. And it struck her that he was living here. Here, in the dark among the moss and the rotting leaves and the dead insects, he was trying to carve out an existence.

'I don't know who you are, but you're not from England. You're African. From Tanzania.'

The eyes stayed steady. Gazed at her. Waited for her to continue.

'You're illegal. And you're in serious shit. Here and back home too.' She moved her tongue around, tried to coax some saliva into her mouth. 'I could make that shit deeper. I'll do it if I have to.'

The head must have tilted a little, because the angle of the eyes changed. They were still focused on her, but the breathing had altered too. It was softer. Deeper and slower. She couldn't tear her gaze away from those eyes. Watching her. Not blinking.

'I'm going to give you something now. You'll understand when you see what it is. You're going to sort it and you're never going to speak about it again. You try and turn it back on me and you'll regret it. I know what the police will look for so I've done some things to the . . .'

She had to break off and press her fingertips to her throat to stop her voice wavering. The compressed air was making her throat dry.

'I've done some things to the body that'll stop them

tracing her to me. If you try to go to the police they'll think it was you who killed her. But . . .' she had to pause again, get her voice in control '. . . if you do this properly, with respect, I'll find a way to help you. I don't know how but I will. I'll find ways to protect you. It's a simple thing. A straight swap.'

For a moment the little man was motionless. Then, his movement barely perceptible, he lifted his head and lowered it. He was nodding.

She wiped her nose and took a deep breath. 'Good. That was all I needed to say.'

She lifted her mask, pulled the webbing down over her wet hair, letting the visor sit on top of her head. Putting her hands on the floor she crouched down next to the chimney mouth, swung her legs round and dropped them into the water. She waited a moment or two, holding the man's gaze. 'One more thing.'

His eyes lifted a little. Questioning.

'I'm sorry. Very sorry.'

Then she pulled up her mask and was gone, lost in a burr of bubbles that broke and spat in the darkness.

71

In the car outside Lindermilk's bungalow Caffery washed down the hospital tramadol and codeine with a can of Sprite Lite. Given time, the drugs might touch the pain, but he knew they wouldn't send him to sleep. Too much had happened today.

He drove to the bottom of the Farleigh Park Hall driveway and sat staring at its blazing lights for a long time, lighting cigarette after cigarette. Now it was dark the CSI team had stopped the examination of Gerber's house. They'd start again in the morning. Maybe they should be looking for human remains, he thought. Misty Kitson's. In the morning he'd tell them that, then go back to see Gerber's secretary, Marsha. Misty had already had some cosmetic surgery on her nose to rebuild it after the damage done by years of hoovering up cocaine. He remembered that much from the files; the op had been done by an Iranian in Harley Street, but maybe she'd wanted more. Maybe she'd had an appointment to see Gerber. *The names might be fake, people get embarrassed*, one of the secretaries had said. Could you have done Misty too, you bastard? Could you?

When he'd smoked four cigarettes he still wasn't sleepy. He left a message on Powers's answerphone – *Call me. Something important* – started the car and headed east, meaning to go home. Instead he found himself thinking again about Amos Chipeta. About what he wanted. He thought of a bracelet of human hair, meant to ward off evil. He found his car meandering, taking him into the sharp dark forest of Stockhill. At just after two a.m., instead of coming into his darkened driveway at Priddy, he pulled off the main drag and into the little lane that led to the Elf's Grotto quarries.

The headlights swept the new leaves on to the crowded gorse bushes. Obeying an instinct that told him to be stealthy, he parked the car just off the slip-road behind some skips and limped the last hundred yards to the edge of quarry number eight.

It was a milky night, the moonlight scattering in an oppressive glow. Low clouds pressed down, holding the light close to the land. Nothing moved in the shadows, no wildlife or wind. He stood for a moment at the edge of the water, his hands on the back of his leg, checking he hadn't opened the wound in the walk here, that it wasn't going to start bleeding again.

The quarry was quiet. Nothing moved. Where does he live? he wondered. Where does he hide?

He went fifty yards round the edge to the place where Ben Jakes had been found, stopped and looked at the undergrowth. Nothing had changed. He went on, anti-clockwise around the quarry, pausing every few minutes to listen to the night sounds, pushing through brambles and dead branches in the places the footpath gave out. He was almost back to where he'd found the scooter when something stopped him in his tracks.

Ten feet away, parked in the undergrowth and covered with branches, was a car. A silver Ford Focus. It looked as if it had been there for a long time. Days, from the way it was covered. But he knew it couldn't have been. He took a step nearer and held his hand above the bonnet. Still warm. Someone had parked it here to hide it. He turned and surveyed the quarry. The water and surrounding trees were absolutely motionless. Was someone else here? Were they watching him now? From the trees? From the other side of the quarry?

The tramadol still wasn't working and his pulse was moving fast as he picked his way through the undergrowth to the back of the car. He looked at the registration thoughtfully. Y reg. A Y-registration Ford Focus.

It came to him slowly. It came like a slow wave.

He knew whose car it was.

Sergeant Marley was bored with the Focus, she'd said. *Bored* with it? He pulled his sleeve down again and tried the boot. Locked. At the quarry the day she'd found the dog, it had been the moment he'd asked her about this car that something had changed in her.

A half-remembered thought edged at him. He stepped back from the car into the undergrowth and stared at the number plate again. He'd seen this car a few times – once was on the day they'd made the arrests for Operation Norway: it had been parked outside a remote house in the Mendips and he'd had time to study it. He narrowed his eyes, remembering: there'd been a PSU-issue kit on the back shelf and something else . . . Something important. A piece of fabric hanging from the boot. A swatch of purplish blue velvet jammed into the lock.

In his pocket the phone began to ring. Startled him. He backed into the trees. Fishing it out of his pocket, he killed the noise as soon as he could.

'Yes,' he hissed. 'What?'

'Jack?' It was Powers. His voice soft and oiled from a night's drinking. 'Got your message. I only just heard what happened. I'm sorry, mate, really sorry.'

'Yeah.' Caffery didn't take his eyes off the car. Purple velvet. Purple velvet jammed in the boot of the fucking car. 'Sure.'

'Where are you? In the hospital? I had someone from the CSI team trying to track you down. They said you promised them your clothes when you got out of the hospital.'

Purple velvet. Car, coat. Car, coat. Misty Kitson's coat. Flea hadn't wanted to search a lake for her.

'And me – have you got something for me? You sounded excited. Was it about Kitson?'

'Kitson.' Caffery repeated it distantly as if he'd never heard the name before. 'Misty Kitson.'

'You said you'd have something by now. Remember?' Powers paused. 'Can you hear me, Jack? Look, just give me the intel you had, what your snout had to say, and we can take it from there. I'll come to you, if you want. Now. Wherever you are.'

Caffery didn't answer. Still staring at the car, he took the phone away from his ear and held it at arm's length. He let Powers speak to the air for a few seconds. Then, using his thumb, he switched the phone off. He stood like that, motionless in the darkness, his arm outstretched, heart hammering in his chest.

There is no God, he thought. *There is no such thing as God.*

72

Looking at it now, it had been clear all along. There was so much to pin on Flea. The tics, the lapses of logic in her behaviour. He remembered Stuart Pearce at Lucy Mahoney's body-recovery site. The traffic cop at the quarry saying that the night Kitson went missing there'd been something wrong with Flea. That she'd been distressed.

From the quarry to his right there came a low, distinctive glooping noise – as if an animal had broken the surface. He dropped the phone into his pocket and backed away from the car, moving silently into the trees, stopping about twenty yards away where he was hidden. He waited, watching the car and the black water reflecting the clouds.

Tiny ripples raced out across the water, as if someone had thrown a stone about three yards from the shore. The surface bulged and broke again. More ripples disturbed the cloud reflections. Someone was in the water. He moved himself further inside the shadows of the trees. More bubbles boiled up, then a head appeared: black and shiny.

It was Flea, the hazy light bouncing off her diving hood.

He wedged himself against a tree so he didn't lose balance while he watched. She climbed up a few ladder rungs, then pulled off the mask and sat on the edge of the quarry, unsnapping the front of the harness, leaning back and lowering the cylinders to the ground. She pulled off her fins and gloves, took a moment or two to turn off the air regulator on the cylinders and got shakily to her feet. She paused for a moment, surveying the quarry, turning around and around. Her wet hair clung to her head and her small face was strained and pinched. When she was sure she was alone, she reached into a pocket in the dry-suit leg, pulled out keys and headed for the car. She didn't open the driver's door, but went straight to the boot and opened it.

Bending down, she wrapped her arms around a large white package. Caffery knew what it contained: he could see the yellowish smudge of bleached hair pressed to the plastic sheeting. He shuffled forward a few paces, pinching his nose hard as if that might make him come to his senses and realize this was just a dream.

Moving slowly, clumsily, Flea dropped the body. It hit the ground with a dull thud. She slammed the boot and bent, catching up the package by two corners of the plastic sheeting. Gritting her teeth in concentration, she leant her weight back and began to drag it along the ground, pulling it out of the trees, out into the hazy, reflected moonlight, out in the direction of the water. It bumped and snagged. Once or twice he thought she wasn't going to be able to get it out of the trees. But she was used to the lumpen weight of a dead body and she fought it. It took her ten minutes to do it, but she dragged it all the way to the edge of the quarry.

She lowered the package close to the ladder, and straightened, digging her hands into the small of her back, circling her head to release the tension. Then something made her stiffen. She turned and looked into the trees.

'Who's there?' She stared in his direction.

Caffery squeezed his nostrils tighter, fighting back the urge to speak. A weight pressed up against his ribcage.

She listened for a moment or two longer. Then, frowning, she began to reassemble her kit, pulling on the fins, leaning back to hitch up the twin tanks, snapping on the jacket.

When she was fully kitted she climbed halfway into the water. Standing on the ladder, one arm wrapped on the rungs, she bumped the body down after her. As it tilted up Caffery could see skin, exposed through the shredded plastic. Torn skin, and muscle, and white-blonde hair.

When Flea'd got the corpse most of the way into the water she paused. She was facing it, one arm around it.

He thought for a moment she was thinking, trying to work out how to do what she was going to do next. Then he realized it was something else entirely. Her head was slightly down, her eyes raised. She was looking into the blank smear that would have been Misty Kitson's face. If it hadn't sounded ridiculous, if it hadn't broken all the rules after what he'd just watched her do, he'd have said she was apologizing to Misty.

He could step out of the trees now, could stand there

motionless in the moonlight, somewhere she'd see him. But before he could do anything she pulled up her mask, wriggled it around her ears, wrapped both arms tightly around the corpse and dropped like a stone out of sight into the dark mirror of the quarry, taking it with her.

Surprised it had happened so quickly, he limped out of the bushes and stood in the pool of water her equipment had left, peering down. Through the bubbles, he could just see the two of them – the black of Flea's head, the frosty plastic shroud around Misty and the wavering of the torchbeam.

Then they were gone. And all that was left were the mirrored domes of bubbles breaking on the surface.

73

Dawn, and Flea had drifted at last to the narrow lanes around her home. She drove steadily, eyes bloodshot, dull, the smell of the quarry still in her nostrils. A mist had come down, a grey, wreathing mist, making the twists and bends in the lanes treacherous. About half a mile from the house a hairpin bend came up fast. She slammed her foot down, wrenching the Focus to the left. The wheels flared out under her, the steering-wheel jerked in her hands, but she held it steady as the car careened around the corner of the narrow country lane, the wheels locking, going into a sideways slide. The tyres screeched, a tree hurtled towards the car. The impact, when it came, shot her forward against her seatbelt and sent pain through her ribs. The airbag inflated, slamming her head back, pushing her jaws together so fast she bit her tongue.

A moment of shock, then the airbag deflated. Her head fell down on to her chest with a jolt.

She sat for a moment, waiting for her ears to stop ringing from the airbag. Blood was welling in her mouth, under her tongue. She held it for a while between pursed lips as she did a mental check of her limbs, her trunk, moving her concentration down her body, along her arms and legs. Her knee hurt – she'd banged it against the steering-column – and her sternum ached where she'd strained against the seatbelt, but she could feel her toes. Could wiggle them.

She opened the door and spat the blood on to the tarmac. Moving creakily, she released the seatbelt, pushed the door open as far as it would go and got out gingerly, not putting too much strain on her chest. The car was tight up against the tree. She had to squeeze herself against it and shuffle backwards.

It was a quiet lane, full of elderflowers and new poppies. Mingling with the mist was the acid smell of crushed cow parsley where the car had flattened the hedgerow. Dew from the overhanging tree had splattered across the windscreen. She walked around the car, inspecting the damage. When she got to the front and saw what had happened she let all her breath out at once. Somehow, maybe more by luck than judgement, she'd got it right.

She went back to the boot, opened it and pulled out the bin liner containing Misty's handbag, phone, sandals and coat. The paint can she'd put in the back had tipped but not spilled so she used her Swiss army knife to lever the lid off and let it trickle out across the boot.

One last look at the car. The headlight that had hit Misty was buried in the tree-trunk, the front wheels had been driven sideways and back towards the passenger seat, snapping the axle out of line. The engine bay and the firewall would have cracked too. The car was a write-off.

Earlier she'd cleaned the whole thing with a rag soaked in petrol, stripping away grease and fingerprints, lifting hairs and fibres. She'd taken two long hours over it, and she was confident. No one would be forensicating this car anyway. They'd have no reason to, as long as she reported she'd been driving it. All the evidence linking Thom and her to Misty Kitson was going to end up in a breaker's yard. The remainder of the petrol was in a small flask in the bin liner.

With the bag over her shoulder, Flea pushed through the hedgerow and set off up through the dewy fields. The sun filtered down through the early-morning haze and, as she climbed, vague ghost shapes to her left and right slowly revealed themselves as stiles and trees. By the time she got to the top of Charmy Down, the old airfield, she had walked straight out of the mist and could see the disused mast ahead of her, glinting in the sun. The remains of her previous fire were still there. A flat circle of blackened grass, dew clinging to it, giving it a greyish pall. She put the bag on the circle, pulled out a flask, tipped the petrol on to the bagged belongings and phone and threw a match on to it.

Having retreated a few yards she sat, waiting for the fire to catch. Beyond, the sky in the east was streaked with dirty pinks and browns. In the valley the mist swirled. The neighbouring hills – places she'd known all her life – rose like dark islands above it. Solsbury Hill was half a mile off and, far away where the gap in the hills led out to Frome and Warminster, another line of smoke, like a finger, rose up into the blue sky.

She kept her eyes on that fire. Her body was aching

from everything that had happened in the last twenty-four hours, and there was a tingling in her fingers that she thought came from the cold of the quarry. But watching that distant fire gave her a kind of peace she couldn't explain. She linked her fingers round her ankles and leant forward, gazing at it.

Look after yourself . . .

It was OK. OK to save herself like this. To do the wrong thing for the right reason. Sometimes all you can do is simply to continue moving forward. Making the choices that keep you alive.

Her own fire made a small whooshing sound and a flame shot up. It dropped, then shot up again, and more joined it, crackling, burning green, orange, blue. A line of silky black smoke guttered and rose into the sky, answering the fire on the neighbouring hill.

The fire of a man she had never met in her life.

74

Some humans have the instincts of animals. It comes from years of living without comfort. Even asleep the Walking Man sometimes appears to know what is happening in the waking world and who to expect. It's as if his slumbering mind can creep coolly out, can float away over the hills and valleys, watching like a hawk those who are out at night. All those who move in his vicinity. And all the time his body lies next to the extinguished campfire, still and silent, only his eyes moving.

That night, as Gerber lay in a Trowbridge mortuary, as Flea submerged herself in the Elf's Grotto quarry, the Walking Man slept soundly and peacefully. He was expecting someone. He had left out a spare foam mat with a sleeping-bag next to the fire.

Caffery arrived at three thirty a.m. He crawled into the bag and fell immediately into a torpid, drugged sleep.

When he woke two hours later in the cold, milky dawn, the mist was freezing and the only sound was the bleak cawing of crows in the high branches overhead. He sat up. The Walking Man was making breakfast. A long thin column of smoke rose from the fire. There was bacon and eggs for two people. Two mugs waiting.

'Morning. Going to be a good one. The mist will clear.'

Caffery didn't answer. The hospital's codeine was still in his system, like something hot and feathery packed into his brain behind his eyeballs. He sat, his hands on his ankles, and gazed into the fire, at the twin tin cups of coffee, at the two frying-pans sizzling on the flames. He couldn't remember ever feeling so tired, so numb, inside and out. His head drooped. He had to jam his elbows into his knees and prop his head on his fingers.

'Why is your phone switched off?' The Walking Man didn't look up from the fire. 'Usually you treat it like a second heart.'

Caffery took it out of his breast pocket. He put it on the ground and stared at it. Not as if it was a heart. As if it was a snake.

'Well?'

'I don't know what I'd do if I switched it on. Don't ask me again.'

The Walking Man shrugged. He scooped the food on to two plates: each had four thick rashers of bacon, three fried eggs, two sausages and a slice of fried bread. He walked all day and he needed his fuel. His plates always brimmed over and he made sure his guests ate well too. He straightened, put one plate next to his bedroll and brought the other across to where Caffery sat. When he saw Caffery's expression, the sick way he looked at the food, the way there was water in his eyes, he hesitated. 'OK,' he grunted. 'OK.'

He straightened, took a few steps away from the fire and crouched to scrape the food off the plate on to the ground. 'The badgers will like you for it.' He went back to his bedroll, walking carefully because he only had his socks on, and if there was one thing the Walking Man had to do, it was care for his feet. He settled down, the tin plate resting on his knees, and ran a thumb and forefinger through his beard, studying Caffery's face through narrowed eyes. 'You know what you've come to.' He nodded at the phone. 'Don't you?'

Caffery was sullen. 'What?'

The Walking Man grinned. 'Crossroads,' he said. 'Your absolute crossroads. And now, *now*, your hand is going to be forced. I don't know why or what's happened but when you switch on that phone you've got to make a decision. Haven't you?'

Caffery stared at the Walking Man. The bastard was right. It had been coming to him as he slept. Hallucinations crossing and double-crossing him. That in the morning he'd have to speak to Powers. He'd have to make the decision. He'd have to tell him what he knew about Misty Kitson.

'And this is the decision that's been coming at you for years. You might not see it but this decision is about whether you stay facing death, or whether you turn the other way and choose life instead. That's all.'

Caffery made a small, contemptuous noise. 'I'm being preached to about choosing life by *you*? Someone who's chosen death? How does that work?'

'Or maybe you're being preached to by someone who's *been chosen* by death.'

'You're not dead.' He studied the Walking Man's eyes. They were blue. Like his own. As if they were from the same family. Except Caffery knew that the wisdom in the Walking Man's eyes wasn't in his own. Not yet. 'You're still alive.'

'Yes. Oh, yes.' The Walking Man looked at his hands. Turned them over and over as if they belonged to someone else. 'It seems I am.'

'You've got a plan. I don't know what the plan is, but it's there. So you haven't chosen death at all.'

The Walking Man laughed – sympathetically, as if Caffery was so simple, just a child. As if it would take him years to come to any maturity of thought or emotion. 'When Craig Evans killed my daughter,' he wiped his moustache, 'when he told me what he'd done . . . when he told me how many times he'd raped her before he did it,' he tapped his finger against his lips, as if for a moment he didn't trust himself to complete the thought, 'when he told me it all, I knew then that the choice had been made. For what she had suffered she had to be comforted. And to comfort her I had to follow her.'

Caffery leant forward. It was the first time the Walking Man had spoken directly about his daughter's death. 'Follow her where?'

'Into the next world, of course. That was just how it had to be. It's the natural way of things. Everything I do, every mile I walk, is my preparation. I have to find the time and the place.' He looked up. 'You don't know what happened to your brother's body.'

'No.'

'You've searched everywhere you can think of.'

'Yes. There's nowhere else. Once I thought I got close. A long way from here. Out in the east, not the west.'

'Yes?'

'I was wrong.'

The Walking Man nodded thoughtfully. He eyed Caffery a little longer then picked up his fork, settled down and began to eat, his eyes on the horizon. Caffery watched him. He noticed how he kept his beard clean of food, wiping his fingers on a cloth. The Walking Man was filthy, from his head to his toes, but there was something strangely fastidious about the way he cared for himself.

'You're not as lucky as I am,' the Walking Man said after a long silence. 'I have no choice, and that makes me fortunate. But you? You still have to choose. And that's more difficult. Particularly now. When there's a new complication in that choice.'

Caffery frowned. 'How do you—?'

'It doesn't matter how I know. What is important is the choice you make and why you make it. Look at me.' He put down his plate and turned to Caffery, his arms wide, his filthy padded jacket falling open to show his torso in the stained thermals. 'You, dear policeman, are learning to judge me for what I am, not for what you think I am.'

'So?'

'So?' He closed the jacket and picked up the plate. 'So be careful to use the same judgement here, Inspector Caffery. Be careful to judge only when you have the whole picture. It will take time but when you can see it all, things may look very different.'

The whole picture. More images came to Caffery. Flea's face that day in her new car at the quarry: the tight, anxious set of her forehead. The look in her eye early this morning as she pulled Misty's corpse into the water. The way she seemed to be apologizing. As if she hadn't meant it to happen.

'And something else.'

Caffery looked up. 'What else?'

'Something I shouldn't need to remind *you* of.' The Walking Man lowered his head and stroked his moustache, his hand hiding the ironic half-smile on his mouth. 'That before you pass judgement on another human being, you should always look back a little. Maybe into your own past?'

Caffery fixed his eyes on the Walking Man. It wouldn't surprise him one bit if somehow the Walking Man knew all about that too: his secret, one he'd carried for nearly ten years now, how back in London there had been a killing. He'd murdered a man there – secretively, and with his own bare hands.

He leant forward and pulled the mobile phone closer. Rested his finger on it. He was so, so tired. Maybe it was true, maybe choice really was the root of all human happiness – and of all human sadness.

'It's time,' the Walking Man said. 'You know it's time.'

Caffery took a deep, weary breath and picked up the phone. He stood, looking at the blank screen. 'Don't watch me. OK?'

The Walking Man gave a long, slow smile. He inclined his head politely and held out his hand, indicating Caffery should move away from the campfire.

Caffery got up and walked in the opposite direction from the trees. He stood at the edge of the hill. The mist had cleared, as the Walking Man had said it would, and from here the land opened up, with all its mounded green forests and glacial ridges. A long way from Bath he could see the misty Avon valley, the vague smudge of the White Horse at Westbury. Closer – from Charmy Down on the other side of Solsbury Hill – another line of smoke rose in the air. It was like the Walking Man's, only this one was darker. Black and concentrated. Leaving smears on the sky.

He switched on the phone, jabbed in Powers's number and, his eyes on the black smoke, waited for the phone to connect.

'Boss. Did I wake you?'

'Yes, you did.' Powers kept his voice low. He coughed a couple of times. 'Jack, what was all that about earlier, then? You put the phone down on me. I called back but you'd switched off.'

Caffery checked over his shoulder to see if the Walking Man was listening. He wasn't. He was looking out across the countryside in the opposite direction, a small smile on his face, as if he had already decided what Caffery was going to do.

'Where've you been? The CSI are going crazy. E District's had people over at your house trying to find you. You're not answering your phone. They've been trying all night.'

'I know. I saw the messages.'

'My guess is you've been with your snout. Am I right?'

'Yes. He's unearthed something.'

The line went quiet.

'It's credible,' Caffery said. 'Very credible.'

Again there was silence. In a dry voice, Powers said, 'Give me an outline, then.'

'Gerber. Gerber did Kitson too.'

'No. No fucking way.'

He looked up at the line of smoke. He didn't know why but it comforted him, that black smoke coming from someone else's fire. It was as if the world wasn't such a lonely place at all. 'She had an appointment with him. Used a fake name – we don't know what. Maybe she talked him into not recording it. Didn't want the press getting hold of it. But as soon as everyone wakes up, when everything comes on-line, I suggest you get some soil people out to Gerber's place. There's a couple of spots out there they could run a ground radar over.'

'Are you sure? Are you absolutely sure about this?'

Caffery didn't answer for a few moments. The wind had caught the black smoke on the far hill and was moving it slowly across the sky. When he'd killed that man in London he'd had his reasons, reasons that still seemed sound and good. Flea's reasons would be clear too, they'd be as understandable as his were. There was nothing in the ground at Gerber's house – nothing except the opportunity to buy some time. Time enough to do as the Walking Man said, to see the whole picture and decide whether to go at things the straightforward way. Or whether to leave

Flea in peace, to make her own mistakes and atonements.

'Yes,' he said calmly. And something in his chest seemed to lift a little as he said it. 'I've never been surer of anything in my life.'

Acknowledgements

I couldn't, and wouldn't, have even attempted to start this book if it hadn't been for one man: Sergeant Bob Randall of the Avon and Somerset Underwater Search Unit. He knows his contribution, he knows how I value it, but there is no harm in the world hearing what a unique, informed and brilliant police officer he is, nor how generous and tireless he has been in helping me, both professionally and personally. I had other help, too, in inching the police procedural details a little closer to reality: DI Steven Lawrence of the CID training unit and Alan Andrews of the Major Crime Review Team, both of Avon and Somerset Constabulary. And, from the Metropolitan Police, Cliff Davies of the Homicide Review Team, who is still after all these years an inspiration and a friend.

It's a rare person who can call many of her colleagues friends, so I am lucky beyond words to both know and work with three extraordinary women: Jane Gregory, Selina Walker and Alison Barrow. Nor could I keep going without the unswerving support of Jemma McDonagh;

Claire Morris; Terry Bland; Stephanie Glencross and Tess Barun at Gregory and Company, not to mention everyone at Transworld Publishers whom I'm honoured to still be working with ten years down the line: Larry Finlay; Ed Christie; Janine Giovanni; Diana Jones; Nick Robinson; the indomitable eco-man Bradley Rose; Simon Taylor; Claire Ward; Hazel Orme; Katrina Whone and Joanne Williamson.

My friends and family who listen and inspire in equal measure are: Christian Allis, John and Aida Bastin; the Billinghams; Kate Butler; Linda, Liz and Laura Downing; the Fiddlers; the Gores; the Heads; Mairi, Moë and Sally Hitomi; Sue and Don Hollins; Patrick and ALF Janson-Smith; Karen Knowlton; the Macers; Rebecca Marshall; Margaret and E. A. Murphy; Selina Perry; Helen Piper; Keith Quinn; Karin Slaughter; Sophie and Vincent Thiebault; Ness Williams; and the ever graceful Gilly Vaulkhard.

And, of course, a big, big thank you to three lovely little girls; first Misty and Daisy, who selflessly lent me their names without holding any conditions about what happened to their fictional counterparts, second, and most of all, a little girl who has surprised me by being the-greatest, and most unexpected, love of all: my beautiful daughter, Lotte Genevieve Quinn.

RITUAL

BY **MO HAYDER**

A Jack Caffery thriller

Nine feet under water in Bristol Harbour,
a police diver finds a human hand.

The fact that there's no body attached is disturbing, but even more disturbing is the discovery a day later of the matching hand and the shocking evidence that the victim was still alive when they were removed.

Recently arrived from London, DI Jack Caffery is now part of Bristol's Major Crime Investigation Unit. His search for the victim leads him to a dark and sinister underworld; a place more terrifying than anything he has known before...

'Hayder has a profound ability to shock
and surprise her readers'
Karin Slaughter

9780553820430

www.mohayder.net